KOREAN
Contemporary Short Stories

Selected from KOREANA Magazine

Edited by Kim Hwa-young

KOREA FOUNDATION
한국국제교류재단

KOREAN CONTEMPORARY SHORT STORIES
Selected from KOREANA Magazine

English translation copyright © 2017 by the Korea Foundation, Bruce and Ju-Chan Fulton, Heinz Insu Fenkl

The short stories in this collection were originally published in Korean in various literary magazines and books in the Republic of Korea. Their English translations were published in lightly edited forms in Koreana magazine (www.koreana.or.kr) by the Korea Foundation, Seoul, the Republic of Korea.

Published by the Korea Foundation, 2558 Nambusunhwanno, Seocho-gu, Seoul 06750, the Republic of Korea
www.kf.or.kr

Printed in the Republic of Korea

Price: KRW10,000 in Korea, USD10.00 outside of Korea

ISBN 979-11-5604-207-5

Copyright Notices

KOREAN
Contemporary Short Stories

Selected from KOREANA Magazine

Edited by Kim Hwa-young

KOREA KF
FOUNDATION
한국국제교류재단

CONTENTS

Korean Contemporary Short Stories and the Search for Universal Truth

The role of the short story in the history of modern Korean literature goes beyond simply being a phenomenon worthy of attention. In Korea, short stories are far more prominent than full-length novels or longer works of fiction. This is true in terms of both quantity and quality. In France, the country of Maupassant, in the United States also, the country of Edgar Allen Poe and O. Henry, and in Russia, the land of Chekhov, the relative importance of short fiction today does not come close. On the contrary, in these countries, compared with the full-length novels which dominate the reading world, short stories (with a few remarkable exceptions) are reminiscent of the practice of writing as a pastime, something authors try their hands at occasionally to loosen up their writing muscles during an idle summer's day.

The historical and sociological background of Korean literature has had a large part to play in creating this elevated status of short fiction within the country. The form of the short story in modern terms first emerged in Korea in the early twentieth century with the beginnings of the inflow of literature from the West. The term danpyeonsoseol (or 'short novel') first appeared in 1906, and in 1915 the first book-length collection of short fiction was published. Literary historians tend to see the 1920s as the period in which the basic form of the mainstream short story was firmly established. It was during this time that, following the founding of the magazine Changjo (Creation) in 1919, there emerged a number of literary magazines and literature sections in newspapers, with many of the major literary works published through these mediums still loved by readers to this day. Unlike the full-length novel which tends to be printed and published in a stand-alone volume, the relatively compact short story is highly dependent on such mediums as magazines and newspapers, for which works were commissioned.

In the case of Korea, the short story is closely related to the tradition whereby new writers are discovered through the Sinchunmunye system of 'annual New Year literary contests.' Sinchunmunye is a gatekeeping system for new writers and poets whereby influential newspapers collect submissions of poetry, short stories and various genres of writing. In early December they begin a process of impartial evaluation with the works judged best announced in the New Year's Day edition of the newspaper in question. For the winners, not only does this mean official recognition as a "poet" or "novelist" and a fixed sum of prize money, but their winning work is also printed in full in a major publication, thus reaching a wide audience. First started in 1925 by the daily Donga Newspaper, a large number of other significant dailies followed suit and continue to run the competitions to this day. Until the 1980s the Sinchunmunye system was recognized as by far the most authoritative institution in the Korean literary community, and was considered the most important step for those wanting to make a career in literature. From the 1990s however its influence has diminished slightly as avenues for new writers to make their debut have diversified, with new writing awards being held by literary magazines, writer-led periodicals and publishers, and the timing of many of these competitions now spread throughout the year.

While there are a small number of exceptions, for the best part of the last century debuting as a writer in Korea meant that the first work a writer would produce or at least have published would almost always be a short story, and for a long time following on from their debut the works they had published were usually in the same medium. As the colonial period ended and Korea gained independence in 1945 there was an opportunity for a great flowering of Korean literature. However, with the outbreak of the Korean War just five years later in 1950 and the hardship of the postwar years, the publishing industry entered into an extended period of decline. In the midst of such hardships, when literary magazines printed works of fiction it was inevitable that with the small number of pages they had available they were usually only able to include short stories limited to a certain number of words. This also influenced the rise of the short story leading to its current preeminence in the world of Korean fiction. Today however, as the publishing industry offers ever more varied, direct and independent ways for authors to reach their readers, the presence and influence of the Sinchunmunye system alone cannot fully explain the way in which writers are still focused on the short story medium.

In addition to this historical backdrop we must also consider a peculiar phenomenon particular to Korea. Unperturbed by the increasingly saturated market, in Korea more than two hundred monthly and quarterly literary publications are printed, and among these, magazines specializing in fiction and all forms of writing total around one hundred; publishing fiction and in particular a number of short stories in each edition. Even now, for every magazine that ceases production somewhere a new one is founded. Of course it is true that among these there are only around ten major literary periodicals which attract interest from a large number of readers, but even the existence of such a plethora of literary publications represents an extremely exceptional situation in the world today. This large number of literary magazines and publications not only provide the many authors who have already debuted a means of receiving commissions and having their works published, they also provide opportunities to increase awareness of emerging talents and are an important source of income for many writers. It is highly likely that the existence of such opportunities leads writers to take a particular interest in short fiction, in line with the limited word count that can be included in an edition of a literary magazine or journal. As time passes and the short stories a writer has had published in such magazines reaches a certain number, they are compiled into a short story collection and published again. The various literary awards (and the generous prize money that comes with them) aimed at short fiction rather than full-length novels also contribute to the pull of this literary form. With the Korean world of literature organized in this way, for many writers publishing short stories (which require comparatively less time to write) in sequence has become something of a writing habit, quite different to the drawn-out pace of writing a full-length novel which takes much longer to reach completion. Of course many authors write short stories while working on novels and have these published in between their longer works. Even so, it is fair to say that the golden days of the short story in Korea have come about in the midst of a deep relationship between the Sinchunmunye system of literary contests, and the presence of various literary periodicals and awards.

However, while this literary sociological environment particular to Korea may account for the quantity of works, it is hard to see how it has brought about the relative superiority of the short story. The rising status of Korean short stories has also drawn the interest of readers, and under such conditions changes have occurred to the scope of the works themselves. Among these is an external change: short stories have been getting longer. If you compare them with the classic works of short fiction by writers such as Maupassant, Chekhov, O. Henry, or Hemmingway, Korean short stories have become noticeably longer. In response to this change, literary journals are now encouraging writers to submit works which do not exceed lengths of around seven thousand words. However, in the case of writers who already have a major following, there is considerable leeway in terms of word counts, with certain works printed in literary journals reading more like novellas. Another change has been internal: a change in the scope of content and change in the forms of description. If readers were to approach Korean short stories with the definition of the short story that was popular in French literary circles around the end of the nineteenth century, that it is "a cross-section of life" and therefore a very simple story, they would no doubt be quite taken aback by the unexpected complexity the developed form is now able to hold. Among Korean short stories there are many examples which rival full-length novels, or in fact display a descriptive structure more complex and intricate than many of the classics. Inside a single short story large numbers of characters may both live and die; the entire lifetime of a character may be laid out with all its twists and turns with different layers of time interspersed and overlapping, each thread in time intricately colored with inner sensations, meditation and contemplation. In this vein, the success of these works lies less in the passive, linear following of a simple story and more in the way in which they demand the active participation and emotional involvement of the reader. It may well be that with their long and detailed methods of description, short stories particular to the Korean literary environment are alluding to the fact that works of literature are a means by which to draw close to the quintessential meaning of life.

The short stories gathered together here were selected from among the ninety-odd translated works of short fiction chosen to be introduced to international readers through the Koreana magazine between 1994 and 2016. Selection was based on the achievements of the stories as works of literature and their variation and honesty in expressing life in Korea. The period in which these works were first published stretches almost half a century from the 1980s to the present day. The authors of these stories range from those who grew up in the war years of the 1950s to the generation of writers now in their forties. Although they each respond to their sensory experience of reality with different depths, heights and temperaments, creating their own unique artistic worlds, if there is something which they all share it must be the historical experiences that have shaped communities across Korea, as well as a certain linguistic reasoning.

For readers less familiar with Korea, the historical experiences dominating the backgrounds of these stories may feel rather difficult to face. For example in 'That Boy's House,' which depicts youth lost to war, the horrendous experiences of the Korean War which broke out in 1950 are implied both directly and indirectly throughout the story. Two young people who knew each other before entering university are separated by the outbreak of war and then meet years later when the young woman has gotten a job in a U.S. army base to provide for her five family members. The young man's older brother and his family all went North and he had heard no news of them. On the other hand "that boy" himself went to war and came back a disabled veteran. As his father follows his eldest son to the North and his mother stays in the South with him, "that boy's" family has been completely destroyed. The short story 'A Bale of Salt' also includes gruesome experiences of the Korean War, as well as domestic violence. The narrator's mother, who has held onto her life by enduring stoically in the midst of terrible hardship, is accused by the recapturing Southern forces of being a collaborator after having fed the tofu she made to People's Army soldiers who came down from the North, but she manages to escape with her life by making her delicious tofu for the Southern soldiers too. At the same time her younger brother disappears and his wife is executed in a peach orchard by Southern forces, while the narrator's violent father sides with those who killed his sister-in-law. Works such as this, which deal with the historical and social effects of the geographical and ideological separation of North and South on the Korean Peninsula, and the confrontation brought about by the Korean War, are commonly called "division literature."

Other short stories reflect the changes in residential culture which took place during in the postwar years of economic growth. For example, 'That Boy's House' depicts traditional Korean Hanok and 'dirt houses,' while offering insight into how these forms of residence contrast with the apartment culture brought about by subsequent rapid development. In 'Words of Farewell,' the anxious and weary footsteps of a mother and daughter visiting a gravesite on a hot summer's day, and the procession of soldiers and army trucks they witness, the untimely death of their scholar husband and father who died searching for a hiding place by a fishing lake after running from their home, references to the Saemaeul Undong, and flyers filled with photographs of wanted criminals—all of the events which create the atmosphere of the story are intimately related to the authoritarianism of the military dictatorship of the 1970s and the brutally oppressive environment it created, an oppressive environment that continued for many years.

The new military authorities that took power following the death of Park Jeong-hee mercilessly suppressed the resistance movement led by university students. In 'Pink Ribbon Days' melancholy remembrance of these times is littered with references to police officers, tear gas grenades, and truncheons, in a short story which shows the generation who spent their university years in the agonizing resistance movement living through their thirties with the wounds of the past.

This is not to say that works of literature can merely be simple testi-

16

monies of historical experiences. Works of literature not only describe the exterior realities experienced by humans, but must by their nature express figuratively the whole of our experience, including that which occurs within the self. Historical realities can only become literature when they are elevated to reflect those issues universal to humankind, those at the root of our being, which transcend the passing of time. In this very way the varied short stories presented in this volume deal with a wide range of creative issues such as life and death, the dignity of existence, poor but happy childhood days, the purity of musical notes, and the sincerity of a traditional storyteller. Historical experience therefore takes on a further dimension, the dimension of universal truth. In putting together this collection, it is my hope that this handful of stories will be an engaging opportunity for readers from all over the world to access the historical experiences and inner truths of Korean people across the generations in a more intimate and intricate way.

August, 2017

Kim Hwa-young
Literary critic,
member of the National Academy of Arts of the Republic of Korea

PINK RIBBON DAYS

Kwon Yeo-sun

Translated by **Brother Anthony of Taizé**

분홍리본의 시절

권여선

A critique of this short story was published in the Koreana magazine in Winter 2010 (Vol. 24 No. 4, pp. 86-87).

© Cha Jae-ok

I t was late in the spring of my twenty-ninth year that I left Seoul. Then, after I had spent exactly one year living in an officetel room in a new town, I came back to Seoul late in the spring of my thirtieth year, just before the rainy season began. At the time I left Seoul I was not working and I was not meeting anybody. Or rather than saying I was not meeting anyone, it would be more correct to say that I did not really have anyone to meet. Likewise, rather than saying I was not working, it would be more truthful to say that I was not being given any work. In any event, as I was leaving Seoul there seemed to be no need to make any kind of choice or decision, I just wanted to live an uncluttered, isolated life.

When it comes to making friends, I tend to be demanding. Of course, I know that I am incapable of being a good friend who will satisfy other people's demanding standards. Still, what you might call a good thing about me is my capacity for comforting myself with the thought that being alone is much better than keeping company with people who are not important. This means that I know how to put up with the loneliness caused by my inability to satisfy my own high expectations. I was living a clear, transparent life without anybody else, so it really is amazing that I was unable to avoid meeting those women just as I turned thirty. Those women, those women of mine.

I brought just five things with me when I moved into the officetel room: a twenty-inch television with a built-in video recorder, a computer, a wardrobe and some white plastic bookshelves, that was all. Wall space being limited, I placed the bookshelves awkwardly so that when you came in, the only thing visible was a narrow passageway.

After moving in, I grew enamored of the large discount store that lay just a five-minute walk away. That vast open space with its huge display counters and wide aisles formed a baroque kind of contrast to my room. Almost every evening I rushed through the store pushing a cart, not to do any shopping but to instill an esoteric sense of ambition into my poor body, that was growing accustomed to my narrow, rectangular room. In my hands as I went back home I would be carrying a bag of onions, a carton of eggs, or sometimes a packet of fresh sole on sale at half price just before closing time. It was one evening after about a month of coming and going between the bookcases with their white shelves and the display counters, not missing a single day. The rainy-season drizzle that had been falling had stopped and as the clouds thinned, the sky broke through, revealing a crimson sunset. I suddenly felt an intense craving for some meat, as though all the fat in my belly had vanished. In the throes of a craving for some hearty broth made from brisket and leg bone, despite the sultry heat, I quickly grabbed my shopping bag.

I hovered in front of the meat counter, which if it had been a bookcase would have been high enough for the four shelves an encyclopedia takes up, and after eying the price tag on some cheap brisket I was looking around in case there was something cheaper. At that moment, an unfamiliar hand was hovering over the pack of meat I had my eye on. In a flash I quickly jerked the wrapped meat into my shopping cart. My rival, showing no particular signs of surprise, went on hovering carefully above the display, intent on choosing another pack of meat with a hand sporting a simple ring and large knuckles. To my surprise, behind the bending woman's broad shoulders loomed the vivacious, triangular face of Ju, who had been my senior at university.

"Why, Cheol-su!"

"Oh, Yeon-hui!"

Ju had no idea that I was engaged in a fight with his wife over meat, and was clearly pleased to see me. That was unexpected, when I recalled the drunken, unfeeling way in which he had declared that it was over between us back in the old days. Before we had exchanged more than a couple of words, we were amazed to realize that we were neighbors, separated only by a major highway.

He was taking some time off before starting a new job, while his wife, who looked older than him, was unwell, despite her robust appearance, and was on leave from her position as a professor. The three of us often met and went drinking together. They had been married for more than three years but they had no children. His wife seemed glad when I said I had a boyfriend. The moment I said that he was currently in Mongolia, she adopted a thoughtful expression and murmured, "Mongolia? Mongolia, of all places." I was on the point of asking if she knew someone in Mongolia when Ju cleared his throat lightly, "Hmm." He spoke with eyes sparkling as if he had just had a good idea. "Speaking of which, suppose we go and eat some Mongolian shabu-shabu? As I get older, eating tasteless food disagrees with me."

The two of them had already explored all the local restaurants, so they took the greenhorn that I was on a tour of a few famous ones. Once we had run out of places worth eating at, they invited me to their apartment. From then on I became their regular drinking companion.

No matter how often I begged his wife not to use a formal style when she spoke to me, she paid no attention. She was the kind of woman who would use honorifics even when she was feeding her pet puppy. He was the only person she ever spoke to without using a polite tone. Even then, she did not use forthright informal language, leaving the endings indistinct.

She never scolded him, but she did sometimes warn him about his habit of smoking cigarettes down to the very end. She herself set the example by never smoking a cigarette more than half way. She was more like a wise guardian angel than his wife.

She was particularly skilled at cooking fish. Among the dishes she produced, my favorite was neither the grilled fish nor the fish stew but fish broiled in soy sauce. After she had carefully blended perilla oil, vinegar and pepper paste to give the basic flavoring, no matter what kind of fish she boiled and served, it was breathtaking. By contrast, she was hopeless at vegetables, which I was good at. She said he was not particularly fond of meat and although she sometimes cooked some, the taste was nothing special.

After a few bad experiences with *soju*, we gracefully changed our preference to wine. As a result, whenever I went to their place I would take along a bottle of white wine from the discount store and his wife usually prepared fish. In addition, their fridge was always richly stocked with all kinds of fruit, so I never needed to buy expensive fruit for myself. Like any middle-class family, they invariably ate fruit, cake or cookies after the meal.

All through the summer they cared for me like some kind of pet animal, trying to fatten me up, while I became their puppy. True, there were times when his wife's use of honorifics in speaking to me was irritating, but again, she was the kind of woman who would never even speak informally to her pet dog. She used to regularly ask after my boyfriend in Mongolia, always employing a very polite formal style. As women often do when they lack feelings of delicate feminine affection, she and I constantly maintained a polite distance.

After meeting the two of them, my tongue got used to luxury so it renounced its previous, abstemious diet and little by little began to follow its own imprudent desires. It had tasted enough fish and fruit, so that meant it started to demand opportunities to taste meat. At such times, I would buy a piece of steak the size of my palm at the store and cook that, or buy some belly or neck of pork and grill that. It felt a shame to be drinking alone when I cooked meat, but since the two of them did not like meat, I had no choice. One day, his wife heard me make some such remark and gave off a sad expression. "But it's only him! I eat meat. Next time you must invite me, at least, Yeon-hui."

To which he added: "I eat meat, too, I just don't enjoy it much."

I felt that courtesy obliged, so one day I bought some tenderloin, prepared chopped steak and invited the two of them to my room. So long as the ingredients were fresh, there was no dish easier to make than chopped steak. You put meat and vegetables finely chopped with scissors into a well-heated frying pan, cooked them over a strong flame, added a liberal dash of steak sauce, and that was it. The couple marveled at my skill in chopping even carrots using scissors and, unexpectedly, did full justice to my cooking. They likewise manifested a vigorous appetite when I prepared fried pork with a hot pepper paste sauce, and when I ventured as far as beef rib stew they nearly made themselves sick with overeating. Yet still he insisted that he did not really like meat, while his wife took care to add that she enjoyed it more than her husband did. It seemed that to them, saying that you liked meat meant that you went mad if you did not eat meat at every meal. As we continued to meet, I could find nothing to prove that they liked meat any less than I did. Rather than not liking meat being a sign of belonging to the middle class, it looked as though they simply said they did not like meat.

If there was a day when I did not go out drinking with them, I would sit at the window of my tenth-floor room and smoke as I gazed at the yellow lamp illuminating the balcony corridor of their apartment block and the glow from their fluorescent light as it streamed out through the small, rectangular window looking onto the corridor. I was imitating Gatsby, of course.

Once, late at night, I witnessed the moment when the fluorescent light went out. That was the room that he used as his study. I imagined the feel of his finger turning the switch off, then the feel of his bare feet walking over the wooden floor toward the bedroom where his wife was. Suddenly I felt a desire to lightly cross the dividing space and hide in their dark bedroom. Then, as if quickly repenting, I wished my nonexistent boyfriend would quickly come back from Mongolia, and crossed myself like some pious Russian peasant.

We stopped drinking at their apartment and instead went wandering around the neighborhood bars after his wife returned to work at the start of the autumn semester, or in other words after our drinking sessions began to be organized differently. It was odd, but as soon as she stopped cooking fish, I no longer felt like cooking meat. She simply stopped cooking because she was busy, I stopped cooking out of sheer idle inertia, having nothing else to do. Rather, it was Ju, who had to take care of his own meals more and more often, who quietly started to cook.

That autumn, he occasionally phoned me. After the phone rang, the automatic answering system would cut in with a programmed woman's voice saying I was out, then invariably his voice would be heard remarking jokingly that I ought to change that woman's message.

"Yes, it's me."

"I went shopping this morning, prices have gone up a lot."

"That's grim news."

"Here's a riddle! It's not as dear as you might think. It's a kind of vegetable that's very often used in Chinese cooking."

"It can't be onions. Mushrooms?"

"I had some fried for lunch."

"Gingko nuts?"

"I quite like gingko nuts, but are they much used in Chinese cooking? This is cheese-colored...."

"Bamboo shoots?"

"Right!"

"Are you saying you prepared Chinese-style vegetables?"

"That's too much bother, so I just fried up some bamboo shoots. They're all right, they have a nice clean taste. Another riddle! The kind of work I want to do."

After the new riddle, he coughed, then laughed lightly.

"Nowadays, there are designers of all kinds of different products."

I said nothing.

"Designers come in all kinds but if you're going to design clothes it takes a special set of skills. With clothes, it's the appearance that matters most, isn't it? I've heard that nowadays there are clothes woven using perfumed thread but there are no clothes with a bitter or sweet taste, are there? This is a kind of clothing where you have to focus on appearance, smell, feel and even taste. It's not something people wear all the time, it's an item of menswear to be worn only at decisive moments.

I was at a loss and he laughed.

"Okay. It's condoms."

"You mean you want be become a condom designer?"

"It's what I keep complaining about; why are there only fruit-flavored or vanilla-flavored condoms? Are we kids? Freshly baked garlic bread, thick bean paste soup boiled up with clams, deep-fried prawns, steamed crab, abalone porridge: wouldn't condoms with those kinds of flavors be to die for? Really hot pepper taste might be good too, but since it's such a sensitive area, we'd better avoid that. Still, a range of savory flavors would be the thing to focus on. Savory enough to make you shudder."

"You're a great feminist, I reckon, seeing how much you've been thinking about women's appetites."

"I'm just being macho, really. Haven't I rejected pepper flavor although I know women are crazy about it? I'm a pepper-protectionist."

"Peppers are part of the environment, so that makes you an eco-feminist."

"Really? The weather's turned cool, what about having a glass of *sake* with an eco-feminist?"

"Sounds good."

I met him that late autumn evening expecting to go and drink a glass of warm *sake*, but he dragged me straight off to a cooperative store. For some reason this guy who said he didn't enjoy meat wanted to buy some milk.

"The wife told me to buy some for her to drink tomorrow morning."

"If she's home you should have come out together."

"No, she phones her orders from school. Pure remote control. I want to buy it now, before I start drinking and forget."

He used to be relatively picky when he was buying a pair of socks. It was only after he had put the salesgirl's nerves on edge by spending a full ten minutes taking out all the different varieties of milk from the fridge, comparing the brands and prices, that he finally deigned to choose one pack of milk that pleased him, checked the expiry date, and paid for it. Told that a bag was twenty won extra, he flatly refused to pay and stuffed the milk into his shoulder bag.

He rarely changed the things he used and he had a rectangular, black leather bag slung over his shoulder that he had carried about since way back. It was what was called a "police bag," the kind that has pockets front and back you can fill with things without undoing the zipper, from where cops could easily take out tear gas grenades, truncheons and so on. At the sight of the bag, my palpitations back from when I had I worshiped him and anxiously sought to spot the back of his head in the scrum of a demonstration, and my bewilderment when he declared it was over between us, came welling up together.

Finally, before we got to the bar he entered a bookstore. After picking books up then putting them down, skimming through about a fifth of their contents, he took out a book card, exchanged the accumulated points for a gift voucher, paid the remaining cost and bought a hardcover book about theory.

In a simple Japanese-style restaurant we ordered *sake* and some snacks grilled on skewers. As he picked at some grilled gingko nuts, he talked about how in the old days they used to harvest six or seven sacks of gingko nuts from the great tree that stood in the yard of their village home. But after his father died a dispute about the inheritance had arisen between the children of his father's elder brother and his own siblings, and ownership of the house had passed into the hands of their cousins, the title to the house being in dispute. Perhaps because they felt bad about it, the cousins did not move into the house at once but nor did they demolish it; for a time they left it abandoned and empty. So when autumn arrived, like now, the villagers came flocking to the empty house and gathered the nuts, on seeing which the second son of their uncle's family had done something incredible.

At that point, Ju drank some *sake* then detached one gingko nut from the skewer and ate it reverently, as though it had been harvested from that tree in his old home.

A stormy rumor had made the rounds of the village. It asked how the sons of the elder brother had been able to grab the house where their uncle had lived for decades as soon as he was dead? Fully convinced that the villagers with this hostile attitude were intending to rob them of the house that belonged to them, the second eldest of the cousins took an ax and brutally cut down more than half of the gingko tree. Perhaps it was beyond his strength to bring down the whole trunk, or perhaps he felt he had sufficiently vented his wrath by cutting down that much, in any event, the partly felled gingko tree slowly died in that unsightly, deformed pose. He had experienced deep grief for his old home through the andante withering of the gingko tree, and now it was with deep feeling that he detached another pale green nut from the skewer and ate it symbolically.

Hearing the year in which the gingko tree had been chopped down, I realized it must have been at the time when Ju had been released from prison and gone to work as an employee in a publishing company producing an obscure quarterly poetry magazine. I could remember clearly how violent and ill-mannered he had been in those days. When I used to meet him in the basement coffee shop in the building housing the publishers, he would ignore me completely. It was not only me. In those times he showed no interest in anything, and was particularly icy regarding anything connected to the past.

"You get nothing by looking back, nothing."

Every time we met, he just kept repeating that, discouragingly, and when we parted he made no attempt to hide his wish not to see me again, the nuance suggesting a breakup. Come to think of it, at that time he was in his twenty-ninth autumn too.

Stimulated by the gingko nuts, he grew quite sentimental and soon began to talk languidly about the past. I laughed and clicked my tongue, sometimes I expressed indignation or added words when I knew the story, all the time drinking *sake* and nibbling at the snacks.

It was a time when friends who prided themselves on being rebellious risked their necks playing at spies pretending they knew each other, so long as they were out of sight of the plainclothes police in some quiet corner of the campus. They always used to have the name, meeting time and address of anyone they were to meet written in tiny writing in a notebook, using a kind of code with abbreviations and numerals, before quickly tearing it out. On the remaining pages they used to write out sorrowfully a few lines of poetry modeled on Shin Dong-yeop's *Geum-gang River* or Kim Ji-ha's *Five Bandits*. But the remaining parts of the campus were as a campus really should be. In every season the lawns were green, the shadows cast by the buildings were dark, the young folk were slender, well-behaved and hard-working. The stone steps leading to the student dining room, memories of how sometimes the sole of a loafer would strike hard against one of the irregularly set stones as he turned to offer a belated greeting to an acquaintance after walking on a few steps. Ten minutes or so spent sitting on a bench behind the Fine Arts College building, female students cutting across the insect-filled lawns in paint-spattered aprons, sounds of instruments ringing out from time to time. A girl's soprano voice climbing gracefully step by step up the scale. The anxiety and fascination as she rose ever higher, as if on an increasingly narrow, steep ladder. The occasional solitude of the lawn in front of the College of Engineering. The rough shouts of the male students who sometimes came racing out. You really have to love those friends. The cool feeling after a hasty draw on a cigarette, overcome with emotion at unexpected memories….

The students who used to play cards on the brightly sunlit window seats in the dining room or on the lozenge-shaped lawn in the angle made by two buildings. The quietness with which children play when out of sight of adults, that tenacious, innocent delight, for some reason made him feel jealous and hurt. If the plainclothes police entered the campus on account of a demonstration, or if a battalion of riot police invaded after a fight at the main gate, hurling various kinds of tear gas grenades, as the explosions of the dreaded tear gas canisters resonated, they would lay down their cards, stand up, and pick up sharp stones with the very same hands.

The saloon bars that used to be lined up near the universities even just ten years ago. The compensations he'd been forced to pay or been paid after getting into fights in various sordid drinking holes. The story of how his student advisor, whom he had not once set eyes on after being designated a problem student, had come hand in hand with his parents, who lived in the countryside, to visit him in prison. The story of the fight he'd had with a member of the editorial staff at the publishing company he had gone to work at on the same professor's recommendation. The grotesque tale he'd heard from that same member of staff of how to cook a bear's paw.

Stories I seemed to have heard and not to have heard came pouring out in an endless stream from his lips. Yet this was the man who, even in the days when he was sharing an office with that same member of staff, had all the time repeated listlessly, "You get nothing by looking back, nothing."

As we were about to part, he tipped his head back and gazed up at the dark night sky. I looked up at the sharp right angle formed by his neck bone.

"How can we just go home and leave that color behind? Let's have one last cigarette first, Yeon-hui."

The two of us squatted on the pavement in front of the crossing where we would have to separate and smoked our cigarettes.

"I don't feel I'm living in the wrong way. Yet living like this fills me with fear."

"When do you feel that?"

He looked at me with a bewildered look.

"It doesn't depend on the time. My lifestyle, my disposition as such make me feel apprehensive. When was my life decided? What is decided, what is undecided? A few days ago I wanted to know the answer, so I took up seven or so pages of A4 paper trying to work it out, and came to the conclusion that it was all decided very early on. The decision was not made as I entered university. Nor was it at high school, or middle school. The decision was already made by the time I started to think. Perhaps from the time I was born. If you go even further back, from the moment I was conceived. In the beginning was the decision."

"Hmm, Cheol-su the fatalist."

He snorted and stubbed out his cigarette.

"Let's call it a day. There's no end to it."

He glanced up at the sky again and stood up, throwing his bag over his shoulder. Just then I pointed at his bag in astonishment.

"Hey, what's wrong with your bag?"

One half of the leather bag was paler than the rest. He turned the bag over with a look that asked what I was fussing about and a cloudy liquid began dripping out. It was milk. When he had squatted down on the pavement, it looked as though he had used the bag for a cushion and squashed the pack of milk. The milk, twice the normal price with its added calcium and other extras, had soaked into the carefully chosen hardcover book of theory and turned it to a pulp. As he stood there looking at me helplessly, I could not help laughing.

After that I often observed, when his wife was not with him, how inside his apparently solid, flawless outside fence he kept a monster of ineptitude that only appeared when his wife was absent. Rather than the question as to when his life had been decided, I was more curious as to when it was that this stupid little goblin had settled inside his fence. If he sat down for a moment on the grass in a park his keys would fall out as he stood up and he would have to call a locksmith who would come rushing along, greeting him with, "You've lost them again!" as he opened the door for him. He often lost his glasses, too, the reason for which was that, realizing he often lost his glasses, he always went about with a spare pair in reserve. I once read an article in a newspaper saying that the subway's lost property office was full of all kinds of things that were really difficult to lose. Reading that there were even people who lost their dentures, I found myself nodding. I felt sure that someone like him who easily lost things went about with a spare set of dentures, which he had then left behind as he got off the train.

The autumn after I moved to the new town passed quietly and peacefully. As I recall that autumn, I find myself with the following questions: Was Su-rim another of his many careless accidents? Was I? Was his wife fully aware of all these happenings? Did he know she knew?

Once the new year came, I spent the whole of January thinking about how I was now thirty. I smoked a lot and drank alone until late every night. For snacks I ate fish fried in a pan. I longed for the fish broiled in soy sauce his wife had made back in the summer, but that was beyond my capabilities. I consumed the sixty croakers in three packs I bought cheap at the discount store within a month. I reached the point when I knew with my eyes shut just when to turn the fish in the pan, I grew skilled at precisely removing even the smallest bones in an incredibly short time but I had no chance to show off. Then one day I was moved by the taste of a couple of strongly flavored pieces of meat from the lower part of a croaker's head, and for the first time in a long while I wrote a passionate poem. In what would correspond to the chin in a human being, a double triangle of dark red flesh was embedded. As I succeeded in detaching it with a skillful twist of the chopsticks, I had the impression I had torn out the croaker's tongue.

I could not even imagine going to sleep without being drunk, immersed in the smell of fish and cigarettes that impregnated every corner of the room. There were many days when I would lie in bed feeling nauseous and not be able get to sleep until the sun had risen high in the sky. Perhaps because of all these unhealthy elements, my thoughts were consumed by the idea of being thirty without any noticeable progress. Like any natural number, all the ages I had experienced and all the ages I would experience had one characteristic in common. There was no reason the first year of my thirties should be more significant than the eighth year of my teens or the third year of my fifties. The only special thing about thirty lay simply in the commonplace truth that every number is special. Yet even now, I still cannot help thinking that there was something special about the way I met those women one after the other when I was just thirty.

Sometimes I think I would have been happier if I had not met Ju and his wife at the meat counter in the discount store. It's futile regretting what happens by chance, of course, but saying it's futile does not stop regret arising. If I remind myself that it's futile, inside my head I remember again the sixty tiny tongue-like pairs of red scraps of meat inside the heads of the croakers I ate all through January the year I turned thirty. If we had a pair of tongues, they might be less useful or they might be more so. I don't know why, but the thought arises in me that if I had had two tongues, my life would have been very different from what it is now. His wife and Su-rim might perhaps have both withered away long ago until they were nothing but a trace of a pair of tongues remaining at the root of my tongue.

I regularly cooked the croakers two at a time, so when the sixty were all gone it was January 31. At some point I got into the habit of looking at the telephone just when it was time for supper, and at some point I stopped receiving phone calls from him. That night I was eating a belated supper as I watched television. The fact that there were no croakers left to cook left me feeling relieved but anxious. Just as I was about to clear the table, the telephone rang.

"This is O Yeon-hui. I cannot take your call now. Please leave a message."

As he had demanded, I had carefully erased the pre-recorded message and left one using my own voice.

"Ah, this woman's message is different."

He was saying it was the first time he had heard the recording of my voice, so how long had it been that he had not called, for goodness' sake? I stretched out a hand and picked up the cordless phone.

"Yes, hello. It's me."

"Why does your voice sound like that? Are you sick?"

"No."

"You haven't had supper, have you?"

"I have."

"You've already eaten?"

He asked as though he was surprised, yet it was already past ten o'clock.

"Yes."

"I'm in front of your building, I thought we could eat supper and have a drink."

"I've already had supper."

"Then come on down and have a drink."

When I said nothing, he added what was clearly a lure.

"Come and see. There's a friend I want you to meet."

"What kind of friend?"

"You'll see when you get here."

"Where are you?"

He gave the name of a fish stew restaurant on the second floor of a building I knew. I hung up and as I glanced at the calendar I realized that not only was I one year older but I had wasted more than eight percent of the time during which I would be that age, and felt it was unfair.

In the entrance hall of the restaurant, a pair of long women's boots were lying askew. The woman sitting facing him had her black hair sleeked down as if she had just taken it out of water, in a style that strongly emphasized the shape of her skull. In some ways she reminded me of his wife but she looked very young, her weight and age both being less than half his wife's.

"I told you about her, didn't I? This is Kim Su-rim."

No, I had never heard him mention this woman. She was working at the publishing company where he had previously been employed; she told me she was in her twenties and unmarried. As he introduced her, his face was marked with a burning desire to fold her up and carry her around in his pocket like Lao Tzu's magic donkey.

"She looks young, doesn't she?"

He asked his question with a smug expression, as though it was all the result of his own efforts. Before I could say anything in reply, the woman spoke.

"Why, this friend looks young, too."

This friend? My eyebrows rose of their own accord.

"I don't think I look particularly young, you know."

"Come on, use familiar-style language."

At her insolent reply, I looked at him.

"That's right, you're the same age after all, so you should use familiar style."

Sensing what I was thinking, he quickly added: "Of course, it's a bit quick, this being your first time to meet."

"If she doesn't do it from the start, she never will, Mr. Editor-in-Chief."

At her pert reply he laughed stupidly.

"That's very true. It's always the first step that counts. There's something I once heard from a professor back in the old days; I bet neither of you know how to cook a bear's paw?"

Now I had heard that story twice at least. He was insisting he had told me things he had not told me and pretending not to have told me things he had. If you make a bear stand on a heated iron griddle, the bear will jump up and down on account of the heat. Once the bear has jumped enough, you remove it and eat the scraps of flesh from the bear's paws that have stuck to the griddle. You treat the wounded bear and then, once new flesh has grown on its paws, you put it back on the iron griddle. He told the story in an excited, flustered tone. If his wife and I had clenched our hands and started pulling at each other's hair, he would not have been as upset as we were.

"Oh, come off it!"

Then his wife laughed. Seeing that my reaction was likewise incredulous, he had gone on eagerly.

"It's true, I tell you. If you have to kill a bear every time you want to cook some bear meat, how much is that going to cost? This way you save its life. It's just the same as when you insert a tube into a bear's liver and extract its bile to drink."

That was it. Any human being would be quite capable of inventing that kind of cruel wisdom. Seeing the direction our expressions had taken, he was completely satisfied. Perhaps on account of that satisfaction, he had told the same story again once when we had been drinking alone. The dance on the heated iron griddle, treatment, dancing again, the meat stuck to the griddle....

As she listened to his chatter, Su-rim kept her head up and sat there looking self-possessed. As I heard him repeat his story for the third time, I could not help thinking about the fate of the bear doomed to experience that pain over and over until it died. If human beings were obliged to live imprisoned in some such repeated cycle of pain until their last day came, surely they would go mad or hang themselves. At the thought of the bear's desolate despair, unaware of death and unable to hasten toward it, I became keenly aware of what a great blessing it was that I knew how to kill myself. I longed to reverently kiss the bear's paws. In order to do that, I would have to once cook and eat bear paw, but he said he didn't like meat, so it would be impossible.

In her closely fitting black leather jacket, tight pants and long boots, Su-rim looked amazingly agile. As she dug the toe of a boot into the earth beneath a streetside tree, she looked like a sturdy, firmly condensed object that had been tossed into the bitter winter's cold. As he loitered smoking a cigarette, he approached me and asked me to let her sleep in my room. She never did anything for herself, she was an expert at making others do things for her.

"It would be best if I could take her to our place but my wife seems to dislike her."

"Why?"

At that moment Su-rim approached us so I had no chance to hear any reply. She had no objection to going to my room. Once she was sure I was going to let her sleep there, while we were on the way she even asked if it wouldn't be a good idea to buy something to drink and some snacks.

In a convenience store we bought several bottles of wine, some beef jerky and some pine nuts. Like him, Su-rim did not much like meat, she said jerky was the only exception. As I opened the door and we entered the room, they both wrinkled their noses disdainfully. He said my room smelled like a vagabond who had spent half the day roaming around a fish market, then half the day chain-smoking in a sealed smoking room at the National Library before walking back home soaking in the evening fog.

While I boiled some instant dried pollack soup, Su-rim finished laying the table. Cheol-su seemed tired and sat dozing in a corner until the drinking started, when he immediately joined in. For some reason, Su-rim suddenly grew excited, busily changing CDs, slurping down wine, smoking continuously. Then suddenly she stared closely into his face and began to hit him with a table tennis ball-sized fist, laughing as she did so.

"Why? Why?"

He seemed beside himself with delight.

"I hate people with artificial teeth more than anything, Mr. Editor-in-Chief."

Her editor-in-chief laughed through his nose, hiding his upper denture. Those were teeth that had been broken in prison. It had nothing to do with anything glorious like torture, I had heard, it was because he had been walking along with his hands behind his back when he carelessly slipped on a patch of ice. I wondered if his habit of giving a slight laugh through his nose without opening his mouth whenever he was feeling happy or had a good idea might not have been because Su-rim disliked dentures.

Su-rim began by reciting one poem, nodding as she did so, then she seemed to reckon that all the poetry books in my bookcase should be invited to serve during the party. Day was already beginning to break when he went back to his apartment across the big highway and Su-rim passed out, collapsing onto my bedding. As she lay curled on the duvet cover, she looked like a black comma printed on a sheet of colored paper. Her skull, small like that of a cat, seemed to serve as a symbol of her peculiar identity. I could not rid myself of the impression that she was capricious and no-good. If I had been a bit more drunk, I might have seized her two feet in one hand, whirled her around my head and hurled her from my tenth-floor room.

When I woke, covered by a single blanket and shivering with the cold, Su-rim had vanished. I crept under the empty quilt. The quilt smelt like a homeless vagabond, but from the pillow rose a heady, fruit-scented perfume. It was the scent of the mousse Su-rim applied like resin to her hair. I quickly turned the pillow over and fell asleep. While I was still asleep, I sensed someone come in. There was the clear sound of someone moving stealthily about the room. I leaped to my feet. As the air shifted in response to my violent movement I detected an appetizing smell of food.

"Are you awake?"

Something like a little black goblin leaped out from the gap between the bookshelves, making me jump.

"Haven't you gone yet?"

"I told you to use familiar-style language. I went down to the store. You want something to eat?"

"I think it'll be hard for me to eat anything yet."

"Then go back to sleep, Yeon-hui."

I felt helpless. Why did she not seem to have any thought of going home? Borrowing strength from my hangover, I went back to sleep again. Some time later Su-rim shook me awake.

"If you sleep any longer your stomach'll go sour and that's not good for you. Try to eat, even if it's just a spoonful."

I got up reluctantly. She had tidied the room that had been in such a mess from our all-night reveling. On the dining table, that until daybreak had been a drinking table, stood a bowl of rice gruel sprinkled with sesame seeds and powdered seaweed, and a dish with chopped kimchi. Oddly, there was only a single set of untensils laid out.

"Won't you eat with me?"

I was still using polite forms of speech.

"I told you, use the familiar style. I can't eat anything."

"You mean you've made this for my sake?" I asked vaguely.

"It's not like that. I don't like meat so I was going to make some vegetable gruel. But now I think about it, I'll be better off not eating."

"My stomach's in a no-good state, too, yet you want me to eat? In that case, you should eat with me."

"No, my stomach's fine."

"Then why?"

"I have a reason for not eating."

Su-rim smiled as if to suggest she was in deep trouble; it looked like one of those bad habits women who want to seem mysterious have. Perhaps because she had just washed it, the tips of her hair were slightly moist. I had no choice but to finish a serving of gruel, then she asked if she should make some coffee. I told her not to bother. I still had no idea when she intended to leave. After I had drunk a glass of water and smoked a cigarette, she pursed her lips and out of the blue asked: "Lend me three hundred thousand won, Yeon-hui."

"Three hundred thousand? But… I don't have any money now."

"You only have to go to the bank and use your card, then let me have that."

My head reeled at her self-assured demand. Three hundred thousand won for a bowl of gruel?

"Just now, on my way to the store, I dropped in at a pharmacy. Once I was back I did the test and it's as I thought. I really don't know why I have such bad luck. It looks as though it must be the eighth week."

I found it impossible to believe that some kind of other life was breathing and growing inside her dry little body.

"I intend to get rid of it now, rather than go on worrying, that's why I'm not eating anything. I'll repay you as soon as I get it from him. I've phoned but he's not answering."

It was not only a matter of lending her the money, I was obliged to go to the hospital with her, bring her back to my room after the operation and let her sleep, then once she was awake I had to hear about the whole wonderful love affair, that she poured out in a flood of tears, during which she had twice become pregnant. While I became privy to a whole set of secrets I did not want, I was obliged to put up with her as she hung around until nine that evening.

"I shouldn't drink, should I? I might get an infection. But Yeon-hui, I really need a drink. I don't hate the guy. I can't stand condoms, that's the problem, it's not Editor-in-Chief's fault. Once you know him, you realize he's really a pitiful fellow. You must know that, too, Yeon-hui."

She spoke those words courageously as she was on her way out of the door, and I was so glad to see her going that I had no time to be surprised on realizing that that pitiful fellow was none other than Ju with his dreams of being a condom designer. I simply nodded energetically to show my agreement. After seeing her off, I wandered around the room for a while, then, although there was no need, I put on a coat, wrote "Refused" on a set of New Year's cards sent by handicapped artists, already a month out of date, and went out to put them in the mailbox. I just had to do something unkind, I could not endure it otherwise. On the way back after tossing the set of cards into the mailbox I entered a noisy beerhouse, ordered a liter of beer without any snacks and downed it in three or four gulps. I deliberately staggered as I wandered the streets, singing through my nose before returning to my room that seemed to be a metaphor for my small, messy soul. The moment I opened the door, the air emerging between the bookcases was thick with the usual, hard-to-take smell. Just then the telephone rang like a kind of signal.

"Wow, I thought I was going to die. I slept all day. I woke up a while ago and went to eat some clam porridge with my wife as she was coming home, now I'm back. Have you had something to eat? Ah yes, did Su-rim leave in the morning? She usually can't sleep a wink in other people's homes, you know. You wouldn't believe how sensitive her nerves are. How do you find her? She's fun, right?"

I gave a thin nasal laugh. I felt like saying something sarcastic imitating his particular style of speaking, to the effect that I had thought she was a no-good woman, and on getting to know her I found she really was a no-good woman. After hanging up, I pulled out all the poetry books that Su-rim had put back in the wrong order thinking she was tidying up and quietly rearranged them in an order corresponding to my preferences. I was putting the last volume back when I suddenly felt that I was compromising my own morals. Perhaps my feeling was similar to the feeling he had had when he said that he constantly felt overcome with fear. Something struck me hard as it passed. Or perhaps I had struck it hard. Something sensitive like a festering sore, something I believed I had abandoned long ago, but that had burst in some cranny and was discharging a fluid, something that filled my mouth with viscous bitterness and made me frown, something that flinched and twisted as soon as it was touched. I rested my forehead on one of the white shelves of the bookcase and wept. As I wept, I reflected that without the freshness descending on the back of my head, what on earth would this being I called "me" be? What was I? What was I?

Perhaps it was a butterfly.

When his wife came to visit me, I was wearing working gloves, tying up boxes of books with twine that I would twist into ornamental knots like ribbons then cut with scissors. The white plastic bookcases were emptying shelf by shelf. I was just thinking that I wanted to visit the vast display counters and wide corridors of the discount store one last time before I left town.

"You're moving out? Without a word to anyone?"

His wife looked at me as she asked, without displaying any great surprise or blame. I had not yet packed my kitchen things and I was able to boil water in the kettle so we could drink some coffee.

"He's pitiful, yes, I know that. But still...."

I intuitively knew what she was talking about. I remembered hearing something of the kind from Su-rim herself. Finally, she added, as though putting a stamp on things: "We've decided to get divorced. It's what he wants."

I adopted a resigned expression. I considered their decision to be something I could not change. Without saying anything, I nodded at this aging woman who was still his wife. An ashen shadow like the fatigue of a warrior at sunset lay over her brow. She stubbed out her less-than-half-smoked cigarette in the ashtray and simply asked, "Is your fiancé still in Mongolia?"

Unsure of her intentions, my expression hardened.

"It seems he's going to India."

I curtly sent my imaginary sweetheart off to India.

"India? India, of all places."

Again, she added that ambiguous "of all places." But I did not ask her if she knew someone in India. We stayed sitting in silence for a moment. Suddenly a fit of curiosity flashed into my mind.

"By the way, you remember that fish broiled in soy sauce?"

"What?"

"I wonder, did you add curry powder?"

"Curry powder?"

Her lips curled upward in a strange smile.

"It's not curry powder."

She did not look inclined to tell me the secret of her broiled fish. Such stinginess was not like her. Perhaps it was her heart wanting to put what had happened in the summer and autumn of the previous year then through the winter and this year's spring in parentheses. I was the same. One such period of total idleness and silence and smells was quite enough. Anyway, she said it wasn't curry powder. Then what was it? Pepper? Bay leaves? But I could not ask anything more.

As she stood up after finishing her coffee, her gaze shifted about anxiously. In the entrance, as she stirred with the toe of her shoe the bits of twine that were lying about she raised her head and for the first time addressed me using familiar-style language: "Was I so docile, to you others?"

I intended to offer some kind of excuse but my throat clamped shut with tension, it was as though the roots of my tongue were being cut in two, and I could not speak a word on account of the pain. Finally the roots of my tongue burst open like a cocoon and two flapping wings emerged. The two tongues wound round each other and tangled together like ribbons. Words came bursting forth, there was no telling if they came from her or from me. Our shoulders rose and fell on account of our madly beating hearts. Like the day in our childhoods when we first learned the words "prick" and "pussy" and kept repeating them over and over again in our heads, the words poured out fresh and clear.

"Wicked creature. Vulgar scum. Birdbrain, thinking of nothing but doing that, day and night. You cheap, shameless hussy, with men that's all you're capable of doing, with women that's all you're capable of talking about, sticking your mouth up there, down there. Have you ever really beaten your breast and cried? Have you ever cursed life until your lips turn pale, not because of a man or a broken heart but because of your own insignificance, your own stupidity, your own incorrigible wickedness? Have you ever sunk to the very bottom and felt intensely that you have nothing left but death, that dreadful emptiness? Have you ever lived the life of a corpse where opening your eyes each morning is hell? Have you ever had a notion of the desolate sorrow where you cannot live and cannot die without it? Surely not. There's no reason you should. You, you just go about treating that one special hole and the skin around it like some kind of sacred relic; you, the only thing you're capable of is taking good care of your body then throwing it as food to men like a pimp; with you, whether it's reading and writing poetry, or crying as you listen to jazz, or having a drink while you recall your student days as if you're squandering your savings, even your preferences, disliking or liking meat or fish, it's all done in order to make a good impression on men; you've replaced the child's upstretched arms begging: Hug me, just once, just once, with an upstretched crotch begging: Do it, just once, just once; with you, you, there's no way."

Once his wife had left I sat near the window smoking a cigarette. It was misty enough that their apartment across the street could not be seen clearly. Was that a butterfly? Something fluttered past me. I opened the window and poked my head out. There was no sign of a pale fluttering object anywhere. In the flowerbeds of the officetel's parking area seen from the tenth floor, red roses stood like stab wounds above a thick growth of dark green leaves. *Plop!* A raindrop fell on my nose. It was about the size of the drop of spittle that had leaped from Ju's lips as he made his impassioned speech. As on that occasion, I laughed as I wiped my nose and flinched. Rain had soaked the bright red palm of my cotton gloves, appearing like blood. I realized that what I had been waiting for was not my boyfriend in Mongolia but some kind of dramatic closure. I had deceived his wife while addressing her affectionately as "elder sister." I had thrust my crotch at the watchful Ju. I had utterly despised Su-rim the sex fiend, yet I had always been so jealous of her. I had disclosed knowledge I did not have. Behind a pretext of isolation I had all the time been dreaming of a dirty complicity.

By the time I resumed my packing, my tongue was stuck together neatly as before. In reality, I do not have two tongues in one mouth. As I tied the twine tightly in ribbon-style knots, I reflected that if the tongue really were double, if there really were a pair of divided desires allowing a moment's respite in which, even if it hurt, my tongue could stand on alternate feet like a pair of bear's feet dancing on an iron griddle, my life would be very different from what it is now. I stood at a crossroads with half my thirtieth year gone and half remaining.

Some years later I heard from an acquaintance that they had not divorced. They had been on their way back after visiting his original home, where there was a withered gingko tree, for some reason. Given his character, that put value on symbolic rituals, perhaps they had gone to announce their decision to divorce in front of his father's grave. On the expressway as they were driving back, one of their jeep's rear wheels came off, the vehicle crossed the central dividing line, made a complete turn and fell on its side. It was very strange. He was driving and he had a twisted arm; his wife who was in the passenger seat fainted briefly then recovered, and that was all. I gathered that the mechanics who arrived to tow the car away, and even the paramedics, looked slightly disappointed by their minor injuries. They underwent thorough examinations in two different hospitals but apart from a minute crack in his arm, there was nothing. I learned that they continued to live together in that new town and still have no children. That's really good, extremely fortunate, my relaxed tongue murmured again and again.

TAENGJA

Yoon Dae-nyeong

Translated by Maya West

탱자

윤대녕

A critique of this short story was published in the Koreana magazine in Summer 2011 (Vol. 25 No. 2, pp. 82-83).

© Kim Si-hoon

Without occasional purification, a person cannot age. An elderly monk told me that; I met him this spring on the boat from Tongyeong to Jeju. He told me that was why he was crossing the sea—he didn't actually need to get anywhere. I was on my way back from Jinhae, where I'd gone to see the cherry blossoms. When I asked him what he meant by "purification," he gestured toward the empty *soju* bottle next to me and the bright red tip of my cigarette, burning down in my hand. Then he added, with an awkward laugh: "This will likely come again, before we reach death."

I don't know if you'll remember. The last time I saw you was at your grandfather's funeral, and that was a good thirty years ago now, though it's hard to keep count. You were just a middle schooler then, with your black uniform and your shaved head. I remember you didn't shed a single tear, even though your grandfather was dead, the same grandfather who insisted on dandling you on his knee even after you were far too big. Face like an angry goat, you just sat on the wooden floor and emptied bowl after bowl of soup. That's the last image I have of you. To think that you, that same boy, are now well over forty—it makes the years seem like some perverse old graybeard with ointment plastered all over his face.

I realize you're probably startled by such sudden contact, but I ask that you resist any urge to ignore this and please read to the end. About a month ago, on the anniversary of your grandfather's death, all his scattered children came back together at the old house. It had been ten, twenty years since I set foot in that house, but I suddenly wanted to see the faces of my brothers and sisters, and so I, too, spent a full day on a bus to make it. Except for your youngest uncle, who lives in Gangneung, every one of us was there. And that was where I heard news of you from your father.

So that's the short version of events that led me to write to you. I'd like to visit where you live. I went back and forth a while, not wanting the request to cause you worry, but I've come to terms with myself, and here I am. I'll make just one request. Seeing one another now and then as we go about our days will be just fine, but I wonder if you might take some time to find me a room. A few weeks to a month is what I'm thinking, but these so-called motels that have become so fashionable these days don't seem the type of place a woman should stay alone. Even if it's rundown and uncomfortable, a room in a private house would be much better.

I think I'll cross over next Wednesday, boarding the boat at Tongyeong. Before that I'll take some time to picnic on my own around Gyeongju, and I'm planning on finally seeing the famous Bulguk Temple with my own eyes, too. This will be my first time, both stepping on a boat and going to Jeju Island, and an incessant little chattering in my old heart tells me it will also be my last.

I know that this letter must be an uncommon bother. Even so, I hope it doesn't make you flee in order to avoid me. Just a few days ago I thought it was still Chungmu, but I called and discovered that the name had been changed to Tongyeong. I will get in touch before boarding the boat there. And make sure to speak to your wife well in advance so she doesn't fuss needlessly. And if you would, don't tell any of our relations that I'm coming for a visit. I just don't want to have to listen to any opinions on whether or not all this is fitting for my age.

Written with care and posted with speed,

From Seoul,

Your Aunt

The name my grandfather gave my eldest aunt was Gyeong-ja. She was born a few years before liberation, so the name likely has no real meaning—just chosen at random, in the Japanese style. If one were to insist on parsing it in Korean, it would be "Seoul woman." But what possible meaning can there be in that? Still, people do tend somehow to follow the path set by their name; it was enough to make me wonder if maybe that was why she lived in Seoul. Then again, until the letter arrived I didn't have a clue that my aunt even lived in Seoul. For thirty years, not a single soul, including my parents, had ever mentioned her to me.

My grandfather left this world in the summer of 1975. At the time I was in the second year of middle school and my aunt, at thirty-five years old, had long since left to marry. All I knew was what I heard in passing, that she lived in a place called Jinjuk near a city called Boryeong in South Chungcheong Province. It was close to some mineral springs, famous for salted shrimp, and not far from Daecheon with some good sandy beaches—a small country town crossed by the Janghang railway line. They said her husband was some sort of porter at the tiny whistle-stop of a station. That day my aunt brought her son with her, a boy just turned seven years old. For whatever reason, her husband didn't come. Not a single person asked why. When I went into the kitchen and asked her myself, my aunt simply laughed rather hollowly and awkwardly stroked my hair with her wet hand.

Skinny and short with a tiny, plain face, even in childhood my aunt never garnered much positive interest. On top of that, even before she started school she had developed a taste for wandering, and before long it was a common occurrence for the entire family to have to search around the neighborhood late at night to look for her, lights held aloft. In part, this rebellion was likely an attempt to get some attention, but its only real effect was marking her as even more of a headache. And as her younger brothers and sisters were born, one after the other, she even fell out of favor with her parents. Considering that Grandfather was the head of the local township, it would have been important for her to be especially well-behaved, but as time passed, she clearly cared less and less. Hanging out with boys, she pilfered melons and apples from neighborhood orchards and, once, even stole and ate a neighbor's chicken. Never considering what she might really be feeling, the family just clucked their tongues, saying the girl should simply never have been born. Still, even a mistake has to be taught right, and so they sent her to middle school—only to have her lock eyes with her disabled homeroom teacher and run off with him in the dead of night, well before graduation. A few months after that, she returned, dressed in tatters, and for the next twelve years, until she finally married and left for good at the age of twenty-eight, she was treated like little more than a servant. Though they never actually drove her out, neither her parents nor her siblings ever took much notice of my aunt. And whenever some small misfortune fell on the household, it was always her who got the blame.

Even as they sent her off to be married, the only hint of celebration in the house was an atmosphere of finally disposing of some age-old nuisance. The decision to lock her away for all those long years had been to serve a single purpose: to erase the rumors surrounding her affair with the disabled teacher. It was all very hush-hush as they searched for a possible husband, ideally from some place as far from home as possible, from some family that wouldn't make a fuss even if word of her past reached them after the marriage. And when a man from such a family was found, they sent her off at the break of dawn without a single hint of fanfare. She was told in no uncertain terms that she was not to return, not even for the most important family gatherings. I was eight years old at the time, and until then I had grown up bearing witness to her situation, though I hardly understood what it all meant. I knew, of course, that she was technically my aunt, but she was regarded as nothing more than a soot-covered scullery maid. I only found out that she had been married off when I overheard some grown-ups talking a few days later. So it was that I didn't see her for several years, not until the day of Grandfather's funeral. And after that, like before, I heard not one bit of news about her. In part, perhaps, this was because as I grew older, I too visited home less and less often.

The letter was written in pencil on a piece of paper with black, narrow lines. To be perfectly honest, my first reaction was not welcoming. A family member with whom one shares every meal is one thing, but families in general are like trees, with each branch growing in a different direction until their tips gradually become strangers—this is the logical, natural way of human life. This is also the reason why it soon becomes so difficult, once one leaves the family home, to get together outside of big holidays. When all is said and done, no relationship is more fraught than that between family members. Even parents and children, if they cross paths too often, will inevitably fall into discord. So to have an aunt I hadn't laid eyes on for thirty years suddenly announce by letter that she would be traveling this great distance for a visit... well, there was no way it wouldn't be a burden. It was easy for her to say a few weeks to a month, but looked at from the host's perspective, the same time frame felt incredibly long. After two or three days, even the visit of a close friend can become exhausting. Be that as it may, as we live our lives we come across situations that cannot be avoided. Personal relations are certainly no exception. Then, as I wrapped my head around all this, it occurred to me how strange it was, for such an elderly person to travel so far alone, and to make the crossing by boat, and I began to worry. I had just experienced it myself this past spring, and I knew that if the waves were even a little bit rough, the nearly four-hour boat ride could be more than a little difficult to bear.

After first alerting my wife about the letter, I began looking into possible places where my aunt could stay that would be close to our house. I started by looking into the rentals they call "pensions," but soon found that the rates were impossibly high. It was peak season for tourists, and each place I found charged more than a hundred thousand won a night; no matter what my aunt's finances might be like, this was too large a sum for an elderly individual to afford. Besides, other than a slightly different façade and a few more amenities, they weren't much different from motels. Next, I looked into new row houses for sale, but none were available to rent for just a few weeks to a month; neither were rooms in private homes. Everyone seemed to shy away from the prospect of taking on a single elderly tenant. In the end, I managed to locate a small room by the sea, but the thought of her sitting there all alone, just watching the ocean day after day, somehow made me uncomfortable. My wife quietly suggested that it might be good to have her stay with us for the duration. After all, what would my parents say if they found out?

Wednesday, July 21, the day of my aunt's arrival, was a day of oppressive heat from morning until night. The boat from Tongyeong docked at Seongsan, which was, in turn, more than an hour by car from Aewol. Eating a bowl of cold noodles, I waited on the pier. Around two in the afternoon, the white passenger liner appeared to the north, far off on the distant waves, and thirty minutes after that *The Mandarin*, crammed with tourists, was entering the harbor. Barely after the boat had fully docked, the tourists began spilling out one after another down the metal stairs, but no matter how hard I looked, I was unable to spot my aunt. I started to feel uneasy, even as I reminded myself that she'd called just that morning to confirm her departure. As the last of the tourists passed through the waiting area, I turned toward the nearby offices, intending to check the passenger list; but at precisely that moment, I spotted two crewmen at the top of the stairs, one on each side of a little old woman, helping her. In her white, traditional *hanbok* top and a long, straight black skirt, she stood out. I hurried over to the base of the stairs to meet her. Her face was drenched in cold sweat. One of the crewmen explained that she had taken medicine for seasickness but had thrown that up too, leaving her completely drained. He advised that I take her to a doctor as soon as possible. With no time for a proper hello, I lifted my aunt onto my back and carried her off the pier and straight to the nearest clinic.

With two IV needles stuck into the back of her hand, my aunt slept deeply for three straight hours. After calling my wife to let her know what was happening, I stepped into the room every half an hour or so and simply stood, looking down at my aunt's face. I suppose it was to be expected, but I couldn't find a single trace of the thirty-five-year-old aunt I had last seen. It was only through a vague recognition of the face's overall shape that I could be certain that this was, in fact, my aunt. Worn out with waiting, I left the clinic for a moment and sat on a plastic chair by the bus stop; there I drank a cup of vending machine coffee and smoked three or four cigarettes. Then I called my wife again, telling her to go ahead and eat dinner without waiting. Seeing the distant waves begin to darken, I pulled myself to my feet and made my way back to the clinic.

My aunt was sitting on a sofa in the waiting room, all cleaned up and chatting with a nurse. The moment I walked in, she stood and reached for my hand, clearly embarrassed.

"I've only just arrived and caused so much trouble already."

"If you were coming from a visit to Gyeongju, you might have used Pohang Airport; why take the boat and make your trip so much harder?"

"Well, I've arrived, regardless, so that's that. First things first, let's get a bite to eat. I threw up everything I ate this morning, and my stomach feels empty."

To the nurse, who had followed us out of the clinic with her bag, she handed a ten thousand won note. Ignoring the nurse's vehement protests, she forced the bill into the younger woman's hand. The evening was growing darker, and here and there on the water the squid boats began to turn on their lights, one by one. We entered a restaurant at the base of Sunrise Peak and ordered a seafood stew with soybean paste, but my aunt frowned, saying it smelled too fishy. People in the restaurant kept glancing our way, possibly thinking she might be a passenger from *The Mangyeongbong*, a special liner that carried passengers from the North. It was her clothes that did it. The gigantic shadow of Sunrise Peak was outlined against the restaurant window, but my aunt didn't even notice. Setting her spoon down on the table, she was grumbling belatedly about the fact that she'd been perfectly fine when they all got on the boat at Tongyeong.

"That damned boat seesawed back and forth so bad, I can't tell you how many times my heart leapt into my mouth."

I've experienced it as well, and there really is nothing that feels quite as hopeless as seasickness. You can't just stop the boat and get off mid-journey, like a bus or a taxicab. Changing the subject, I began asking about the earlier stages of her trip.

"How was Gyeongju?"

Her face clearing immediately, she replied.

"It was very fine indeed. It was hard, walking all the way up to the main gate, but once inside Bulguk Temple, even a dunce like me couldn't help feeling a bit holy."

"You really wanted to see the temple so badly?"

"And why not? I've wanted to see it since I was fifteen years old, so it was a fifty-year-old wish finally fulfilled. Besides, seeing Dabo and Seokga pagodas, too, after a lifetime of just looking at them on our coins, it felt like now I could really be done."

To think that in this cramped little country, there were those to whom Gyeongju represented such a distant pilgrimage. But then how had she ever thought to come all the way here, to Jeju Island? I didn't feel I could ask, but I felt, once again, a suspicion that had crossed my heart several times since first receiving her letter. Was she just using my being here as an excuse to come and sightsee?

As we left the restaurant, I mentioned that I had been unable to secure a place for her to stay, and that she was welcome to stay with us for the duration of her trip and get all the rest she needed. At first she didn't reply, almost as if she hadn't heard; it was only in the car, well on our way home, that she spoke. Near and far, countless little boats lit up the night sea like a vast fish market. After watching the water for a while, she spoke suddenly, as if awakening the night.

"But you see, the thing is...."

Her tone was cautious, but it was clear that I was being chastised.

"I know you're busy, but was it really such a chore to find a place for me to stay?"

I didn't say a word.

"I know. There is such a thing as duty. But you know, I've spent my entire life watching my every step under other people's roofs, and now that I've come all the way here, I don't much care for the idea of having to watch myself under your wife's roof."

"She's not like that."

"No one's like that in the beginning. But then one day turns into two, and things start to get uncomfortable—that's just human nature. And I don't know about now, but as far as this aunt of yours can remember, you're not the most easygoing person yourself. It's in the blood. And as you well know, our family, we're all quiet as can be, but we're also cold as stone on the inside. Even when we get together, the way we each just slip away one by one, leaving without saying a word—it's like temple folk."

Maybe that's the reason why, but one day I, too, just stopped going back home. It just felt as if all we had left in common with one another were bones, not blood. But then again, seeing all those bones hurry back into position whenever there's a big holiday or some kind of reunion, it seems almost mystical. Especially since those of us who've crossed some family convention or custom, even just once, aren't actually allowed to join at will. And it's not even a family with the kind of standing where allowing such a thing would carry any great significance.

"Tonight, since there's no avoiding it, I'll stay with your family in your home, but tomorrow, as soon as it's light, just go get me a room in a motel."

I stopped the car in Hamdeok and walked down to the shore to relieve my bladder in the darkness, then got two cups of coffee from a vending machine in front of a corner store. My head was already aching at the thought of what my wife's reaction would be if I followed my aunt's instructions. It was, of course, obvious that having my aunt stay in our home for a few weeks to a month would be hard on her, too, but my wife was the kind of person who always put duty first when it came to personal relations.

As we sat next to each other in the car, drinking our coffee, I spoke.

"I'll do as you ask, Aunt."

I decided that this would be best.

"I'm sorry to be so much trouble, but, yes, it's the only way I'll be at ease. But you know, this coffee, why is it so strong? It's okay to leave the rest, right?"

As we passed Jeju City, getting closer to Aewol, I remembered the face of a man from Wando Island who now lives near our house. This person, I thought, might be able to help me find a place for my aunt to stay. He is in his mid-fifties, and had been living on Jeju Island for twenty years or so. Up until a few years earlier he'd worked for the Forest Service as a logger, but one day he was injured, his shoulder hit by a falling cedar tree, and he was in the hospital for eight full months. He retired after that, and had been living on the compensation he'd received ever since. His wife ran a restaurant named Wando in downtown Aewol. Though he was fully recovered, his wife had such a scare that she refused to let him do any kind of work. I met him while fishing along the breakwater, which eventually led to our sharing a few drinks and growing quite close. Since we lived near one another as well, every now and then we would get together for a meal with our families, or bring each other a good side dish or two.

When I called up the man from Wando and explained the situation, he offered up a surprisingly simple solution. In the foothills of Aewol there was a quiet, secluded little house where one could both see and not see the ocean. It had been built in the spring to rent out to tourists, but its business permit hadn't come through yet, so all the rooms were empty. The owner, a man in his late forties, lived on the upper floor with his wife, but it would be easy for renter and owner to simply ignore each other, and besides, the place had been built like a private home, so it wouldn't feel like a motel.

The next day, I headed over before breakfast to take a look at the house. Luckily, the owner and his wife were out in the front yard cutting grass. The moment I mentioned the restaurant Wando, the owner said he'd already spoken to my friend, and asked me where I lived. As usual, the thought of an elderly tenant completely on her own was cause for some concern. But when I replied that I lived nearby, he said that then I might bring her along around lunchtime to settle in. On top of that, he cut the price of the room in half, though I hadn't even asked. He told me not to feel unduly indebted, since they were unable to take on official paying guests for the time being anyway.

Happily, my aunt liked the house very much. Saying that the stairs might be a bit difficult, the owner gave her a room on the ground floor. It was a two-story house, and one had to climb all the way to the roof to see the ocean in the distance. Still, the front of the house looked out over an expanse of wide open fields, so there wasn't any sense of being closed in. While my aunt was inside her new room unpacking, I received a phone call from the man from Wando, and about ten minutes after that he rode up on his motorcycle. He announced that he was on his way to go fishing.

"It's hot out today. Why don't you come along, nephew, and enjoy the cool breeze?"

Now this man, too, was calling me "nephew."

"My wife doesn't like it when I fish during the day; she says my face gets too sunburned."

If I go fishing three or four days in a row, the color of my face darkens and my body gets thinner. My wife hates it, saying I look like some sort of wanted criminal.

"So where is your aunt?"

Perhaps drawn by the commotion outside, my aunt stuck her head out the window and looked over at us. When I announced that this was the person who had recommended the house, she insisted on bustling all the way out of the house, bowing her head low to convey her thanks. With an invitation to come by their restaurant sometime, the man from Wando hopped back on his motorcycle and disappeared between the potato fields. Upon his departure, my aunt turned to me.

"But why is that man's face so dark? To my eyes he somehow looks like a cattle thief."

I replied jokingly: "It's true, I hear he used to be a mountain bandit. Even now he'll still feed on anything, beast or fish, as long as it's alive."

"Makes sense. Tsk, tsk. I'm grateful to him for finding this place for me, but I'd rather not see him again."

I suggested that we take a walk to catch the breeze, now that we'd found her a room, but my aunt shook her head.

"You must have wasted your whole day yesterday. Use today to study. If you get curious, just drop by in a couple of days or so. I still feel a little out of sorts, so I'll just rest for a day or two."

And with that, she inquired, rather belatedly:

"Does your father know that I've come here?"

Taking into account what she'd said in her letter, I hadn't bothered myself to make any calls to inform him. Father is my aunt's second eldest brother, making him about five years her senior.

"Good, good. I'd prefer it if you didn't mention it, even later on, after I've left. It was my intention from the beginning to just come and go without a sound."

When I returned to the house after letting a day go by, I found my aunt pulling weeds in the yard with a kerchief wrapped around her hair. She said that the owner and his wife were out to the village market that opens every five days. When I asked her why she didn't go with them, she replied that she hadn't been asked. When I asked if she'd care to go to the market as well, she retorted she had no interest in trailing along after other people.

My aunt and I drove slowly along the coastal road, heading west. The day was as oppressively hot as ever, but the sky was completely clear, as in the wake of a typhoon. At Hyeopje, we stopped for a break and had a couple of sodas. I took a few photos of her, and to my surprise she didn't complain or avoid the lens. Looking at her through the camera, I suddenly felt what might be meant by the concept of "blood," and felt a kind of quiet surprise. It was only then that I realized: Blood relatives become so familiar that we begin to avoid them, but in moments like these, when we glimpse them from someplace hidden, we can, at last, feel close to them again.

"The color of the water is so pure, like jade."

The waters of Sehwa-ri and Hyeopje, near Seongsan Harbor, are known to have the most beautiful color of all the seas surrounding Jeju Island. It was the tourist season, and the shore was teeming with people swimming and sunbathing. At the sight of a little old woman in a white traditional top and black skirt, carrying a handbag, everyone turned away to giggle. Completely unaware of the effect she was having, my aunt took a long breath, muttering to herself.

"It's so clear it's almost embarrassing. It doesn't feel like a part of our country."

Regardless of what things look like from the outside, the lives of people are much the same wherever they may be, and those of us who live here on the island have our problems just like everyone else. Prices are high, even as each year the fishermen's hauls shrink more and more, and fewer and fewer people seem interested in eating tangerines. There are even those who abandon their fields and take their own lives. And it's not as if the weather is always clear. In winter, clear days happen about as often as national holidays. Storm warnings sound practically every other day, making it difficult to even venture out of doors. People from the mainland are prone to depression, especially in winter. But summer is no different: typhoons come so frequently that many honeymooners spend their entire stay getting rained on. So they even say every side of the island—north, south, east and west—has its own weather. Staring off at Biyang Island in the distance, my aunt was silent for a long, long while.

When we got to Gosan, my aunt and I went for a late lunch at a restaurant called "The Pearl Divers." I saw then that my aunt's eyes had grown bloodshot. I don't know if it was because of the salty sea air, but her coughs were growing more frequent and she kept on spitting globs of phlegm into a napkin. She told me all that sun was making her dizzy, and that we should drive back through the mountains instead. The roast-ed mackerel and hairtail soup arrived, but before long she put her spoon down yet again, saying it just didn't taste right.

"Is there someplace where we can get some soybean paste? I'm not talking about that sweetened stuff they sell at the supermarket. I mean real Joseon soybean paste, the kind you make at home. That's what I need to deal with this phlegm and settle my insides; ever since I got here I've just been bloated, feeling nauseated all the time."

No matter where they go, old people always talk first about water and food. It's said that as people age, they crave the foods they grew up with. There was no way that the food here would suit her. In the same vein, it's said that people from here who move away from the island start craving *jari* sashimi and *hanchi* squid, and that this is why they come back. In the end, our taste becomes our memory, our past.

"That fellow from Wando runs a restaurant in town, so let's drop by on the way. I've had a taste of their soybean paste, and it suited me very well."

As soon as I brought up the man from Wando, my aunt clammed up, a look of disapproval on her face. We took a look around the market in Moseul Harbor then went along the Northwest Scenic Byway, and by the time we got back to Aewol it was evening. We went directly to the Wando restaurant and asked for some soybean stew. The man wasn't there; he'd left at dawn to catch some parrotfish and hadn't yet returned from the ocean. After a taste of the soup, with its slices of young zucchini and green chili, my aunt suddenly asked for the woman in charge of the kitchen. She and I, of course, knew each other well. I wondered if this time, too, some-thing about the dish had bothered her, but when the lady came out my aunt stood up from her chair and grabbed her hand, exclaiming:

"Where are you from? Could it be Chungcheong Province?"

Though obviously a bit startled at first by the sudden outburst, the woman's expression grew easier, and she was soon laughing bashful-ly. "That's right," she said, explaining that she was from Dangjin in Chungcheong.

"My, my, to think I came all this way to meet someone from home. I knew the very instant I tasted your soybean paste."

Neither my aunt nor I were from Dangjin. Even so, she seemed pleased just to meet someone from Chungcheong Province. Their eyes growing misty, my aunt and the wife of the man from Wando spent a long time sitting together and chatting about this and that. By the time we headed back to her place, my aunt had been given a huge heap of soybean paste for her own use. Stepping out of the restaurant, she reached into her handbag, pulled out two bright green fruits, and handed them to her new friend.

"It's not for eating, I know, but I picked them in Chungcheong Province, so take them. You can smell their scent now and then, when you miss home, and it'll ease your heart."

Then, as if she'd only just remembered, she handed several to me as well. They were *taengja*, hardy oranges. The fruit of a tree known for its unusually fierce thorns.

"What did you bring these for?"

After a moment's hesitation, as if she had just been reproached, she mumbled her reply.

"Well, let's see."

"What do you mean 'let's see'?"

"Well… have you heard that saying that if a tangerine crosses some place it becomes a taengja? I just suddenly remembered it, and so I picked a few to bring along."

When I had peeked inside her bag a bit earlier, I'd spotted more than twenty of them. All put aside, I felt a flash of surprise at my aunt's response. I remembered it from an examination I had once taken, it was an old Chinese saying that a tangerine will become a taengja if it crosses the Huai River.

"Some part of my idle little heart wondered if maybe bringing taengja fruit across water would turn them into tangerines, so I brought them with me."

Without thinking much of it, I put the taengja she'd given me in the console of the car. As soon as we arrived at her place, the rain and wind picked up considerably. When I called the automated weather hotline to check, I learned that a typhoon was headed our way. Knowing well the power of such storms, I suggested that she come home with me for the night, but she shrugged me off, saying that it would be a waste of rent not to stay in her room.

The typhoon raged all night, tossing the entire island like a bundle of straw, and showed no sign of abating even past sunrise.

Together with my wife, who worked Monday through Friday at a foreign language academy, I headed over to the rented house early in the morning. My aunt was still in bed. Her complexion had soured completely overnight, but she insisted it was nothing but lack of sleep and told us not to worry. Despite my wife's pleas, my aunt was determined to stay in her rented room. Sending my wife back home with the car around eight thirty, I went into the kitchen to prepare breakfast—but this, too, my aunt wouldn't hear of. I noticed then that two china dishes had been set side by side next to her bed. One held the soybean paste, wrapped in a plastic bag; the other was filled with a heap of taengja fruit. The taengja looked untouched, fresh and green, as if they had been transported in sawdust. In the end, we settled on a simple soybean stew, and my aunt and I sat down to breakfast at a table set for two. My wife had packed and brought over a number of side dishes, but it was decided that these would be saved for later, and so they remained unopened.

Suddenly, in the middle of the meal, my aunt's eyes began to redden. It was so abrupt that I didn't dare to ask what was wrong. Feeling awkward, I remained quiet for a moment, then slipped out of the room and headed up to the roof. Watching the fiercely tossing waves of the distant ocean, I smoked one cigarette after another, and thirty minutes had passed by the time I ventured back inside. In the interim, my aunt had cleared away the dishes and was getting dressed. When I asked her where she was going on such a day, and without a car, she suggested that we call a taxi and go back to Gosan. Though she hadn't mentioned a thing the day before, she claimed that the view from Gosan's shore of Chagwi Island kept coming back to her, and became quite insistent about wanting to return there to treat me to a plate of sashimi. Still concerned, I said that we might wait until the storm had passed and make the trek then, but there was no reasoning with her. She said that there was something urgent she needed to discuss with me. At that, I gave in, and called the local taxi company to find out the rates and arrange for a cab to come to pick us up. It occurred to me, too, that the whole undertaking might actually be preferable to simply sitting around in the room all day when no one had any idea when the storm might pass.

After taking one highway out of the neighborhood we turned off about halfway down and went directly to Gosan. The rain poured against the windshield in a steady stream, as if buckets of water were being emptied on top of us. It was so bad that the windshield wipers weren't enough to secure a safe level of visibility. By the time we finally arrived at Gosan, drilling our way through the storm at a steady twenty kilometers an hour, it was nearly eleven a.m. Tourist season or not, because of the worsening weather most of the sashimi places were closed. When we made our way to "The Pearl Divers" once more, just as we had for lunch the day before, the sole waitress was asleep, taking an early nap in a small room off the entryway. The young woman seemed startled, as if she, too, couldn't help wondering why on earth anyone would be out on a day like this. It was only when she recognized us from the day before that she leapt into action, hurriedly clearing a space for us and readying a table near the window with a view of Chagwi Island. But thanks to the rain and wind, even the island, just a ten-minute boat ride away, was only a faint outline.

We ordered triple-tail sashimi, giving instructions to thoroughly boil the head and bones for a soup, like with beef bones, until we were done with our meal. After a first round of Hallasan *soju* and then another immediately after, my aunt reached into her bag and pulled out a pack of cigarettes, lighting one.

Apropos of nothing, she started her story.

"The story of my life to date is one that no one has heard so far. So for you, too, it will be new. An entire lifetime, it's lain quiet in my breast, but for some reason I don't understand, coming here has brought these old memories back to life, clear as day, like flipping through photos in an album."

My mouth dry, I took another gulp of *soju* and lit my own cigarette.

"It was precisely a year after your grandfather passed away. About mid-August by the solar calendar. One day, a blister appeared on my husband's hand. It all started with a pretty bad temperature and complaints about feeling itchy, and soon each of his fingernails began oozing some foul-smelling discharge. Thinking it was some skin disease, I bought some medicine in town at Gwangcheon; he took it for ten days but it didn't do any good. When I said we should go to the hospital, he refused to even consider it—he was full of fear. I'd heard somewhere that wild rose root was good for such things, so I boiled some and tried having him soak in it, and when that didn't work either we even tried lye. By this point it wasn't just his hands any more; these big white marks had started spreading around his groin and his eyebrows. Then someone said it might be albinism, so we tried applying ground garlic and even an ointment made from burnt mercury powder. Nothing worked. His skin just kept on rotting. We wrapped his hands in bandages but this red-black pus would soak all the way through so often that we'd have to wake several times in the night to change his dressings. And even then, he kept it all hidden, behind closed doors, refusing to budge an inch and go to the hospital. It made me burn up inside, watching that, and in the end I started getting the white marks myself. Then, and only then, did he agree to wrap himself in a blanket and scurry to the hospital in Hongseong. When the doctor saw him, he was so shocked he had to turn his back to calm himself."

Just listening to the story, the hairs rose on the back of my neck and I felt the need to scratch here and there. I didn't need to hear anymore. It was clear enough what the disease had been. These days they call it Hansen's disease. In the olden days they'd called it, simply, leprosy. With all the modern medical advances, I'd heard it was now considered no more than a skin condition, easy to treat, and even cure, if discovered in its early stages. But back then, at the time of her story, it had amounted to a death sentence from the hand of God himself.

"They said he had to be isolated immediately and sent to a leper colony in Eumseong in North Chungcheong Province. It was the only logical step for us to take, but my husband flatly refused to listen to the doctor. I can still remember all the names of the countless medicines that he was given: Promin, Ciba, Diazon, DDS, Rifampicin, Lamprene… I found out that they were basically just disinfectants, all of them, and the sight of him taking those pills by the fistful with every meal made me want to die. And every time he took the pills, he would complain that his stomach burned, and mix MSG into his rice then dump all that into a bowl of Coca-Cola to eat—it was so disgusting to watch that every time I was the one who ended up in the kitchen throwing up. Whether through good or bad fortune, the medicine worked for me, and before long I was back to normal; but my husband, because he'd waited so long, didn't see much progress. His right hand ended up looking like a used kitchen sponge, all mashed up without a single finger left, and his eyebrows fell out. He spent all his days hidden in his room, under his blankets with a wool hat on his head. Eventually, though, all those powerful pills had some belated effect, and by early winter his symptoms stopped progressing. Still, there was no way he could live a normal life anymore, not in that state."

Through the rain, Chagwi Island showed itself for a moment before disappearing again.

"Anyway, we had to eat, and so I kept us alive, alternating between working days at a salted shrimp factory and spending my nights working at a cannery. I don't know if you know this, but when a woman goes out to earn for the family, there's something that bad husbands will do. I'm talking about the way they'll find any excuse to beat their wives. I'd come home at dawn, exhausted to the bone, and at least every other day he'd start beating me with that sponge of a hand—I don't know how it hurt so badly. Every time, my little boy would wail from the room across the hall, and, you know, more than the pain of the blows themselves it was that sound that ripped my heart in two."

I poured another shot into her empty glass. The sashimi sat on the table untouched. The fish head and bones were still in the kitchen, boiling away.

"But it's not like those days lasted for very long. The next year, right around when the azaleas started blooming in the mountains, he jumped in front of a passing train and ended his own life. It was a quiet night. So quiet that it seemed almost as if I'd crossed over into the next world myself. It was quiet like that for a few days in a row—suffocatingly quiet. Two days later, when we were burying him in the mountain, the azalea blossoms all looked black. I couldn't squeeze out a single tear. But the whole world was so desolate; no one would have heard my crying anyway."

We exchanged the empty *soju* bottle for a new one.

"A few days after we wrapped my husband up in a straw bag and buried him in the mountain, I put my son on my back and left Jinjuk for good, right around daybreak. All I had with me was just enough money to rent a room somewhere. I made my way up to Seoul with no real plan at all and found a room in Sindang-dong, some wreck of a place with a tin roof. Then, I set up shop as a fishmonger. That was April of the year 1977. My boy was nine then, and he became my Buddha. He was such a good boy; every day without fail, when he got back from school, he would come to the market and help his mother run her stand. He was a good student, too. He studied engineering in college, and got himself employed at a famous company. He's in the U.S. now, with a good job, married with one son and one daughter. A few years ago I heard they got permanent residency."

I had seen this fellow once before. He was, of course, my cousin, and was about seven years younger. I met him in 1983 or so, at an annual family gathering that always took place at the Sudeok Inn, below Sudeok

Temple. The gathering lasted two nights and three days, but in all that time the fellow never opened his mouth, like some sort of deaf-mute. He was a middle schooler at the time, I think, and he looked the part of a model student, with his white face. He was tall, too, maybe taking after his father. After the gathering, when we ended up seated next to each other on the train back to Seoul, I made a few attempts to start a conversation—but even then he still wouldn't answer. Watching him as I did over the course of a few days, I felt that the boy was filled with hostility toward his maternal relations. It was only when we arrived at Yeongdeungpo Station and I stood up with my bag to get off the train that he spoke:

"Mother was so insistent I go, so I did, thinking of it as a kind of field trip—but me, I have a different last name, so no one can say I belong to your people. So isn't it ridiculous to shove a family tree in my face and blindly demand that I memorize it? I mean, after all this time you all treated my mother like some sort of subhuman?"

When I asked him why he had come, if this was how he felt, the bold young man replied:

"I don't know if you know this, but the great painter Yi Ung-no once stayed at the Sudeok Inn. Did you see the two big boulders by the entrance to the inn? Etched into them is a work of abstract Chinese calligraphy by Yi. To be perfectly honest, I came to see those. And see them I did, for three straight days, so there won't be any need for me to go back to the Sudeok Inn, ever again. Well, take care of yourself."

So this boy who dreamed of becoming an artist had grown up to enroll in engineering school. And, indeed, just as he had hoped, we never did cross paths again.

Starting out as a fishmonger, by the time her son was entering middle school my aunt had opened up a food stand at the entrance of Sindang-dong market. Around that same time, she explained calmly, she met a widower who ran a nearby fruit and vegetable stand, and the two of them became intimate. He had a daughter who attended the local girls' high school. Not wanting to draw any undue attention, they decided to forego a wedding ceremony and simply move in together, but it wasn't to be— the daughter in question, shocked by the whole situation, ran away from home. Still, she told me, they stayed together despite it all, and for a couple of years or so she managed to live a life that wasn't so terribly lonely. The price, though, was great. During that same period, people working at the market used to gather together once a month to chip in a small sum to a group fund, with a different member each time getting the chance to take home the whole pot. With more than a dozen members, it was no small amount they pooled together each month. As was the custom, they all took turns being in charge of the money, but when it came time for her new common-law husband to take the position, he took it all and ran, disappearing from their world as if he'd been planning it all along. And that was just the beginning. The other members, knowing all about her relationship with the man, mobbed her house, breaking her belongings and even threatening her with a wooden club, demanding that she return the stolen money. At her wits' end, my aunt temporarily registered her address as being in Uijeongbu, some distance away, and moved her household to Yeongdeungpo as soon as things seemed to quiet down a bit. Then, she changed her line of work entirely, opening up a tiny draper's shop.

Up until he graduated from college, her son worked every kind of part-time job imaginable and used every spare moment to help my aunt at her shop. Because he had lost his father at such a young age and needed to help support his single mother, he was exempted from mandatory military service. Upon graduation, he was offered a position at a major corporation that necessitated a move to their local facility in Incheon, and so he began to live on his own. Though Incheon is really not so very far from Yeongdeungpo, my aunt insisted that the commute would be too difficult and used the rental deposit of her own apartment to set up a place for him there. Sadly, from then on she would no longer see him very often. Not long after his employment, the young man married the daughter of a doctor of traditional Chinese medicine from Bucheon. The following year, his wife gave birth to their first son. And not long after that, his company offered him a position in the U.S. Ever since then, it was only once every two years or so that he visited Korea. And now that they had permanent residency in the U.S., even those visits had turned into occasional phone calls during holidays.

For years, my aunt ran the draper's shop; it had not been long since she shut it down that she purchased a forty-*pyeong* apartment in the up-and-coming Bundang area. She explained that this was so that she, her son, and his family could all live together when they returned. It was after this retirement that she had quietly made her way back home to attend the gathering for the anniversary of Grandfather's death. And on her way back up to Seoul, she stopped by Jinjuk, too—the place of her marriage and exile at the age of twenty-eight.

After a lifetime of hard work, finding herself alone with nothing to do in that Bundang apartment only made each day more difficult to get through. That was why she decided that she would take the opportunity to go to all those places she had heard so much about but never dreamt of actually seeing. She packed her bags and headed first to Gangneung and Sokcho on the East Coast. Then, she spent two nights at the Donghae Tourist Hotel at the base of Seorak Mountain. There she rode the cable cars and made a trip to Naksan Temple. The morning she was scheduled to leave Seorak Mountain, she rose early and bathed at Cheoksan Hot Springs, then boarded a bus from Sokcho that took her southward through Pohang and on to Gyeongju.

The letter to me had been written the day before she left her apartment in Bundang. Gyeongju in particular, she told me, had called to her heart; she mentioned several times that she would like to see the flowers there in spring. She explained that when she left Jeju Island, she planned to cross over to Wando Island, dine in Haenam, then spend a night in Chunhyang Village in Namwon. Then, since she expected she would be a bit worn out, she would board an express bus at the Namwon terminal and return to Seoul.

After we returned from Gosan, my aunt seemed as if her mind was more at ease. That night, back in Aewol, she told me that everything was fine now, and asked that I not come back to see her for the time being.

The afternoon after the storm passed, I got a phone call from the man from Wando. It was five days after the trip to Gosan. In the intervening time I'd had another visitor from Seoul and ended up spending three full days as both his guide and drinking companion. A photographer involved in environmental activism, he had come to photograph the pine trees in Yeongsil along the Halla mountain range and the forest of nutmeg trees in Gujwa Village. I had never met the man before; we were introduced by a forestry scholar I'd known for some time and respected deeply. This kind of thing came up now and then, and wasn't cause for much concern, but as it turned out, this so-called environmentalist had a great affection for drinking. So for three straight days I not only had to trek all over the island, I also had to drink with him until the wee hours of the morning. Not surprisingly, by the end of his visit my body was as exhausted as could be and I was having trouble getting any work done.

The reason for the phone call was that the man from Wando had slaughtered a pig that morning and he was inviting me to join him at the breakwater that evening for a barbecue. Around two months earlier I had received a similar call from him telling me that he had killed a dog under a bridge. I felt bad about having refused to join him then, but told him that this time again I was unable to accept, because I needed to go check on my aunt.

"Oh, don't worry about that. Your aunt happens to be right here with us."

Startled, I asked, "And where might that be?"

"The restaurant! Where else? So hurry along, and bring the missus!"

I had told my wife about the incident with the dog, and ever since she did her best to avoid the man altogether. For her, to personally butcher an animal was beyond the pale. And when she learned that the animal in question had been a dog, she headed straight for the bathroom, dry-heaving, to brush her teeth. In the month after I made the mistake of sharing this information with her, every time I did anything with the man from Wando I could sense her disapproval. And yet, my aunt was there with him now.

As I found out when I arrived, it was all because of the connection that began with the soybean paste. Without much else to do with her time, my aunt had fallen into the habit of going for walks all around her place to while away her days—and just two days ago, she had walked all the way to downtown Aewol without even realizing it. It occurred to her then where she might go. Since they were both from the same place, my aunt had simply walked into the restaurant without any ado, and the wife of the man from Wando had welcomed her like a sister. Yesterday, in fact, my aunt had helped out with the restaurant's dishes, even putting off her own dinner, then had a bite to eat with the family and gone home to her rented room on the back of the man's motorcycle.

The man from Wando purchased the pig at the market held every five days and handled the business of readying it himself, all in the backyard. I'd seen him do that once before, and I had a hard time keeping the contents of my stomach down. First, he slit the pig's throat, then caught the blood in a bowl and drank it on the spot, like rice wine. Then, he slit the pig's belly and ate part of the liver. Then he removed the huge pile of intestines, sorting out the parts to use for *sundae* sausages, then digging a hole in the ground and burying the rest. He was unusually skilled, and so all this actually took less than an hour. After witnessing the whole process, though, I found I simply wasn't able to eat any of the meat. The pig was cut in half, lengthwise, and stored in the refrigerator. A portion would be served in the restaurant, and another would be boiled to make a thick soup that would become a staple dish at their own table for the following few days. Yet another portion, set aside in advance, was earmarked for grilling and eating with friends and neighbors at the breakwater. This very day, in other words, was that day of celebration. The meat itself was wrapped in a black plastic bag; after loading it into his little van, the man from Wando hurried everyone along, exclaiming that we needed to get to the breakwater before the sun set. I looked over at my aunt, who was sitting at the table peeling garlic, and examined her face.

"Well, what shall we do?"

Wiping her hands on her skirt, she slowly rose to her feet.

"Shall we go along just to see what it's like? After getting that ride home on his motorcycle, it doesn't feel right to say no."

We started out as a party of four, but as soon as we arrived at the breakwater, the man from Wando's younger sister and her husband showed up in a car loaded with boxes of *soju* and beer. Out over the breakwater the sun was dipping, turning the waves into a teeming mass of blood-red light. It gave a red tone to all our faces, as if we were standing around a campfire. Soon the meat was grilled and served, together with soybean paste and scallions and garlic, wrapped in red lettuce and tucked into our bellies with the help of some *soju*. After a few rounds of drinking, the man from Wando, acting as if it had just then occurred to him, introduced his younger sister and her husband to my aunt. Casually, he went on:

"This is my youngest sister here. Fate's been hard on her. She married and moved to Suncheon at twenty-two, but within five years her architect husband was killed in a drunk-driving accident. Then for ten years after that she saw all kinds of trouble, raising two kids on her own. I just couldn't stand by and watch any longer, so the year before last I told her to pack up her things and move on down here to Jeju. And this fellow here, her current husband, well, he buried his first wife seven years ago, and was raising his kid alone, too, living a chaste widower's life, so they were really kind of in the same boat."

I learned later that the man was a police detective who investigated violent crimes.

"I met this fellow too while I was out fishing, and you know where? Why, right here, on the Aewol breakwater. The breakwater here is like a community center in mainland terms. Anyway, we got to drinking, and it occurred to me that he was pretty alright, see? So the third time we drank together, I invited my little sister here, and introduced them. And after that, whenever there was occasion to drink, I always made sure she was included. She enjoyed it, too; she wouldn't have come if she hadn't. And then last fall we had ourselves a wedding at the town hall, and they moved out of their rented apartments and even got a new place. They do very well for themselves now. And you can't imagine how well the kids get along with each other."

The couple in question simply turned their faces away and giggled along. About two hours later, they were the first to leave, saying that they had an ancestral ceremony to see to the next day. The night was deepening, but our surroundings were lit, the lights from the nearby squid boats as bright as a full moon. My aunt, too, had taken some bites of the meat, occasionally pouring herself a half glass of *soju*. Eventually, the fully inebriated man from Wando broke into a song called *The Pier*, banging his chopsticks on the grill from beginning to end. Next, declaring it to be his wife's turn, he got her to sing *Chilgap Mountain*. It was, naturally, my aunt's turn after that, which led to a minor tussle.

"Come, now, you've come for a good time, so let's have a good time!"

Shaking her head from side to side, she firmly refused.

"Not once in my entire life have I ever sung a song, so you give it a rest and just pour me another drink."

After filling her glass to the brim, however, the man from Wando resumed his campaign.

"All the more reason to take this opportunity and sing us just one song. Come, now, do it for your nephew."

"I can't."

But even when his own wife stepped in, entreating him to stop, the man from Wando wouldn't give up.

"A little bird told me that you've been eating our family's soybean paste, and if that's the case you've got to sing to earn it! Do you know how hard my wife here slaves away from autumn to spring to make that stuff? It's not the kind of thing we hand out to just anyone."

Nervous, I glanced over to take in my aunt's expression, but happily it didn't seem his words had actually hurt her feelings. Apparently wanting to leave, she brushed at her knees and gathered her skirt about her, rising to her feet. She stared off over the breakwater at the countless bobbing squid boats, her gaze cold. For an instant, her small form swayed against the lights as if ready to take flight.

And just like that, she began to sing. The sound of the waves made it difficult to hear her voice clearly. As I concentrated, leaning closer, I realized that it was a song I knew: *The River Hill Where the Waterbird Cries.* Her voice went on, alternately thin and green as a piece of shredded scallion, then thin and red as a sliver of red pepper, until finally disappearing without a trace into the blowing wind.

By the time we returned, it was midnight. Perhaps she had overexerted herself, but as soon as she stepped into her room, she flopped wearily down onto the bedding. As I lingered, reluctant to simply turn and leave her, she spoke.

"Go on. You're expected at home. I'm tired, it's true, but I'm feeling good."

"When did you start drinking?"

"Why, am I not allowed to drink? It's been over twenty years, so no point in someone coming along now to worry. Without alcohol, what would I have done all those long, endless nights?"

"And cigarettes?"

"About ten years for those. I quit a few months back, but on days like today, spending time with people and having a drink or two, I find myself thinking of them again. It's not the kind of thing I should say in front of you, but your aunt here quite enjoys drinking and smoking. When my anxieties deepen I actually prefer them to people."

...

"Yes, I know. Even so, Buddha is still to be found in humanity."

"I'm going to head out. Sleep well, and rest here tomorrow instead of going to the restaurant."

As I moved to leave, my aunt raised herself up from her bed.

"This time, too, wait a few days before you come back, if you would."

She longed to see a lotus flower, she told me, her expression pleading.

Ever since she'd gone to Seokguram in Gyeongju, she said, the thought of lotus flowers just wouldn't leave her.

As luck would have it, my wife happened to have the day off from work, so the three of us went to the arboretum together to see the lotus flowers. The floating blossoms were a clear, luminous pink, covering the surface of the water as if Buddha himself had descended that same dawn and left them as his blessing. The three of us sat together on a bench by the pond and spent a full two hours gazing at the lotus flowers. We could see bright red carp and goldfish weaving their way in and out between the green stems. After a crowd of Chinese tourists had bustled past, my aunt spoke.

"Whoever was behind its creation, the world is such a pretty thing. There are moments now when it occurs to me that everything I see I'm seeing for the last time. It's all so beautiful it brings tears to my eyes."

"It's much too early for you to say such things. You don't often see a grandmother who takes a boat all the way from Tongyeong to Jeju all alone, on a lark."

My aunt laughed.

"Well that's just because I had nowhere else to go. Now that I've been here a few days, I keep thinking that I ought to build a little house here and just quietly spend what time I have left."

Until that point, I had assumed that she was simply being sentimental, but as I listened, I saw that that wasn't the case.

"I could buy maybe fifty *pyeong* or so of land and raise a roof to make a room—that would be good enough, don't you think? I've set aside enough money that I could do something like that. I could leave it to you, too, later on. Would you drop by a real estate office for me?"

My wife was pretending she couldn't hear the conversation, and I, too, found myself at a loss for a response.

"I guess you don't like the sound of that."

"What will you do with the place in Bundang?"

"That place—I could be in that place until the day I die and not a single soul would come by to see me, so I don't think it's anything I need to hang on to. Besides, who knows when that son of mine will actually come back to Korea? Just waiting there, taking care of the place like some sort of ghost—it exhausts me just to think about it."

While my wife went to the snack stand to pick up some refreshments, my aunt launched into yet another set of complaints.

"Animal or human, if you have enough kids, at least one of them will inevitably turn out to be off. In our household that was me. All the rest listened to our parents; they were smart and stayed on the right path. So all my brothers are college professors or government workers, and even my sisters are wives to school inspectors or teachers. They all live good lives. But for whatever reason, ever since I was born I've just been found lacking in this or that—always something. At school, I was always the worst student among us, and though I was a girl all I did was play, going unwashed for days on end, like the boys in the neighborhood. It was early on that my parents turned their gaze elsewhere. Then, when I came back after running off with that lame teacher at age sixteen, even my brothers and sisters turned their backs on me. Still, I don't hold any grudges. The only reason I hid in that kitchen like a ball of soot and bore out those twelve long years was the promise I made that lame-footed teacher."

My aunt's voice had weakened, souring like a batch of old cabbage kimchi.

"He was a very famous man, you see, from Hansan. The night we ran off, he took me on a bus to Gap Temple, in Gongju. After a few days in a motel there, however, we had no place to go. So without any other choice, he took me down to Hansan. There, he had just an elderly mother. Thatched huts are all well and good, but I've never seen such a run-down thatched hut in my life. Still, I thought of it as if I'd married into the family, and I headed straight for the kitchen. As I was making rice, though, I realized that the elderly mother, far from being as frail as she looked, was going to be a force to be reckoned with. She called me out from the kitchen and declared that she refused to accept some urchin from the street as her daughter-in-law, and ordered me to leave. Once she found out that her son had actually quit his position at the school and come down for good, she took straight to her bed. And so I had to nurse her, but she refused to touch any food I had made. Even so, I did my best to accept this as part of my fate, and I bore it all for a full hundred days. My husband was a gentle, sensitive man, and just didn't know what to do, stuck in the middle as he was. Day by day he grew thinner and thinner, like a reed. Then one day he quietly called to me from outside the gate, and told me that I should return home, and that we would reunite later on, when the timing was better.

Before that day arrived, he would find another teaching position and we would gain the permission of both our parents and even have a proper wedding. I wept and wailed and clung to him, but he was cold as stone then, despite all his gentleness. So in the end I was basically thrown out, and I packed my bags and headed home."

"It was late when I arrived, and I stepped through our front gate ready for anything. But not one person said a single word to me. They were in the middle of dinner, and every one of them, spoons and chopsticks still in hand, just came on out into the open living room and just looked down at me where I stood in the middle of the yard. They just stared and stared for a long time, without saying a word, until somehow, automatically, my feet just took me over to the kitchen. I waited for three years in that kitchen, cooking day after day, waiting for him to come from Hansan for me. But I never heard a word. After five years I went there myself. His elderly mother had already passed away, and he was teaching at the local elementary school. Married, you see, to some other woman. When I asked him how this happened, he told me it had just happened, just mumbling one thing or another. Apparently, ten years earlier, his mother had borrowed some sacks of barley to eat from the butcher in the next neighborhood, and they'd never been able to repay the debt. Then, some time before she died her mind had begun to go, and she began insisting that she wanted the butcher's daughter as her daughter-in-law. She pitched fit after fit, saying that she needed to see a daughter-in-law before she died. At any rate, what is there to say to that? Especially when even the butcher's daughter followed me back out of the house, hanging onto my ankles and weeping her apology? By God, I may not be any prize, but she was the homeliest woman I'd ever seen, with a face like the shell of a walnut. Then again, what can you expect from the daughter of a butcher? Anyway, after he calmed her down and sent her back home, he picked a couple of green taengja fruit from the school fence and handed them to me. 'I'll come to see you,' he told me, 'when these ripen to yellow.' I believed him, and I left Hansan, and it struck me, just how cruel my fate really was."

"Did he come?"

"He did come, but it didn't do any good. Afraid of drawing any notice he just sat, huddled on a little stool at the bus station for an hour or so, just sighing over and over without saying a word, and then he left on the same bus that brought him. The only thing he told me was that his second child would be born soon—each word a nail to my heart. That was all, and that was the end."

"So you never saw him again?"

"He came again once before I went to Jinjuk to be married; he'd heard about it somewhere. He told me he wished me the best for my marriage and my new life. He came just to tell me that."

…

"I don't want to keep harping on it, but on this trip, before I came here, I stopped by Hansan. I looked him up at the village office. It turns out that he retired from the school long ago, and now he lives alone in some apartment in town. The same year he retired his wife died from cancer, and all his children have moved to the city, only coming back to visit once or twice a year. Then he said something that felt like a kitchen knife being stabbed into my back. He said I should move down to Hansan and we should live together again. I was so angry, I picked up a stone that I'd been rolling around with my foot and threw it at him. Then I walked all the way back to the bus station."

I responded carefully:

"Was that so hateful to hear? The suggestion to live together again?"

"What I hated was me, for listening. I walked all the way to the station, but he didn't come after me. I waited a while, and there was still time until the bus would leave, so I took a taxi to the school he used to teach at. I wanted to see if the fence was still there with all its taengja fruit."

"… It was there, wasn't it?"

"It was there."

"So, that's where you got them."

"Yes, that's where I got them. I was just thinking about the past, and so I picked a whole armful and brought them back up to Seoul. And the day after that, I left for Seorak Mountain."

After a pause, I ventured:

"What about going back to Hansan one more time?"

My aunt sighed, a big, deep sigh, and then replied:

"Will going back turn the taengja into tangerines?"

Unwilling to let it go, I went on, insistent:

"Well, you could take a sack of tangerines with you from here."

"That's very easy to say. But it's not such an easy thing to do."

The day was gradually darkening, so she and I rose from the bench. We dropped my wife off at our house, and as we made our way back down to Aewol along the mountain road, my aunt suddenly asked me to stop the car.

We stopped at a big, open cabbage field spread along a low foothill of the mountain. Getting out of the car and facing the cabbage field, my aunt pulled her cigarettes from her bag and put one in her mouth. I lit it for her. Her small, wrinkled face appeared for a moment in the flicker of the lighter, only to disappear again into the darkness. Down past the thousands of *pyeong* of cabbages, the town and then the ocean lay in the fading twilight. When I looked back, I saw that during my momentary distraction she had actually entered the cabbage field. Before long, I heard it: from where she stood, far enough out that her outline almost disappeared into the darkness, came the sound of weeping, rising and falling like a song. It was her, the same aunt who hadn't shed a single tear in the face of the ocean. Instead it was here, in a cabbage field, that her heart, blocked up for so many long years, finally and laboriously began to open up. The sound of weeping gradually turned into a faint wail, continuing on and on for some time.

Back in her room, she spoke:

"I'm sorry you had to see that—sorry and embarrassed."

"Get some rest. You'll feel better in the morning."

Ignoring my reply, she went on. I was remembering the cabbage field we had left behind in the darkness.

"He was on his way home from a visit to our house. I went out to see him off, you see, and the sight of him, limping along ahead of me in the growing darkness—it just broke my heart. Back then this aunt of yours was just a girl, and uncommonly bold. I sped up to catch up with him, and I reached out and pulled on his sleeve. 'Quit staggering along like some kind of cripple,' I told him, 'and just get up on my back. I'll carry you anywhere.' That was in a cabbage field. He was shocked, and he stopped in his tracks, and then he just sat down on the edge of the cabbage field and started to sob. Like some sort of stray cat, I just stood there, looking down at his heaving shoulders. After a while, he raised his face, and asked me if I was sure I wouldn't regret it. I'd already decided, so I told him, 'Come what may, I'll never look back.' And so we left, together, that night, along that road."

Finished speaking, my aunt lay back on her bedding and closed her eyes. I stayed where I was, staring down at the floor of the room. At some point, I realized that she had fallen asleep.

The next afternoon I went fishing and ran into the man from Wando, who had some unexpected news. My aunt was shopping around for land. She had stopped by the restaurant that morning, he said, to ask for his help. So they went to a real estate agent together and spent the rest of the morning looking around. He mentioned something called a "steel house." They were cheap, these houses, and if you had the land, building one could be done in just a few days, if you hurried. These days the technology was so good that even a rush job like that would stand up to high winds and be easy to heat. The only problem was the land. No one sold land in plots as small as fifty *pyeong*. The smallest lots approved for sale were all at least two hundred *pyeong*.

By the time I packed up my fishing gear and made it up to her vacation rental, my aunt was lying in bed covered with blankets despite the midsummer heat. The sight of her face didn't look promising. She was drenched in sweat, and she was coughing up yet more phlegm. It seemed likely that the windy night we'd spent grilling pork on the breakwater might be catching up with her, and now she was truly ill. When I suggested that we head to the hospital, she replied that she had already been, and gestured toward a package from the pharmacy sitting by her bed. After staring blankly at the package for a moment, it struck me that this simply would not do, and I spoke, my voice colder than I intended:

"Rather than build a house here, I think it would be best for you to go back to Seoul."

Without asking why, my aunt simply closed her eyes.

"This could all end very badly. I know it's summer, but all it takes is one bad encounter with the ocean winds and older people from the mainland are never the same again. It's not the kind of thing that a doctor can fix, either. What if our relatives were to find out that you're here like this, ailing away? What would they say? I don't know if I could handle that."

"I understand, so you needn't keep pushing."

"My wife, too—she hasn't been able to sleep right these last few nights. She keeps saying it's not right, to start, that you're staying out here, on your own, and she's been sick with worry that you might be getting ill. She keeps nagging me to bring you back to our house."

"Everyone gets sick when they get older. And it's not as if I haven't thought about returning to Seoul myself. The man from Wando told me this morning that it doesn't seem right to him either, for an elderly family member to show up and be around like this. It's all true."

"I'm sorry I'm not able to make your visit more comfortable."

"No need for such talk. When I got on that boat to cross over here I had no plans of causing such a fuss."

"What's important is your health. And once you've recovered, you can go back down to Hansan."

"Hansan… Yes, Hansan. When I ran my draper's shop, the only ramie cloth I carried was made in Hansan. It's not that I don't want to go. It's all I've thought about, ever since I got here."

"Then what are you waiting for? It's not like you have to worry about what people might think, not anymore."

"I just don't have the strength anymore to cook and clean for a man. If it's just me, I can make do with a single bowl of soybean soup, but my back will break if I have to set three meals a day for someone."

"If you don't go because you're worried about setting meals, you'll regret it forever."

My aunt laughed weakly.

"So I should listen to you, then, and go back again one more time?"

"He'll be waiting, too."

"Do you think so?"

A cool breeze poured in through the open window.

"You know, the reason this aunt came to see you—it's because back when I was living the life of a scullery maid, you, and you alone, still treated me the same as everyone else. You were so young, but I must have seemed pitiful to you, because every evening you'd hang around the door to the kitchen for a few moments and say a word or two to me before heading to your room. It was a great comfort to this aunt of yours back then. So don't be too angry with me for showing up so suddenly and causing you so much grief."

That night another typhoon hit, tossing and turning the island for three straight days before moving on toward Japan. After a two-day delay with all her bags packed and ready to go, my aunt boarded a boat to Mokpo from Jeju Harbor, exactly fifteen days after she arrived.

On the way, my aunt stopped by the Wando restaurant to return the soybean paste she still had left over and to say farewell to the lady of the house. It was the Wando man's wife who first raised her hand to her eyes, dabbing away at her tears; saying that she'd grown attached to my aunt already, she handed her a box wrapped in cloth. Tangerines from Seogwipo, she explained, bashfully, and went on to wish she had something more to give.

My aunt said that she was heading to Wando Island as she had planned. The thought of such a long journey worried me all over again, and I tried to convince her that she should get on a plane and go straight to Seoul, but she protested, telling me not to stand in her way on this point, at least. The man from Wando, who had been listening quietly up to this point, suggested a compromise: my aunt could go to Mokpo and take an express bus to Namwon. It would be a much less difficult journey. Stepping out of the restaurant, my aunt turned back to look at the man from Wando, and said that the grilled pork and *soju* from the evening on the breakwater had been very tasty.

The boat to Mokpo was due at nine thirty in the morning. We had started out from the vacation rental early and had plenty of time, so I asked my aunt if she might like to go to the arboretum again to see the lotus flowers. After thinking a moment, she shook her head and changed the subject.

"How about we find some *noji* tangerines instead?"

Noji tangerines are grown naturally in an open field rather than in a greenhouse. Like apples or pears, they put out white blossoms in the spring, and are harvested beginning around late October. It would be months yet before they were ripe for picking. Without trespassing into some stranger's field and stealing them, there was no way for me to get my hands on any *noji* tangerines.

"What on earth for?"

"Well, I brought taengja fruit with me, so I want to take tangerines back."

"But the lady at the restaurant already gave you a box of tangerines to eat."

"Now you've turned dense as well. Who said anything about taking them back to eat?"

I had some vague sense of what she meant, so I headed first toward the tangerine field by the arboretum. No one expected anyone to pilfer such green, unripe summer tangerines, and so no one was standing guard; it didn't take much to pick a few. I chose five, ones that looked to have particularly thick wedges, and put them into my aunt's bag. Then we headed to Jeju Harbor.

I stayed in the passenger terminal for a while, watching the ocean through the window until the boat my aunt was on disappeared into the distance. Back in the parking lot, I opened the console to find that over the course of fifteen days, the taengja fruit within had wrinkled further, yellowing and blooming with mold. They gave off a strong scent of rot. But instead of throwing them away, I left them where they were.

I couldn't stop thinking that I had pushed her away; the thought kept needling my heart, and so on the way home I stopped by the arboretum and looked around the lotus pond. This day, too, the lotuses were in full bloom, floating on the surface of the water. The goldfish and carp made their leisurely way through the green tangles. After ten minutes or so I began to make my way back out of the arboretum, only to discover a solitary taengja tree standing between several large plane trees. The office I used as a workshop was right nearby, and so I'd been to the arboretum nearly every morning as part of my exercise routine, but this was the first time I'd ever noticed it. Each of its thorn-covered branches was bursting with the little green fruit.

As the days turned into weeks after my aunt left that morning on the boat to Mokpo, I still didn't hear from her. Could it have been that she was truly hurt?

Late in October, as the taengja and tangerines grew yellow and ripe, I heard about her death the way I might hear about a stranger's, during a casual phone call with my father in Seoul. He mentioned it in passing, that on the Tuesday of the second week in October, she had passed away from lung cancer, and that she had been buried in a cemetery in Bundang. She had found out about the cancer five months earlier. Her son had flown in from the U.S. just barely in time for the wake, and then left again as soon as the funeral was over. Quiet but stern, I demanded to know why on earth he had waited so long to tell me such news. Apparently taken aback by my reaction, my father was silent for a moment, then simply hung up. And so I never did manage to tell him that just last July, my aunt had come all the way to visit me on Jeju Island.

LIGHT'S ESCORT

Cho Hae-jin

Translated by **Brother Anthony of Taizé**

빛의 호위

조해진

A critique of this short story was published in the Koreana magazine in Spring 2015 (Vol. 29 No. 1, pp. 82-83).

© Kim Si-hoon

I n the crowded walkway leading to the unfamiliar airport's immigration gate, I suddenly stopped and looked around. That melody, which had gently enfolded the round, transparent world where snow was falling, was once again ringing in my ears. With flights delayed on account of the sudden bad weather, people whose schedules had been turned upside down jostled past me brusquely as I stood in their way. Through the windows could be seen the dark runways of New York's international airport, where snow was piling up, and planes with lights glimmering faintly through every window. "It's snowing," I muttered quietly, as though realizing it for the first time. Just then, the melody that only my ears could hear seemed to grow faintly louder. Ever since I met Gwon Eun again, ever since I managed to clearly recall the scene I found behind the rusty, dented front door, that melody had from time to time made its way, through long intervals of time, to wherever I happened to be standing. When that happened, all I could do was peer silently into the world from which the melody was resonating. There were times when that world was a tiny, cold room without a kitchen or even a bathroom; sometimes it was a snow-covered Sunday playground; and occasionally it was a sickroom redolent of chemicals. And always the only inhabitant of that world was Gwon Eun.

When I was reunited with Gwon Eun one year ago, twenty years after our first encounter, in a book café in Ilsan, I truly could not remember her. Gwon Eun was living in Paju, and I had come to nearby Ilsan in order to meet her for an interview, that was all. In those days I was a journalist for a magazine, responsible for a section devoted to interviews with young achievers who seemed destined to play a leading cultural role in the future, and Gwon Eun, a young photographer noted for taking photos in some of the world's hottest locations, was the subject of that week's interview. Most of what she told me that day was impressive, even moving. Her account of how she began to take photographs while learning to use a camera a friend had given her was interesting, but all the episodes she recounted, poised between life and death, clearly reflected the intensity of her passion.

As the interview came to an end, large snowflakes could be seen falling beyond the window of the book café. "It doesn't look like the snow will stop soon." As I was saving the text of the interview, I murmured to myself, and Gwon Eun replied in a low voice: "When the clockwork winds down, the melody will end and the snow will stop for sure." Her statement was not one that ordinary people would think of; it struck me as funny and I playfully asked if it was a riddle, but she merely smiled and said nothing more. Once the interview was over we left the book café and parted at the crossing light after a loose handshake. After taking a few steps I happened to look back and could see Gwon Eun in profile, as she stood with her head bowed silently beneath the falling snow. The snowfall was increasing in intensity yet still she did not move. I briefly thought of going back to her and offering to share an umbrella, but felt uncomfortable at the thought of the silence that would surround us while huddled close together. So I turned and headed for the subway without looking back again.

In retrospect, the things she said to me during that meeting, such as the reason why she took up photography or the mentions of clockwork and melody were all hints. Even the way she stood motionless in the cold snow might have been a sign to me. But little did I realize at that moment that what she had been trying to give me on that day was a kind of key that would open times gone by that I had all but forgotten.

Feelings vanished in the order they had come. The melody grew faint, the conversation we had shared faded from memory, the street scene with Gwon Eun standing in falling snow gradually grew remote. All that remained were the white snowflakes that had been settling on the asphalt, on Gwon Eun's collar, and on her shoes. When I came to my senses and lifted my head, those snowflakes quickly blended into the snow falling beyond the airport windows.

By the time I emerged from the terminal, caught a bus and reached downtown Manhattan, it was past eleven at night. The snow fell against the evening neon signs, the garish billboards followed one another endlessly, but I frequently lost my sense of direction in the center of the big city, as though cast adrift in a maze with no exit. While I was on my way to the hotel where I had booked a room, the idea that this gaudy city might be part of someone's dream grew ever stronger. The dream, that is, of a lonely girl sitting alone in a small, cold room winding up over and over again a snow globe's clockwork, immersed in a snowbound world, who would fall asleep as the melody began, without time to shed a single tear. But why was it so cold in her dream?

After that interview in Ilsan, my next meeting with Gwon Eun might have been because of a snow globe. Before she phoned to thank me for the article based on the interview, I had visited the children's section in an apartment store to buy my niece a Christmas present and there I discovered a snow globe, which contained all the clues needed to solve Gwon Eun's riddle. Forgetting completely that I had to choose my niece's present, I stared fascinated at that round, transparent world where a melody played and snow fell as the clockwork turned. Gwon Eun, who stood there helplessly in the falling snow as though she had nowhere to go, was inside that world. It was only then that I realized the image of her I had glimpsed that day on the street had all the while been occupying a corner of my mind. If I suggested to Gwon Eun, when she made her courtesy phone call, that we should have a drink together, the only explanation I can offer is that it was on account of the snow globe. Never before had I met again privately with anyone I had interviewed, I never felt the need to. If I had not met Gwon Eun a second time, and so not heard about Helge Hansen's documentary *Person, People*, I would almost certainly have lived my entire life without knowing who she was.

As it stands now, I regret nothing.

It must have been a few days after Christmas. Seoul's end-of-the-year fever was at its height; there were crowds everywhere. We met at a subway station on Euljiro, where my magazine's office was located, and headed for a nearby bar. As soon as we had been served beer and something to nibble, Gwon Eun told me some unexpected news. She said that in one week's time she was off to take photos of a visit to a refugee camp in Syria by a group of volunteers, composed of pastors and missionaries. At the time Syria was in the middle of a civil war, notorious as a place where foreigners were often attacked or taken hostage. I was worried, but I felt unable to tell her to think again, or say she ought not to go. It was entirely her business, and I felt reluctant to change the filmography of a young photographer I scarcely knew with my interference. Besides, I could hardly try to diminish her enthusiasm when she believed that, if she held a camera, she could easily avoid danger. Moreover, she was a professional photographer who had already been in other troubled regions.

"So what kind of photos do you intend to take?" Finding nothing else to say, I asked absently as I rapidly emptied my glass of beer. "Why, photos of people, of course," she replied. "The tragedy of war is something you have to find, not in metal weapons or ruined buildings, but in things like the tear-filled eyes of a young woman recalling her dead lover while she applies makeup before a mirror. War is all about ordinary people who, if there had been no war, would only have cried as much as you or I." I stared at her in some confusion as she spoke with fluid eloquence that made her words seem to have been prepared in advance. Perhaps I was looking too serious, for she suddenly laughed and explained that she had merely been quoting another person's words. "It's something Helge Hansen said." "Helge Hansen? Who's she?" "She's my favorite photographer. You might say it was her influence that made me start venturing into areas of conflict." Therefore, on hearing that this photographer had for the first time produced a documentary and eager to view it at all costs, she spent hours scanning the schedules of various indie cinemas, visiting all kinds of movie-related sites, inquiring about DVDs and video files. But that documentary had never been shown in Korea, and was nowhere to be found, on DVD or other formats. Finally she was able to watch Helge Hansen's only documentary, *Person, People*, thanks to a friend that was studying cinema in Japan and who managed to obtain a file with some difficulty and sent it to her. From that documentary, discovered because of her interest in Helge Hansen, she came to know about the woman named Alma Mayer. "It's odd," Gwon Eun said. To adopt Gwon Eun's expression, she and Alma Mayer, totally unconnected like passengers embarking on ships that had left port in different ages, with different histories, shared a similar experience, as though the two totally distinct ships carrying each of them had briefly gone adrift near the selfsame island, enduring the buffeting by the very same winds and waves. Therefore, she said, from that time on, whenever she had time she used to write letters to Alma Mayer. Gwon Eun laughed as she spoke, seemingly embarrassed. That laugh struck me as somehow familiar, and I stared at her across the table, until momentarily our gazes met awkwardly. "So did you receive any replies from Alma Mayer?" I blurted out, hastily averting my gaze and pouring beer into her empty glass. "I write them in my private blog, like a diary. In Korean, of course. Anyway, Alma Mayer can't receive my letters. She died in 2009." I stopped pouring and looked at her. Then what does she expect to get, writing letters to a woman she had never met and who was already dead? I was naturally curious about what the experience she shared with Alma Mayer might be, but I did not want to rashly pry into another person's affairs. Casually, I changed the subject. Our conversation meandered into how incredibly the cost of housing was rising and other nothings such as our ages—in the vague mid-thirties—but in my heart, Gwon Eun's words did not vanish but remained, congealed.

At about ten in the evening we emerged from the bar and before we went our separate ways I spoke up once more. "By the way, I've solved your riddle. What you said about a place where the melody stops and the snow ends when the clockwork winds down." Instead of asking what I meant, she simply looked at me in silence, as though waiting for me to go on talking. "But do you still like toys at your age?" I joked, but she did not laugh. Just then an empty taxi stopped in front of us. She got in while I stood by the taxi bidding her a conventional "Have a safe ride home." "Thanks," she said. "The camera...." "What?" Just then the taxi moved off so that I could not hear anything more of the additional clue she was giving me about a camera.

A small cold room, and in that room when the light comes on a snow globe with the clockwork wound down, then every time I leave the room the orange light of shabby alleys that used to fill my eyes, then hurrying to that room one late autumn day, clutching a camera... It was only after a little more time had passed that these clues slowly came to me, step by step, like footprints on a snow-covered playground.

The next morning, New York was covered in thick fog. Seen from the ninth-floor room of the hotel, the streets of New York looked unreal, like some ancient city submerged underwater; they felt remote like an illusion perched at the tip of the seesaw known as eternity. Like a city in the childhood dreams of Gwon Eun, who had been obliged to wander about lost, on the verge of tears, with the secrets I had yet to fathom completely hidden inside.

I left the hotel and as I reached Manhattan's Anthology Film Archives I could see the sign announcing the special screening of *Person, People*. I had come to the right place. On a table set up in the lobby there was a display of photos of an attack by Israel on the Palestinians five years before and leaflets about *Person, People*. Picking up a leaflet, I walked to a seat in a corner of the lobby. The leaflet introduced Helge Hansen, the director of the documentary, as one of the survivors when a relief truck heading for Palestine was attacked in Egypt in January 2009. It described the reason why Helge Hansen made the documentary: "Because in Norman Mayer, who lost his life in the attack on the relief truck, and his mother Alma Mayer, who thus lost her only son, I see the value of the courage displayed by individuals who fall victim to the violence of history. I am a survivor and it is my belief that survivors must remember the victims."

After folding the leaflet flat, taking care not to crumple it, and placing it in my bag, I went into the theater. It was early on a weekday, yet more than half the seats were taken. I had only just found an empty seat and put down my bag when the lights dimmed and I found myself filled with unanticipated tension. As the screen grew bright and the title appeared, the tension did not subside; I was trembling to the very tips of my fingers.

The documentary began without any subtitles or narration, showing photos of many people fixed to the wall of a mosque in Ramallah, the Palestinian capital. The wall of the mosque was like a gigantic album and from each tattered photo a man, a woman, an old man, a child, silently looked out at the world, each with a different expression. The camera lingered at length over a scene in which a young woman in a hijab walked falteringly up to the photo of a young man and kissed it devoutly, her eyes still moist, bidding us to imagine her weeping for her dead lover as she applied makeup before she came out to the mosque.

The opening shots were short but powerful, then we were inside the relief truck. The six passengers, including the driver, were laughing occasionally as they talked, then the truck stopped and they unfolded a map and consulted one another. Perhaps because shots of the other passengers had been edited out, the main focus was on Norman.

According to one article I found, Norman's death became a major issue in American society and gave rise to a long-running debate. The facts of the matter are compelling: a relief vehicle was attacked, in breach of international law and practice—relief vehicles were not attacked even in wartime; an American, a retired doctor, died in the attack; and most of the relief goods the truck was carrying had been bought by that Jewish doctor, who had spent his life savings in the process. The poignancy of it all sharpened the shock and outrage, and the audience followed the story captivated. Once interest in Norman had built up, his mother Alma Mayer became the focus of attention. All the media tried to interview her, day after day, and messages of sympathy came pouring in from all parts of society except the Jewish community. She refused every request for an interview and ignored all the expressions of sympathy. She did not go out, invited no visitors, took no phone calls. Helge Hansen was the only outsider she met with in connection with Norman's death, and that was only after she had seen the images of Norman's final fifteen hours that Helge Hansen sent her, images that would later form the core of her documentary *Person, People*.

Three months after that second meeting, when I learned of her misfortune from newspapers and the evening news, I was not particularly troubled. I was surprised, certainly, but it was not quite a shock; I felt a mixture of emotions but they were painful enough to make me forget ordinary life. Even if I had tried to dissuade her in that bar, she would surely still have set off. Besides, what right did I have to challenge her decision? It was easier on one's mind to think like that. At that time I had recently moved to a new job at a movie magazine, so I had little time to keep thinking about Gwon Eun. In my new workplace there were new relationships and new kinds of writing, and I was obliged to adapt as quickly as possible. I gradually forgot Gweon Eun. Indeed, I unconsciously tried to forget her and I almost succeeded.

Gwon Eun's name, which had remained faintly at the back of my memory, once again came so close I felt I was touching it when suddenly an older colleague quit the magazine and all the tasks he was in charge of were turned over to me. Among my new responsibilities was reporting on a documentary film festival to be held in New York, and among the materials about the festival he had prepared I found a mention of Helge Hansen's *Person, People*. I learned that the documentary was favorably received by the critics when it was first released in 2010, and had been invited to several international film festivals that year. There was also an announcement from the organizers of the festival that there would be special screenings of *Person, People* to mark the fifth anniversary of the unprecedented attack on a relief truck.

From that day on, I often thought about the things that Gwon Eun told me when we met at the Ilsan book café and the bar in Euljiro. Late in the evening, when all the reporters had left the office, I would sit there searching the Internet, determined to find out everything about Gwon Eun. Memories did not come rushing into my head in a sudden flash; instead they trickled into my consciousness bit by bit from somewhere far away. Her confession that she had come to photography thanks to a camera a friend had given her was the first clue; that moment at the streetside in Eu-ljiro when, after getting into the taxi and saying thank you, she mentioned the camera, bobbed up as another clue. In any case, whenever I looked into her world in my memory, snow was always falling. That world was round and transparent, and so long as the snow was falling a familiar mel-ody was ceaselessly ringing in my ears. And there was that unrealistic talk we had about a snow-covered school playground on a Sunday afternoon. "When you press the shutter, light flashes past inside the camera." "Re-ally? Where does the light come from?" "It must be hidden somewhere inconspicuous." "Where?" "Behind a wardrobe, or in a desk drawer, or somewhere like an empty bottle…."

Before setting off for New York, I enquired about the hospital where Gwon Eun was and paid a visit. As I expected, she was extremely sur-prised to see me. As she told me the depressing news that after three oper-ations to remove the shell fragments embedded in her legs, it was doubtful whether she would ever be able to walk again for the rest of her life, her eyes flashed oddly dark. "Do you still have that Fuji camera?" I asked after a long silence; she looked at me piercingly for a moment, then, still facing each other, we both broke into awkward laughter. In the end I was not able to say that I would come again. Before I left the hospital room, she gave me the address of her private blog on a piece of paper. She added that there was a letter she had written to me on the blog, but she too did not say anything suggesting we should meet again.

When I reached home I turned on my notebook and opened her blog. I found a letterbox that contained twelve letters written to Alma Mayer together with one for me. I sat at my desk and read straight though all the letters, after which I went to the bathroom and took a long shower. As I dried myself with a towel, I stood in front of the steamed-up mirror over the washbasin and experienced the illusion I was looking out through a window at a blurry world where there were no such things as right or wrong choices. It was not a bad illusion but the steam soon vanished. In a whisper I questioned the mirror, where my reflection was growing clear again, "So are you happy now?" No reply came from the blurry world, but from behind my back came the grating sound of a door handle turning. I felt that I knew what it was without turning around. That door would be a rusty, dented front door and the thirteen-year-old boy who had opened the door impulsively would be blinking his eyes, unaccustomed to the dark, as he asked: "Uh, this is Gwon Eun's home, isn't it?"

On the screen, Alma Mayer is explaining her lengthy seclusion:

"I simply could not tolerate the way people were dressing Norman up in terms like 'conscience of the age' or 'last hope of the Jews.' Believing that if someone is hidden behind inflated terms like those, they can become witnesses to justice without ever actually doing anything, somehow, seemed to me like pure hypocrisy. It's like pretending not to know things that you could have known if you had only tried to know, then later claiming you can't be blamed since you did not know. I remember all those non-Jews who were appalled at the horrors of the Holocaust only after the war was over. I was not angry. Then and now, I just feel numb. A kind of lethargic disillusionment, that's all."

The scene changed as the documentary summarized Alma Mayer's past. Born in Belgium in 1916, Alma Mayer overcame discrimination against her, both as a Jew and as a woman, to join the Brussels Philharmonic Orchestra as a violinist in 1938. But when the order for Jews in Belgium to register was issued in 1940, she was dismissed from the orchestra and seemed doomed either to be confined in the ghetto or deported to a concentration camp. At that point her sweetheart Jean, who played the horn in the same orchestra, prepared a hideout for her in the cellar storeroom of his cousin's grocery store on the outskirts of Brussels.

Windowless, that cellar was dark unless a lamp was lit, whether it was early morning or midday. At times, even with open eyes, vague images seemed to hang in the air as if in a dream. Then, if she blinked once, without fail an unfamiliar street would appear, and in that street the only lights burning would be those of shops selling musical instruments. If she cautiously pushed open the doors of those shops and went in, members of the orchestra she had not seen for a long time would welcome her joyfully. Each one would sit down before their instrument, then they would strike up a lively dance or march, and whenever their eyes met hers they would smile warmly, as if they were whispering: "Nothing hurts; so long as we're alive we exist so that every pain is comforted and healed." Her heart warmed, she would remain absorbed in their performance for a while, then if she blinked again the melody, the players and their smiles all vanished. Every time the sweet illusion vanished, she would feel even more lonely, more dejected. As she dreamed she was eating her fill of food prepared by her mother, her lips would move unconsciously, then if she suddenly woke she would feel unbearably cold, as if she were out on some windswept plain, all alone. Once every two weeks, Jean would come to the cellar bringing a basket with water and bread, but in those days, he was poor like everyone else, and so it was never enough to last for two weeks. The basket might have been light and shabby, still Jean never forgot to spread at the bottom a sheet of music he had composed. On days when she saw the brightly lit shops, she would take out her violin and perform those pieces, keeping the bow some distance away so it did not touch the strings, on an unlit stage, devoid of any audience's applause, in silence.

"Those pieces composed by Jean were a light that enabled me to dream of the future in that grocery store cellar, where I had every day been thinking only of death. So I can truly say those musical scores saved my life."

After speaking at some length, Alma Mayer slowly raised her head and smiled slightly, for the first and last time during the interview. In my darkened seat, I unexpectedly found myself smiling with her.

"Uh, this is Gwon Eun's home, isn't it?"

Although the door was open, I did not immediately go inside but instead repeated my question several times. The rusty, dented front door led straight into a dark room, where the only source of light was a round, transparent snow globe. What brought me to that small, cold room where almost no sunlight entered was not something I was in control of. After Gwon Eun had been absent from school for four days, the homeroom teacher summoned me as class president and another student, a girl serving as vice-president, and asked us to go and see what was wrong. The moment we left the teacher's room, the vice-president said she had a piano lesson and refused to accompany me, so I set off alone for the address written on a scrap of paper and found my way to that front door. As my eyes slowly grew accustomed to the darkness, Gwon Eun came into view, wearing a shabby overcoat and covered with a blanket. Just as Gwon Eun rose and switched on the light, the clockwork of the snow globe wound down and stopped.

It was a room without any adjoining kitchen or bathroom. A portable gas stove and a kettle, together with a plastic washbowl holding toiletries revealed the room's multiple functions. I could not even begin to imagine what that thirteen-year-old girl ate or how she lived in that poor, unheated room. I learned that Gwon Eun's only family, her father, used to leave home for a minimum of one or two months up to a maximum of six months at a time. "Keep that a secret." As she spoke she held out a glass of water. "I'm not an orphan. I'm never going to go into any kind of home." I could think of nothing to say and the water I was gulping down had the distinct metallic taste of disinfectant. Grimacing, I put down the glass, said "Okay," and quickly left the room. The next day I reported to the homeroom teacher that Gwon Eun was sick. All said and done, there was nothing much wrong with saying that. The young homeroom teacher, who had only recently been appointed, did not seem to pay much attention to my words. After that, I often found myself imagining that Gwon Eun might die. Even just imagining that Gwon Eun died was enough to fill me with panic. There were days when I had the illusion I could hear the other children in my class whispering it was my fault that Gwon Eun died.

After that, I visited Gwon Eun's room several times without being told to do so by anyone. It was simply that I disliked the panic and the imagined blame falling on me; I had no other plan. The only things I could take to her room were comic books I had finished reading or trifles like new batteries for the snow globe. "Off you go now. I'm okay." Being alone with a girl in the same room felt awkward, yet I could not leave so easily and while I stayed hovering she used to push me in the back as she spoke.

Once I left Gwon Eun's room and walked down the narrow sloping alley that led to the road, the orange streetlights, the kids vanishing hurriedly down the alleys, the broken doors of the communal toilet and the dirty toilet bowls glimpsed through them, and worst of all the bulldozers crouched like furious wild animals on vacant lots—all these ghostly sights used to loom vaguely like something not of this world. More than half the houses on the hillside, built roughly of cement and planks, were derelict. Like Gwon Eun, I was only thirteen. There was nothing I could do about the hunger and cold Gwon Eun had to endure in that isolated room in her ruined neighborhood. When I happened to come across a Fuji camera in the wardrobe of my parents' bedroom, without a moment's hesitation I went running blindly to Gwon Eun's room clutching the camera to my chest, because it looked to me like something that could be sold secondhand for a bundle of banknotes. Contrary to my expectation, Gwon Eun did not sell the camera. That was only natural. To her, the camera was not simply a device for taking photos, it was a path leading to another world. She must have loved the magic moment when she pressed the shutter and masses of light came pouring out from every corner of the world to enfold the subject. But then, once she had pressed the shutter and that light vanished from the viewfinder, surely she must have felt more lonely and depressed, like Alma Mayer? Like the landscape not included in the frame of a photograph, all of that lies now in the domain of things I cannot verify. Possibly forever.

Once she had used that camera to photograph everything inside her room, Gwon Eun gradually began to venture outside in quest of more scenes to capture, and she came back to school, too. Yet I did not approach her and start a conversation as soon as she came back. It was probably because I did not want to give anyone the impression that I was close to Gwon Eun, who always wore the same clothes. Gwon Eun likewise often acted as though she could not see me. So in the end we never became friends but each kept the other's secret. I never revealed to anyone that Gwon Eun was pretty much an orphan, and she pretended to the very end not to know that I had stolen the camera from my father. One day a couple of weeks before the winter vacation I heard the news that Gwon Eun had gone with her family to live in some remote region. A rumor spread that her father had been found dead on a rubbish dump near a gambling den, but nothing was certain.

Countless hours have passed since then, and now Gwon Eun writes this letter to an Alma Mayer who no longer has an earthly address: "In that room, to which Father rarely came home, I dreamed the same dream nearly every night, and since I did not want to dream that dream, until sleep came I would wind up the clockwork of the snow globe and immerse myself in a world where snow fell for one minute and thirty seconds, then just before the melody ended I would pull the bedding up over my head and shut my eyes quickly. In the dream I wandered though an unfamiliar town, one that I was visiting for the first time, calling my mom until I awoke. My routine never varied." Pausing, Gwon Eun is silent for a moment. I likewise maintain my silence. Only a few days later does Gwon Eun open the blog again and slowly write: "Sometimes I would lay my brow against the cold wall and pray fervently, asking that the clockwork driving the room stop, that I might stop breathing. Until the camera came into my hands, that was my only prayer. So...." The sentence following that "So" was repeated in the single letter that Gwon Eun wrote to me. In that letter she called me "Class President." Of course, twenty or so years had passed, she felt hurt that I had not recognized her, but on the other hand she also thought it was fortunate, she wrote in that letter. She asks me: "Class President, do you know the greatest thing a person can do?" I shake my head. "Someone once said that saving the life of another is the greatest thing, one [gift] that is given to few. So… No matter what happens to me, President, you need to remember that the camera you gave me saved my life. Eun." That letter was saved to the blog on the day she and I drank beer together at Euljiro. After saying thanks, she got into the taxi and left, and inside the taxi as it made its way through the streets of Seoul, she thought that for once she must write a letter that a living person could read, a really useful letter.

It was only in 1943 that Alma Mayer was able to leave that cellar storeroom. Jean heard that someone had reported her to the German police and once again helped her to escape. She went with him to Switzerland and they parted in a Swiss border town. By that time she and Norman were already connected at their hearts, but since she had not yet realized it, she said nothing to Jean. She first became aware of Norman's existence after a severe bout of seasickness in a third-class cabin on a steamer bound for America. Arriving at Ellis Island, the gateway to America, in November 1943, the first thing that Alma Mayer did was sell the violin that had been like an organ in her body. With that money, she was able to get a place to live and she did not have to work until Norman was born. Five years had passed since the end of the war before she heard that, incredibly, Jean was alive. But Jean was now married and had a family, and she did not inform him of her survival or her whereabouts. In her mind, Jean had already done too much for her, risked too much for her. She did not want to give him any more trouble. Rather than a lover's pride, it was more a matter of human courtesy.

Until Helge Hansen sent her the film, however, she had no idea that Norman had long been following the course of Jean's life. For almost a full thirty years, Norman had frequented an unlicensed office on the outskirts of New York that secretly collected and provided personal information about individuals. Once a month or so, Norman would visit and learn about Jean's current doings, sometimes even receive a photo. But he only took the information, he never let Jean know of his existence, never wrote a letter or phoned. He did not agree with his mother's idea of human courtesy but he wished to respect her choice, thinking that in this world there are sometimes untruths that are close to truth. In 2007, Norman received the final piece of information about Jean, a kind of pamphlet with a photo of Jean's funeral and the location of his grave. "Sorry, Norman." The office manager who had dealt with Norman's business for so long and had grown old with him, offered him a cigarette. On finishing the cigarette, Norman left the office, went on past his parked car and walked aimlessly. Jean Berne, from French-speaking Belgium, had dreamed his whole life of being a composer yet had never published a composition, a nameless horn player who once past forty was excluded from even a small provincial orchestra and was never invited to perform solo anywhere…. On that day, as he had recalled the information he had been receiving for nearly thirty years, Norman made a resolution:

"I resolved that in my own life I would repeat the one great thing he did in his life, in saving the life of a worthless woman about to die in war. I believe that saving the life of another is the greatest thing, one [gift] that is given to few. As you can see, I am already old. Before I get any older, I want to commemorate his memory by acting as he did."

Once Norman had finished speaking, a somber silence filled the relief truck. The camera focused in close-up on each passenger in turn, then gradually zoomed away. The screen was slowly fading out. Just before it turned completely black, like a sudden slap to the back of our heads, the sound of a powerful explosion filled the cinema. The lights overhead flooded the room, the final credits were rolling on the screen, but my ears were burning as if they too had been blown apart in that blinding moment behind the sound of the explosion. At the very end of the credits came two names together with their dates of birth and death—Norman Mayer and Alma Mayer, who died at home two months after her interview with the director. The clockwork that had made both their worlds turn had wound down and stopped in 2009.

Even after the final credits had come to an end, I remained sitting there, unable to take my eyes from the screen, until someone lightly tapped my shoulder. Turning, I found a middle-aged black woman carrying cleaning materials standing behind me. Looking around, I saw all the seats were empty. Shouldering my bag, I quickly left the building. The morning fog had lifted, and unexpectedly dazzling winter sunshine was beaming down, filling the street with light.

I slowly merged with the Manhattan streets that were billowing with light. After a few blocks and a corner, the place loomed into view. A place that absorbed all the street's sunlight, unable to close its gaping mouth; I walked step by step toward the display window of a store selling musical instruments. Inside, all kinds of instruments were on show, including violins and horns. If Gwon Eun had been with me, she would surely have begun to imagine Alma Mayer and Jean Berne, each holding their instrument and playing. Perhaps with an escort of light, after tightly shutting her eyes then opening them. No wonder. What melody continues to resound in that world even after the clockwork winds down and the snow stops, and sometimes passes into other worlds and breathes life into vanished memories, too, were things I now could understand.

I looked toward my feet.

As the snow began to melt, the footprints inscribed in it were gradually fading away. A few steps in front of me I could see Gwon Eun's little form from the back, crouching hunched. A Sunday afternoon, with nobody except us in the snow-covered school playground. Little by little, as I approached Gwon Eun, her posture grew clearer, she was pointing her camera at footprints someone had left in passing. "What are you doing?" Those were the first words I addressed to Gwon Eun after she came back to school. Tearing her eyes from the camera, Gwon Eun looked at me with a surprised expression, as I repeated my question in a gruffer voice. "Why are you at school?" "There are visitors at home, I've nowhere to go…." "But what are you doing here?" Gwon Eun made no reply but instead gestured to me to squat down beside her. Bewildered, I squatted down at her side, then she pointed at footprints whose outlines were becoming blurred, and said: "There's light inside those footprints. Don't they look like little boats loaded full with light?" "Oh, really…?" "And hidden in here, too." "What?" "When I press the shutter, there's light flashing past inside the camera." "Is there? Where does the light come from?" As soon as I showed interest, Gwon Eun, who had never once looked at me, gazed at me with an excited face. She had still not begun to speak, but already I knew. I knew about the brief moment when the masses of light that at ordinary times lie folded thin behind a wardrobe, or in a desk drawer, or somewhere inconspicuous like an empty bottle, the moment the shutter is pressed, that all come streaming out and enfold the subject, and about the rapture of visiting another world every time you take a photo; I already remembered all those things. Gwon Eun began the tale that I already knew. The sunlight reflecting off the music store's display window was shining on her alone.

A BALE OF SALT

Koo Hyo-seo

Translated by **Brother Anthony of Taizé**

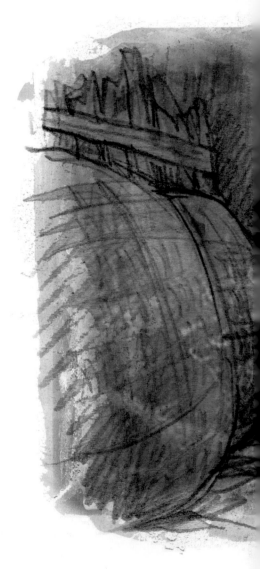

소금가마니

구효서

A critique of this short story was published in the Koreana magazine in Winter 2008 (Vol. 22 No. 4, pp. 85-87).

© Cha Jae-ok

*F*ear and Trembling: written by Soren Kierkegaard, translated by Munetaka Iijima, and published by Hakusuisha (『恐怖と戦慄』, キルケゴール 著, 飯島宗享 譯, 白水社).

He told me once that it was a book my mother had read. I was never able to ask my maternal cousin again if that was right, if it really was a book Mother had read. When I found the book in my cousin's bookcase, he had been dead for three days. It was like a bequest from him. If I had found it only three days earlier, would I have been able to ask him about it? Had it really been Mother's book?

It was not possible. Even if I had heard it directly from my cousin, when I had first came across that book in his bookcase, I would have stared blankly down at the cover, at a loss for words. No matter what answer I heard, it would surely not have relieved the doubts in my confused mind as I held the book. Was he saying that my uneducated mother had read Kierkegaard, and in Japanese?

Until just before he died, my cousin had told me this and that story about my mother, but he had not gone so far as to explain why she had read Kierkegaard.

In addition to that book, there were a few more of Mother's books: *Dream of Geumsan Temple, The Sad Tale of the Gisaeng Gang Myeong-hwa, The Legend of Kim In-hyang, Autumn Moon Sympathy, Kim Ok-yeon...* that kind of thing, nothing particularly surprising. Novels, in Korean. She had not attended school, so she had not learned to write as a child, yet Mother had no difficulties in reading and writing. However, because she had mastered writing in her twenties or thirties, she was weak at spelling and knowing how to space words. While I was stationed at Chupung Pass during my military service, Mother wrote a letter including the usual opening phrase, "Inho, sea what I have written." The platoon leader, noticing this, asked what kind of sea she thought there might be in Yeongdong, Chungcheongbuk-do Province. I, being accustomed to Mother's spelling, had no difficulty understanding her meaning.

Still, Kierkegaard was not what I would have expected. As for *Fear and Trembling*, I remember reading it when I was about twenty-two. I still have it, wedged in a corner of my bookcase, but I do not recall her ever saying that she had understood it while I was reading it.

Why Kierkegaard? How much could she possibly have understood of Kierkegaard? I examined the passages underlined here and there. The underlining was in pencil. Occasionally short notes were visible. Clearly they were in Mother's handwriting. But I cannot read Japanese. I was obliged to check against my old Korean translation. Amazingly, the portions that Mother had underlined and the portions I had underlined were frequently identical.

There was one who was great by reason of his power, and one who was great by reason of his wisdom, and one who was great by reason of his hope, and one who was great by reason of his love; but "he" was greater than all, great by reason of his power whose strength is impotence, great by reason of his wisdom whose secret is foolishness, great by reason of his hope whose form is madness, great by reason of the love which is hatred of oneself.

Kierkegaard was the youngest child, born when his mother was already forty-five. Strangely enough, I too was the youngest, also born when my mother was forty-five. Therefore Mother might have felt an affinity with Kierkegaard. But that was not all. They were also similar in having had six children in all, of whom several had already passed on. The way the daughters had not received an education on account of the father's opposition was the same, too. Even the way I, like Kierkegaard, suffered from back problems was the same. If she had read that book before I was born, then at least those similarities with me could not have been the reason she read it. But even this aside, the other similarities were sufficient for Mother to have felt an interest in Kierkegaard. Nonetheless, the fact that a work by Kierkegaard was sandwiched between popular novels of the time left me with a strange and uncertain feeling.

Finally, my unrelieved apprehensions received the beginnings of a solution in the three characters of a name inscribed on the last page, while developing at the same time into suspicions of a quite different order. Not that it was really a different order. These were ancient suspicions that I had ignored, not wishing to examine them closely, and that I had therefore forgotten as life went on.

"Property of Pak Seong-hyeon." The name was written in the margin of the copyright page containing the date of publication and the name of the publisher. The penmanship was elegant. Despite the long passage of time, the writing still preserved the turquoise hue of the ink. That dimly emerging turquoise hue tugged gently at my thoughts, which were struggling to go on ignoring something.

So originally it had not been Mother's book. Whether the owner had lent it to her or given it to her for good so it had become hers, it was clearly quite different from the book originally being Mother's. It was a moment testifying to a substantial relationship between Mother and the owner. Heard as a rumor. I had been a child born of rumors.

Uneducated, an avid reader of popular novels, mastering Japanese *katakana* and *hiragana* scripts, finally even reading Kierkegaard, and in those days there had been Pak Seong-hyeon, the only Christian in the village and the only person to have studied in Japan, the father of the rumors.

Mother's intellectual prowess must have been far greater than I had realized. Besides, there would have been the book owner's constant, prudent care and discrete guidance. Judging Mother's educational level and estimating what had been the level of her relationship with the book's owner came down to the same thing. It could be that *Fear and Trembling*, which had left me with a strange, curious feeling, might in fact have been for those two neither strange nor curious.

That Mother's skill at deciphering what she read was out of the ordinary was a fact that I had experienced at least occasionally since childhood. There's the *Tojeong Bigyeol* (a work of divination by Tojeong Yi Ji-ham (1517-1587))—an ancient book I still own—well, Mother was the only woman in the village who had read it and could explain its meaning. Calculating the relevant signs of the sexegenary cycle from the numbers of a person's birth date then deducing good and bad fortune was not something just anybody could do, while interpreting without hesitation the most significant sentences, made complex by analogies and symbols, was quite impossible without considerable experience.

In the first ten days of each new year, the womenfolk used to come crowding to our house. They reckoned that consulting the book would show them their fortune for the year. The reason they all came crowding together into our house was partly because the only copy of the book in the village was there, and besides, Mother was the only person capable of reading it. The fact that they knew there was no husband around also made it easier for the womenfolk to gather in our house.

Once the winter sunlight began to shine onto the door with its paper lining ornamented with leaves of mugwort and morning glory, Mother would open the book and put on her reading glasses.

"You say you were born in Gimyo year, in the eighth month?"

In addressing both older people or younger people, when they consulted the book Mother's style of speech varied subtly. She talked down to them.

"Ah, well, let me see… the eighth month, the twenty-ninth… I think."

In contrast, whether younger or older, while they were consulting the book they addressed Mother in honorific language. Between a person discerning fortunes and her clients, such an exchange of covert granting and tacit acceptance of power was considered necessary.

Coming to the third month, cast fishing line into river or lake, catch fine fish; board a raft, cross the sea, clouds scatter, bright weather comes….

Once she began to cast the fortune for the coming year, month by month, the client inevitably grew tense. *Chrysanthemum and maple are better than peony; wind passes through reeds, flocks of geese scatter.* Naturally, with words such as these, whose meaning could not be grasped no matter how hard one listened….

Whether the message was good or bad, with their fortune for the whole year depending on the book, anxiety was inevitable. Still, Mother did not readily disclose the meaning.

Unvaryingly, a client's expression would gradually darken, her head grow heavy. If Mother just left it at that, it seemed the client would stop breathing for good. As time passed, the face would harden, the cheeks sag.

At the wintery start of the new year, curiosity, misery at being illiterate and fear of the future would start to fill the room. Until Mother gave at least some little hint, the women would sit there as if about to drop dead. That was how it looked to me.

Only when the tension filling the room seemed to be on the verge of exploding would Mother utter a cautious, "Very good!" The client would be so unnerved by that time that she would not hear her. She would only come back to life after somebody sitting close to her had poked her in the ribs, repeating, "She says it's good." Then the client would let out a loud, long sigh. The atmosphere in the room, that had grown quite rigid, would abruptly relax and the women's faces would grow bright with understanding like the sunlit window paper.

Irrespective of what was actually expressed in the book, Mother's "Very good!" alone would set free the client's constricted breath. Such was Mother's unlimited, unsurpassed power as she played with the life and death of those women with that single "Very good!" or "Ah, good!" Similarly the owner of the book by Kierkegaard had once been fascinated by her far-from-common appearance.

Infinite resignation is that shirt we read about in the old fable. The thread is spun under tears, the cloth bleached with tears, the shirt sewn with tears; but yet it offers better protection than iron and steel.

Pak Seong-hyeon, there, fascinated, behind the image of Mother. Was that what had made Father unable to take it any longer? Born posthumously, I had only been able to gain a sense of my father from the memories of Mother in her lifetime, my sisters and, finally, my maternal cousin.

Father had been a strange kind of person. Yet from what I'd heard about him, I always found Mother even stranger than Father. In the course of a life in which she had endured the unspeakable from him, had she never once answered back?

Father violently mistreated Mother, all the time proclaiming an ancestry of which he was in fact completely ignorant. Every time he beat her up, Father boasted of an ancestor, a general, who was falsely rumored to have been awarded the posthumous title of Second Minister in the War Department after dying in an attack against the enemy during the Chinese invasions of the 17th century. General or ancestor, whatever he might be, to Mother he was nothing more than a demon or ghost that troubled people. After she had been beaten up by Father, Mother's face would be swollen like a pumpkin in autumn. The village shaman used to click her tongue, saying: "Why, that husband of yours takes his wife for an enemy warrior."

Less than three days after the birth of a daughter, Father dragged her out into the yard by the waist of her pants, cursing her for lying around at her ease when there was no one to help with the work. You wonder where that daughter came from? In a millet field swept by an icy midwinter wind, Father, drunk, was sitting astride Mother, throttling her. Unable to breathe, Mother's face had turned a shade of bronze. The red remains of dried millet stalks shaking in the wind were like streaks of blood emerging from Mother's body. Father was raping her with explosive fury. I had just turned twenty and my eldest sister's face was expressionless as she told me the story of the origin of my second sister, two years older than myself. When I realized that the births of their various children were all uniformly nothing more than the dregs of hatred, resentment and anger, I felt fortunate that I could not so much as remember my father's face. Several times he gave Mother a sudden kick in the behind that sent her toppling face down into the cauldron where tofu was boiling, and he frequently shoved her face into the tray of tofu she had spent the night making.

Father used to take the money from the sales of tofu and hand it all to the woman who was the last barmaid in the village. She boldly, brazenly served as his whore. Even when the barmaid approached Mother at the communal washing ground and addressed her in familiar terms within earshot of several others, Mother did not so much as bat an eyelid. The tongues of the other women wagged about how the descendant of the Second Minister in the War Department beat his own wife and apparently stuffed the barmaid's nether hole, but Mother mutely went on with her washing.

Father had wanted to marry but he owned absolutely nothing. He had spent a year doing farm work for the parents of his future wife, who lived on the far side of the hill and were as poor as he was, then married her. Traveling back and forth from work he came to know of the existence of Pak Seong-hyeon: he had returned after studying in Japan, no less, the good-looking son of the richest farmer in the district. He adored my mother but had come up against his family's objections. That was all. Mother never so much as cast a careless glance in the direction of the Paks. It was only after their marriage that Father discovered that Mother could read and write Korean and even had a good knowledge of Japanese. Father's sexual mistreatment and his debauchery did not involve his children. Father's impotent fury, unable to vent itself against the strict Park family, manifested itself in a craven violence against Mother.

If I reflected on how Father's wrath could have lasted unchanged for so long, perverse though it may seem, I used to wonder if it was not because of an affection for her that he could not let go of, something that could hardly be sensed from the harsh memories of my mother, my sisters, or my cousin.

At any rate, even without being fully convinced, given Father's strange personality, it was not completely impossible to guess at the reason behind Father's violence. Rather, what was utterly incomprehensible was what lay behind the method and attitude of Mother in dealing so ineffectually with Father while she lived with him.

Beatings that went on for hours on end behind the room's locked door used to take their children's breath away as they waited outside. Father's shouts and curses seemed about to bring the house tumbling down. Punches and kicks rang out against Mother's body and each one made the children wince. What was strange was the way Mother was never once heard to groan or cry out while she was being beaten like that. When at last the door opened and Mother was tossed out, she would always look as wretched as a sheaf of rice emerging from the threshing machine. With her face swollen and red like an old pumpkin in fall, the first thing Mother looked for was her children as they waited outside the door. In the midst of that maelstrom, spreading her arms as wide as could be, she would gather her children to her breast. No sound of sobbing or groaning could be heard from her. What the children hugged to her breast could feel after a short time was the far too rapid thudding of her heartbeat and the hot, chestnut-sized tears falling onto their heads.

Mother blamed nobody. She never uttered any complaint. She soaked a huge quantity of soy beans and ground them on a hand mill. All day long she fed the fire beneath the cauldron. When it was finally done, she would first of all bring Father a block of hot, steaming tofu. Once he had downed the whole block of tofu with *makgeolli*, Father would go out to piss. Once she grew older that was how Mother lived, and I longed to be able to understand her but my oldest sister said there was no way of knowing a mother like her.

Living in that way, Mother's insides must have gradually deteriorated, yet, incomprehensibly, she was never once sick until the day she died, and she lived to be ninety-seven. As she was dying, her expression was bright and peaceful. It was like the death of a queen who had never once in her life known hardship.

One became great by expecting the possible, another by expecting the eternal, but he who expected the impossible became greater than all.

Not that she was fully consistent in showing a resigned expression and a serene face in every circumstance. When my second sister fell out of the jujube tree and died, Mother went crazy.

Sister had climbed the jujube tree fearlessly. She had gone up to collect eggs from a bird's nest, then slipped on a branch soaked by rain, falling headfirst into the ground. Striking the ground, she lay spread-eagled and her breathing grew intermittent.

Ever since shrikes had started to bring bits of straw and pile them up on a branch of the jujube tree, the children's eyes had begun to shine. It was because of the thoughtless bragging of a neighbor's child, claiming that birds' eggs wrapped in spring onions and baked in a fire were so delicious they were just out of this world. It was less because of the appetizing way he mimed chopping onions into pieces with a knife and more because they were mad about any meat baked in a fire. The eggs laid by the two hens were carefully controlled by Mother; without exception they were enclosed in a long twisted-straw pack and sold on the next market day. If ever a hen failed to lay, the whole family fell under the darkest suspicion. Meat, even on special festivals, was excluded from inhuman, cold-hearted Father's table. As for eggs, there was nothing left to share with the children, who had to make do with the luxury of smelling them. To such children, even the eggs laid by the ownerless shrikes in the sky might be considered a bounty.

By the time Mother arrived at the foot of the jujube tree, the child was already dead. The villagers who had got there first shook their heads. She had already lost her eldest son to a disease, then the daughter two years younger had died after being pulled down into the well by the bucket; it looked as though she was doomed to have her children die in a series of misfortunes.

Mother picked up the child and put her on her back. She glared with bloodshot eyes at Father when he said she was already done for. "Do you think that because they were born as the dregs of anger and hatred, it doesn't matter if another of them dies?" she screamed. Father tried to stop her, saying it was too late, there was no point, but she pushed him out of her way. She pushed with such force that Father, who was bulky in size, tumbled for ten furrows.

She had often urged Father to cut down the jujube tree, since snakes clustered at its roots, but Father insisted it was needed for the offerings in honor of his distinguished ancestor. Now it seemed he had killed a child for the sake of a few jujubes. White foam gathered on Mother's lips as she shouted she would either cut it down with an axe or burn it down. Not just Father, all the villagers told her it was hopeless. It was already growing dark, it was too far to the hospital in the main town. If she ran those ten miles, Mother would die too. They said she should kill a chicken, boil many eggs, and perform a ceremony for the repose of the child's soul.

Mother paid no notice. She swore harshly at the people there. Foam flew from her lips. Mother went darting off like an arrow into the dark, while rain kept falling, carrying the child on her back as if she was possessed.

If they said there was no hope, it was in part because the distance was too great for the condition the child was in, but mainly because the local stream was swollen at the end of the rainy season. The stepping stones had been submerged long ago and the fierce current was strong enough to engulf an ox. Father and the villagers all knew that after just a few miles, she would be stranded. Only Mother in her madness knew no such thing.

Day dawned and she had not returned. They believed she must have fallen into the stream with the child and drowned. A few of the villagers set off with Father at daybreak to look for mother and child. One man said he had heard someone screaming fit to cough blood close to the stream late in the night. He said that the voice, mingled with the sound of the wind, was no human voice, it had sounded like the ghost of the fellow who had fallen into the stream and drowned a couple of years before.

Then the villagers and Father came across a huge willow tree that was lying across the stream. Beside the stump of the tree, that seemed to have just been felled, there lay an old saw with bloodstains on its handle.

Every time she recalled that day, Mother would display the scars etched deep in her palms. Climbing along the willow tree, crossing over the stream, Mother hastened on in the dark. As she sped heedlessly along the muddy road, Mother heard the darkness calling out, "Sorry, I'm sorry, Mom." The girl on her back was weeping in fear, mingled with groans. The mad jolting of her mother's body had stimulated the girl's weak diaphragm. She revived, hacking and coughing. Her mother squatted in the mud, embracing her daughter and weeping, "My little girl, my little girl."

"Here now, if you're going to die, eat well first." As the eggs emerged from the hens, Mother fed them to the child after she left hospital. She ate so many that boiled eggs became the food she detested most of all. Even now sister refuses to eat eggs, saying they smell of chicken shit.

The frenzy that had threatened to possess her completely and her reckless optimism had saved the dead child. Thus Mother was sometimes fierce, frightening, so tough that even Father and the rest were no match for her.

As a matter of fact, she was capable of browbeating others into submission without so much as a word or the slightest change in her expression.

Sun-deok's mother, chattering away at the back door, saying I was Pak Seong-hyeon's child, told how she had been kidnapped by Mother in broad daylight. She had dragged her as far as the shed where the bier was stored, out in the middle of the fields, had gone inside, then after about the time it would take to smoke a cigarette emerged rubbing her hands. She looked as though she had simply relieved herself. That day Sun-deok's mother came creeping home on shaky legs like someone who had been possessed by a spirit then released again. No one ever knew what had happened inside the bier shed. Neither Mother nor Sun-deok's mother ever spoke of it in their lifetimes. But from that day, whenever Sun-deok's mother came face to face with Mother she used to wet herself as if she had just seen one of the great guardian spirits in the flesh, while the village women would stop their smiling as they calculated the dates of Father's death and of my birth.

"He" keeps silent—but he cannot speak. Therein lies the distress and anguish. For if when I speak I am unable to make myself intelligible, then I am not speaking—even if I were to talk uninterruptedly day and night. Such is the case with "him."

In our house there used to be three straw bales full of salt. There were always three of them. In the dark shed behind the kitchen, at half-a-step intervals, they stood enshrined in a row on a platform of large stones. As time passed, their girth would gradually shrink, and by their height or by the way they were raised up on pedestals, they were like three Buddhas in a temple. That is why I feel obliged to say they were enshrined.

They had been there long before I was born. From time to time they were replaced by new bales, of course, but to my eyes they seemed always to have been there without any change. A white pottery bowl was placed beneath each one. Into the bowls the golden brine fell drop by drop.

The shed was always dark. A trickle of water issuing beneath the outside storage terrace flowed through there, so it was always thoroughly damp. Even when it was not the rainy season the bales of salt kept up their flow. They let fall their brine like tears.

Unlike sacks for rice, the bales of salt were loosely woven with old straw. They had to absorb plentiful darkness and moisture if brine was to be produced. The brine served to make the tasty tofu that everyone enjoyed. The tofu Mother made was famous in the surrounding region. It was her tofu that fed the family and kept it alive.

Chill dark, downright damp, together with solitude. If I happened to enter there, that grim atmosphere would lick disagreeably at the nape of my neck. For a while I was held motionless by the dark and damp, then with a shudder I would make an effort and violently escape. Cold, salty brine emerged from that space. The way such brine consistently produced warm and savory, soft and white, tasty tofu was for me mysterious and strange.

That shed brought out goose bumps even on the hottest days. Going in there might have been a way of avoiding the sweltering heat, but our family almost never frequented the place. Only Mother spent her summers there. When Mother emerged from the shed after a lengthy period inside, her appearance was that of a bale of salt impregnated with darkness and dampness and solitude. When she had been beaten up by Father and her whole body was a mass of bruises, she used to spend long hours there. Indeed, it seemed certain that her body found healing there.

The North Korean People's Army came South. They demanded food from Mother. There was already tofu in the house, and piles of beans. Overnight, Mother turned all those beans into tofu, and they held an unruly party. By that time Father was already in hiding. Mother was branded a traitor. She was not the only one. Her younger brother, my maternal uncle, who had managed the boat that night was also labeled a traitor. They had transported the North Koreans' supplies to the far side of the stream. When the South Korean army advanced North again, her uncle fled, leaving behind his old mother and two-year-old son, the cousin who had shown me Mother's book, as well as his wife. The boat, their livelihood, was confiscated, their house demolished. Our aunt was executed in the village peach orchard by the rightist youth brigade using a heavy scythe.

Mother too was tied to a peach tree. Even when she was coughing blood, our aunt kept denying her husband's treason, insisting they had been forced to do it at gunpoint, but Mother did not imitate her. Even when her clothing had been torn off and she was being beaten with a peach tree branch so that scraps of flesh were torn off, Mother remained silent.

Once Father emerged from the cavity beneath his sister's privy, claiming he had hidden to escape being requisitioned by the People's Army, he became a member of the youth brigade's action corps. For him that meant tagging along at the rear of the group, casually carrying a stick, but on the day Mother was taken to the peach orchard there was no sign of him. Someone told me he had been instructed to stay away. The person watching from among the peach trees as Mother faced imminent death had been Pak Seong-hyeon.

Pak Seong-hyeon was not a casual member of the action corps like Father. He was the son of the richest farmer in the region, a Christian who had experienced intimidation while the People's Committee was in control; the motivation for his participation in the corps was bound to be different from that of people like Father. His family's property, entirely confiscated by the People's Committee, had already been returned to them, but since his religious beliefs had been harshly threatened, he was unable to let those troubled times pass quietly. As a result, the woman he adored was here before him in a situation in which she seemed sure to suffer severely.

Yet this paradox turned to Mother's advantage. The authority temporarily bestowed on him was Mother's salvation. That the members of the action corps were all starving was something Pak Seong-hyeon knew full well. Just as the People's Army had done, he commanded her to make tofu for them. When she said she had no beans, he replied that they could use the beans in the storeroom in his house. Freed from the peach orchard, Mother once again boiled tofu day and night. The two main rooms in our house were being used as a shelter for wounded soldiers. Those soldiers survived on the tofu Mother made while they were waiting to be evacuated.

Mother, snatched from the jaws of death, reckoned the bales of salt were her benefactors. Clearly the tofu and Pak Seong-hyeon were also benefactors. Through this incident, Mother could feel once again that Pak Seong-hyeon's mind was unchanged. It also served to confirm the still unallayed suspicions of the villagers and of our father. The families of the dead victims viewed Mother, the only traitor to have been spared, as an immoral woman.

Mother simply made tofu. Just as she had said nothing when tied to a peach tree, she endured the villagers' whispering and the now even fiercer violence of Father in silence and indifference. As for Pak Seong-hyeon, who had saved her life, she never so much as looked at him, let alone uttered a word of thanks. The eye of the storm had passed through the heart of the village, but after the uproar Mother just went on as she had before, making tofu. She winnowed the beans in a wooden dish, turned the hand mill all night, poured out brine and boiled the cauldron. Setting a plank on a trivet, she would lay on it a cloth bag full of fresh tofu. As a finishing touch, she would set twenty pottery disks with a lotus flower pattern in rows on top of it, lay another plank on top and weigh that down with a millstone. For Mother, sleeping, waking up, breastfeeding the baby and making tofu was all in a day's work. Like breathing, done in silence.

In order to safeguard his faith, Pak Seong-hyeon became leader of the patriotic youth association. Having realized through bitter experience that without the state his faith would find no safeguard, he took the lead in becoming a loyal citizen devoted to the Republic of Korea. Mother's brother was among the missing, his wife had been wretchedly executed. With his mother dead, Mother's three-year-old nephew was as good as orphaned. Their property had already been confiscated, thus her whole family had been destroyed. Therefore it was strange that Pak Seong-hyeon's book had come into Mother's hands. She clearly did not enjoy preparing the food for ancestral rites, but Mother had never shown any interest in Christianity, either. In addition, there was Father ever ready to respond violently to the slightest suspicion with blows and kicks. And she had a book of his, one even signed with his name. Why? How? Besides, when could she have read it? As ever, here too Mother was silent.

It is great to give up one's wish, but it is greater to hold it fast after having given it up. It is great to grasp the eternal, but it is greater to hold fast to the temporal after having given it up.

My maternal grandmother built a shack of mud and reeds on top of the demolished house and lived there with her little grandson. Our aunt was buried in a hole in the ground with the bodies of the seventy-three other traitors. All hope of our uncle returning seemed to have vanished. Not owning so much as a hand's breadth of land, Grandmother could not even plant vegetables. She boiled a soup of horsetail grass and wild millet rubbed between her palms. In winter not even this was available to her. That long drawn out penury, lasting from the summer drought, through autumn and winter was more terrible now that the troubles had come.

Her own mother, shriveling up like a dried pollack and her nephew, his belly sticking out like a dried pollack's, might have been close nearby, yet Mother could do nothing. She already had nine mouths to feed. More fearful still was Father's glare, ever on the watch in case any provisions might leak out. If Mother said she was going to visit members of her family, she could not help being acutely aware of Father's stern expression glued to the back of her head. Standing at the side of the yard, Father would watch Mother's retreating back until she was out of sight.

When Mother was cooking gruel, she used to add an extra measure of water. She managed in that way to obtain one extra serving of gruel. This she would place inside an empty water jar. When my eldest sister went to draw water, she carried the jar on her head. By great fortune, the house of our grandmother was beside the spring. On her way to draw water, Sister would deliver the bowl of gruel hidden inside it to the house. Equally fortunately, water had to be fetched every day. In this way, Grandmother and Cousin were able to escape dying of hunger.

Every time she went to the spring, bearing the pot on her head, Sister's legs would be shaking dreadfully. Father seemed to be glaring at her from all sides. Every time my fifteen-year-old sister, who always used to be hungry from the watery gruel, thought of the bowl of gruel inside the water pot, she would swallow her saliva. Mother always used to worry whether she might not put her lips to the bowl of gruel along the way. Yet my eldest sister never once put her lips to the bowl. Mother called my admirable sister a good daughter. She called her that until the day she died. I remember Sister sobbing at the rites for Mother. Since she kept calling her a good daughter, I used to challenge her, asking if she realized how hungry and weary she had been all her life.

When Grandmother finally died, our then five-year-old cousin had to come live with us. It meant one more mouth to feed. Since everyone in the village knew him to be an orphan with nowhere to go, Father had no choice but to put on a show of accepting our cousin. Inside the house, it was another matter. He furiously asked why he should be obliged by fate to have to feed someone from his wife's family.

Our cousin was unable to sit straight at the meal table, he was always twisted, with one eye on Father. He would even jump at the sound of Father merely putting his spoon down. Mother could do nothing to protect him. It was the same as if he had been made to eat out of doors. Had he eaten? Had he slept? On account of Father's threatening attitude, nobody dared show any interest in him. Even Mother feigned indifference. She made as if she could not see him gnawing at sorghum stalks to fill his hungry stomach, and she took no notice when his lips and fingertips were smeared all over after he had been catching and eating grasshoppers. Mother must have realized that the only way to keep him near her at all was to ignore him completely, almost as if he was not there.

At primary school, that he entered at the same time as my elder brother, he soon revealed intelligence beyond his years. He knew Chinese characters they had not studied, and he displayed such outstanding skill in calligraphy that he wrote out in formal style the memorial inscription "江湖砲手參戰碑." On the day when the county magistrate and township mayor, amazed by the advent of such a prodigy, came to offer their congratulations to Father, he went into a rage like a man who had been disgraced.

Wanting to belong in our household, Cousin acted as if he was stupid. For even the simplest calculations he would ask my brother about each step. In the presence of our family he never looked at anything resembling a book. The only time he could read or write was when he was alone at home with Mother. Having no paper or inkstone, he would write in the sand with a twig from the persimmon tree. He knew, as the family did not, that Mother had books concealed that she read.

Cousin left home when he was fourteen. My elder brother had started middle school but the moment cousin completed primary school, Father dragged him off to the fields. One winter's night, having been forced to spend a whole year working like a borrowed ox in the fields, Cousin left carrying a bundle of books Mother had prepared for him. Mother's last exhortation to him was: "Come what may, you must read and write." Inside the bundle were the old books that Mother had read. In addition, seeing he was only a cousin, there was a truly amazing sum of money in there, too. It was incomprehensible. Money was entirely under Father's control, as Cousin knew very well. It was too large a sum for her to have collected penny by penny without any help.

In actual fact, if he had held on just a little longer, Cousin would have been free of Father's contempt and ill-treatment. For only half a year after he left, Father died.

But that was after he was gone. For a long time no one heard any news of Cousin. By the time the newspapers announced he had won the President's Prize for calligraphy, Mother was no longer alive. He had become a professor in some provincial university. I had thought Mother might have kept in touch with him, but when I visited him, he did not so much as know that Father had died so soon after his departure.

Even when I told him of Mother's death, he showed no great surprise or sorrow. He simply gazed up at the sky in silence for a while. Then he asked me: "Do you know what your mother's hope was?" Had Mother ever had a hope? If she had, surely it had vanished the moment she married Father. Seeing that I had no immediate reply, he went on: "My hope, your hope, that's what it was." "What is your hope?" I asked. He laughed awkwardly. "Since you and I can read and write freely, it's been fulfilled. If I still have a wish left, it's to write a memorial tablet to be set up in that peach orchard over the grave of those seventy-three poor souls. Will you do that if I can't?"

In the end he died without fulfilling that wish.

He who loves God has no need of tears, no need of admiration, in his love he forgets his suffering, yea, so completely has he forgotten it that afterward there would not even be the least inkling of his pain if God Himself did not recall it, for God sees in secret and knows the distress and counts the tears and forgets nothing.

I have the impression that someone once told me I was not my father's son. Because I was born ten months after Father had left this world. Counting by the solar calendar, not the lunar, he said. If it was really so, and if so how, I don't know. Mother never said anything. And I never asked her. How could I ask Mother whose child I was? I might ask myself, it was not something I could ask Mother.

Father died ten months before I was born. Father had been forty-seven. It was because of the clan registry.

Once the war was over, a new clan registry was published. In the registry, brought up to date after thirty years, all the recently born children's names were recorded in full. In the old days, not even the main branch of the family had a copy of the clan registry. Until then, if someone wanted to consult the registry, they had to go all the way to Yeongheung township where the tenth generation of the Suncheol family line was living, walking, then by bus, then crossing the river. The cover of the newly revised registry was not only thick, it was black and shiny. It was no longer called a clan registry but a genealogy, the word printed in gold letters. One set of ten volumes was allotted to each senior household for the first time. There was no longer any need to go all the way to Yeongheung. Father coveted that genealogy. He longed for our house to have a copy, even though we were not a senior household. Father, who every time he beat Mother up would drag in a mention of his ancestor, the Minister for War, and never did cut down that snake-ridden jujube tree because he needed it for offerings to his ancestors.

Father was waiting for an opportunity. The eldest grandson of the senior family, Father's second cousin, was fully aware of Father's intention. Father, who knew there would be neither opportunity nor justification for simply removing it, finally took decisive action and stole it. The eldest grandson, realizing the genealogy had vanished, came running after Father. The confrontation took place on a bridge, and Father rolled off the bridge together with the book. He struck his head on the stones of the dried up streambed, spent four days without recovering, then breathed his last breath. The grandson was twice summoned by the police but at the family's insistent entreaties, Father's death was classified as having been caused by an accidental fall.

Father died on Mother's knees. There was no way of knowing what last words they exchanged but until his last breath Father clasped Mother's hand tightly. All his life, he had done nothing but beat her up, but she did not withdraw her hand from his until the strength had completely gone out of him. Nobody could guess what might be the meaning of the tear that flowed from Father's closed eyes. Even in death, Father seemed a riddle.

Pak Seong-hyeon, mistakenly thought to have been my father. In every way his life was the antithesis of my father's. After being head of the patriotic youth league he once even ran for election to the provincial assembly, but finally his end was no different from Father's. Carrying a shotgun, he was out hunting deer when he fell into a boar trap and his heart was pierced.

The man who had set the trap was a pockmarked fellow named Cheon from the lower village. During the war he had gone missing together with our uncle, but then had reappeared, minus one arm. He earned a living by hunting and slaughtering. The nickname "One-arm" was added to the original "Pock-face." He used to be better at carrying out difficult tasks than those equipped with two arms.

Among the seventy-three poor souls buried in the peach orchard had been his father. He could not avoid the suspicion that the boar trap had been a deliberate plot, a means of revenge, but after being questioned more than twenty times, he was cleared of suspicion and released. Whether or not there had been a plot, the death of Pak Seong-hyeon, falling by accident into the boar trap and dying on the spot, had been the end of him, no more, no less.

The only one to enjoy a full span of life and close her eyes peacefully was Mother, who had spent her whole life exhausted and in misery. Her skin was amazingly white and soft for someone of ninety-seven. Her daughters exclaimed, "My, so soft, my, so pretty," stroking Mother's face as she lay there. As her consciousness began to waver, her children clung to her, shedding tears. "You mustn't die. You should live another thousand years, ten thousand. You're entitled to it."

Whether or not she heard them, Mother spoke, barely moving her lips, "You're… still… alive…." Then she named the sons and daughters who had died more than sixty years before, and as if absorbed for a moment in some private grief she twisted her lips. There were sons that even we had forgotten and could not recall. "So you can go now and see those sons and daughters," my eldest sister said, wiping away tears. Mother smiled faintly, as if to say she understood. Immediately after that her ninety-seven years of life here on earth ended.

To the very end, I never was able to ask Mother whose child I had been. I did not ask. That spring day, with pink azaleas covering the hills, Mother rode in the bier to lie beside Father. The white paper flowers decorating the four corners of the burial site fluttered in the breeze. All her life she had willingly accepted the dark and humid as though she detested herself, protecting her children with love, and now her body, purified like pure white salt that has given up all its brine, was lying in the flower-adorned bier. Her twenty children and grandchildren in cotton mourning dress followed behind lumpily, like fresh tofu. Watching those lives, so abundant, solemnly continuing, I finally murmured, as I wept alone, "Your life was great."

The many tears that came pouring out then were salty and sour like brine, but also sweet and tasty like Mother's tofu. Now, as I compare the underlined portions in the two books, I finally realize, although I still cannot fully understand it, what had made it possible for me to underline precisely those portions was the fact that Mother's hand was guiding mine.

THE WAYFARER NEVER RESTS ON THE ROAD

Lee Ze-ha

Translated by **Brother Anthony of Taizé**

나그네는 길에서도 쉬지 않는다

이제하

A critique of this short story was published in the Koreana magazine in Spring 2016 (Vol. 30 No. 1, pp. 84-85).

© Kim Si-hoon

The sun was setting on a day a couple of weeks before the Lunar New Year; the Year of the Pig (1983) was hastening to its end. A Sokcho intracity bus stopped briefly at the Mulchi crossroads and several passengers alighted. A few men obviously equipped to go hiking in the mountains, with rucksacks over their shoulders or carrying utility totes, exclaimed at the cold as they straightened their thermal jackets and donned their hats, then began to walk toward the roadside shops; following behind them, a somewhat older man trudged along, seemingly on his way home from buying fish downtown; he was carrying a parcel. The man who got off last simply stood there blankly, looking as though he had been hit by a tram. Before him, stretching as far as the eye could see, lay nothing but the sea.

He had boarded a bus at the Seoul terminal almost on an impulse, and had been looking out at the water occasionally as they rattled along, but now, when the sea suddenly loomed beyond the window as the bus came to a halt, it provoked totally different feelings in him. And so, at the very last moment, driven by a sudden urge, he quickly descended from the bus. It was like a cliff that had appeared out of nowhere, blocking the way ahead.

Though the road was not as busy as in Seoul, here too vehicles, whether tourist buses or whatever, whizzed by; the water began right at the edge of the asphalt of a road that looked like a wide open plaza, being three times the width of a four-lane highway. Unconsciously, he shuddered, then hesitantly began to cross the road, as though skirting a cliff.

Perhaps for the safety of vacationers, trough-like cement planters lined the roadway, but as they were buffeted by gusts of wind so strong that it seemed like the tarmac was about to rise and stand upright, they looked extremely small and crumpled. After clambering down the two-foot-high embankment, he walked out onto the ten-meter-wide strip of gravel and put down the bag he was carrying. Just as he was bending down, a shout rang out: "Stop! Don't move! Step back three paces! Leave that where it is."

The sentry who had approached, with his gun drawn, glanced into the bag he had been opening and then relaxed his expression.

"What's this?"

"Goddammit…" he replied, "Can't you see? A table of numbers and roasted rice flour."

"What?"

Inside the bag there was nothing but a few pairs of underwear, a toiletry kit and a plastic bag. As the soldier crouched down, examining the plastic bag, the thought, "You might have been dead by now," flashed through his mind. If he had been a spy, he would not have let the chance pass. What idiot would carry his gun in his bag?

"What's this? Looks like powder… quicklime?"

He glanced scornfully at the soldier who was rubbing together the fingers he had withdrawn from the bag.

"Didn't I tell you? It's rice flour."

"Stop fooling around with me! Oh, what the hell… Scatter it somewhere and get back up there quickly. Go on, get back up there, quick."

During his military training, some fifteen or so years back, he had witnessed an accident when a recruit, at a loss what to do when holding a grenade with the pin pulled out, had thrown it awkwardly and blown off another recruit's arm. All around people were stamping and pointing and shouting, but that recruit merely sidled away with his face flushing ever more deeply; the moment he grabbed the plastic bag from the soldier he felt anger rising in him, as if his face too was blushing like the recruit's. He picked up his bag and climbed back up toward the road without a word.

The windows of a couple of restaurants, displaying paper signs for *maeuntang* (hot fish stew), could be heard rattling hard despite the distance.

When he opened the door of the restaurant to his left and went in, the men who had gotten off the bus with him were sitting around the stove. They paused in their drinking to look over at him. One man, who had been carrying a rucksack, looked as though he recognized him and did not immediately turn away, but he paid him no attention and made his way to a corner, where he set himself down on a rickety chair.

"Why's the guy still not here? Does it mean he's failed?"

"No way! There are so many of them around here… it'll be the opposite."

"The opposite?"

"I only hope those girls won't be all over us… you know, if you make a pass at one, the whole lot of them come and stick to you."

"He'll surely have calmed them down in advance. General Kim knows what he's up to… if there are too many, we can enjoy them too, I don't mind two or three…."

"Hey man, you shoot the moment you're in, quit bluffing…."

"What do you mean? I'm not done yet. It depends on what you've got. Once it finds the right pipe for itself, it'll go for an hour or more…."

"Hey, stop bickering, we're all getting older. It's over now."

From behind the men, who sniggered and began to grow noisy again, an older man opened a side door and approached him.

"You want *maeuntang*? It's all there is."

"What kind of fish?"

"Flatfish… that's all we've got, too. And *soju*?"

"A big bowl of that, just one bowl. And some rice…."

He gazed briefly at his clasped hands, then unfolded them and from force of habit took out a cigarette.

"Can I have a word, please?" When he had finished the soup and rice the woman had brought him, the older man approached him again from the direction of the side door, smoking another cigarette, his eyes closed wearily. By then, the companion the group of men had been waiting for had arrived noisily, they had all left, still chattering, and the place was empty. They seemed to be a rowdy bunch, intent on lechery under the pretense of mountain climbing. The fellow wearing a beret who had appeared midway through the meal had brought along with him four or five young women, at which point the others began to squabble as the pairing didn't work. "Didn't I tell you I don't need one?" the man with the rucksack said, sullenly. "I said I didn't need one; what are we supposed to do now you've brought too many?"

"Don't make such a fuss… Show me anyone who's against it. I brought one each, so what are you going on about? You really don't need one?"

"No need."

"Don't bother if you don't need one. I'll deal with it… Anyway, no one will lay a finger on your girl. All you have to do is pay."

"You goddamn pitiful excuse for a man…."

"You'd better say that to your wife, I mean, all that eunuch talk…."

Calling the women by their names, "Yeong-ja," "Chun-ja," as they sat with deliberately wide open eyes, the man with the beret led them outside; the last to leave was the fellow with the rucksack, who turned to him as he was going out.

"Coming up the mountain?"

He did not reply, hesitant, to which the rucksack man pulled down the brim of his hat. "If you take the same road, come up to the White Snow Inn. You can play go-stop with us, or whatever you like...."

Outside, the men could be heard calling a taxi. He put down his spoon and listened. Despite the fact that they had come to sell their bodies, the laughter of the women that mingled with the men's was much livelier than theirs.

"Don't say anything; just come with me." The older man led him to a room beyond the side door. The restaurant seemed originally to have been a kind of lean-to shed projecting forward, and beyond the side door there lay the yard of a small old house with flat eaves. Apparently there was no separate kitchen, for here and there on the back porch and in the yard were strewn shabby bowls and steaming cauldrons. "This is the room..." the older man said, after wrenching the door open. He looked in but then made no sign of further movement, and instead, merely standing in front of the stone wall, turned his head toward the older man.

"Could you escort that gentleman to somewhere near Wolsan?" the older man said. "He said he would pay a hundred thousand won. He's over eighty and he's been like this for the past three days."

"He's really sick!"

He glanced once again into the room, then made a move to turn away, thinking to himself that today was a truly ill-fated day. "Why do you ask me?"

"After waiting three days, I couldn't find anyone fit for the job. I reckon you could do it, couldn't you?"

"There are taxis, why ask me?"

"Cars can't get up to Wolsan. There's no road... no telling which side of the Armistice Line you're on...."

...

"It's a matter of getting somewhere close. You can go as far as Seo-hwa."

The person "fit for the job" the older man referred to should clearly be someone who looked physically strong enough.

In the room, an old man with his head twisted to one side was lying down, his eyes wide open as if in a state of shock, while a woman with an expressionless face, wearing a nurse's uniform, was sitting with her back against the wall, looking at them.

"Surely you could take him?"

"Carrying him on my back?" The older man looked angry. "Didn't I tell you they'll pay a hundred thousand won in addition to the fare?"

"I'm on my way to the mountains. It's not possible."

"You're too uptight and hard to people you've met on the road. How much do you want?"

"What do you mean?"

"Won't you do it?"

"Find someone else."

"Please don't try to force him, mister."

The woman dressed as a nurse spoke in a dull voice from inside the room. Unclear whether it was the sick old man or the nurse who had offered to pay, he turned on his heel and made his way out, feeling uneasy.

Once in front of the restaurant, he looked across the road but the sea, which had been a dark green color, had changed to a thick gray, and there was no sign of the sentry. But surely if he set one foot on the gravel of the beach he would emerge from somewhere with his grating voice.

Having caught a bus heading for the mountains at the road junction, he gazed out at the fields that were already being consumed by the spreading dusk, but found himself unable to shake off that feeling of unease. It might just have been a discomfort emanating from the sick old man, but his feeling seemed rather to have been caused by something about the woman dressed as a nurse. He had been unable to tell at all whether her face was that of a girl barely twenty years old, or whether she was thirty, or nearly forty. In the room, a low sound of *pansori* singing could be heard from a radio cassette, and even under the naked light bulb he had been unable to perceive clearly the outline of her face, but it had awakened in him a strange sense of repulsion. The old man, with his thick overcoat and luxurious fur muffler, looked to be the fastidious patriarch of a wealthy family. His condition seemed to have worsened while he had been convalescing in the hills and they were apparently on their way back. It was clear at first sight that he had suffered a stroke, and if the older man had not mentioned the Armistice Line and if he hadn't seen those wide open eyes of the sick old man, he might perhaps have accepted the proposal.

Getting off at the stop where the inns were he found the White Snow Inn, and the man with the rucksack, who seemed to have been expecting him, beckoned from a second-floor window, his back to the light.

"Come on up, you can't miss it."

As he was going up, the man was standing at the head of the stairs, about to come down. "Don't take a separate room," he said, "we've plenty with four. We only asked for three rooms, but the landlord asked us to take an extra one for gambling... even though this is the place we stay every time we come, damn it... those guys will just sit up all night. I don't enjoy go-stop. Why don't you come along to view the waterfall tomorrow morning? Get some exercise?"

"Didn't you invite me to play go-stop?"

"Just play for a couple of hours, then get some sleep. It's no fun, anyway. When you go somewhere you ought to come back with a clear head; not that, all day, all night...."

He glanced around the room the man with the rucksack showed him into, but without putting down his bag he followed along behind him. The second room seemed to be the man's room, and the gambling was going on in the third room. The girls, one squeezed between each of the men, were laughing, serving drinks and snacks, or helping count the winnings; that seemed to be why they had been summoned. "Hey, you there, school-girl, today you look after this man in place of me... by the way, have you eaten?" Still speaking, the rucksack man caught hold of one of the girls and made her sit beside him. "If you're going to stick to him, stick like a rice cake," another girl said, throwing an odd glance at him.

"Win or lose, make sure you're asleep by midnight; if you get overheated you'll ruin yourself. I'll call you tomorrow morning... I must go and practice yoga in my room."

Having arranged for him to join the party, the man went out.

One member of the group briefly summarized the rules of the go-stop game they were playing using flower cards. He made no comment and pulled out his wallet, realizing that the stakes were quite high. At the slightest mistake, he might lose his fare home.

They say the fun of gambling lies in watching the players reveal their true character. Once the game started, they fell silent as if someone had poured water over them. They seemed to have invented various rules in order to raise the stakes, only the girls kept on chattering or at times burst out laughing, making the players raise their heads. The girl sitting beside him seemed very young but she looked as if she had been hit with a cotton bat. From time to time she would pass him a snack or refill his glass, but she did not say a word. Perhaps the fact that she was surplus to requirements had worn her down; they say a woman who can't attract a loving touch at home will be unwanted even in a bar.

Around nine, one of the girls picked up some of the money that had been collected as a kind of tip at the end of each game, stood up and went out. Then, coming back, standing at the door she said, "Mr. Kim, phone call."

"So early?" The man she had addressed as Mr. Kim frowned with a flushed face and stared at the girl, but the other men urged him on: "Don't keep her waiting, have your fun and come back." The man rose and went out. Some time later, they returned together.

At eleven, another man was called out to the phone, then came back; half an hour later another went out. By that time he had figured out what answering the phone meant, and unconsciously glanced down at the money piled before him. It was when they were losing that they went out, had sex and came back, as a way of exorcising their bad luck. It was past twelve thirty when the girl who had been sitting beside him called him from the door to answer the phone.

He followed along behind her without saying a word; when they reached the room at the end, where the bedding was already spread out, she began to take off her clothes.

"I'm not doing it," he said. "Besides, I wasn't losing, so why did you call me out?"

"You really don't want to?" The girl looked at him, expressionless, her hands on her skirt.

"I can't get it up. I'll give it a pass."

"I'll help you out. Come here."

"Damn it!" he said, "I told you I was giving it a pass."

"Really?" the girl asked. "Hey! Great!"

Still the same, her face showing neither the gladness she had expressed nor anger, the girl came up to him, put her arms around his waist and kissed the back of his head. "Let's wait a bit before we go back in there; then please say that the reason the phone call took so long was because it was an overseas call. Promise?"

A lengthy overseas call… as he sat awkwardly beside the girl, he suddenly felt weariness sweeping over him. He was winning a little, but he reckoned that even if he left after staying just another half hour, the others wouldn't glare at him.

It was exactly two forty-five when he stood up and went to his room, where he passed out for about two hours, then near daybreak awoke to find someone shaking his shoulder. The man with the rucksack was looking down at him, pursing his lips with an odd expression.

"Get up. There's been an accident. Some time after four thirty, one of the girls suddenly began to vomit, then fell back. Lying on her back, she passed away. Looks like a heart attack…." As he listened, he unconsciously thought of the girl who had been sitting beside him and felt anxious.

"The girl called Miss Choi?"

"Did you have some kind of hunch? I suppose you had your phone call with her, but of course I'm not suggesting…."

He tried to say "No," then gave up and stared at the man. "Was that what gave her a shock?"

The man with the rucksack looked at him narrowly, as if at a loss for words, then forced himself to smile.

"You've had a shock, too, old friend. You should go on down first. The police'll be coming, since we've reported it… anyway, we're civil servants. There's no need for you to get involved in any trouble, is there? You'd better get out of here first."

He asked how things would be settled, whether a doctor had come, but the man with the rucksack merely replied that it had almost certainly been a heart attack, then fell into a heavy silence. Feeling uncertain whether he should express thanks or embarrassment, he left the inn. It looked like the other men were sitting together in their room debating what should be done. There was no reason why he should remember the names of each of the men he had been introduced to in such a setting, but on realizing he had not even had a chance to introduce himself to the man with the rucksack, he stopped heading downhill and instead started walking up again. After about a mile, he reached the resort area, where the Swiss-style building of the Park Hotel caught his eye. Children with weird hairstyles on a school outing were peering out from windows here and there or loitering in front of the closed souvenir shop. The low-lying, slate-gray sky was streaked with red in one direction, but with the shadow of the mountains that hemmed in the valley on both sides, and the icy chill in the air, the scenery was still veiled in hazy mist. On the grounds of the hotel, a grotesque statue of E.T. towered over him, crude and obscene, while from the valley rose the sound of nearly frozen water. He regarded the monster, which could have come hundreds of thousands of light years from some distant star, with a sense of horror.

The words "Anyway, we're civil servants" refused to leave his mind. When he said those words, there was no knowing whether the man with the rucksack meant that since they were civil servants they would take full responsibility, or with that status the matter could be easily resolved. If they said that someone who was not part of their group had been involved, surely the matter could become unnecessarily complicated. Such situations are bound to become nasty for people involved in delicate public proce-dures, like it or not. Even if the result of the investigation was clear, the police would keep asking what that person was doing there, why he was there. If by any chance the cause of the girl's death had something to do with the gambling, matters could become even more complex. *You mean you bought women with those coins from the stake money? I am not sure how thick-faced you all might be, but wash your mouth out first before trying to tell that crap to the judge. There's no way anyone would believe you.*

He loitered near the cable car station waiting for the hotel's coffee shop to open, then drank a cup of tea, so that it was nearly eleven before he got back down to the inn. It was completely deserted.

"Those people from the culture department?" The landlord pretended not to know that anything out of the ordinary had happened, then perhaps realized that he had been a guest too, and grew angry. "Those rotten hicks said they were from the culture department; my, what a filthy world… They went down together with the policeman."

"Where to?"

"The police station of course, where else?"

"Did a doctor come?"

"What could he do if he came? I feel sorry for the girl. Why are you asking? Did you do it with her too?"

The landlord kept grumbling about the culture department but he could not gather whether he was talking about a newspaper or a broadcasting station or what. By police station he must have meant the one in Sokcho.

He boarded a local bus heading for Sokcho but then changed his mind and got off at Mulchi; he pushed open the door of the restaurant and went in. It was completely empty. After throwing himself down on a seat carelessly, he waited for the older man to emerge. He guessed that Wolsan must be a remote village somewhere at the far end of Inner Seorak Mountain. Once he had passed close to Inje and he recalled having heard a similar name there, Wolhak or Wolsan, and although it must be near the Armistice Line, he did not know how far the road went before it was blocked, but if he hurried he could take the old man somewhere near there, at least, and perhaps then take the boat across the Soyang River as far as Chuncheon. From Chuncheon he would be able to catch an early morning train to Seoul.

He finally had to shout through the side door before the older man came out, and looked at him blankly, with no sign of recognition.

"Are those folks still here, the sick old man?"

"They've left."

"Did you find someone?"

"No way… They left at daybreak, saying they would just go to Wontong and wait. They took a taxi but it'll be even harder to find anyone up there. What use is money when you can't even get where you want to go? Go and ask up there. Why, did you change your mind?"

"You said it was possible to get in as far as Seohwa? From there, could I get to Chuncheon today? I really have to…."

"It might be difficult. They'll be checking everyone thoroughly."

Even if the road checks were intense, the trip should not take half a day. He looked impatiently at the man and moistened his lips.

"That's no good. I have to work tomorrow."

He was on the verge of saying something like "even if the world ends" or "I'm a civil servant," but restrained himself and ordered something to eat.

It was already two by the time he boarded a bus for Gangneung in front of the restaurant; at Gangneung he changed his mind and took a bus heading for Gyeongpo, just after four. He got off at the lakeside and began to walk absently toward the water.

He had to admit that although he had kept his wife's ashes for a long while, it was not out of a sense of attachment but because he had so far been unable to find the right place to scatter them. He might have done so at the crematorium or somewhere on a hillside, but that day he had come out carrying her ashes and then, because he was feeling weary, had simply

gone home, stuffed her remains among a mass of junk, and had completely forgotten it for some three years.

"I'm not from Wonsan."

Recalling something his wife, confined to her room for five years with
what the doctors called valvular heart disease, had carelessly muttered one
day, he thought of looking for the plastic bag, but he was not completely
sure that his wife's birthplace was anywhere along the East Coast.

He had asked her, "If not Wonsan then where?" But she had been unable to reply. Even though she had been tossed here and there in confusion
soon after her birth, she should have retained some memory of when and
in what village she had been born, but she knew nothing. There were times
when the dialects of the Southeast and Southwest were uttered together,
at other times his wife spoke casually using the accent of the northerly
Pyongan Province, so that perhaps her speech gave support to her tales of
endless bleak wanderings, but he had never been able to *fully* accept his
wife's total ignorance of her roots because when he first came to know her
in a street full of bars in the midst of a market, where she was working as
a peddler, he had been attracted by her intelligence. If she had grown up
in an orphanage, she might have heard something by hearsay or someone
might have given her some information, wrong though it might have been.
If not, surely a couple of place names ought to have been lurking in the
depths of her memory? His wife used to grow flushed as though she had
suddenly developed a stutter and then struggle, muttering nonsense, before
finally shaking her head.

Talking of Wonsan was her improvised response to his saying he was
from Kaesong, she explained. At the time he had only laughed, but the
way that memory had risen so clearly in his mind only now, as he was
about to cast away the last remains of his wife, made him feel strange.

They had come just once to Gyeongpo on their honeymoon some ten
years ago. Then, as now, the off-season holiday resorts were often dreary,
and this place, with the lyrics "The moon rising in your wine glass, blah
blah blah" ringing out, was no exception. The shuttered sashimi restaurants along the deserted seafront looked crushed as they bowed their slate
roofs and endured the wind, while in front of the few that were open a
handful of fish were cowering or floating motionless in cement tanks shel-
tered under the eaves, bathed in fluorescent light even in broad daylight,
reminding him of bleak deserts.

After pointing to one fish that had its snout cut off, he went upstairs to the dining room and ordered a drink. The floor was unexpectedly warm. The woman explained it was a needlefish and that they did that because it kept poking all the other fish with its sharp pointed beak. He opened the window and took out the plastic bag. In the Southern regions, the wind usually reversed direction at nightfall and blew seaward, but when he tilted the bag, the ashes swirled around, rose, then passed over the roof and went blowing off in the other direction, toward the lake. He tossed the empty bag into the wind and sat staring out at the darkening horizon.

It was already dark when he awoke from a drunken doze, sprawled across the table. The thought that he ought to go back kept nagging at him, yet he did not feel inclined to get up. After inquiring whether the restaurant was also an inn, and at what time the first bus for Seoul left in the morning, he washed his feet downstairs then climbed back up to his room. The woman followed him carrying a load of bedding, explaining that they had no registration cards on hand, before she added, "There's a young lady if you want." He shook his head and spread out the blankets.

He thought she had given up but soon after he turned out the light and lay down, the telephone lying abandoned in a corner rang. "Sir, there's a nice young lady."

He hung up abruptly without answering, but when it rang again about ten minutes later he unthinkingly sat up. Eager to put an end to the woman's rambling persuasion, he asked, "How much for a short time?" Then he added: "I need to sleep some more. I dislike whining so send her up later, around ten, after telephoning first."

As his relationship with his wife had been strained for quite some time, he had grown accustomed to relieving his physical tension about twice a month. Since that had also been the time when he was studying on his own to pass the exam for the fifth level of the civil service, it might have been inevitable. Once his day's work was over, he would sit down at his desk, for he had quit drinking, and his eyes would glaze over. He wondered what he was doing, living just like a schoolboy preparing to retake the college entrance exam, and would go out for a breath of fresh air. That led to him giving in to the temptation of buying a woman. By the time he discovered how such temptation actually helped him to concentrate on his study, it was already too late to stop anyway. For something that was really no better than masturbation, he naturally turned to bar girls or women in alleys, and he usually took precautions, but today he felt uneasy since he was not prepared. Awakened at ten by the sound of the phone ringing, for a moment he thought of asking her to bring a condom, but then gave up, feeling too uncomfortable. Perhaps for that reason, once the woman arrived he went rolling downhill and came in a flash. After paying the woman and sending her away, he turned off the light and went back to sleep.

In the grim weather, a portion of the lake was glittering in the morning sunlight, as though it was frozen over. The road curved past it, circular like a playing field, then stretched ahead, while in the middle of the road some ten yards ahead a woman was walking at the same pace as himself, her back and shoulders visible. His consciousness was awake but he could not decide if it was a dream or if he had just awakened from a deep sleep and was on his way to catch a bus downtown. Apart from himself and the woman, there was nobody else out walking; the whole background seemed to have withdrawn into the distance and was covering everything in a kind of misty slow motion. He had the peculiar feeling that all the movements and all the sounds around him were coming to a halt together.

"Why have you come here on such a cold day?"

"Really I'm not sure... but come to think of it today is the anniversary of my wife's death...."

It had been the woman who asked and he had replied, yet clearly the woman walking ahead of him had not turned her head. That was not all. He could also hear the faint sound of *pansori* music like that he had heard from behind the side door at the restaurant in Mulchi. He dismissed it all as irrational and realized that the remarks were from the conversation he and the woman had the previous evening before they embraced. That had been the end of their talking and the woman had lain back with a very strange look on her face. Now it was being replayed as though it had been recorded and stored away. Moreover, seeing how that was overlapping with the sound of a radio from another time and place, it was evidently an auditory hallucination. Ahead of him, his field of vision shrank as if a screen was being spread in front of him, while the air grew thick like a burning sandstorm. With her back still to him, her image came speeding toward him at an alarming rate, as if it was being enlarged, while her pace quickened into a run. She was racing toward a vehicle that was looming larger as it approached. Ignoring this foreboding warning, with all his might he kept himself from turning around and setting off toward the road leading seaward, then, exhausted, collapsed at the foot of a pine tree at the steep roadside. Even without lifting his head, he could picture the scene with people shouting and children noisily heading in that direction. He saw the woman of the previous night falling dead, blood trickling from her nostrils, and the large hands of a policeman covering her with a tarpaulin.

"She ran right into me, deliberately," the driver was gabbling, standing with unfocused eyes before the car she had rammed her head against sideways. Wondering hesitantly if he might check the woman's face once more, after a desperate effort he rose to his feet.

There was nothing in sight. The road beneath his feet went stretching ahead but the woman whose back he had seen and the vehicle that had run her over were nowhere to be seen; nor was there any trace of the people who had gathered out in the distance and caused such a commotion. He shook his head and finally realized that his wife's death a few years ago had suddenly come sweeping over him as a phantasmagoric reality. He fumbled for a cigarette with a sweaty hand.

Once in central Gangneung, having gotten off at the wrong stop, he walked a mile or so to the terminal. There, changing his mind again, he hesitated, wondering whether he should buy a ticket back to Sokcho or whether he should take the route to Inner Seorak, branching off at Yangyang. If Sokcho came back into his thoughts, it could be because he was still troubled about the affair of the man with the rucksack and the bar girl. His intention was to snoop around the police station to see if he could peek inside, before crossing over Jinburyeong Pass and heading for Wontong.

He bought a ticket as far as Yangyang, then with an unpleasant feeling, as if he had failed to brush his teeth, he bought some bread and milk for his breakfast; now he was staring out through the bus window. He realized that the city that had looked so clean during their honeymoon, seen again ten-odd years later, was nothing of the sort. He soon realized that it was not so much the city that had changed, that the difference was mainly in his own heart, yet he was quite unable to understand why, or calculate just when, in what amounted to only a short period of time, the quagmire in which his heart was so deeply mired had begun to form. It might have been pity for his wife, or something triggered by his own feelings toward a world from which his wife had vanished. Despite her physical condition, what might be seen as his wife's vitality, her clinging to life, had been tough and strong as eulalia grass. Despite repeated miscarriages, his wife kept wanting to get pregnant, and up until the very moment when she was finally incapacitated, she held on to her stretcher. Once she was forced to remain bedridden, as the years passed by in that condition, she constantly fretted about everything; perhaps it was another form of that same obsession. *Living like this, I'd rather do away with myself...* When she would roll her eyes and grumble like that, it was not that he wouldn't sometimes rebuke her with "Okay then, go ahead and die." But if he never once made such a remark even to himself, how could she have had the heart to commit such violence against herself?

"The buses have stopped running for today. You can only go as far as the spring village."

Even after hearing the woman behind the ticket counter, which he had headed for after arriving at the Yangyang terminal, he simply stood there blankly, his money held out.

"They can't leave because there's a blizzard warning; how many times do I have to tell you? The snow's about to start. Shall I give you a ticket as far as Osaek Village?"

"Any tickets for Seoul?"

"You'll have to go to Gangneung and take an express bus there. But in the afternoon they'll probably stop running from there too."

If it was going to snow, how much did they expect to fall? If the roads were blocked around here, there'd be no going anywhere. The safest step would be to return quickly to Gangneung and head for Seoul at once. Avoiding a man who was pursuing him, repeatedly urging: "Take my taxi, I'll give you a good price," he asked himself why he still wanted to head for Wontong, when that meant making a mess of everything and being away from work for at least one day, perhaps three or four. If that goddamn old man had not had such wide open eyes, if the luxurious muffler wound around his neck and that overcoat had not aroused his resentment, or if that cheeky nurse with her stuck-up expression had not so shamelessly offered him bait... all those things had stirred up bad feelings, still they did not add up to a good pretext for not going, while an ominous feeling was telling him that he could not simply head for home with this uneasy feeling bothering him....

"Didn't I say I'd take you, even risking that we'll be blocked at Wontong?"

"Is that why the buses aren't going? It seems they're going as far as the spring?"

"Nothing doing there. Do you know how many people will be coming down off the mountain to the spring? You'll have to pay whatever they ask."

"If I get to Inje, will I be able to catch a boat?"

"Would the boats not leave just because of some snow?"

It seemed the taxi driver was merely saying whatever came into his head, but he had made up his mind, so he stopped walking and gave in to the man who was pursuing him.

He knew that it ought to take no more than two hours to reach Wontong. He would have accepted the fare the driver charged if he intended to see the scenery on the way or if he felt he could trust what he had said. Still quibbling over the fare and not really trusting him, when they finally reached the spring at Osaek, people who had come down off the mountain could be seen here and there beyond the car windows.

"Look at them; rushing about like frogs before it rains, aren't they?" The driver stopped the taxi, lowered the window and put out a hand. "It's coming down hard."

He felt that the man was exaggerating to a ridiculous extent, but for some reason he experienced an odd feeling of release at that moment, as if he had finally stepped off a treadmill that he had long been trapped on.

As they crested the Hangyeryeong Pass, snowflakes glistened in a sudden blast of swirling wind. Lowering the window, he took out a cigarette.

In fact, it was not until the taxi had come all the way down as far as Wontong that snow really started to fall in earnest. Together with a blinding wind, it soon grew into a blizzard and within two hours white walls were piled up in all directions, so that he and the village he had reached were completely imprisoned.

Intending to send a wire, he asked where the post office was, but the woman at the restaurant who brought his stew gave no reply, merely looked him up and down, turned on her heel and hurried back inside. Numbskull, looking for a post office in a place like this, her face seemed to express utter amazement, so that he was overcome with embarrassment and fell silent. With the traffic blocked by the snow, he would be absent from work for three days... he felt almost dirty at using such a lame excuse when he was merely one of the lowest-ranking employees; perhaps for just one day, but not for three days, he thought, as he stared blankly at the snow-filled wind as it kept rattling the store window like slaps on the cheek. The three-way junction seemed to form the center of the village and among the houses in sight only three or four at most seemed to offer accommodation, yet he felt awkward at the thought of searching from one house to another. Should he happen to find the old man and the woman, what would he have to say to them?

He dashed into a store he noticed across the road from the restaurant, bought a plastic raincoat for hiking, slipped it on, and when he came out again the wind seemed to have grown slightly less violent; by then it was around three in the afternoon. Despite signs announcing themselves as "inns," the majority were ordinary family homes where, in rooms and yards, snowbound hikers with anxious expressions were chattering loudly or shaking off the snow, while empty rooms loomed as dark as caverns.

In the sixth house, which appeared to be the last, when he looked and inquired there was again no sign of the woman and the old man, but there he encountered two men on the same quest.

"Those people are looking for the same folks," he was told, and on turning around saw through the snow flurries two men perched on the ledge of a wooden porch looking across at him.

"Are you looking for Mrs. Choi?" The slimmer of the two stood up.

…

"Have you asked at all the inns here?"

"They're not here."

He answered vaguely, without thinking, then with a perplexed expression looked at the man as he approached him.

"We've looked for them all the way from Seohwa." The man reached under the projecting eaves and spoke in a sociable tone as he looked up at him, then smacked his lips, "There's no sign of them."

Suspicious questions as to why he was looking for them ought normally to have come from their side in challenging tones, but as they walked together back to the junction and sat down in a coffee shop, nothing was said.

"Seohong, Wolhak Village… we've looked everywhere. You know, the guys have been conducting an extremely thorough search."

By "the guys" he seemed to mean the soldiers performing road checks. The slim man sipped his tea, occasionally stared outside and smacked his lips, while the more heavily built man, apparently the driver, kept his eyes lowered, barely moved and said nothing.

"I happened to see the sick man in Sokcho for a moment and so I've come after him."

As the man chattered away, he sensed the overall situation and when a chance came he felt obliged to tell the whole story from his own perspective in simple terms.

"Well now," the man spoke in an admiring tone. "So that's how it was. It's only human to want to get near your birthplace, isn't it?"

The enthusiastic reply seemed pointless so he just stared at the man. The nurse called Mrs. Choi, who on her own volition had taken a patient away, was trying to escape to somewhere with the moribund old man. So the only solution was to catch her and bring them back... The reply did not fit with what he had been chattering about just before. "This is who I am," the man had said as they sat down, handing him a card on which he was identified as "Executive Director, S Company."

"Was the nurse named Choi in charge of the old man?"

"She was seconded from the company hospital. That girl's impossible... that's why she's acted like this."

"That girl, Mrs. Choi" struck him as a strange mix of labels, but since it was none of his business, he just looked out of the window.

"What shall we do?"

Finally the other man said something.

"What shall we do? We have to get to Inje... They'll be there without a doubt."

"But we looked pretty much everywhere in that direction as we were coming up here, didn't we? Won't they have headed for Baekdamsa Temple?"

They had probably driven up via Hongcheon. Even without unfolding the tourist map bought at the terminal, it was clear that the road up to Baekdamsa Temple via Outer Gapyeong would by now be a hell fierce enough to make even ghosts tremble. Wicked woman... he was pretending to grind his teeth, but the man looked so much like an actor playing the role of a child that he had to keep himself from laughing aloud.

"You can come with us. After all, if you intend to head for Seoul that will save you the fare."

"How, in this snow? I mean, thanks, but...."

"We should be able to get through. We can. If we don't get to Seoul by tomorrow the president will be furious."

He was at a loss how to respond to the man's offer. With things growing increasingly tangled, supposing that they did find the old man, once the nurse started to present her side of the story, he might find himself caught in an even stickier situation. He was only guessing, but he had a clear impression that the men's relationship with the nurse was not the usual employer-employee relationship. Dimly sensing a serious conflict between the old man and his son, he followed the two men, hoping they would be similarly unable to find the missing pair at Inje.

The Mercedes they had come in managed to force its way through on what had looked to be a hopeless journey. Though the wind blew fiercely and the snow continued to fall in white sheets, the car ploughed its way forward without any particular trouble, but that very certainty only plunged him into deeper gloom. Neither driver nor companion said anything further. Outside it was already growing dark but he felt increasingly convinced that he should not ride with them all the way to Seoul, even if they came up empty at Inje. If the snow slackened off during the night, the boats would be running the next day.

"Wait here. I'll just take a look…."

Stopping the car at the first inn as they entered Inje, the man went inside, then emerged and beckoned to them, standing with his back against a street lamp. "I've found them. They're here. Come on…."

Then something unexpected happened. The driver lowered the window but made no attempt to do as the man said.

"Why aren't you getting out?"

As the man drew nearer with an agitated expression, the driver said, "Let's just drive on."

"What are you talking about, you filth?" The man slapped the driver's cheek through the open window. Holding a palm to his slapped cheek, the driver bowed his head for a while then meekly got out. As he watched the two walking together, he hesitated for a time, completely at a loss.

Up until now, he had been nothing but a total outsider, but now, feeling that if a fight were to break out he should try to stop it, he too got out and hesitantly walked toward the inn. He paused in front of the room indicated by the shoes left on the step outside, then feeling embarrassed he went and loitered on the nearby wooden porch.

"Take this and give me the contract." He could hear what the man said but, unexpectedly, he spoke in a low voice. "Does that mean that everything is settled?" The woman's voice too was quiet. He heard the man say, "The president admires Mrs. Choi," then the woman replied, "It can't be helped; please thank him." He moved to one side as the door of the room opened and the driver emerged carrying the old man on his back, together with the other man, while the woman stood just inside the door as if seeing them off.

"Ah, you again!" the nurse spoke in that same voice devoid of any hint of emotion. "What are you doing here?"

The driver with the old man on his back looked unsteady, so he was obliged to follow them under the pretense of providing support; the old man with his eyes still wide open made his heart thump again. It looked as though his lower body was completely paralyzed, matching his eyes.

"Aren't you getting in?"

As he was getting into the car, the man turned and noticed that he was standing some distance away. He nodded to indicate that he wasn't. The car advanced some ten yards then stopped and the man again put his head out.

From the man's lips came curses flying in a kind of roar. He unconsciously started to move toward him, upon which the man's head vanished and the car drove off.

The woman, who had come out of the inn, approached. He was looking at her, perplexed. He simply could not understand why the man had suddenly acted that way.

"You didn't leave, I see," the woman said. "Why have you come here?"

Embarrassed, he mumbled like an outcast child. It was the second time he was asked this question. He could have replied that he had followed them because he had felt uneasy about the way he had neglected the sick old man. But the old man was no longer there, after all. The woman seemed to have paid for the room and was now standing there with her suitcase in her hand. She still had her white cap perched on the back of her head and a black coat draped neatly over her uniform, but despite the growing darkness she showed obvious signs of weariness, almost as if she had been beaten.

"Didn't you ask me to take him to somewhere close to the Armistice Line?"

She laughed weakly. "You are a step too late. If you had come yesterday, things would have turned out differently…."

"Didn't you say you would be at Wontong? That old fellow at the restaurant in Mulchi…. "

"We were in Wontong," the woman replied.

He looked at her oddly, wondering if she was lying. "You didn't take a room anywhere?"

"I found a room but not in an inn. I didn't like having people coming and going, all staring. Then I gave up and brought him down here. If you had arrived yesterday we would not have been able to meet. You would never have thought of asking at ordinary houses, would you?"

Sensing a hint of mockery in her voice, he said nothing.

"Still you meet those you are destined to meet," she observed, and sensing his sullenness laughed again. "Let's go somewhere else. I'll buy you supper. You'll be leaving for Seoul tomorrow?"

"Maybe, it depends if the boats are running."

"I have to go to Gangneung then head for Jeongseon. I need to see my father first."

"Is that your home? Everyone's from Gangwon Province, it seems…."

"Are you from Gangwon too? I'm from Yeoryang, not Jeongseon… Have you ever heard of Auraji River?"

He was on the point of saying: "I'm not from here, but my dead wife was," before giving up. "Auraji River?"

The woman, who was by now covered in snow, led the way, not to a restaurant but into another inn. Uncertain, he paused but the woman, looking back, urged him on. "There's no proper restaurant here. Why don't you have supper here, then you can go and sleep in another inn?"

The woman went out to shake the snow from her coat and order food, and in the meantime he spread his hands on the heated floor where two cushions were laid. Perhaps due to the pointless fatigue he had endured for the last two days, his eyes closed. What excuse was he going to offer once back at work…?

"What did that guy say when he swore at you before running off?" The woman seemed to have washed up, she looked fresher when she came in, then sat leaning against the wall looking at him.

"Didn't you hear?"

"I heard something, but it wasn't clear. What did he say?"

Wondering why she was so interested in the curses, he merely stared into her face.

"'I knew it. You bastard...' or something like that, perhaps? 'I knew it. Enjoy yourself with that whore...' right?" She repeated the words clearly.

He looked hard at the woman before turning his face away, as if he saw something he was not supposed to see.

"If you heard that kind of language, I deserve it. That's what I did, even preparing the documents...."

"Was it the contract the guy talked about?"

"Yes," the woman lowered her eyes. "I was charged with caring for that old man for two years. They made a request at the hospital I worked for. I had no choice, it being the firm's hospital. They asked if I could undertake a special job, not a matter of washing him or taking care of his bodily functions. The moment I heard what was involved I thought I should have a contract. It doesn't exactly specify the dirty things I had to do."

"Would an eighty-year-old have the strength for anything of that kind?" he asked, suddenly feeling angry or at least bad-tempered. "Hadn't he had a stroke?"

"Have you ever heard of what they call a hot pack? A water pouch applied as a poultice... a kind of hot-water bottle. What the Japanese call *yudanpo* is a bit different but... I spent two years acting as a hot-water bottle. The contract called it 'special nursing.' I absolutely insisted on inserting that term... Recently they began to feel uneasy about the contract. I had forgotten all about it, but the boss, being such an asshole...."

"So you ran away?"

She nodded and returned his gaze with an odd expression. "They all knew we were coming here. Where else would he go, if not here? Even before he fell ill he had been saying all the time that he wanted to go to Wolsan Village. That was why he kept fighting with the boss... Since you made your fortune here in Seoul, you should think of Seoul as your hometown; the boss used to bully him and the old man only grew more stubborn... it was just an excuse. It was merely his way of getting back at his father for everything he had against him. Do you know what the old man's nickname was in the old days? 'The Jindo Bulldog,' a combination of a Jindo dog with a bulldog, you understand? Then this winter he collapsed. Feeling sure he wouldn't last till the end of the year, I took him away. Even if he can't speak, once he starts to pester...."

"With all those worries, you still brought along the contract?"

She laughed sadly. "Who knows what may happen? I've had enough hard times in the hospital from people who make trouble because of greed, even when they can't walk or move. And the boss was looking for an excuse to sack me, too... The boss means to stand for the National Assembly next year. Every topic of gossip has to vanish...."

Supper was brought in on a table. The woman poured out beer but he did not feel like drinking so he put the glass aside and picked up the chopsticks.

"And I came following after, without having any idea...."

"I knew you would come here, didn't I?" The woman, who had been eating busily, lifted her head with an undefinable expression. "I had thought of going to Seorak Mountain for a few days of rest, but it was no good, it was beyond my strength. I was waiting there because I remembered something I heard once from a fortune-teller in Myeonmok-dong. Why Mulchi? At thirty I would meet someone bearing three coffins beside water... that person was my husband in a previous life...."

"Do even nurses say things like that?"

Her expression turned playful.

"Look at this." She laid her chopsticks aside and held out her palm. "Have you ever seen palm lines like this?"

He looked casually at the jumbled lines that seemed to have been cut with a sashimi knife, then asked mischievously:

"You mean that before and after I dropped by there, nobody appeared to take your hundred thousand won? Still it's not me, surely, and what's that about someone bearing three coffins or something?"

"Who said it was you? Don't count your chickens too soon... I just knew you would come... Show me your palm; you never know...."

She stretched out her hands as though dealing with a patient. As she began to behave like a child, obviously with her guard down, he gazed at her.

Pulling his arms back, he casually asked, "So, are you still a virgin?" before immediately regretting it.

"Does a virgin think nothing of talking like this? When I first arrived in Seoul I didn't even know how to eat *bibimbap*. I thought the vegetables and the rice were supposed to be eaten separately... In those days I was a virgin." Her tone suddenly became dejected. "I am no virgin."

Seized with an awkward feeling, he looked down and began to force food into his mouth. She too kept silent. After she had carried the meal table out and come back, she took a piece of paper from her pocket.

"They gave me my severance pay just now. What should I do with this check?"

Not understanding her reasoning, he looked up, at which point she went on, still standing, "Shall I tear it up?"

"Are you out of your mind?"

"Tearing up the money I've earned doing that, is that something that makes me a mad woman? It's three million won... I could rent a room for Father with that, but...."

"Don't be silly," he said. "What do you solve by destroying it? You would only be making a fool of yourself. How old are you for goodness' sake?"

"Then I'll tear it up. Far better to be a fool."

The woman's hand that held the check began to tremble. She was weeping as she said, "I can't do it...."

Her body came crashing down. At a loss what to do, he embraced her in his arms but sensing the deep groan that was sinking down into his bowels, he had to keep his eyes wide open. If they had been on the road, she might have died too.

He did not know how he escaped from the room. As soon as he started to rub her back, the woman stopped crying, and he vaguely recalled how, between sobs, she had repeated: "I can't endure being alone any more...." It was certain that he had repeatedly rubbed his cheek against hers, but he could not be sure if he had said he would come to fetch her the next morning, nor if he had asked her whether she would go up to Seoul with him.

Once outside in the alley, he found he was carrying a bottle of beer; he must have brought it with him from the room.

He went into the first inn that caught his eye, took a room, and once the bedding was spread on the warm floor, he undressed and sat down on it, leaving the door that looked onto the yard slightly ajar, and began to drink from the bottle as he watched the snow falling outside.

The woman who brought in the table with breakfast, which he had not ordered, informed him that a boat would be leaving at ten thirty. He heard the faint sound of a drum being beaten which seemed to have awakened him.

"It's a ceremony for the dead," the woman told him. "Last year a kid slipped on the icy road and fell into the lake. The child was from the scholar's family, just over the hill...."

Shaking off the woman, who was offering to carry his bag, he went across to the other inn, where the nurse was apparently waiting, for she immediately opened the door and emerged as he arrived. Avoiding each other's gaze in embarrassment, they walked down the alley and he set off quickly for the pier. During the five or so minutes it took to reach the landing along the path they did not speak a single word.

While they watched the boat with the shaman slowly coming toward them from over the horizon, he handed a note with his address and office phone number on it to the woman.

"Will you come up straight away, once you've visited Yeoryang?"

"Yes."

"We have to be prepared to earn two incomes for a while, I guess. If we're going to set up house...."

"Are you talking about that already?"

"I have to catch this boat. Can you find a bus?"

"They should be running. They're already clearing the snow, it seems."

Even though only one boat had been canceled the previous afternoon, the railing of the ship was already crowded with hikers and other passengers who were chattering with anxious faces as they shifted their weight from one foot to the other. The ceremony seemed to be over but as the boat used for the ritual drew in, the shaman stepped ashore and began to sprinkle water around from a gourd. Then she threw aside the gourd and snatched a fan and a bell from her assistants, who were carrying an hourglass drum and a barrel drum. She began to ring the bell and the drummers began to beat the drums once again.

"Be careful," the woman said. Unable to tear her eyes from him as he crossed toward the boat, the woman suddenly began to smile as she stood on the jetty, so he turned his eyes away as if dazzled and lit a cigarette.

Dragon King, god of the East Sea, the East,
Ksitigarbha, god of the West Sea, the West,
Naraka Hell, the world of woe and tumult,
Behold and see, behold and watch over us!
Smoothly come down please, smoothly....

A fire was lit near the shaman; people who had come to see others off and some local children gathered around it.

By the time he realized what was happening, the shaman who had approached the woman, dancing all the way, was holding out her fan.

"Take this!" the shaman screamed.

Boundless expanse of blue water,
Sacred tree, souls of the wretchedly dead,
I never expected to see you again.
Oh, my daughter, my pitiful daughter,
To the netherworld ninety thousand leagues away,
You left and now have come back....

After reciting her lament, the shaman once again screamed with glistening eyes. The nurse's face was flushed crimson. The shaman kept holding out her fan as if she were pushing it toward the nurse, whose body staggered backward, floundering. The nurse then dropped her suitcase and seized the fan with both hands; she seemed to be shuddering violently. The cap fell from the back of her head.

"Hey, what's going on there? Isn't that a spirit coming down into her?"

"Why, that's a nurse...."

From among the onlookers along the railing of the passenger ship could be heard sympathetic voices as well as clacking tongues. Cries of "Darling!" rang out, either from his dead wife or from the nurse.

Just as he took one step forward, about to leap from the ship, the woman's gaze changed. Tearing at her clothes with one hand, waving the fan with the other, she set about dancing.

The ship listed as it floated on the water. A sound of water ebbing from beneath the keel rose up, while above the snow-covered peak across the water a giant palm was suspended.

Unable to tell whether it was a dream or an illusion, he stared with wide open eyes at the lines on his hand, which he had hitherto taken no notice of; they were running confusedly, crisscrossing his palm, forming three squares.

WORDS OF FAREWELL

Oh Junghee

Translated by **Bruce and Ju-Chan Fulton**

별사
오정희

A critique of this short story was published in the Koreana magazine in Fall 1994
(Vol. 8 No. 3, pp. 62-64).

© Kim Si-hoon

J eong-ok closed her eyes and leaned against the sliding glass door to the veranda. She had transferred the hard-boiled eggs from the cold water to the mesh bag along with a few *chamoe* melons from the refrigerator, and was about to step down to the yard. But the very moment she noticed her father, his hair closely cropped, squatting on the lawn—was he pulling clover and weeds from the tufts of overgrown grass?—she thought she saw the fence around the yard receding and a transparent form moving in front of it.

When she opened her eyes the sensation was gone, like a momentary dizzy spell. In the dense, voluminous stillness she noticed only her father's outline, distinct against the fence, whose white paint had long since flaked off, leaving the bare boards damp and rotting from the persistent rain.

What had pierced her vision and disappeared like a fleeting sliver of sunlight was nothing more than a sensation of movement, without apparent shape or texture, but it made her feel she had viewed the essence of the sudden impulse that had brought her here to her parents' home.

What could I have seen? she wondered. Was it simply an illusion, water vapor shimmering in the sun? Or could it have been the unseen hand—the unseen power—controlling the unfamiliar figure of her father and his desultory weeding?

She peered toward the yard looking for even the slightest movement that might have caused the illusion. But her attentive stare caught not a breath of wind brushing the tips of the leaves; there were only the sluggish, automatic movements of her father's elbows. The old man's thin shoulder blades were wraith-like, his sleeveless ramie shirt sweaty, and she wondered if this simple task was too much for him.

What precisely was this sensation that visited her at unexpected moments, a sensation she felt intimately acquainted with?

It had happened the previous evening too. When she entered the front gate, her boy sound asleep on her back since the bus stop, her mother, who had been watching television on the veranda, rushed out and took the boy in her arms. At that moment the familiar but unanticipated sensation raked her skin, leaving her with goosebumps, though she realized it was only her father she saw, curled up in his armchair at the front of the veranda. The sun had set some time before, but there he was in his dark glasses, leaning slightly forward and staring off into a corner of the yard, which seemed darker for all the fragrant roses in full bloom.

"Why haven't you turned on the light?" she had asked, touching the back of the armchair. "You're getting bitten by mosquitoes. Won't you go inside?"

"You're right—they're eating me alive," her mother had complained as she slapped her bare calves and forearms over and over.

The humid night air, thick and sweet as if with pollen, had stifled Jeong-ok.

"Is he sleeping?" Her voice was louder as she struggled to shake off the darkness, viscous and heavy with the fragrance of the roses that ceaselessly bloomed and withered on their viny bushes from spring to autumn. Her mother had shaken her head, eyes fixed on the television screen.

Her father had been off in his own world, drawing random figures with his finger on his knee—first a circle, then a square within it, and confined inside that a triangle. You might have thought he was sending signals to an unseen place beyond the dark. Like calm water at dusk, he had seemed to blend with the ever-thickening darkness.

Now the boy was trying to shake loose the date tree's half-ripened fruit. His upturned face looked like a kite floating in the air.

The ring of the doorbell pierced the air. Though a visitor could have seen through the gaps between the fence boards whether anyone was home, the ringing continued, persistent. Jeong-ok donned sandals and ran to the gate.

As soon as she released the bolt, the gate was pushed open and two dark red faces pressed close to her. Propping themselves against the gatepost and blocking the entrance, the visitors stuck out shriveled hands.

Jeong-ok briefly scrutinized them. Silently they extended clawlike hands toward her eyes.

"Don't come inside. Stay there," Jeong-ok said in a choking tone that sounded like someone else's voice. She took a hundred-won coin from her pocket and dropped it into one of the palms. The recipient looked hard at her and grinned. The sunlight glinted on his hairless eyebrows.

"Who is it?" came her mother's voice from inside.

"Lepers."

"When they're gone, pour water on the gate and then sprinkle it with salt."

Jeong-ok washed down the gatepost with a basin of water and scattered a handful of coarse salt about it.

The boy wrapped his arms around the date tree, shook it again, retreated a few steps, and located the fallen fruit among the tufts of grass and pocketed it.

The hand of a passerby shot up above the rose bushes that trailed along the fence and plucked one of the straggling sprays.

"Are you ready?" asked Jeong-ok's mother. She stepped down to the yard.

Jeong-ok glanced at her and turned away with a wistful smile. Her mother was quite the stylish woman with her pink dress in a cloud pattern and her loosely knit summer bag. Her makeup was sumptuous.

"You'll have to take the Kanghwa bus past Ojong-ni," Jeong-ok's father faltered, not looking up from his mechanical weeding as they prepared to depart.

"Don't you want to go inside? It's getting hotter by the minute," Jeong-ok said, reaching toward him. But with a wave of his hand he dismissed the gesture.

"Lunch is on the table. Help yourself, and don't go skipping it." Her mother's hint at the length of their outing was waved off as well.

Her mother opened her parasol, squinting to place the sun. Her dyed hair, a brilliant steel blue in the sunlight, rested firmly on her head like a wig, not a strand out of place, not a telltale gray hair to be seen.

"Are they beggars?" the boy asked. Gently holding the hem of his mother's skirt, he watched as the lepers pressed other doorbells in his grandparents' alley. Jeong-ok placed her hand on his head, not really knowing why she did so. Whether the boy took her gesture to mean "Yes" or to mean "Don't be scared" he questioned her no further and scampered off ahead of them.

Their bus was packed. Yes, it was the weekend, Jeong-ok told herself, but most of the passengers appeared to be fishmonger women rather than tourists. The empty plastic basins stacked on the floor of the bus reeked of fish and left little room to stand. The strong smell of tidewater permeated the women's clothing and hair. Remembering the name of the port where the bus route started, Jeong-ok guessed the women were on their way home from an early round of peddling. The boats at that port, bearing romantic names such as *Sea Gull*, *Billow*, and *Golden Wave*, would be lying at anchor, smelling of engine oil; from there they would leave for the small islands of the West Sea. The women's unseemly chattering would take some getting used to.

Jeong-ok stood clutching the back of a seat near the door, straining to keep from being knocked off balance. Her son, head and all, was out of sight among the other passengers. There was only his desperate grip on her skirt to assure her of his presence. *You don't have to hold on so tight,* she wanted to tell him. *Mom won't ever lose you.*

Now and then she twisted around so she could spot her mother, buried deep within the overcrowded bus. She could still see the back of her mother's hand, its tendons swollen, gripping a handrail. And she could see her nephrite jade ring. The stone was too big to be genuine, its shade of green too deep and undistinguished.

"Is this your skirt, Mom? Is it you, Mom?"

The boy's small face, more troubled than she would have thought, surfaced among the throng. Might the skirt be someone else's? He forced his head back and looked up. His forehead was creased with a few thin wrinkles that made him seem wise beyond his years.

A man sitting in front of Jeong-ok read her face at a glance and lifted the boy toward his lap but then released him, for the boy had looked at him warily and begun shaking his head obstinately, tightening his grasp on his mother's hand. An awkward moment of tension rose from the boy's instinctive wariness and the uncalculating thoughtfulness of the man, who appeared surprised and embarrassed at the little one's stubborn and seemingly hostile rejection. Jeong-ok dispassionately observed the man's outstretched hands hesitate, harden, and come to rest on his knees.

Her arm clutching the seatback drooped from the weight of the bag with its eggs, melons, bottles of soft drinks, and other refreshments. "Let us off at the checkpoint," Jeong-ok said, craning her neck toward the bus girl. She had already made several such requests.

"Still a ways to go," the young woman replied without lifting her head. Amid the crush she was somehow able to keep her nose stuck in a magazine.

The bus was passing the Kimp'o rice fields. The rice plants formed a dappled green background beyond the heads of the passengers. The fresh color caught Jeong-ok's eye. It looked like they had been washed clean by the previous day's rain. While this vast green, gently swaying velvet apron sped through her field of vision, a hot, sticky breeze blew up through the windows from the blacktop tar.

When the bus stopped and three young people dressed for a hike boarded, blocking her way to the front, she felt uneasy again. "Are we getting near the checkpoint?" she called out, impulsively pushing one of them in the back as if she were about to get off.

Only then did the bus girl turn up her small eyes at her. "I know when to let you off. You don't have to keep asking. I'm not deaf, you know. Really! It's the next stop," she snapped irritably.

Why do people have to act like that? she feebly lamented. She felt her face burning. If only she could liberate herself from her feelings, so easily hurt. She was well aware that her indignation at the bus girl's insolence was accompanied by rage toward herself for lacking the courage to express that indignation, a rage that seethed deep in her heart, covered up and festering.

"Mother, come up front," she called, pushing the strap of her bag higher on her shoulder and seeking the boy's hand. How extraordinarily clear her voice sounded to her.

She straightened the boy's clothing by pulling down his shirt, which had crept up under his suspenders. The laces of his sneakers had come undone and his fresh white cotton socks were smudged all over.

"That way, maybe?" said her mother when they got off the bus, indicating an unpaved road to the left that skirted the checkpoint. Dust-covered *chamoe* melons and tomatoes languished on a low platform in front of a small franchise shop at the intersection.

Jeong-ok nodded, though she had never been here before and knew little about the area. She covered her mouth because of the dust, which obscured her vision like the misty spray from an atomizer.

Dust, there was only dust. The roofs of tiny shops and the vegetable fields beside the road lay tranquil under their coating of the mist-like stuff. How odd: was that what radioactive fallout looked like? It was chalky and ash-like, ghostly and dreary-looking, as if stilled by the relentless sunlight. She wondered if this fantasy was a reaction to the muggy fish smell of the bus, which still pervaded her, or perhaps to the green rice plants swaying vividly beyond the sticky black asphalt.

But this image of barren desolation disappeared as soon as she turned down the dusty road and saw a bulldozer coated with ocher-colored soil come to a stop on the shoulder. Sparks flying from their pickaxes, men were digging up rocks embedded in the road. Women carried large sacks of gravel on their heads. The roadway was being scoured in preparation for a coat of asphalt, and only enough space was left for a single row of vehicles to slip through.

Jeong-ok, her mother, and the boy cut across one of the bordering fields to a rough path of gravel culled from the road. The jagged bits of rock pricked Jeong-ok's soles.

An endless line of honking cars passed by on what was left of the road, leaving no time for the dust to settle. Coolers and reed mats could be spotted beneath flapping trunk lids. *That's right, it's the weekend!* Jeong-ok exclaimed to herself. This realization cut to her heart, for reasons she did not clearly understand.

In one of the cars a girl in a sun hat was resting her chin on top of the back seat, which was covered with embroidered hemp. Her gay smile slowly disappeared in the dust. "It's the weekend." This time Jeong-ok mumbled it, enjoying the wistfulness of the phrase.

The boy had walked but a short way when he started dragging his feet and whining. Jeong-ok smiled to herself. She had pretended not to notice his longing glances at the ice cream back at the shop, and this must have disappointed him.

Stopping to reason with the peevish boy, she kept falling behind her mother. The older woman, clopping along a few steps ahead, kept unstrapping her sandals and shaking the soil from them. She seemed oblivious to the drone of the bulldozer and the gravel being poured on the road. The white parasol held obliquely over her head looked unmoored, like a stray balloon at an amusement park.

The boy looked back and froze. A military convoy had appeared, one troop truck after another. Jeong-ok gripped his hand more tightly and hastily dropped down to a path that ran through the field, away from the road. She couldn't keep her heart from pounding the moment she saw the procession of onrushing vehicles. Was it the incongruity and coldness of those bright headlights in the midday sun?

The soldiers in the trucks looked down with stony expressions. The tractors and automobiles silenced their horns and moved aside in a jumble, clearing the way for the convoy.

The trucks rolled past with an earthshaking rumble, their massive wheels coated with the same ocher soil as the bulldozer. Again the boy stood stock-still, gaping at the gigantic procession. Dust-streaked hair falling across his eyebrows, the boy's sweaty, grimy face looked pathetic and wretched.

Jeong-ok turned and lifted the boy onto her back.

Her mother had stopped and was looking at them. "Why don't you let him walk instead of doing whatever he asks," she said with a frown.

"Still far to go?" Jeong-ok asked, shifting the boy so he sat straight.

Her mother looked around uncertainly, though she had been here once before. She took the bag from Jeong-ok, whose hands were clasped beneath the boy's bottom. "There's a road heading uphill somewhere around here," she murmured. Then she went into a small wayside shop.

The shopkeeper pointed to the dirt road, which stretched straight ahead. "Go another hundred yards or so and take the side road on the left."

Jeong-ok bought an ice-cream cone and secured it in the boy's hand.

"We'll have to walk a good hour or more," her mother groused. "And look at the condition of the road." So saying, she took the lead and set out briskly.

It was hot. Jeong-ok's arms kept sagging under the weight of the boy, who reacted by pulling on her neck with his sticky hands. Her hair was sweaty and tangled, falling into her eyes and blocking her vision. More than once she stumbled and nearly fell. The unbroken procession of trucks continued.

A girl toting a baby on her back stood in a furrow in the field, waving at the convoy. One of the women who had been carrying gravel squeezed between two trucks, crossed the road, and stepped down to the field. She removed the towel wrapped around her head and dusted off her clothes with it. Then she took the baby from the girl, unbuttoned her blouse, and gave the baby her breast. The girl picked some blades of grass and waved them in front of the suckling baby, laughing brightly. Turning its head to and fro in pursuit of the grass, the child released the nipple and wriggled its arms and legs, trying to grab the flickering blades. This brought another burst of shrill laughter from the girl.

Jeong-ok's mother covered her nose and mouth with her handkerchief and walked on, then turned and spat heavily.

A column of soldiers appeared behind the procession of trucks as it snaked around a seemingly endless bend in the road. Helmets squeezed flushed faces, and the green uniforms were darkened with perspiration, the insignias, perhaps polished to a luster before the march, barely visible beneath their coating of dust.

Watching the dull green column of soldiers marching by in silent rhythm, Jeong-ok felt the nebulous shroud of anxiety in her chest hang heavier. To ease the oppressiveness she approached her mother and whispered, "It's a military unit on the move, isn't it?" Not waiting for a response she asked another question, realizing as she did so that her mother wouldn't know the answer. "Where do you suppose they came from? They probably left at dawn."

A bird with enormous wings draped with steel netting, flying through the night in pursuit of the sun and stealing into the gray of early morning. Footsteps treading heavily across her chest every dawn before she woke up.

A black cloud scudded across the sky, veiling the sun and casting shade across the scattered clumps of reddish brown soil, the green column of soldiers, the vales among the hills, and the thickets of tangled brush before drifting away.

Jeong-ok's back was sticky with sweat where the boy clung to her.

"Wouldn't you like to walk awhile? That's a good boy."

So amazed and curious was the boy at the sight of the column, so different from the pictures he had seen of children playing soldier, that he came down without a fuss. The ice cream, melting as soon as it left the freezer at the shop, streamed from the cone, leaving the boy's fingers and mouth soiled and sticky. Jeong-ok wiped him vigorously with her handkerchief until the area around his mouth was scarlet like new skin. The boy scowled and shook his head furiously.

Jeong-ok's mother looked back and urged them on: "If you keep poking along like that it'll be sundown before we get there." What was left of her thick face powder, eroded by sweat, had been darkened by the dust. "The man at the store said it was the first side road..." She seemed flustered that her memory was so hazy. Time had clouded her eyes and she must have been wondering if she would spot the fork in the road that was somewhere to the left. But her worries were short-lived. Across the road, in front of a franchise shop at the corner of a side road between vegetable fields, stood a crude signpost, "Entrance to Memorial Park."

Jeong-ok stood the boy before the pump in front of the shop and drew water. She threw the boy's ice-cream cone in a trash can and washed his dusty face and feet.

The march of the soldiers continued. Perhaps they would see the end of the column when they came down the hill from the cemetery. She wondered if the tedious march would ever end.

Her mother soaked her handkerchief in cold water, carefully wiped the nape of her neck, then slipped the handkerchief inside her dress and mopped the sweat from her chest. Jeong-ok poured water over her own feet without removing her sneakers. She was about to tell her mother, *If you wash your face, you'll feel much fresher; the water's nice and cool*— but thought better of it. With her face powdered thick and pale, her hair black like a crow's feathers, and the line of her mouth vividly accented by her gaudy lipstick, her mother looked ready for burial. Maybe she would stay mummified when she died. Jeong-ok smirked at this sudden impertinent thought.

A small group of young people in bright windbreakers and tight jeans passed by carrying guitars. The sunlight resting on the rifles atop the soldiers' packs gave Jeong-ok a chill. "More people die from futility than fear"—he had said this once, as if he were a terrorist.

The boy moved behind Jeong-ok and began whining again. It was impossible for him to know the purpose of the tedious military march on this hot day, or the reason his little legs, having stumbling over jagged stones, now had to tramp incessantly along this parched, hilly road that bore only weeds and dust.

"Let Grammy give you a piggyback ride," said Jeong-ok's mother. But the boy, now on his mother's back, refused to budge. Instead he stared at his grandmother as if he had never seen her before, then looked away.

"What a silly brat! You think Grammy has thorns on her back?" She tsk-tsked.

Jeong-ok couldn't blame the boy, for he had yet to become familiar with his grandmother, whom he saw a few times a year at best.

She looked at her watch. Two hours since they'd left. Without realizing it they had already walked an hour or so.

She kept thinking they would see the cemetery around the next bend in the hillside road.

"Let's have a short rest," said her mother. Sitting down under a tree next to the road, the older woman shook sand from her sandals and dabbed at her sweaty face with her handkerchief. Despite the parasol, her face was turning ripe red in the fierce sun. Jeong-ok swept her palms across her own puffy, burning face, wondering if the swelling would ever go down.

The tree had a burly base and offered thick shade. The procession of soldiers still commanded Jeong-ok's attention. By now they were faint specks in the distance, but she felt if she looked carefully she could make out their backpacks, filled with emergency rations, bedding, and weapons.

He had left as if it were wartime.

"Where are you going?" Jeong-ok had asked with parched lips. It was first light, and he was about to leave, shouldering his tackle bag and carrying a fish net and creel.

"Well, it'll have to be someplace with a lot of fish."

"The keys will be here." Jeong-ok made sure he watched as the keys to the front gate and the door dropped with a clink into the mailbox mounted on the gate. If he stuck his hand through the slot, he could retrieve them without difficulty.

"If someone comes looking for you," she asked after a pause, "where should I tell him you went?"

"To Heaven's Pass and the Stream of the Gods," he shot back. It sounded like a password. The next moment he'd produced a vague smile, as if trying to soften his curt response.

"Don't sleep out in the open if you can help it. It's bad for you."

Bad for you! Jeong-ok forced a smile as she ruminated on these words. *Tobacco is bad for your health, so if you're going to smoke, do it in moderation. Sweets are bad for your teeth. The nighttime dew isn't good for you.* She realized that these common reminders, which gave her a sense of routine and comfort, were absurd and laughable.

The entrance appeared: "Anshik Memorial Park." It seemed so sudden, after all their waiting. The realization that this was their destination took a moment to sink in.

"Here we are."

But for her mother's words Jeong-ok could have bypassed the place and walked on forever.

A wide path cut through a grove of acacias. There was no sign of the cemetery. Jeong-ok was briefly disconcerted, having imagined a visible demarcation between the cemetery and the mundane life they saw around them. But the path was merely a connection with the road, merely a part of the hill, lying long and slender like a backbone. She wondered if she really wanted to see the realm of the departed—the wandering souls—or if she only wanted to sense colors, smells, the stillness of forms she had never experienced before.

The path went gradually uphill through the acacias and finally came out at a small wooden building with a sign hanging lengthwise from it that announced, "Memorial Park Office." One end of the shabby structure contained the office, the other a small shop that sold incense, candles, liquor, and such. The office looked something like a real estate agency. From outside she could see a telephone on a metal desk and a map of the cemetery on the wall that at first glance resembled a detailed map of the capital or one of its districts. Two men were playing chess, one wearing a sleeveless undershirt and the other a reservist's camouflage shirt unbuttoned from the neck to the waist, exposing his chest.

"Excuse me," said her mother. As the older woman poked her head inside the office, the two men simultaneously looked toward the door.

Jeong-ok's waterlogged sneakers had dried out but her swollen feet felt squishy and uncomfortable inside them. She stopped at the pump in front of the shop and splashed more water on them before following her mother into the office.

"The sale ended a long time ago." The men returned to their chessboard.

Jeong-ok's mother took from her bag a thin, light brown envelope containing a contract for a lot. "I know—I bought one of the lots."

The man in the undershirt sluggishly turned back to them.

"I was here once before, but I don't think I can find the lot this time." Jeong-ok's mother glanced at her daughter, then approached the man and gave him an affectedly sweet smile while unfolding the contract.

"Block D, 9-3. It's up on top. Follow the path and take your third right. Then you'll find some steps," said the younger-looking man in the reservist's shirt. His unnaturally dark and thick eyebrows twitched at every syllable he ejected.

"It's a special lot, forty-eight square feet. For my husband and me," Jeong-ok's mother added impatiently.

"Did your beloved…?" the man in the undershirt asked, suddenly courteous, trying to identify the two women.

"No. My daughter happened to be visiting, so I thought I'd show her the lot. We hardly see her because she lives in the countryside."

She glanced at Jeong-ok, then produced a shy smile for the man.

Jeong-ok looked outside at the boy, who was dangling playfully from the pump.

"If the family is bereaved, let us know immediately so we can have the burial mound prepared. Rounding up the gravedigger takes time. But that's what we're here for. We handle everything."

"I would hope so. That was one of the first conditions when you sold us the lot. And of course you'll take good care of the grave. That was one of the conditions for paying you a maintenance fee."

"All the special lots are in the upper section; you were lucky to get one of them. It looks down, and you've got an open view in front. What more could you want? Dead or alive, we've got to be able to look down...."

"And that's why it's special. What a difference in price! We knew what we were doing when we paid extra for that lot."

Her mother seemed ready to chatter on forever about the lot. But when the men resumed their seats at the chessboard she reluctantly folded the contract, put it in her bag, and left the office.

Rounding the spine of the hill, Jeong-ok uttered a low exclamation and closed her eyes, dazzled by the burial mounds spreading across the hill like boiling, seething blobs of lather. Although the cemetery was supposed to be terraced, the closer she approached, the more disordered it appeared. The mounds and their gravestones were of uneven sizes, and most of the mounds were overgrown with weeds. The epitaphs on the small granite stones, provided by the cemetery office as specified in the contract, were difficult to decipher among the weeds, because their Chinese-ink lettering had been rubbed out, leaving only an indistinct engraving.

The burial sites were separated from the pathways by blocks set in the ground, but most of the blocks were missing, broken or worn away, allowing dirt to sweep down onto the walks. Perhaps the summer's rain was also to blame?

"A damn cheap operation if you ask me," spat Jeong-ok's mother. "Where's all that maintenance they're supposed to be providing? They want us to pay the fee on time, though." Her tone had been different with the men in the office.

The boy's face turned pale and he said nothing, perhaps apprehensive at the stillness of the cemetery and the graves looking like a heap of warts on the back of a hand.

As the man in the office had explained, the path they were to take had steps, or rather the semblance of steps formed by people's footprints and almost buried by soil. In reality, it was no different from a steep mountain trail.

The sun was hot. The boy started sweating again. A mole cricket darted across the whitish path, its short shadows resembling musical notes.

"Where are we going?" the boy asked Jeong-ok with an exceedingly doubtful look.

"Well…." She was momentarily perplexed. The boy wasn't yet old enough to understand that people have to die and leave everything behind.

"Why did it take you so long to come see us?" her mother abruptly asked.

Her mother had asked the same question when taking the sleeping boy from her upon their arrival the previous night. But Jeong-ok couldn't remember her answer. Had it been, "No one to take care of the house"? Or, "I was kind of busy"? Since her mother hadn't followed up with, "Mr. Yi must be on vacation—where's he off to?" it had probably been the latter.

"I was kind of busy," she replied, frowning. Their vacant home in Vernal Stream and the empty mailbox with the two little keys inside flashed across her mind. The boy's tricycle would be lying in the corner of the yard.

She couldn't explain to her mother that it had been difficult for her to leave home because she was waiting for some brief word from him; that the uncertainty of the situation had made her willing to believe even an unsubstantiated report.

A sense of urgency, unlike her habitual anxiety whenever he left the house, dazed her now, obscuring her vision.

She recalled the sound of the telephone, probably ringing even now in the empty house, and the questions lying in wait inside the silent, unanswered receiver.

"Hello, may I speak with Mr. Yi?"

"He's not home now."

"Would you happen to know where he went?"

The voice inquired after him politely and persistently, without a sign of irritation. A friendly male voice, its sole concern the well-being of the other party, but giving absolutely no hint of what murky, hidden purpose existed at that end of the line. She was flustered by these calls, realizing instinctively from the speaker's acute professionalism that he would get the answers he sought.

"Hello, may I speak with Mr. Yi?"

"He went out to play *paduk*."

"Could you tell me where?"

"I think it's a place called the Hope Club, but I'm not positive."

"Do you happen to know if he was planning to meet someone?"

"Well, he doesn't tell me anything about his outside affairs, so...."

Although he hardly ever left home, he obstinately refused to answer the phone.

"Did Mr. Yi go out again? Somehow I feel like we're playing hide and seek."

Though its tone was light, almost droll, the unseen voice kept searching tenaciously for any trace of his trail—a trail that might have stopped at a place he had visited.

"He went to the barber shop."

"Is it near your house?"

"Yes, it's called the Springtime of Life."

"A fine name. Hahaha...."

That day, after coming home with his hair neatly barbered for the first time in a long while, he finally took some scissors and cut the telephone cord. But after he left, Jeong-ok had the line reconnected.

"Did a burglar do this?" The repairman chuckled as he looked down at the section of line severed so decisively by the sharp blades.

As soon as the line was reconnected the voice crawled out as if it had been hiding in the severed cord.

"Hello, may I speak with Mr. Yi?"

"He's not here—he went fishing."

"Oh? Fishing?"

"He often goes fishing," Jeong-ok said, raising her voice for emphasis.

"Did he go with somebody?"

"Well, I'm not sure. Sometimes he goes by himself, sometimes he goes with a group."

"Would you happen to know where he went?"

"He said something like the Stream of the Gods. I think he said he had to walk in quite a ways from Heaven's Pass."

"Well, if he comes home with a big catch, Ma'am, cook up a nice peppery stew with it. I'll drop by for a taste." The voice roared with laughter.

Although Jeong-ok distinctly heard the caller hang up, she imagined his laughter still bursting through every little orifice in the receiver. The man seemed to have been beside himself with delight, but at the same time listening keenly to the sound of his own calculated staccato laughter.

As Jeong-ok listened to the laughter, her despair at her husband's departure—his figure gradually becoming dim and then vanishing—flashed vividly through her mind, as it always did. "Where are you?" she asked over and over, listening to her voice circling in vain about the empty house.

Where could he have gone?

"There's no reason for them to be looking for me," he had said.

The ocher earth spilled down the narrow trail and found its way between her toes.

The "special" lots, as they were called, occupied the crest of the steep, narrow path. Because they were not marked with serial numbers, Jeong-ok had to rely on her mother's somewhat unreliable memory to find the correct one.

Again she took the boy on her back, the path being too narrow for two to ascend side by side. Evidently her mother was bewildered by the sight of all the graves. Before, there had been only the burial sites, leveled to be sold.

Taking out the cemetery plan attached to the contract, her mother traced their path from its starting point and began matching the graves with the numbers on the plan. At the same time, she repeatedly shook the earth from her sandals, perched first on one leg and then the other, tsk-tsking all the while. She had been relieved to have arranged for her husband and herself to be buried together here, but now she appeared regretful that the lot had to be in a public cemetery.

The hill that had served as their ancestral burial ground was in North Korea. In the North, Jeong-ok was told, the family would make a temporary grave in the yard when there was a death in winter; not until the ice melted could they hold a second funeral and a proper burial on the hill.

"To get up here, a corpse would have to stand up and walk," said her mother as she slipped on the sandy ocher soil. She grasped the weeds, grown like tousled hair, and panted as she crawled up the trail.

Stopping momentarily to catch her breath, Jeong-ok looked back; the path they had crept up seemed far away. Much lower, on a ridge across the valley, seven or eight men with shovels were busily hollowing out a grave—to all appearances a burial.

He had always gone up in the hills at dawn. Jeong-ok, fast asleep then, never caught sight of him leaving the house and would wonder when he had slipped out. Whenever she heard the clank of the front gate in her fleeting dawn dreams she was seized by a desperate feeling that she would never see him again. To erase the desolate sensation that she was falling apart, she would soothe herself even while she was dreaming: It's only a dream, she would think, and when it's light and I wake up he'll be back, brushing his teeth at the faucet outside just like always. Her dawn sleep was too short and her dreams disturbing. Once she had considered following him, but she never did. Not only because she liked to sleep through daybreak. Rather, they had an unspoken agreement that dawn was the one time of day when absolutely no one was to interrupt him. He felt compelled to spend his day napping, playing *paduk*, taking some light exercise in order to sleep at night—fumbling to repair the gutters, say, or pushing the boy along on his tricycle. Since a dawn stroll was supposed to be good for one's health and since she considered it his personal ritual, she refrained from showing the slightest sign that her sleep was ever disturbed.

About the time he returned and stepped inside, accompanied by the cool outdoor air, Jeong-ok would rub her drowsy eyes. Then, after covering the boy with the quilt he had kicked aside, she would rinse some rice and put it on the stove.

"Why don't you sleep some more?" she would say nonchalantly, as if talking to a patriarch who had diligently swept the alley in front of the house early in the morning. Then she would turn and murmur inaudibly: "I don't know anything. I'm just an ignorant woman. But I've never thought of that as bad luck. I'm a woman who plants flower seeds in the soft, warm soil after the rain and watches the buds and the blossoms in joyful wonder. If I'm not greedy, I can live a mundane existence day by day, like others. And I have a future: our son. But if he hears this he'll probably answer: 'You say, let's plant some seeds and live a simple life, but why do you want to do that? It's because you're anxious to see the flowers, isn't it?'"

It was because they constituted the world in which the boy was to live that Jeong-ok thought about the time and space that would follow her death—what she called the future. She would leave behind her flesh and blood in that world.

"Goodness! It used to be just a ridge, and now all these people have come to rest here…." Sighing, her mother looked in turn at the map and the graves, then pointed to one of the lots and shouted, "There it is!"

The empty rectangular lot, divided by cement blocks buried among the weeds, was smaller than Jeong-ok had expected. Perhaps because of the burial mounds heaped around it, this lot, the only empty one in section 9-3, looked more cramped, as if hollowed out of its surroundings. Right beside the lot was a sparsely sodded mound that looked new. Jeong-ok wondered if a family had recently visited the grave following the third-day-after-the-funeral memorial service. Collected there were a bunch of withered flowers, a piece of white paper blotted with letters in Chinese ink, leftovers from a meal partially wrapped in newspaper, an empty bottle of some offertory beverage, paper cups, and other odds and ends. Perhaps a downpour had prevented the visitors from cleaning up. Nothing unusual about a shower in the summer, she told herself.

Thinking that Jeong-ok was wondering how two people could possibly be buried in this narrow lot, her mother sheepishly tried to vindicate herself: "It's not that small, you know. After all, it's for two people. Look, compare a grave for one and a grave for two—see the difference?"

The flat grave site was a bed of weeds. Jeong-ok found it difficult to imagine that someday the tightly clotted earth separated only by the weeds' tough roots would be turned up and a huge mound formed atop it.

The boy's amazing ability to harmonize with new situations and people, that special quality of kids, made the graves seem no longer strange to him. Jeong-ok was relieved not to have to explain to the inquisitive child this different world in which they were intruders: "Where are we?" "This is where the dead are buried." "The dead? What is dying?" Who indeed were these people called the dead? she asked herself. They were people who had lived in the same era and experienced the same events as she. People she hadn't known, whom she had brushed past indifferently on a street corner, whose eyes had lightly made contact with hers. They were people who had risen in the morning and fallen asleep at night, people with whom she had experienced sunlight, wind, snow, and rain. She had been born at a certain moment in their lifetimes, and at a certain moment in hers they had humbly departed. How awfully fortuitous to have shared the same era with them, and yet she hadn't had the slightest premonition or indication of their deaths.

The city center was visible in the far distance. Though the day was clear, the city looked dim and hazy; it gave her the impression of a crudely tinted photograph.

Suddenly a breeze gathered. A stream of cool air touched her forehead and she saw a blurry remnant of the city, which the wind seemed to have driven toward her.

A sound carried by the breeze brushed her ears, now disappearing, now returning. So far and faint that she thought she might lose it in a single instant of inattention, it was like the continuous striking of a gong or a small drum—or a combination of the two.

As soon as the breeze passed, the sound disappeared and the city receded. The sun felt hotter. She watched her mother sitting on an outspread newspaper, slapping her calves, and wondered if ants were crawling up them.

"I wish we had some shade," said the older woman.

But there could be no dense thickets, no trees with thriving roots on this denuded graveyard hill. Otherwise tree roots would reach into the burial pits and tangle themselves—or so people said.

The sun was directly above. Their shadows were squashed beneath their feet and their unsheltered, exposed bodies turned crimson.

The cloth lining of the bag felt damp. Wondering if something was leaking, Jeong-ok emptied the bag of its soft drinks, melons, and other contents and arrayed them on a white towel she'd spread over the grass, the arrangement suggesting a pleasant picnic was at hand.

Was it because of this? Jeong-ok murmured to herself. When her mother had causally asked her at breakfast if she wanted to visit the cemetery, had she readily agreed because she envisioned finding there the solitude and absolute peace of the dead? Had she agreed to the trip even though she could barely imagine venturing forth in this scorching weather with the boy in tow?

She uncapped the soft drinks and the carbonated beverages bubbled and dripped from the openings. There was only this indifferent fizzing of the froth to break the deathly stillness. After sprinkling some of the overflowing foam on the ground to appease any thirsty spirits in the vicinity, she took a sip and passed the bottle to the boy.

"We should find some shade," muttered Jeong-ok's mother. But she spoke in vain. There was nothing to produce a spot of shade except the tilted, open parasol. Pointing to the shade it provided, she said to the boy, "Come here and sit."

The boy's face was the color of a ripe tomato. He took a sip of the soft drink, and after a throaty *k'aaaa* he smacked his lips in satisfaction.

"Little rascal, listen to you already," said his grandmother. "You figure on being a big drinker some day? Does your daddy do that?"

Jeong-ok and her mother burst into laugher. The boy, pleased with the response he had elicited, repeated the guttural sound—this time louder.

"It looks fairly large," said Jeong-ok. "I guess it is for two people. The location is good, too." Though she thought differently, she said this to satisfy her mother, who had taken pains to emphasize, even to the men in the custodial office, that it was a double lot.

"Large? Are you kidding? It's too narrow for two. Even though there's just one mound, they'll be digging a hole for each of us, so they should have made it about as wide as two single lots." Her mother shook her head: this would not do. It hadn't taken long for her to change her tune.

"You know, when they bury two people," her mother went on, "they make a little hole between the graves to connect them before building the mound. We did the same thing when we buried your grandparents. Then we found a better location for the graves, and when we dug up the coffins we found that the holes had been shaped into a nice, smooth passage. You see, the two of them were always visiting each other." Blushing slightly, she broke into a shrill laugh. She had no doubt that a couple buried together would be tied by fate in the next world.

There was a secret game Jeong-ok had played with her friends when she was a girl. It had likely originated in a book of folktales. According to one of the tales, if a girl touched her forehead with one of the ornamental silver knives that women used to carry to protect their virtue, then looked into a round mirror on a moonless night, the face of her future husband would surely appear. And so the girls tried it, despite their apprehension and their disdain at this venture into superstition. It was difficult at their age to resist curiosity and the temptation to see their future mates. No face appeared in the mirror, of course.

Jeong-ok, however, continued the game for some time. As she sat in bed alone and looked into a mirror darker than the room whose light she had extinguished, she earnestly wished to encounter the face of her future husband.

They were now man and wife, he had said after their wedding. He no longer seemed a stranger, and his face had become as familiar as if she had known it in a previous life.

Although she had been seized even then by a vague sense of failure, she had gripped his hand and pledged to be a faithful attendant, to be obedient and true. "Yes, we are really man and wife," she had said. And then for the first time she had seen a face in the mirror on a moonless night.

He was walking along a road, his footfalls raising dust, his parched mouth full of the scorching sun. The sunlight became a fire in his heart. There was no respite from his thirst. He could not remember ever having been free from it. Wanting to rinse the flaring fever from his mouth and soak his burning feet, he glanced around in vain for a cold stream.

On he walked.... A path through a field, lacking any trace of human life; the sound of unripened kernels swelling involuntarily inside verdant, growing rice plants; the sound of new ears of rice drying in the blazing sun.

He wondered where the reservoir could be. He was beginning to feel the weight of his tackle bag with its fishing rod and other gear. The stiff new straps, not yet broken in, dug into the joints of his sweaty shoulders and chafed them.

Surely the girl at the inn had said it was about five miles to the reservoir. While telling him this she had stolen several glances at his new set of fishing gear. Was it simply his imagination that he had read suspicion on her face?

It was almost ten when he woke up that morning; the sunlight had penetrated deep into his room. Upon opening his eyes, he usually listened closely for any movement from outside before getting up. A radio was blaring the latest episode of a soap opera. Otherwise it was quiet.

He got up and opened the door. A girl was wiping the long wooden veranda, her bottom up in the air. She gave him a smile. It was the girl who had brought him dinner after he had checked in the night before.

"Shall I bring you some breakfast?"

He shook his head and, toothbrush in mouth, stepped down to the yard. The girl followed and filled a washbowl for him, as she had done the previous evening.

"Are you going to be leaving today?"

"Where am I, anyway?" he countered, looking at her puffy checks. It was strange. Since leaving his house he had become indifferent about the names of his destinations and the places along the way. Every place was exactly the same—was that it? But whenever he woke up in a cramped, untidy room in an unfamiliar inn he would shake his head fretfully, trying to remember where he was.

"This is Chinnae-ŭp. You didn't know?" The girl stared at him, trying to figure out who he was. This time the suspicion was obvious.

He took a different tack: "I'm wondering if there's a place to go fishing around here."

"About five miles down the road there's a reservoir just full of big fat fish," she responded, her expression softening. "I hear they're swarming because several people have drowned there." Giggling, she pretended to shudder.

Just then an announcement for a movie thundered from a speaker on the roof of the theater across the street. Listening to the repeated notice of the screening, he asked himself, *Why not take the girl?* He didn't want to be noticed, so having a companion might be safer than being all alone; blending into a crowd would be even better.

"…What's the meaning of that dream you told us about? It's not like the dreams we have. It's difficult to understand. We're not here for your lectures." And then the tone eased. "Use simple words we can all understand." They burst into guffaws and patted him on the shoulder. But their eyes were not laughing. He shrugged off the hands. But he couldn't rid himself of the feeling that he was forever caught between the links of a chain that would tighten mercilessly until they crushed his shoulders.

"Would you like to go see that movie?"

"I'll get scolded if I go out with one of the guests," the girl answered primly. She then turned the radio still higher.

He had had to wait nearly an hour for the first showing to start. Afterward he could remember only a few scenes—a speeding car crashing, turning into a fireball, and plunging into the sea; close-ups of kabuki actors, their powdered faces white like masks. This proved he had been thinking about other things throughout the film. Even so, he had shed a few tears while watching it. Why?

Before the lights came on for intermission, he looked at the clock next to the red "No Smoking" and "Hats Off" signs. The hands stood at two o'clock. He decided to sit tight awhile; it would still be blazing hot under the midday sun. Skipping breakfast had made his stomach sour, so he bought some pastries and yogurt at the snack bar. The pastries reeked of preservatives.

He also wept a little during the second showing—and at the same scene. There was a blizzard of confetti, and balloons of various colors rose and filled the sky. Celebrants in peaked hats holding lanterns decorated with dragon heads shouted in wild abandon, their faces bubbling in laughter. And suddenly he was teary-eyed, overcome by the scene of a woman on the verge of childbirth struggling through a milling throng on a slum street where ragged clothing had been hung out to dry on every balcony.

The colors of the film looked dull on the old screen, and the subtitles were completely illegible. From the corner a baby cried out in terror. The sound echoed violently from the high ceiling of the dark, nearly empty theater.

He left in the middle of the second showing. The sun seemed scarcely to have moved. He walked toward it, shaking his head to dispel the fog in his mind—such a feeling of unreality. The people in the peaked hats dancing in abandon, the wretched, exhausted woman about to give birth, and the crying baby—were they the scenes and sounds of yesterday? Just now? Tomorrow? Walking a road that was indistinguishable from a life he remembered having borrowed for himself and lived—yesterday, the day before that, or much further in the past—for the first time he thought he understood why he had wept. It was because of his son. It was because there was an inevitable beauty to the sight of people making their way through life, even though the life his son would wish for, like the peaceful life he desired for himself, could not in the end be realized.

Jeong-ok's mother was peeling a second melon. A magpie flapped toward them and came to rest on the ground. At the sight of the black form flying into this space filled with sun and stillness, she paused. Jeong-ok instinctively looked at the boy. He had been sitting bored, blowing into an empty soft-drink bottle with a deep whoosh, but now, his eyes like saucers, he set the bottle down.

The sounds from the ridge across the valley occasionally rode the wind to their ears. Jeong-ok now recognized them as a gong and cymbals, but so faint and distant were they that she wondered if she might be imagining them.

Her mother briefly squinted at the magpie and resumed peeling the melon.

The boy began creeping toward the magpie. The bird couldn't conceal its hostility toward the unexpected visitors. Its firm, spry wings had a blue sheen, and its stomach was white as snow. It fixed its glistening, seemingly mocking black eyes on the boy, though it couldn't have seen anything so unusual in him.

The boy sensed the bird's antipathy and his eyes grew tense. He tiptoed closer, clenching his fists and breaking into an amiable smile of childish cunning. But when he was just one step away, the magpie shook its wings and soared off.

The dispirited boy looked at Jeong-ok as if to complain. She shrugged.

The magpie flew freely in the still white void and then returned to earth, the desolation of midday seeming to weigh heavily on its steel-colored wings. Every time it hopped from one gravestone to another the boy would approach it. He tried his best to muffle his footsteps, but the bird never failed to slip away into the air. When the boy finally gave up and dropped his arms to his sides, the magpie flew near, keeping close enough to sustain its opponent's interest. The bird now had a firm grip on the boy. It was casting its net and entrancing him.

A white bus came up the road in a cloud of dust. It turned at the foot of the hill where they were sitting, then halted at the bottom of the hill opposite. The doors opened and a funeral party emerged with a coffin. The coffin bearers slowly led the mourners up the hill. As Jeong-ok had suspected, they were heading toward the open grave far below them where the gravediggers were waiting.

The boy chased after the magpie and careened among the gravestones, which towered above him as if they had a life of their own. Unnoticed by the two women, he had removed his sneakers and socks, enjoying the sensation of the grass under his bare feet. And then he tried a new game, embracing head-high gravestones and spinning around them.

To Jeong-ok the boy resembled the magpie the way he dashed about in the glare of the sun. He seemed to have forgotten that she and her mother existed. For the first time she saw him from afar as if watching someone else's child. Who was this boy romping around innocently in shorts and a T-shirt? Was he the boy she had met so often in her dreams, desires, and thoughts before she became pregnant?

Before her pregnancy she was forever imagining children running to her. Although she had no particular face in mind for the baby who would be born after inhabiting her womb, the boy bore not the slightest resemblance to any of the children who had run to her from out of the future, some of them halfheartedly and others spreading their arms in joy. Who was this boy of hers?

If he were to walk straight ahead where this paved road forked in three directions, the narrow streets of a town would likely appear. At the left fork stood a board with the Buddhist swastika and an inscription, "Bota Temple, 6 miles." The path to the fish-filled reservoir seemed to be to the right.

After hesitating a moment he saw a small shop at one of the intersections. On its glass door were advertisements for noodle dishes. He went in. Although the smell of the preservatives in the pastries he had eaten at the theater came up whenever he exhaled, he was still famished.

There were two long tables inside. Hearing him enter, a young woman peered out from the living quarters attached to the back of the shop. Her face was puffy, as if she had just risen from a nap.

"Could I have some *ramyeon*?" he asked, looking over the menu.

The woman emerged, buttoning her blouse. "Would you like an egg in it?" She began wiping one of the tables.

"On second thought, could I have soup noodles instead?" he hastened to ask, recalling the repulsive smell of rancid chicken fat that he associated with *ramyeon*.

Without answering she turned toward the shelves, sweeping up her disheveled hair and fixing it with a pin. She took down a bundle of noodles from a shelf where boxes of matches, bottles of liquor and soft drinks, and other goods sat covered with dust.

As he waited for his meal he smoked a cigarette and read in turn every single flyer posted on the wall: a slogan for the government's New Village Movement, a slogan urging increased production of foodstuffs, and posters containing photos of most-wanted fugitives—together with their offenses and the rewards offered for their capture. All the while he dusted off the basketball sneakers he was wearing by tapping them against the cement floor. A tractor rattled by with an awful din and a succession of housewives and grandmothers with loads on their heads came in to buy candles and incense.

Frogs were croaking in the stillness of the late afternoon. It looked as though it would rain by nightfall.

Finally his meal was ready. The woman served the noodles in their thin anchovy broth, then set some radish kimchi and chopsticks beside them on the table, making a separate trip for each item.

An elderly woman entered the shop with a young woman in mourning clothes who had a toddler in tow. "We'd like some candles."

The shopkeeper gave a faint, knowing smile. "On your way to the temple, I see."

"It's the seventh and final observance," the old woman whispered, glancing at the younger woman.

The shopkeeper rummaged through the shelves, then brushed off her hands. "We're all out," she said, shaking her head.

The women purchased a bottle of *jeongjong*, and with this offertory rice brew and some sticks of incense in hand, they left with worried looks.

The woman in mourning had gripped the boy's hand and remained silent throughout.

"If his highness knew there was a ceremony today, why couldn't he stock up on candles?" the shopkeeper grumbled. "All he ever does is...."

They must have been profiting from the visitors to the Buddhist temple.

"So the temple's holding a service?" Regretting having requested a spoonful of hot pepper, extra work for the shopkeeper, he tried to ingratiate himself with her. The white skirt of the young woman fading into the distance caught his eye as it moved in and out of sight through the door of the shop.

"Today is the Buddhist All Souls' Day," the shopkeeper replied. "They're on their way to Bota Temple, over the hill." Noticing his eyes were still following the hem of the white mourning skirt becoming faint in the distance, she added: "I guess they're finally having the forty-ninth-day observance. They're from the upper village. The kid's father drowned in the reservoir seven weeks ago."

He stirred the hot pepper into the broth, and some insects in the condiment floated to the surface like shreds of white rice bran.

A baby cried from the back of the shop. While the shopkeeper sat looking vacantly outside, her cheek resting against the door frame, liquid saturated the swollen front of her blouse, spreading and darkening it. When the crying became a piercing scream, she sluggishly rose and went into the back room.

The noodles were plentiful but flavorless. For one so hungry, he now had virtually no appetite.

He paid the woman as she was nursing her child and left.

"Looks like they're opening the coffin," Jeong-ok's mother said, squinting. She must have been watching the scene unfolding below. The seven loops of white cotton broadcloth around the black coffin were being untied.

"What for?" said Jeong-ok.

"So the bones stay white. That's the way they do it down south. Apparently the moisture in the wood can stain the bones yellow."

Jeong-ok gazed at her mother's face. The lines and furrows that crosshatched it stood out clearly in the sun. All the makeup had been wiped away except a touch of blue eye shadow. After slowly chewing several bites of melon the older woman realized she was being observed, and her face hardened. Jeong-ok got to her feet, stretched her arms high, and took a few deep breaths. She could now see the spectacle of the funeral more clearly.

The corpse was being lowered into the grave on a mortuary plank containing seven holes in the shape of the Big Dipper. All the bereaved women had prostrated themselves, and now they began wailing in unison. Then some of the men, clad in black and wearing hemp mourning hoods signifying their close relation to the deceased, each scooped a shovelful of earth into the grave and stepped back. Another round of wailing rose from the women, still prostrate in their white mourning garb, their heads lowered. Next, a man in black without a hood respectfully bowed toward the grave and shoveled earth onto the corpse. He was followed by the women. Jeong-ok was reminded of officials taking turns with a shovel in a memorial tree-planting ceremony.

The mourners transferred their shovels to the gravediggers, who sprang to work and quickly covered the corpse with soil. Then came the tamping and liming of the earth. The gravediggers, each with a long pole, descended into the grave. Their heads barely rose above the ground. An old man kneeling languidly at the head of the grave began to sing, and the gravediggers fell into two rows. Alternately face to face and back to back, they stamped the earth while responding to his calls in ringing voices. Their tone was sorrowful and slow. Though Jeong-ok could not hear the words, the melody was distinct.

While the old man, hoarse by now, smoked a cigarette and cooled off, the gravediggers showered the grave with another layer of earth mixed with lime. A lull in the wailing and singing made the sound of the gong and cymbals faintly audible.

Leaving her parents' plot, Jeong-ok walked from one burial mound to the next, stopping at each stone to peruse the name and dates engraved on it. Some people had lived almost a century, others barely a decade. In each case she was struck with wonder, for she was alive. There were people still living who had already arranged for their graves. And someone dead at seventeen. Another at twenty. The face of death differing with their ages. But these memories were only shadows in the hearts of those who knew these people at death, and memories would, in their turn, inevitably become dim and soon be forgotten.

On her next visit she would stand here again. The boy would be lanky by then. Would he remember this day? Would he remember their forced march on a scorching summer day buried in his past?

She was brought to a halt by the sight of cream-colored roses wrapped in cellophane lying in front of a burial mound. Once fragrant and charming, they had withered in the hot sunlight, but their leaves still looked fresh and green because of the water droplets gathering inside the wrapper. Traces of yesterday's shower were evident. Looking closer, she saw hardened depressions made by high heels in the cramped plot in front of the mound.

Finding here the traces of the rain she had watched the day before while lulling the boy to sleep in her arms on the veranda of her house in Vernal Stream, Jeong-ok recalled the elusive feeling that had accompanied an image she had seen in that rain—the familiar image of a young woman bringing cream-colored roses to her beloved's grave. But then she shook her head, realizing that rain was virtually a daily occurrence in summertime. The rainy season was over, but the pattern of sudden thunder and lightning followed by clearing had persisted like some celestial prank for a month or so.

"He must have been caught in that rainstorm," the officer at the police substation had said.

The creel, fishing rods, folding chair, and other items the policeman delivered to Jeong-ok were still damp. The ink had run all over the appointment book and identification card found in his jacket. There was nothing to identify in the photo on his identification card. Like a face from a forgotten past, it was unfamiliar and indistinct, lacking the stamp of his personality. This sensation was accentuated by his short hair in the photo, which had been taken before men started growing their hair long.

The policeman scrutinized Jeong-ok with curious eyes, then pointed to the boy, who with his hair covering his ears and forehead might have been taken for a girl. "Is this your... son?"

Jeong-ok lowered her head. "Yes..." Then she added, "He's an only child," answering the policeman's unspoken question.

The boy's eyes never left the gun at the policeman's side.

"It doesn't take long for the river to rise when it rains... The island gets cut off and then submerged. For all I know he might have swum away, but we're continuing the search. It's easy for outsiders to get into trouble there. If there's no rain, it's quite safe and there's no problem. It's not that far to shore, and the water only comes up to your waist... Last year a man was camping there with his kids and they got caught in a downpour in the middle of the night. He never knew that when the rain comes that island disappears."

The policeman went on at length with his explanation, his tone more kindly as he sympathized with the young widow.

As Jeong-ok was picking up the items of fishing gear one by one, the boy shouted with joy: "Aren't those Dad's? When he took me last time...." He remembered having gone fishing with his father on a long summer day the previous year. The boy hadn't been fishing since.

Jeong-ok went with the policeman to the scene of the "accident." The island had been formed by sand deposits in a wide stream that flowed into a river. It lay bare in the water, a flat, small white oval that reminded Jeong-ok of a fish belly. It seemed impossible that this solid-looking island could have disappeared overnight in the rain.

The sparkling sands danced under the blazing sun.

The local people all agreed that a lantern had glimmered on the island of sand till late at night. And then the rain came pouring down.

A man had come fishing. He carried his gear to the island, making several trips through the waist-deep water. At the side of the stream he gave a youngster some change and asked him to get a pack of cigarettes. Early the next morning, worrying about a net he had set in the stream, the boy went out and found a piece of clothing snagged on a bush. It was the jacket the man had been wearing the previous evening…. The boys who lived along the stream repeated to Jeong-ok word for word the story they had told several times already to their neighbors and the police.

"He didn't catch anything, not even a chub. We told him the current here is too strong for fishing, but he just laughed."

The next day one of the older boys rowed to the junction of the stream and the river and scooped up a folding chair spinning against a rock and a creel floating downstream.

"It was a wild storm—so windy and rainy we couldn't put up an umbrella," someone else said. "I was out late, and on my way home I saw this light coming from the island."

Some people living nearby had taken a boat downstream as far as a long, rounded dune and searched for his body with long poles. No trace of him could be found.

Jeong-ok affixed her fingerprint to some forms and was given her husband's belongings by the policeman.

"I understand he teaches at a college."

"Yes."

"Does he often leave home by himself like this?"

"Well, summer vacation started early... and fishing is one of his favorite pastimes."

"Actually, since he teaches at a college I suppose he can do what he wants with his time even when school's in session. But you know, it's quite a ways from here to Vernal Stream, and we're not all that well known for fishing…."

The policeman was obviously trying to uncover the significance of the disappearance of this stranger who had come here on a hot summer day. At that moment Jeong-ok was seized by a violent urge to tell all. Her throat itched to pour out the flood of words: *He's a lecturer at a provincial college, and we've been married five years now. One day everything became off limits to him. He's like someone who's been declared legally incompetent—he doesn't have any rights or responsibilities. And he has to have a regular checkup, like he picked up syphilis or something. The only time he can travel is during his naps or when he's having a long dream. And that's why he began sleeping all the time. The way he sleeps with his mouth open—it's just like he's dead, so I get frightened, and several times I've shaken him awake.*

But then, pushing these words deep into her heart as she always did, she asked: "Would you happen to know where Heaven's Pass and the Stream of the Gods are?"

The policeman considered the question then shook his head. "Never heard of them. I'm sure there aren't any places around here with names like that."

If they're not around here, where could they be, with names like Heaven's Pass and the Stream of the Gods? she had wondered.

After her husband's departure she had pored over every map she could find—detailed maps that showed cities, towns, and townships. But Heaven's Pass and the Stream of the Gods were nowhere to be seen. No surprise there—by now she always expected this sort of thing.

Perhaps because of the blueness of that dawn, when she heard those place names from him she had visualized a vertical cliff with no handholds, an azure sky above it that had never opened itself to view, and a blue gorge—the kind where trout are said to gather in the chill water to cool their red, feverish eyes.

The tamping feet quickened and the calls and responses accelerated into a quick tune. The gravediggers wheeling about the hole appeared to grow out of it like leeks shooting up from a storage cellar. They were lavish with the lime and stamped the earth hard. Dancing and spinning, their legs almost completely visible now, they were the only people to be seen. The sun had driven the mourners to cover under an open tent.

He sat beside the stream, removed his sneakers, and soaked his whitish, blistered feet in the water. It was astonishingly refreshing.

He bent to look at the various shapes and colors of the stones in the stream bed. His reflection appeared first. The colors of the stones seemed to flow with the water.

He broke his reflection by stirring the water, then collected some of the stones. Worn, rounded stones lay flat, others were upright. When he took the stones from the water, their colors faded.

"A lizard wearing a pretty flower-print dress said to a baby mouse, 'When the full moon rises, go find me a purple pebble. Make sure it's purple. Then I'll make your wishes come true...' But the mouse couldn't find a purple pebble no matter how he tried...." Only dimly awake, he was listening to Jeong-ok's monotonous, mechanical voice as she read to their son. He thought: A purple pebble—if it's purple but not a gem, how pretty and marvelous it could be…. "And so? So what happened?" the boy eagerly asked, his legs fidgeting. Jeong-ok was reading the story without conviction or interest; she must have told it several times already…. So, could the little mouse find a purple pebble? he wondered. Before he could hear the end he began drifting off to sleep. Of course, he told himself, after some impossible adventures, sacrifices, and ordeals that little mouse would obtain the purple pebble and have his wishes come true. All children's stories are like that.

He arranged the stones he had taken from the water. As they dried and lost their luster they soon became common and ordinary.

There was a rock in the garden of their house in Vernal Steam that in form and color was difficult to distinguish from a tree root. Brought home some time ago from one of his fishing trips, it had been left alone in a shady corner of the yard, where it was now growing a coat of damp moss. The boy thought the rock grew a little every night. The little rascal's brain was full of stories about magic. He believed that those buried deep in the earth could overcome death and rise from their graves in response to a spell: *suri suri masuri*. The boy's tiny gestures and expressions, which he had never fully appreciated, pricked his heart with pathos.

"You're putting up a smokescreen. Are you... a poet?" they had asked sarcastically. They thought they had discovered his weapon. But this was unfair of them: he had wished to be an advocate of common sense, not so much a poet.

He began to throw the assorted stones back in the water. They struck a large rock rising from the stream, throwing sparks and leaving faint white marks. The last stone whirled into the water, and he rose. The sun was near the horizon. If he set his mind to it, he could probably reach the reservoir before dark. If he walked without stopping he could see the sun become a gigantic fireball and make its illusory descent beneath the horizon. Then he could watch the night set in.

A new mound soon rose from the soil that had been hurriedly dug up.

The clang of gong and cymbals sounded much more clearly and urgently.

It had taken place within twenty minutes at most. The boy had been taking such a long nap. Covering the sweaty boy's stomach with a towel, Jeong-ok suddenly remembered she hadn't picked up the laundry she had taken to the cleaner's right after winter. Before summer was gone, she thought, she would need to have her husband's autumn clothing ready for him to wear.

Locking the house and gate and dropping the keys in the mailbox, she ran to the cleaner's. She was back with the laundry in no time. For a moment she stood outside the wall surrounding their yard and strained to hear whether the boy was crying. Inside it was just as quiet as before. But then she reached into the mailbox. Although the keys were there, something was strange, different. But at the same time it was as if a thoroughly familiar sensation had brushed across the back of her hand. She drew out the keys, which were crudely embossed with the head of a lion, and studied them. They didn't seem twisted or scratched. When she unlocked the door and entered the house she felt even more keenly that someone had been there. Not that the door was open or that the shoes in the vestibule were disarranged. Nothing had changed. The boy was still asleep with his arms outspread; he had kicked away the towel over his stomach. Only after a look around the house did she understand: it was the faint odor of tobacco.

She flung down the bag of clothing and dashed into the kitchen. She didn't know why, but since he had gone, it was always his appetite that came to mind whenever she thought of him. There was no sign he had touched anything, only a glass of water almost empty.

But there in the bathroom hamper were the roughly folded clothes she knew so well. It was as if the master of the house were taking a bath.

"Where are you? Where are you?" she whispered, as if wary of others' ears, though she knew he wasn't there. Only then did she pick up the telephone. There was only the incessant dial tone seeming to whir about her ear. Not really knowing what she was trying to find, Jeong-ok picked up two cigarette butts from the ashtray that were still moist with saliva; feeling like a veteran detective she inspected them.

As she usually did before starting the wash, she searched the pockets of the clothes he had left. It was clothing from a restless journey, permeated with the smell of the many places he had been, of the wind, the sunlight, the dew, and the people he had crossed paths with in places she had never visited.

The pockets yielded a wrinkled movie stub, whose stamped date was almost illegible, an admission stub to an amusement park, a grimy handkerchief, some flakes of tobacco. But where was the note he might have left?

Then she saw the clear imprint of his lips on the cheeks of the boy, who was fast asleep. There was no need to investigate further.

He was gone forever. Just as he had gone into hiding, leaving only his shell on a pile of sand that had disappeared in an overnight downpour, he had merely changed his clothes and vanished. It had been at most twenty minutes, but that was time enough for him to be far away by then.

She put her lips to the sleeping boy's cheek. The boy rubbed his eyes in annoyance, tossed about, rolled over, and went back to sleep.

The heap of reddish brown soil was being covered with turf. Her mother watched, unblinking, as if to fix a mental image of the burial from start to finish that she could review at some point in the future. She had lifted her dress above her knees to prevent it from being soiled and wrinkled, and her legs—once more proud and vigorous than the grass in a meadow—lay there as if cast aside, fleshy but withering, their veins faintly varicose.

The boy appeared from behind the stonework in front of a family plot whose mounds were backed by a semicircular wall. He ran to Jeong-ok, settled in her lap, and leaned back.

She passed her fingers through the boy's hair, which stuck to his sweaty forehead. She looked into his eyes. It was precisely when she looked in those eyes that she was conscious of her husband. And in those eyes she saw something new: the piercing eyes of her father-in-law in a faded, yellowing photograph. Despite the round chin that she associated with her own family, the boy's eyes gave an impression of perspicacity unbefitting a child. She could immediately spot that small face among the jumbled thousands of children flocking into her imagination. But his distinctiveness would disappear before long. He would grow and couple with a woman from a different family, and after he had fathered a child, his unique characteristics, inherited from his father and grandfather, would gradually wear away. Later they would be unfamiliar, those faces of children to be born with her husband's surname, as unfamiliar as people buried long ago.

When the mound had been dressed in turf and a simple tray for the offering set before it, the mourners emerged from their tent. While Jeong-ok was engrossed in the scene, a buzzing swarm of blowflies attached themselves to the melon peels at her feet.

She looked tenderly at her mother's face. Someday she herself would be holding a farewell ceremony for her mother on this very spot. She would someday be pouring a glass of *jeongjong* over her mother's burial mound and burning a piece of offertory rice paper.

Black smoke rose. The empty coffin was being burned. Her mother sighed.

A moist wind gathered. India-ink clouds billowed up from one side of the sky and covered the sun.

The ceremony below had concluded. The mourners gazed at the sky. Perhaps anxious about the unmistakable prospect of a soaking shower, they hastened to fold the tent, roll up the rush mats, and pack the ceremonial vessels.

The gravediggers surrounded the smoldering embers of the coffin and stirred them into flames with sticks.

The jagged row of white and black figures moved steadily down the hill among the burial mounds.

The tall, coarse grass of neglected graves began to tremble eerily in the moist wind, its color darkening in the gray void.

Perhaps sensitive to sharp drops in air pressure, a flock of birds filled the sky, their wings fluttering. They seemed to have risen from every ridge and hidden gorge. Suddenly they began swooping in low circles all over the cemetery, cawing back and forth. Jeong-ok saw that they were magpies.

Now the birds were perched motionless on every gravestone. She stiffened at the sight of them. For the first time that day she felt panic.

Startled by the enormous gathering, the boy locked onto her arm, his face filled with fear.

The mourners had reached the foot of the hill and boarded the bus, which started up with a tremendous racket.

"Let's go," said her mother.

Jeong-ok silently helped the boy with his sneakers, then wrapped the melon peels, eggshells, and other scraps in newspaper and put it all in the mesh bag, together with the empty bottles. She wished to leave no trace in the empty plot. Otherwise, how horrible it would be if the next time she came these remnants prompted her to try in vain to relive the hours she had just spent here.

"Are you planning to go back home today?"

"I'd better," Jeong-ok replied without really thinking about it. She had intended to stay several days with her parents, but she now sensed in her mother's tone a hint that she should return home. And now that she had responded, she felt like hurrying back, as if something urgent awaited her there, as if she had left the house in Vernal Stream empty forever and not just for a day.

"There might be a path this way too, maybe a shortcut." Her mother pointed out a ridge opposite the path they had climbed. Along it was the trail to the new grave the mourners had just left.

The sky darkened even more. The path dropped steeply. Jeong-ok lifted the boy to her back. The clouds were massing overhead.

The more they descended, the nearer the gong sounded.

"No two ways about it, we're going to have a shower," said her mother as she folded her parasol.

They passed the grave and were eyed by the gravediggers, who were partaking of the food offered in memory of the deceased. Turning their heads, the gravediggers followed them with drink-reddened eyes until they were out of sight.

They rounded two bends in the path and a Buddhist temple seemed to leap into sight at the edge of the hill. The kaleidoscopic tricolor design of the eaves and columns had been touched up; the paint looked fresh enough to smear at the touch of a hand. The incessant sound of gong and cymbals came from a dark sanctuary identified as the Hall of Hades by a plaque hanging at its entrance. It was the sound they had heard all along from the hill.

"Must be a ceremony," Jeong-ok's mother whispered faintly in her ear.

Thick raindrops began to spatter on the ground as they entered the temple courtyard. A cast-iron pot was suspended above a fire of pine branches in an outdoor cooking hearth, and acrid smoke was spreading over the ground.

A head poked out from the outbuilding that housed the kitchen, and a middle-aged woman in a nun's habit emerged. With her short permed hair and long rosary she gave the appearance of an untonsured nun or a shaman.

"A ceremony, is it?" asked Jeong-ok's mother in a congenial tone. Moving close under the eaves of the building she perched herself on the edge of the veranda. A sly, artful smile—the kind Jeong-ok associated with the elderly—appeared on her face now that she had achieved her ulterior motive of escaping the rain.

Through the open door of the Buddha hall they could see colored lanterns hanging everywhere from the ceiling. They would have been the ones displayed on Buddha's Birthday a couple of months before.

"It's the Paekchung ceremony," the woman replied without interest, having determined that the new arrivals were neither supplicants to Buddha nor regular benefactors of the temple.

"Well so it is," said Jeong-ok's mother. "That's right, it's July fifteenth." She turned to Jeong-ok, who was sitting beside her, and said loudly, as if this news had taken her by surprise, "We'll see a full moon on our way home."

The lines of rain became a driving wall of water. The runoff from the eaves bounced off the ground to form new lines in the air, leaving small grooves in the earth.

What could have drawn her here? Jeong-ok thought with a faraway look as she listened to the gong and the chanting of the sutra. The sonorous sounds penetrated the rain more clearly now. Was it love?

Jeong-ok checked her watch. The night would be well along by the time she and the boy returned to Vernal Stream after a three-hour bus ride. By then would the clouds have lifted and the moon come up?

"We're going to see a full moon," her mother said again.

Jeong-ok turned to her, wondering if she had heard correctly. Her mother was gazing absentmindedly at the rainy courtyard.

The faint smell of incense lingered in the rain. It was Paekchung, the fifteenth of July by the lunar calendar. A ceremony for the dead, a day for the departed. A full moon, a lambent night. Taking the boy on her back, Jeong-ok would walk the steep, dark road to her house in Vernal Stream, which was already the stuff of memories.

THAT BOY'S HOUSE

Park Wan-suh

Translated by **Brother Anthony of Taizé**

그 남자네 집
박완서

A critique of this short story was published in the Koreana magazine in Spring 2013 (Vol. 27 No. 1, pp. 86-87).

A younger friend who had been living in an apartment told me recently she was moving out to live in a house with a garden. I automatically replied that it sounded like a good idea, but I did not get the name of the neighborhood where she had bought a house. I seem to have fallen into the habit of not paying attention to what people say. Ever since I realized that one sign of growing old was a conspicuous decline in one's ability to remember names and numbers, my habit of listening to such things absentmindedly seems to have grown stronger. Instead, I became intensely curious about what the house and garden looked like, how many rooms it had, what the view was like. Yet that was not really what I wanted to say.

I too, several years before, had brought to an end a lengthy period of life in an apartment and moved into a house with a garden. The first night, as I lay alone in that isolated house, wondering what on earth I had come all that way in quest of, my decision seemed so pathetic that I was unable to sleep. A beautiful view, fresh air, peaceful surroundings, some degree of solitude, surely those were things I had long been dreaming of? What more could I hope for? All the time I was living in the apartment, equipped with every kind of convenience, even its value as an investment guaranteed, I had been constantly feeling that something was not right. But what exactly was it that had not been right? The way my secret, silent memories slowly lost their significance until finally they were nothing, just an empty feeling, was not the apartment's fault, and likewise the house did not breed such memories by itself. The more recently a house is built, the more it simply imitates the structure and conveniences of an apartment. Thus, one might expect to settle in without much discomfort; it ultimately depends entirely on the owner. Why was it only now that I realized that I was a helpless person who was incapable of even changing a faucet? Actually, that was the most terrifying of my anxieties on that first night in my new house.

But still, it was spring. The moment I went down into the garden the next morning, I saw lovely, delicate shoots springing up from the ground, and I seemed to hear them saying: "We're glad to see this world's light, we're happy together," so that I felt a response springing up inside myself, "I'm glad I moved here." It was an unexpected joy, and a consolation. That friend was twenty years younger than me. She was still far from reaching an age when sacrificing practical interests and convenience to gain at most a few flowers, marvel-of-Peru or rose moss, does not seem to represent any kind of loss. Perhaps it was because of those cautious misgivings that I held back from asking aggressively: "For goodness' sake, what are you hoping to find, giving up an apartment and moving to a house?" Irrespective of what I might or might not think, my friend moved and then told me about the new sights of her unfamiliar neighborhood. Since it was an old residential area mainly inhabited by respectable middle-class folk, she had been expecting a settled kind of atmosphere, but perhaps because it was close to a university, all day long she only had to look out the window and the bustling vitality of the streets meant there was never a dull moment. I asked the name of the university. She said it was Sungshin Women's University.

"Sungshin? But surely that's in Donam-dong?" I asked, slightly taken aback. "That's right," she replied. Only now the neighborhood had been divided up into several parts, each one with a different name, and she told me the new name. I knew the area like the back of my hand. I asked the exact location; it was between Sungshin Women's University and Seongbuk Police Station. The last house I lived in before I married had been located between Sungshin Girls' High School and Seongbuk Police Station. My family had moved to another neighborhood at almost the same time as I had got married, so that I had never had a chance to go back there. Even if a chance had come, I would probably have avoided it. I had left that neighborhood fifty years ago. Fifty years, that's a long time. Donam-dong is no remote locality. It's not far from the city center. In those fifty years, how many times must I have traveled along the street up the hill beyond Hyehwa-dong, passing through Miari, Gireum-dong and Suyuri. It has been a long time since the Dongdo Cinema that I used to frequent disappeared. I must have noticed it had vanished as I looked through the window of a bus or car. Squirming, twisting my head painfully to look behind, I bade a sad farewell to Jean Marais and Charles Boyer on the fuzzy black-and-white screen. Did that mean my friend had gone to live in a Korean-style house?

Since I had never once been back after leaving, I could still quite vividly recall the neighborhood as it had been then. Those tiled Joseon-style houses, dignified like an elderly lady with her hair drawn back in a bun, and suitably dilapidated. My friend said no, it was a modern two-story house, built so that the basement and upper floor could be rented out separately. There were not so many Korean-style houses left, she added, and those that remained had mostly kept nothing but the traditional tiled roofs, the interiors having been transformed into cafés, fast food places, or fashion stores. She added that since a university had been established there, it was only natural that the residential area should turn into a student neighborhood. Well, yes. Had the things I could vividly remember as having been there ever really existed? I felt sad, and relieved at the same time.

My friend set a day for me to come and see the house. On account of repairs to the house and tidying up the garden, my friend often phoned me for advice, and each time, rather than reply to her questions, I would indicate curiosity about this or that aspect of the neighborhood, which bothered her since she took it to mean I was pestering her to hold a house-warming party. I was the only guest invited and since the repairs were not completely finished she suggested we eat lunch somewhere nearby then go home for a cup of tea. She came all the way out to the Sungshin Women's University subway station to meet me. I told her that I could meet her anywhere, she only had to say where, but I was grateful that she did not listen and came all the way out.

The neighborhood I followed her into was not the old Donam-dong I had stored in my head. It stretched out, bright, sophisticated, lacking nothing, a typical university neighborhood bustling with vitality. Given the university was still relatively new, the vitality was not overflowing noisily; rather it gave the impression of classy poise, intent on self-restraint, perhaps on account of the traditional Korean tiled roofs that just occasionally struck my eye, quietly perched over shop windows decorated in the modern style. My memory flustered, trying to think whether those really were the same Joseon-style roofs. My friend had gone exploring in advance and the restaurant she had chosen served seafood stews. It was an excellent choice. Various kinds of vegetables and flavorings could be added to a basic selection of seafood according to taste, and cooked on the table; the resulting taste had intensity and depth. The price, too, was reasonable. Cheap, tasty and plentiful, it was an outstanding meal. Our table was beside a large plate-glass window, and the feeling of being in an outdoor café was not at all unpleasant. Nowadays society does everything for show, whether it be eating, dressing, earning money, or making love. In the distance, at the foot of the hill, could be seen the lofty campus of Sungshin Women's University. When I emerged from the alley where my former home used to stand, I could see Sungshin Girls' High School at just the same angle, just that far off. Had I been eating lunch on the site of my old home? I began to feel strange. When I asked this aloud, my friend suggested that we try to find the house where I used to live first, before going to her place.

I thought that it would be easy to find the house once I had found the Angam Stream. That was what we used to call the little stream that emerged in the Seongbuk Valley and flowed past our neighborhood after passing Samseon Bridge and Donam Bridge. Since the water was plentiful and clean, the local residents would head for the Angam Stream whenever they had a load of washing to be done. Alongside the stream ran a street wide enough for pedestrians and cars to pass each other, while beside the stream weeping willows dangled their branches, so that in those days, when cars were few and far between, it was sufficiently quiet and romantic for people from other neighborhoods to come and enjoy a stroll there. The Angam Stream, that pierced my mental map like a major artery, was nowhere to be found. It was invisible. What was I looking for, some kind of waterway? I should have known that it had been covered over long ago. Yet even if it had been covered, I felt that the stream and the road beside it taken together ought to have left space enough for an eight-lane highway.

When I first visited Europe, in the 1980s, and saw the River Seine, I found myself thinking: "Why, that famous River Seine is barely wider than the Angam Stream," so much had the stream of my memories seemed like a wide river. Emerging from our house, I could see the grim rear view of the Seongbuk Police Station with its wide yard, just across the stream. Our family could surely not have lived very long with the view of such a building without feeling a corresponding sense of detachment. The modern neighborhood possessed no such wide side streets, however after the covered-over stream, the next target was the police station. We found it at once. I was not the one to find it; from the spot we had been circling around my friend pointed a finger, "There it is!" It was only then that I realized we were standing midway between the Catholic church and the Sinseon bathhouse. My former home had been in the alley directly behind the bathhouse and that boy's house had been behind the Catholic church. The church and the bathhouse had both stood by the streamside road. The church must have been enlarged or rebuilt, for although it was still in the same place, its exterior looked very different, much larger, but the bathhouse was exactly as it had been in those days, right down to the name. That bathhouse had remained just as it was fifty years before, although surely fifty years was time enough for it to have turned into some kind of spa, sauna, or *jjimjilbang*. Because of that wretched bathhouse I was obliged to believe that this not-so-wide side street was the covered-over Angam Stream. The street in my mental map was not a real street, it was nothing more than the street I had been hoping to discover. In the alley behind the bathhouse, the old houses with their Korean-style roofs had not survived. Multiplex housing had invaded the area and it was impossible to even identify the exact site of our house.

We went to my friend's house, looked around, and drank tea. It indeed had a garden, though not a very big one. The previous owner had not looked after it, leaving it like an empty lot, but my friend seemed to have fallen for it. Since it stood on somewhat higher ground, it overlooked the whole neighborhood. Where would that boy's family house have been? My friend went raving on about the various kinds of trees she was planning to plant there the following spring. Moving from pine trees, silver magnolias, flowering cherries, azaleas to fruit trees such as cherry, plum and jujube, then on to perennials such as peonies, tree peonies and iris. I gazed at my friend as she went on multiplying endlessly the number of species she would cram in her palm-sized garden, but my thoughts were elsewhere. I am not sure why the thought arose, but I kept thinking that that boy's family house might still be standing.

His family moved to the area beside the Angam Stream less than a month after we moved there. I had accompanied Mother to the hardware store and as we were returning home, carrying humble items such as a bucket, a dustpan, a shovel, a rattrap and so on, we came across his family unloading their belongings. The owner of the house they were moving into greeted Mother gladly. Mother grudgingly responded with a cold expression. She was an elderly woman some ten years older than Mother, with a very bent back. Apparently she was a distant relative. Even if Mother was above her in terms of their position in the family tree, she was clearly her senior in age, and such standoffishness was not typical of Mother. Standing beside her, I was both disconcerted and amused. I knew why Mother was acting in that way. She had previously enjoyed living in ever larger houses but now, for reasons she could not explain, she found herself in circumstances where she was obliged to make do with a far smaller house. Compared to the neighborhoods where she had lived before, the houses here were much cheaper, and moreover the house we had moved into was ridiculously small for three generations to live together, what with a daughter-in-law and a grandchild "small as a nose-picking," as Mother put it. So it was only natural that Mother should feel embarrassed in front of other people. Yet at home, she was more forceful than ever. If our large family had managed to avoid becoming homeless, and owned a home, even if it was just a shack, that was all thanks to Mother.

Regardless of whether Mother was happy or not, the old lady beamed as she urged us to come in and view the house, and insisted on taking us inside. Claiming she wanted to show her house to unwilling visitors amidst the fuss and bustle of moving, she appeared to be both overkind and rather silly. A few strapping fellows were carrying bundles into the house. Some were workers, but others were sons and sons-in-law. Belongings packed for moving show plainly a family's standard of living. Mother must have been disheartened at the sight of elaborately decorated wardrobes, antique stationary chests, nicely finished étagéres and so on, while I cringed before roughly tied bundles of what looked like several thousand books. The old woman's house, too, that we toured, unable to resist her insistence, was on a different scale to the ordinary run of houses in that neighborhood. Although there were several trucks parked in front of the house, the street was wide enough for them not to be in the way of passing cars or people; the house was located in an alley leading off the main road. We could see that it was a blind alley, but it was wide and it was a space that the house had all to itself, there being no neighbors to share it with, so that it looked like an outer yard. Nor was that all. Looking toward the house, no front gate was visible; instead, as in old palaces, a stone arch could be seen. The arch opened onto the garden in front of the men's quarters; the front gate leading to the women's quarters was located at a spot where the wall attached to the stone arch made a ninety degree bend. For some reason, I was more impressed by the graceful old arch than by the awe-inspiring lofty gate with its threshold of stone. Compared with traditional houses with their ordinary tiled roofs, it looked to be in a class of its own.

One of the youths who had been unloading the furniture was lingering beside us, indicating that he wanted to be introduced, and the old woman presented him as her youngest son. He was affable and good-looking. As she gazed at her youngest with a contented smile, her face was full of wrinkles. Given the difference in their ages, it would surely have been more suitable to say he was her grandson, so that she seemed even sillier than before. The youth was dressed in working clothes but he was wearing a school cap, so I immediately recognized he was attending a high school in the same neighborhood as the girls' high school I was attending. In those days, there were more than ten middle and high schools for boys and girls crammed into the area stretching northeastward from Gwanghwa-mun, including Sinmunno, Anguk-dong, Gye-dong and Susong-dong, so that it did not strike me as some kind of strange coincidence. I felt relieved since the school he attended was considered by the kids in my school as being a not-so-special, mid-range kind of school, so I could get over my feelings of inferiority. Something similar happened again not long after-wards. On that day, since the whole house was in such disorder, we only peered at the main building from the middle gate then went out again, but the way the old woman had so kindly insisted on showing us around seemed to have stayed on Mother's mind. She was six or seven years older than Mother, but she was only some kind of distant niece on the maternal side, so that it would be alright for her to treat her like a stranger, but since she had been so kind, Mother seemed to feel that she had to return at least once, and had apparently gone bringing a gift of matches. "That family's eldest is a high official working in the main government building, the daughter-in-law is extremely courteous," she reported, with indications of being seriously jealous. Still, she did not forget to add a word or two:

"But so what? When she got married not only was her family of a lower standing, her husband was much better looking and had studied a lot, so that her older relatives worried they might not get on well together and even now she has a hard time with her old man."

"You mean that old woman even told you that?"

"Do you think I have to be told before I know? Seeing how she can't avoid getting her own hands wet when she has such a well-mannered daughter-in-law. The way she is good to others, too, has become a habit, showing how inferior she feels toward her husband and his family. I don't know why a rich man's wife lives such a miserable life, poorly dressed with hands like rakes."

I reckoned this was my self-assertive mother's way of consoling herself. Finally it fell to me to provide Mother with a sense of superiority. Once I had become a university student, I went out with her to buy shoes and we met the old lady. Mother boasted that I had been admitted to Seoul National University and we were on our way to buy some shoes. It would have been enough to say I was going to attend university, I suppose she added the name because of her pride that no university could be more prestigious than SNU. The old woman's youngest was also entering university. It was a good school, but it was not Seoul National University. At the sight of Mother's bragging, for the first time in my life I felt proud of being a good daughter, and took it as an encouragement.

When it was time for school, the peaceful, beautiful street leading from Wonnam-dong to Anguk-dong used to be filled with school children, boys and girls, in their uniforms. If I found the streets less crowded than usual, that meant I might be late and I would start to run. The school I attended was famous for the way the principal would keep watch at the gate himself and scold any students who arrived late. Since I was particularly interested in the students from the school the youngest boy of the stone-arched house was attending, our eyes met several times along the way to school. But I would rapidly look away, without seeing if he had recognized me or not. It was not that I was being especially good or sly; in those days such things were taboo. On learning that we had both entered university, the first thought that came to me was a premonition of thrilling freedom, since we would no longer have to act in that way if we met. I was such an innocent that my heart would race when I only imagined the freedom of being able to go to the movies without tucking in the white collar of my uniform, so it was no unusual emotion.

Repairs to my friend's house were far from complete. Once an aluminum sash had been fixed to the rear veranda, a truck arrived bringing topsoil for the garden. As I was about to take my leave amid all the confusion, she came after me, insisting that she would accompany me as far as the subway station. Perhaps because the search for our old house had shown just how poor my sense of direction was, she treated me as a helplessly impractical senior who would never be able find the subway alone. As I walked along I kept looking around and trying to refuse help until at last I mentioned that boy's family house. The harder you try to hide or cut short any talk about something involving a boy and a girl, not a Mr. Kim and a Miss Lee, the more you arouse the other person's curiosity. With the face of a girl just beginning to enjoy love stories, my friend became my guide. She reckoned that since we knew now where my old house had stood, it should not be difficult to find that boy's house if we started from there. His house had been behind the Catholic church, across the concrete bridge beside the Seongbuk Police Station, beside the main road. Although the house had been a step or two off a side street, the main road had run alongside the outer garden. There could be no hope that such a spacious property would still be a family residence in such an increasingly thriving university district. Of course, the kind of family home I was thinking of was a two- or three-story Western-style building such as the one my friend had moved into, not an old Korean-style mansion. Contrary to my expectations, aloof from the arrogant currents of time, that house had remained intact, an old-style house with a tiled roof. Perhaps because the other houses, their main gates shunning the main street, had all been transformed into four- or five-story buildings, the house which had formerly looked more impressive for being a step or two further back now looked sunken. The space in front, which had formerly opened onto the main street, was now closed off by an iron gate; that was the only difference. The gate was firmly shut. Because of the gate, the old house behind seemed to have opted for seclusion, surrounded by modern buildings on both sides but refusing all contact with them. From breast height, the iron gate was composed of bars you could look through, but trees had grown so densely inside that the stone arch could barely be seen. The trees must originally have been planted so as to leave room at least for someone to pass between them, but the branches had spread into such a dense tangle that there was not even space to peer through.

The thought that houses too might have a kind of soul made my heart shudder as though touched by a sliver of ice. The house with a stone arch once had an abundance of trees and flowering plants, not only around the men's quarters but in the main courtyard too. At the back of the house there was a cellar for storing oleanders, pomegranates, plantains and suchlike, plants that could not survive the winter outdoors. In May, when the lilac in the garden of the men's quarters was in full bloom and came over the wall, people passing in the street would all look above the arch, flare their noses, then slow down or stop, as if hoping the fragrance might permeate their clothes or bodies. I climbed up onto the stone base of the iron gate, raised myself to my full height and peered inside, but apart from confirming that there was indeed an authentic traditional tiled roof, there was nothing else I could recognize. Traditional roofs take a lot of work. In addition, nowadays it has become very hard to find good tilers. Even before, the pay for a tiler was three times that for a plasterer. It is easy to end up with someone who has not been properly trained, an unskilled worker who believes all the rumors about the rate of pay. When you see the wretched, dilapidated state of the roofs of the old Korean houses that have happened to survive among the city's forest of high-rise buildings, you soon realize what irresponsible nonsense all this fuss about preserving traditional *hanok* houses really is. The rows of concave tiles on that house's roof were so even and smooth that it seemed they must have been overhauled almost every year. If a homeowner did not skimp on the money and effort needed for such troublesome upkeep, it would never be someone obliged to stay living there because they could not sell the house, it would be someone wealthy who loved such old houses. I was moved and happy that boy's old house had found such an owner.

The boy's family had left the house soon after I left to get married, so that in the time since then the legal ownership might have changed as many as ten times. Yet still, the way trees had become so thick in the outer yard that I could not so much as peek through the stone arch left me feeling sad. The trees had dense, glossy leaves like spindle trees, only taller. When I wondered aloud what kind of trees they were, my friend immediately said they were Bodhi trees. She knew all about the names of trees. And not only trees; I knew that there were times when she would not be able to simply pass by a flower whose name she did not know, but would insist on finding out its name. If she said they were Bodhi trees, that was surely right. Only they were nothing like the Bodhi trees I knew. I had seen a Bodhi tree just once. When I was much younger than I am now, I had taken a trip through a sultry region steeped in Hindu culture and our bus had stopped for a break in a remote village. The spot chosen to shelter from the scorching sun by the group of some twenty tourists, as if by common accord, was in the shade of a Bodhi tree. The towering tree, more than thirty meters high, had a gnarled, twisted trunk that went soaring up without a single sprig of leaves then spread its plentiful foliage like an umbrella far above. Our guide told us that it was a Bodhi tree. There was no reason to suppose it was the same tree as that beneath which the Buddha had attained his awakening, but this tree looked so merciful and majestic that it was easy to understand why it had been called a Bodhi tree. Perhaps that is what is meant by sacred. The impression I received that day had been so powerful that I had never once thought that there might be Bodhi trees in Korea. Our country does not have the climate for such gigantic trees to grow. So what about the linden tree celebrated by Müller? But surely those trees growing densely in the outer yard and blocking my view of the stone arch were too petty to dream sweet dreams under? Those trees were in no way similar to either of the two different images I harbored, the Bodhi tree or *Lindenbaum*. Yet I did not want to let go of the name "Bodhi tree" that my friend had produced so promptly. Perhaps the thought that a house has a soul had not been not a sliver of ice but embers instead?

Once back home, I looked it up in an illustrated guidebook. It was a comprehensive listing of the trees growing wild in Korea and the Bodhi tree was there. Yet although I looked at the photo and read the simple commentary, there was not enough to enable me to decide whether those were Bodhi trees or not. Still, I firmly consigned to memory the explanation that in autumn its globular fruit, some six to eight millimeters in diameter, took on a red color. One day, when the gingko trees along Sejongno in the city center had suddenly erupted madly in pure gold, the purest yellow that they had been storing up deep inside themselves, I took Line 5 on the subway, but instead of going home I changed to Line 4 at Dongdaemun Stadium. The bagful of books I had bought at Kyobo Bookstore was really heavy but I had no choice. I got off at Sungshin Women's University Station. There was no question of my having no sense of direction. I headed straight for that boy's family home. Being alone, I had no need to hide anything. The iron gate was tightly closed as before. They were listed as being deciduous but those dense green leaves had merely lost a little of their gloss, while still perversely forming a screen between me and the stone arch. However, among the leaves bunches of three or four red berries were dangling from the jagged forked branches. Perhaps in the summer they had been the same color as the leaves, so that I had not noticed them. How long would it take for these trees to grow high enough for there to be room to dream sweet dreams in their shade? Some fifty years? Timewise, I went in the opposite direction to the Bodhi trees and slipped into an illusion that a young person as lovely as jade dreamt sweet dreams in that luxuriant shade fifty years ago.

The next time I met that boy, there were nothing but women and children left in our house. I hated being lumped together with "women and children" but gradually accepted it. This was what our family had become once the war had swept over us. The men, passing via Seongbuk Police Station, were no longer of this world. The war had been on for over a year, but still the front line kept advancing and retreating just a few miles to the north of Seoul, with the people in Seoul who had not managed to flee all nothing but paupers. Since everyone was poor, real paupers were quite rare. The working people were all women. It was not only our family; it seemed that women and children were the only people left in the city.

Having heard that you could earn the price of side dishes by picking radish tops at Ttukseom and selling them, I set off together with my sister-in-law at dawn. If you followed the Angam Stream on and on, endlessly southward, the stream vanishing here, then reappearing there, you reached Salgoji Bridge and Salgoji Meadows. Depending on how much we paid, the owner of the perfectly square field allowed us to pick radish tops and carry them away. Thus far we had done like the other folk; from there on we could not do like the others. The others clamored to be given more; we held back, asking if we could not be given less. Because the bundles of radish tops were so enormous, we would often drop them to the ground along our way back home. By the time we reached home it was getting dark. The others had already bought rice and side dishes with what they had earned by selling their radish tops and were already cooking their evening meal. Even if we had time to sell ours, the bundles had suffered so much from constantly falling to the ground that they had lost their value.

After that I found a job on the U.S. military base. Even before, a woman from the neighborhood who did cleaning work on the base and who felt sorry for us had said she would introduce me, but that had made Mother jump, declaring that she would rather starve than see me doing such work, and I was not allowed to go. The woman had actually said that there would be something better than cleaning for a university student like me, but Mother seemed to understand that to mean there was a vacancy for a whore. Either because the failure of our radish top gathering was a shock to her, or because hunger overcame her scruples, Mother finally allowed herself to be persuaded, as if surrendering, and I was given a simple job on the base. That solved the problem of food and housing but poverty grew increasingly sordid as the days passed, because the family felt humiliated at being fed and housed with money earned by a daughter working for the U.S. army.

That winter I met the boy again on a tram as I was leaving work. He looked glad to see me. He addressed me without hesitation as "*Nuna*," elder sister, which seemed odd. I felt at ease, and at the same time sad. It was late and the tram was almost empty, but while we were there we could do little more than express our extreme pleasure at meeting like that. Alighting at the terminus, we entered a dimly lit bakery. It was a poky little store selling things like homemade donuts and steamed buns. Having ordered some steamed buns that gave off a sour smell of *makeolli*, I began by asking why he had called me "*Nuna*." The reason was simple, he said. Since we had begun university in the same year, we should be the same age, but he had begun primary school when he was only seven, so he was almost sure he must be a year younger. He was right, it was a plausible way of reckoning. He was wearing military uniform. It was not the shabby uniform ordinary privates used to wear: above sharply creased blue serge trousers such as American officers wore, and brightly polished boots, he was wearing a fur-lined parka. It was a time when, as I was working on the base, I was longing to make the acquaintance of, if not a U.S. officer, at least a Korean officer. In wartime, an officer in a smart uniform symbolized power, like a knight mounted on a white charger. It did not even have to be an officer. Any young man with guaranteed status would be a gift from the gods, I felt. Before we had even started on the buns he asked the shopkeeper to wrap them and suggested we leave. He said he knew a streetside cart-bar that was okay. Then why had he not suggested going there to begin with? I was not happy with his inconsistency but since he was a gift from the gods I did not want to lose him. I followed him one tram stop back to Samseon Bridge. There were lights beside the stream. They came from lamps whose pallid glare made faces look ghostly. I did not mind the smell of carbide. It was even plainer than the bun shop yet, oddly, it was not at all seedy. Later I learned that the boy was especially averse to seedy places. Of course, nobody really likes them, but he had an immediate physiological reaction to them, like someone eccentric who cannot stand a certain smell.

In the tent-covered bar that evening I saw for the first time a nine-hole briquette stove. On a stove where powerful flames were rising from every hole of a coal briquette perched an iron cauldron with *odeng* broth aboil.

The aproned man in charge welcomed us nonchalantly. Putting into china bowls egg and tempura, chunks of radish, fried tofu and some kind of meaty gristle that he added a skewerful of together with *odeng*, he poured on boiling hot broth. The broth, the things on the skewer, even the eggs, were all a dark soy-sauce color. Yet the taste was strong and somewhat sweet. The owner said nothing, as if struck dumb, and seemed uninterested in us.

"Has anyone in your family been wounded in the fighting? We only have women and children left…."

I spoke quickly, before he could ask.

"Only Mother and I are left…."

"Really? In that big house? How many were you before?"

"Seven. Mother, Father, my older brother, his wife and their two children."

"That's terrible. You mean even the children are dead? Yet you weren't bombed…."

"Who said they were dead? They went North. Brother was a leftist, you see."

"We heard he was a high official in the government; Mother was jealous. So even people like that can turn into leftists!"

"High official? Brother was generally recognized to have a brilliant mind; he could probably hold a post like that in the North."

"Then what about you? Where do you stand?"

I simply could not put together the family of a defector deserving persecution and his slick military uniform, so I questioned him nervously. When it came to the suffering, humiliation and surveillance the family of a so-called commie had to endure, I had experienced it until I was sick of it. It just went to show that there are no gifts from the gods anywhere. My face fell with bitter disappointment. He said nothing in reply but started to cautiously gnaw at the tendon-like meat on the skewer, slowly, like an old man. His jaw movements were thorough and concentrated, as though he was determined not to miss anything of the faint flavor of the meat hidden within. Yet without the least sign of greed. Once he had completely chewed and swallowed everything, he addressed the owner: "Hey, fellow, the gristle I ate last time at least smelt like a boiled Yankee army boot; not this, though. Would it be too much to ask you to give us one of your old shoes from under the floor with a bit of a stench to it?"

"Here, that's enough of that. Soon you'll be asking me to steal my mother's rubber slippers and serve them boiled." The two men sniggered. Their laughs harmonized well together. I grew tense as I listened to them exchanging banter. Unexpectedly, they began to discuss a book they were currently reading. They seemed to be close enough to lend each other books. I found myself thinking foolishly that they were conscious of my presence and were making fun of me. He thrust some money toward the owner and stood up. When he tried to give him his change he waved his hands and told him to buy his mother some rubber slippers.

"Valiant disabled veteran, sir! I know it is my duty as a citizen to serve strong beef bone broth, but funds are way down below floor level! I'm very, very sorry."

The owner saw us off, scratching his head without the least indication of being sorry shown on his face. The moment we were outside, I questioned him:

"Why, he called you a disabled soldier. What does that mean? Your four limbs all look intact. Have you been lying to that simple fellow? Who are you, really? Come on, speak up, quickly!"

He replied in a low voice. We walked from Samseon Bridge along the Angam Stream, past the bathhouse, up the alley and by the time we reached my house he had finished, as though it had been made to match that distance. It was not far. So his tale was terse and condensed.

When the North Korean army entered Seoul in the summer, for some reason his older brother had not been purged and had continued in his regular job. But since a person only really has his two legs, it is obvious that he cannot count on anything more than them, so when the Communist army retreated at the end of three months, he went North with them. At first he had gone alone, leaving his wife, children and elderly parents behind. But the world was turned upside down again that winter, and when the Communists occupied Seoul a second time, his brother had turned up, intent on taking his family with him. His wife and children were ready to follow him without a word but for his parents it was different. The reason was that, after the Communists retreated and Seoul was liberated, their younger son had been drafted into the South Korean army. And because their son was in the Southern army, the family had so far been spared much of the hardship inflicted on the families of those who had gone North. So the parents were confronted with an insoluble dilemma. Finally the elderly parents had decided to separate. The father would go North with the elder son and his family while the mother decided to stay behind and wait for her younger son the soldier. For that reason, on returning home after he had been wounded in the thigh and received an honorable discharge he found that his elderly mother was left alone in that large house. In the meantime she had turned into an old woman and far from embracing her in tears, he abused her terribly, asking what devotion she had expected to receive, waiting for him like that. The very thought of how free he would be without her took his very breath away so that even now, he said, he was constantly berating her.

Such things happened in the turmoil as the world turned upside down, righted itself, then in a flash turned upside down again and again, and that was what had happened in his family. When a whole nation is writhing in agony, how many ordinary citizens can hope to escape unscathed? So we felt no sympathy for each other. The sufferings we endured were our daily bread, like kimchi and rice. If there was a family that remained intact, where nobody had died or been hurt, people would have found their self-satisfaction so intolerable that they might even have plotted to kidnap their only son. That night I could not get to sleep. The carbide lamplight shimmered pale over his beautiful face, at once aloof and melancholy, his strong body still perceptible even through the thick parka; I sensed that a dangerous breeze had blown over me. We had not expressed mutual feelings or anything like that, but did we not sense a foreboding of similar misfortunes? Like a young girl walking down a street who encounters a strong gust of wind that sends her skirt billowing upward, I felt at the same time a sudden surge of yearning and a burst of shame making me want to pull down my skirt quickly and squat on the ground. In order to economize firewood, our whole family slept together in the main bedroom. I could hear the peaceful breathing of our surviving family, two widows and two small children, all sound asleep. Surely relief at having reached a level where things could get no worse could not coexist with peace. Still, peace is so much more sacred than the survivor's feeling of sorrow. Thus I confronted the yearning for danger that whirled within me.

Almost every day he was waiting for me when I came off the base. The people working there were a varied lot, ranging from illiterate to university graduates, but they were all people with some kind of guilty secret. Many were draft dodgers. It was not officially approved but they could wear a military uniform and received an illegible identity card, so if they were determined they could shout and bluster their way into avoiding inspection. Those grubby, unsavory men wanted to know everything about the smartly uniformed, healthy and brash looking young man. I ought not to have said he was a close relative, like a younger brother. Nobody believed me. As a disabled soldier with all his limbs intact, he was an object of envy. Think what you like; we enjoyed such things. They increased our happiness. Just as silk dresses and jewelry are meaningless unless people feel jealous at the sight of them, the same is true of a boyfriend who does not inspire envy. He was handsome, so the more I saw of him the more I wanted to become pretty. I could feel the sap rising inside my body. He said I was like a jewel. That was a compliment better suited to a younger sister than a girlfriend. It was not very sexy, but I came to like the expression. Jewel-like eyes, jewel-like tears, jewel-like dew, jewel-like waves… no matter where you added it, the word glistened.

That winter was the most jewel-like winter in my life. Apart from the banks of the Angam Stream, there were not many places where lovers could go. Once we entered university and could get to know the places that had been forbidden while we were in high school, the war broke out and Seoul lay in ruins. Fortunately there were cinemas that survived. Wartime cinemas had no heating. He would sit hunched up beside me and slip his fur-lined gloves, turned inside out, beneath my feet. If you just turn up the palm of a glove, the five fingers stay crumpled up inside and if you fit them over the tips of your toes even the coldest of feet will thaw and start to grow warm. I wonder how he came by such a wonderful idea. It killed two birds with one stone. Not only did my frozen toes keep warm, it allowed me to feel content at being so cherished. Since we mainly watched movies at the Jungang Theater, we could easily walk to Myeong-dong. The buildings along Jongno were all in ruins and almost all the inhabitants had left Seoul, so there were few houses still occupied on the residential streets; it was wartime and the silvery lights of Myeong-dong were unreal. We savored freedom in light, like moths. We found a wonderful regular café, discovered an expensive bakery, came to know the delight of buying cute, unnecessary accessories in boutiques. Apart from such places, in Myeong-dong there were also imposing, showy jewelry stores where the main customers were high-class whores keeping company with U.S. officers. In their spacious recesses there were dim corners decorated like parlors so even from outside we could clearly see voluptuously made-up customers elegantly sitting cross-legged like Western film stars, basking in the shop owner's flattery. Since there was no sign of any customers merely standing there looking around, we did not dare to venture inside. Instead, all the jewels that I laid eyes on, standing outside glued to the window, became mine at some later time. I liked his wild promises better than the jewels themselves. Even without any desire beyond ogling expensive jewelry, dating cost a lot of money. He was unemployed, unable to earn a penny, and although I was earning, I had a family of five to support. Our dating practices did not go so far as to despise the sanctity of family support. In those days, disabled veterans had no pension. His easiest source of money was his old mother. He had berated her, saying she should have gone North with her elder son and her husband, and not expect any devotion from him for having waited, and he kept tormenting her. He would have had a hard time surviving if it had not been for her ingrained habit of never serving him rice without side dishes to go with it, yet he did not realize it was more than he deserved.

He kept pestering her for pocket money. I learned from my mother that she used to take clothes out to sell at the market, and even walk around with a basket perched on her head hawking vegetables. She was bent almost double, far more than when they had moved into the house, and Mother said it was amazing to see her balance a heavy load on her head then spring to her feet and start walking. My mother would also sometimes take things to the market to barter. Even though Seoul seemed to be empty, if you went to the local markets they were swarming with people. In such places brimming with vitality, there was no distinction between those buying and those selling. Everyone kept spreading things out, selling them, then buying what they needed. Since the owners of the market stores had mostly fled South, there were only a few shops open. Fierce life-or-death bargaining matches took place everywhere, beneath the eaves of the closed stores or in the market alleys. After Mother had met that boy's mother and helped her lift a load onto her head, her expression was bitter and blank for a time. She seemed to be able to feel pity for her now, seeing her as a mother whose pride had been wounded, instead of as the wife of a rich man with a successful son. However, our mother's pity was only a comfort to herself, it was not applicable to that elderly mother. On several occasions, when her son was being cruel to her, I saw that old woman with her bent back, looking far older than she really was, enjoying herself as if she were watching her last-born performing cute tricks. As I watched her smile at her son, wrinkles spreading like ripples from the corners of her puckered lips, even after he had taken all she had in her purse, I recognized that the person who should be pitied was my mother. By simply coming back alive her son had completely fulfilled his filial duty. Perhaps for that reason, I did not tell him to stop cruelly exploiting his old mother, even though I disapproved of it.

Still, if he needed more than just pocket money, he would make an expedition to Busan, saying he was adapting to circumstances. Between him and his elder brother there were two sisters, one of whom was a doctor. Since she had fled Seoul and reached Busan, where she had found work in a large hospital and was able to earn a regular income, she was his main source of cash. That sister was useful to him in many ways. If his mother would not give him enough money, he would threaten to go down to Busan and beg his sister, then she would sell some precious antique to raise money. His extremely refined mother disliked intensely the way her son troubled her married daughter. But her kind-hearted daughter, wishing to help with her mother's living expenses, would summon her brother down to Busan. On days when he was in Busan, I used to feel lonesome and morose, so I would stay in bed, sobbing quietly in secret. It made no difference even if the people in the market raised the roof with their noise, without him Seoul was just empty. It was absolutely intolerable that the last surviving couple should be separated. Even though I told myself to endure that fleeting meaninglessness, that feeling of emptiness for just one more day, I waited for him so desperately, so passionately, that I used to think that death would be preferable. He never once came back later than the day he promised to return, but every time he came back he had to take his punishment. A greater consolation than usual, that meant enjoying extravagant fun that was beyond his means in some brightly lit spot. So I cannot say that I never encouraged him to shamelessly exploit his mother and sister. And my demands for extravagant fun beyond his means were not limited to material things. He not only enjoyed reading poetry, he had memorized a number of passages as well. Walking down unlit alleys, mile after mile, or in the tent-bar by Samseon Bridge, on a spot illuminated by the pallid blue carbide lamplight like stage lighting, he would recite poems by Jeong Ji-yong or Han Ha-un in a low, intense voice. He had memorized poems by a lot of other poets, but those two were the only ones whose poems I recognized on hearing them. Since he only performed in that uncalled-for manner when there were no other customers, the bar owner used to listen in silence. After hearing everything, I would thank him, saying I felt I had been enjoying some huge luxury. Such words were to him higher praise than any applause. If poetry was a luxury for us, might not the material luxuries we enjoyed together also be poetry? What enabled us to endure those grim, poverty-stricken, chaotic times was neither austerity nor resentment nor ideology; it was luxury. It was poetry.

Ultimately, though, the luxury that cost least of all was to be found in the men's quarters of his house. The building, adjacent to the stone arch, was built in an L shape; the main house was likewise constructed in an L shape and if the two had been built close together the result would have been a square; but they were not, they were separated by a considerable space and were therefore independent of each other. Not only did the men's quarters have its own yard, it had the stone arch so that it was possible to communicate with the outside world without using the main gate. Looking onto the yard, with a wooden *toenmaru* running along its entire length, the main room had been a study shared by his father and elder brother; on the side running toward the inner quarters was a smaller room where he said his brother had pursued his hobby alone, away from his wife and children. His hobby seemed to have been listening to music. The room contained a record player, a rare object in those days, and two walls were packed to the ceiling with records. My ears were not at all accustomed to classical music. For that reason I harbored a sense of inferiority toward him, while he, sensing that, tried hard to be especially kind. But when he played Beethoven's *Ninth Symphony*, to see if it might appeal to me, I exclaimed that it was too noisy, it would wake his mother, and turned down the volume, at which he looked incredulous. Even so he did not give up. He began to play songs that I had been accustomed to hearing during music classes in school, such as *Heiden-röslein*, *Largo* and *Lindenbaum*. He treated the records with extreme care, seeming to caress them. While one record was playing he would choose the next, breathe on it and wipe it with a small brush. That brush was not originally designed for cleaning records, it might have been used for applying makeup. It was a soft, delicate brush that reminded me of a Western woman's eyelashes. I used to feel that if I touched that brush, seemingly soft yet stiff, an electric current might shock me. It was perhaps on account of his skillful yet sensitive fingers, making it impossible to decide if he did it because he wanted to stroke the records or to remove the dust. As he listened, he would quietly hum in a sensuous manner as if caressing the rich voice of some foreign tenor whose name I had no need to know. I could never decide if the brush was the humming or if the humming was the brush. As sense of touch and sense of hearing blended together, the result was a moment of exquisite intoxication. The record he used to play most frequently was *Lindenbaum*. The lyrics were a poem printed in the textbook we had studied during German class in the last year of high school. "*Am Brunnen vor dem Tore, Da steht ein Lindenbaum: Ich träumt' in seinem Schatten, So manchen süßen Traum*"—as I listened to him humming along with those words, I felt as though every last hair on my body was standing on end. How far have we come from those days? Did we really ever have such days? Where am I now? It was a kind of crisis consciousness. Once May came, the garden erupted in blooming profusion. I had not realized there were so many kinds of flowering trees and plants. In addition to the intensely fragrant white lilac and the purple iris, flame-like azaleas, sensuously scented oleanders, pomegranate flowers like the lamps in the red-light district, breathless gardenias, all flung their blossoms wildly and passionately as if flirting with abandon. Since the garden had only been planted after they moved in, he said that for him too it was the first time to see such a fine display of flowers. The excess of irrepressible energy that brought all those flowers into full bloom seemed to shake loose the foundation stones and the gates until the ancient house was rolling like a drifting boat. We sensed a premonition of crisis so strong we longed to embrace each other. Luxuries costing nothing are so dangerous.

Once the war was over, my family urged me to marry. I met men, examined qualifications, met a suitable man, got engaged, had wedding invitations printed. For me that was a natural order of things, like graduating from one school and moving up into a higher level. The first time I told him was when I gave him his invitation. His face expressed incredulity, disbelief, and he suddenly began to sob violently. He had been busy recently. The government had come back to Seoul, his sisters had returned too, if house prices were rising they meant to sell, so the house was put on the market, and so on; he seemed to think all this had happened while he had been so busy there had been no time to bother about a girlfriend. Yet it had been in the cards from the start. I wept with him. Because parting is sad. There was nothing false about my tears. But at graduation ceremonies, no matter how bitterly children may cry, it's never because they want to stay in school.

The moment I realized there could be no doubt about those leafy trees in the outer yard of his house being Bodhi trees, I walked away as if fleeing. But I could not go far and kept walking around the neighborhood that was centered on the now underground Angam Stream. It was some ten years ago that I heard he had died. We had never met again. Just as he was for me an eternally beautiful youth, I might have been for him an eternally jewel-like girl. At the time we had been blind followers of Platonic love. We had embraced it simply out of fear of pregnancy. I smelt a coal briquette burning somewhere. After the war, coal briquettes spread quickly and it is no exaggeration to say that for me married life had been a story of endless struggles with coal briquettes. But the smell drifting near was not that stale odor, rather it was a smell of longing, mixed with a whiff of carbide lamp. I relaxed my stride and went floating along, guided by the smell. Under the eaves in front of a store bearing a sign "Briquette Galbi" a series of briquette firepots were lined up waiting to be kindled. Retro fashion had finally got as far as coal briquette stoves, apparently. The interior looked dark. I opened the door, made of planks to resemble the front gate of an old-style house, and went inside. A man sweeping the floor informed me that they did not open until five. There was no sign of a carbide lamp anywhere. I really just wanted to sit down somewhere and rest but the man doing the sweeping looked so unenthusiastic that I said nothing more and went out again. The neighborhood's gingko trees, their color just as beautiful as those on Sejongno, were lightly shedding their leaves. I longed for coziness. And for warmth. I pushed open the door of a brightly lit coffee shop and sat down near the window. Seen from inside, the street with its falling leaves was like a scene from an animated movie, perhaps because of the cheerful, carefree movements of the young people passing by. The distance separating me from them was not just a matter of age, we were two species as remote from one another as East and West.

Occasionally I used to hear reports about him, not very bright ones, and I would feel ill at ease. Why had things turned out as they did back then? Thinking about it in retrospect, I loathed myself, my temperament, too quick to make decisions, for falling out of love with him as though it was someone else's affair. Some time ago, watching a program on the National Geographic TV channel, I felt as though I had found the solution to something I had long been wondering about. Perhaps I had been wanting to find an answer for so long, not that it really was the right answer. The program showed how birds go about getting a mate. Everyone knows how males usually try hard to woo females by song, gestures, display, but the most interesting was a bird that wooed females by building a nest. That was the first time I had heard of such a bird. The males would snap off strong branches with bright green leaves, build a sturdy, square home, fashion an arched door to come and go by, even adorn the interior with sprigs of red or yellow flowers. Each female would inspect the various nests and then choose the one that pleased her best, and mating would occur.

Right, and in those days I was bird-brained.

It was the right answer, and it struck me like a thunderbolt. With no thought of saying small would be fine, I wanted to hatch cute chicks and live in a solid, safe house. His house, like my family's house, leaked on all sides, was cracked and would soon collapse. The houses were wrecks, where chicks could never be hatched; for the sake of my still unborn chicks, I had no alternative but to reject such a house.

I began to feel uncomfortable sitting there. It was not a place for me. The tearoom, that also served snacks, was full and some young folk, mostly couples, cast longing glances at the empty seats at my table before going out again. The owner sent daggers in my direction. The Briquette Galbi place must have opened by now. Vivid before my eyes I saw an elderly person slowly walking past it, nostalgic for the smell of coal briquettes and carbide lamps. Who could it be? That melancholy old person with nothing but memories left to hold onto.

Reluctantly I stood up. The young couples sitting close together holding hands cared nothing if one elderly person came in or went out, but I felt embarrassed as I left, as though they were somehow mocking my obscene chastity in those days. The whole world is a mat spread out for those young folk to enjoy themselves on; so where should I go? Let them squander their youth, then. Squandering when the blood runs hot is no sin, it's a virtue. Saving it up, unable to squander it, does not mean it will always be yours. I comforted my sulking heart before those young people.

THE STORYTELLER'S TALE

Lee Seung-U

Translated by **Brother Anthony of Taizé**

전기수 이야기
이승우

A critique of this short story was published in the Koreana magazine in Fall 2010 (Vol. 24 No. 3 pp. 81-83).

© Cha Jae-ok

W hat happens is always the same, or at least similar. Such is life. In what ways is someone different really different? In those days, carefully scrutinizing some five free magazines and two free newspapers, circling or underlining things then phoning to check whether the information published there was correct, was my main daily job. Not an ideal job, for sure, but it's tough to find a job that suits you. A series of experiences soon taught me that the more enticing something looks at first glance, the more careful you should be. Most available jobs were positions as salesmen and low-level salesclerks who were obliged to get rid of hard-to-sell products using whatever feeble methods they could find. For example, you have to ignore any ad that promises five million won a month. Likewise anything inviting applications as director-general or joint investor. Mornings I would spend operating the vacuum cleaner and the washing machine; I don't know where all the dust comes from, despite sweeping and dusting every day, and since you can't spend a whole day like that, in the afternoon I was obliged to go shopping for something to eat that evening. My wife usually came in after seven. Twice a week on average she would work overtime. On those days she came home after midnight, usually stinking of drink, and out of some kind of mean-spiritedness she never warned me so I could make less effort preparing supper. Perhaps she never told me because I never asked, that's true, but I had no way of knowing if that was the real reason why she never told me. Just like most working men who come home in the evening after a day at work, I would relax, after a day spent bustling about at home, and watch television. My evening hours were rich and diversified like a well-filled meal table, with dramas and news and comedy shows. I sometimes got the impression that I spent the whole day washing, cleaning and cooking food in preparation for the evening's viewing.

That kind of daily routine can be a bit boring, but once you get used to it, you can create a sort of rhythm in the monotony—by reading the magazines in a certain order, for example, or deciding just when to go shopping—once you have learned how to quietly enjoy such things. If I spend several hours with my eyes fixed on the small print of the magazines, I vaguely begin to sense that my mind has been tamed and is moving automatically; at such times I feel a bit befuddled, rather like after taking some strong cold medication, and my nerves gradually relax. I long to let my consciousness go slipping away stealthily; a bit odd, at least, not too bad, I reckon. I might say it's as though, while things are being used, they draw the user into their own order. Strange, isn't it? I lived like that for fifteen months. What does that figure of fifteen suggest? Do you wonder? You can guess, I reckon, you'd probably be right. It means that until fifteen months ago I too used to go out to work. It's no simple matter, losing your job, as anyone knows who's been through it. You may pretend it doesn't matter, explain one way or another why it doesn't matter, but in the end you can't say it doesn't. And even if you do, so what? A sentimental poet of the 1950s once said: "Human life is not lonely, and it's as vulgar as a magazine cover." I think he also realized that life isn't vulgar because it's like a magazine cover, but rather that a magazine cover is vulgar because it's like life. I have just begun to understand that a little… that life in the midst of loneliness can never be vulgar. Just as a magazine cover cannot be lonely, so life cannot not be vulgar.

I grew accustomed to it, and it quickly became part of my daily life, but then something happened, something that obliged me to interrupt my dull-as-ditchwater routine. I'm going to tell you about it, so just listen. It must have been about three in the afternoon. A phone call suddenly came from my wife, who had gone out early that morning. By that time my nerves had grown quite flabby, dulled by the words in the magazines. A woman's voice said I must come out quickly, at once. I'm sorry to say that at first I did not recognize it as my wife's voice. I reckoned it was either a wrong number or a crank call, and quietly hung up without saying a word. It was a method my wife had taught me. If you're home during the daytime, as anyone with experience knows, you get all kinds of odd telephones calls. The most common is from real estate agencies, saying they have reliable news of a redevelopment area in which you should invest. Sometimes a youthful sounding woman's voice says she wants to be your sweetheart. Nowadays telephone companies keep calling, insisting I should transfer my number. My wife recommended that if I received any such calls I should say nothing and simply replace the receiver quietly. Among her friends there were people who had replied in the wrong way, and after that had been pestered day and night until they changed their phone number or even moved house. It was not so much on account of my wife's advice, more so that I did not want the ordered, dull routine of my daily life to be disturbed that I tended to hang up immediately on any caller I did not recognize. That was usually the end of the matter. But this time it was different. The telephone rang again. I thought that the same person as before had dialed the same wrong number or was playing the same game and just let it ring while I concentrated on scrutinizing the innumerable, amazingly simple combinations of words in the magazines spread out over the floor. But the phone did not seem inclined to stop as it normally did, rather it seemed to be becoming more insistent. Thinking that it sounded like the cicadas whose cries made midsummer days feel even hotter and more irksome, I moved lazily and brought the receiver to my ear. It's rather childish but I was about to whisper in a low voice, "This is the crematorium." But even before the receiver had reached my ear, the same voice as before came shooting out like bullets flying: "What are you doing? Why did you hang up without saying anything?" The voice was so determined and full of conviction that I abandoned the joke I had prepared. I could not simply put the phone down again, either. I racked my brains, wondering who on earth this woman might be, with her rather rapid, husky, nervy voice. It was no good, I could not put a face to it. I had no choice but to cautiously ask who she was. "You mean you don't recognize the voice of the wife you share a house with? For goodness' sake!" Now it sounded like her voice. "Is that you, dear?" I asked in a slightly dispirited voice. She continued with her barrage: "How could you possibly forget the voice of your own wife? I only went out this morning! For heaven's sake, it's living proof of how rarely you think of me; really, it's too bad." I cannot really say if I rarely think of her or not, but I could not agree that the act of failing to instantly recognize her voice on the phone was in itself living proof of how rarely I thought of her. If you're going to quibble, it wasn't even my fault. In all that time she had never once phoned me during the daytime hours I spent at home, so from the start she was eliminated from the list of people who might possibly be calling. Using a tone suggesting that she would have a lot more to say about the topic but since the matter was urgent she was putting that off for later, she urged me to come out at once. I did not know what was the matter, but it seemed to be urgent. In a slightly intimidated voice I asked, "Where? Why?" "Where? My office, of course. No, wait, there's no need for you to come here, you can go straight there. Note down the address." What was she talking about, I asked, annoyed on seeing the tidy order of my dull-as-ditchwater daily life beginning to unravel. "Look, it's a very important client of ours. We have to keep him happy. The usual narrator's sick. She still meant to come out but she really can't, she's got a raging fever, she says. Taking medicine has had no effect. There's a really bad cold going around, you know. None of the other narrators are available. I would go if I could but I have an appointment at the same time. I've arranged to meet the person in charge of Silvertown, we might be going to sign the contract, I can't not go. Anyway, you'll have to take over as narrator just for today. It's not difficult. I'll send you the materials in a file, together with the customer profile and a map. Open your email now. There's still an hour and a half, so you can do it if you hurry. You'll have to dress neatly. You'd best wear a suit with a tie. Comb your hair and shave, too. Okay?"

My wife's declaration that she was going to start working came some three years after she began attending lectures on writing fiction organized by a literary association, and at that time I had been loafing around for fifteen months after losing my job overnight when the team I was in was dismantled during a restructuring at the office. It was undertaken, they said, in response to the economic downturn and changes in industrial structures. She declared that, even if she went on attending, she had no hope of ever becoming a novelist, but I have no way of knowing if that was true, and it's hard for me to express any opinion since I never had a chance to see anything she had written. It was not that I did not ask her to show me her work. I expressed a degree of interest. But my wife always put it off, "Later, later." It was not a matter of: "What does someone like you know about novels?" But still it made me feel sad inside. It is certainly true that, even if I had read what she had written, I was not qualified to judge whether or not she had any hope of becoming a novelist. It does not really matter whether she had any such hopes or not. It might perhaps have been the reason why she decided to stop studying novel writing, but it could never explain why she made up her mind to go out to work. Every time she looked at our bank statements and sighed, saying: "Somebody will have to earn some money," there was nothing I could say.

At first I thought she was uttering some kind of complaint, simply because it's hard living like that. But it was not that. There was no pondering over where to set up an office, she never went out to ask anyone's advice, nothing upset the usual atmosphere. I felt anxious, ignored, until at last, feeling sad, I finally asked: "What kind of work are you doing?" At which she replied in a flash, as though she had been waiting for the question, that she had an idea. After a slight pause, she asked, "Have you ever heard of '*jeon-gi-su*?'" Supper had been cleared away and we were vacantly watching the evening news. "*Jeon-gi-su*? What's that? An abbreviation of something to do with electricity (*jeon-gi*)?" I replied casually, and at once my wife, smiling brightly with an "I knew it" expression, started to explain the word. She spoke smoothly and without hesitation as though she had been preparing for my question and had memorized everything. She seemed enthusiastic. "In the Joseon era, there used to be people who would read aloud professionally from storybooks at the roadside where many people passed. There's a record of it in a book called the *Autumn Room Anthology* written by a scholar, Jo Su-sam, early in the 19th century. Around the time of the Japanese invasion of the 1590s, Chinese romances such as the *Romance of the Three Kingdoms* and *Water Margin: Outlaws of the Marsh* reached Korea, and their influence provoked an increased interest in novels and stories. As a result, in the later Joseon period professional story-readers appeared on the streets of Seoul; they received a regular income to read aloud from novels or tell ancient stories. Those people were called *Jeon-gi-su* (Storytellers)." Such was her explanation. Those people would set themselves up in a place where there were many people passing, and mostly read from ancient Korean storybooks such as *The Tale of So Dae-seong, The Tale of Sukhyang, The Tale of Simcheong,* or *The Tale of Xue Rengui.* All of that came, of course, from the *Autumn Room Anthology.* Beginning at the start of the month, performances were held on the first day beneath the first bridge, on the second day beneath the second bridge, on the third day in front of Inhyeon Palace, on the fourth day at the entrance to Gyo-dong, on the fifth day at the entrance to Daesa-dong, on the sixth day in front of the Bell Pavilion, then on the seventh day the order would be reversed, up and down, throughout the month, starting again the following month. "In those days, you might call it a kind of new profession. There were no proper pastimes and the simple folk of those times had no way of enjoying any leisure activities, so listening to the storytellers must have been one of their rare moments of pleasure. So of course they were immensely popular. They mostly lived outside the eastern gate, and earned a meager living from the coins tossed to them by the audience, but that was not all, of course. Playboys from rich families, or older women with nothing to do, as well as girls from *gisaeng* houses must surely have provided extra support. What do you think? Fun, isn't it?" This was

the first time I had heard that people with such a job had existed in the Joseon period, but since I could not begin to see what she found so thrilling
about it, suspicion and stress emerged in equal parts. I simply asked: "So
what? Presumably people like that vanished once literacy rates rose and
book distribution increased. Instead of listening they just read. But what
about today? Is there anybody in need of a storyteller? What, are you
saying you're going to read to people as a job?" I asked, displaying some
surprise. I also think I wanted to express in that way my disappointment to
my wife, who had told me it was what she called a new business idea. My
wife's notions of business were less than satisfactory, but I was unhappy
with myself for not being worried by that. I tried not to provoke complicated emotions by adding: "I understand what you are saying, but surely
there's too great a difference between the Joseon era when the storytellers
were active and today? First of all, in those times only a limited number of
people could read, and there were very few things available to read. And
as you mentioned, there were no proper pastimes and people had no way
of enjoying any leisure activities. Storytellers were bound to be popular in
such a context. Everything is so completely different now. There's nobody
who's unable to read, we're flooded with books, and despite that, since
we're flooded with so many even more amusing and entertaining things,
we're in a situation where nobody pays any attention to them. Of course,
there must be people who are unable to read books even though they
would like to. I'm not sure how many there might be, but so far as I know
lots of audiobooks have come onto the market for people like that."

Although she agreed in part with my opinion, my wife did not change
her mind. She reckoned that either I was taking no notice of my contem-
poraries' profound solitude and alienation or I was underestimating them.
"The number of people living isolated in their own little inner space is
surely greater than the number of illiterate people in the Joseon era, or at
least it's no smaller. I mean all those poor souls who confine themselves
in a dark emptiness, like a black hole, unable to expose their faces to the
world's bright light because of fear and anxiety. Inside, they long desperately to communicate, but they are incapable of expressing that desire
outwardly, that is another characteristic of such people. They hope that
their isolation and emptiness will be dissolved in some hitherto unseen
way, through some kind of extremely private, secret process in which their
isolation and emptiness are not advertised. They do not want the fact that

they are isolated individuals to be revealed, let alone the fact that they are yearning for communication." If I did not go on quarreling, it was not because I agreed with her. Rather, for some reason, I was feeling reluctant to hear anything more and it was only after a little more time had passed that I realized that my reluctance was somehow related to the liking for my inner state of isolation that had begun to grow within me. In fact, my dull-as-ditchwater, well-ordered daily life was no different from a black hole-like emptiness.

My wife got together with an old university friend who had earned a fair amount tutoring students for the university entrance exam, set up a site with the appropriate name of "Seoul, 21st-century Storytellers," and went into the storytelling business in earnest. When she handed me her business card, "Seoul, 21st-century Storytellers, Lee Yeong-ran, Head of Planning," her expression was a mixture of excitement and pride. This storytelling business, that proclaimed itself to be a visiting program with home study materials, began, as you may know, with a membership system, recruiting and educating people known as narrators who would read books or tell stories, and sending them out to members. It's still the same now, the principle being that a suitable book should be chosen in consultation. But there were people who decided on a title for themselves. There were those who asked for a digested version of a specific book, while others asked to be read a newspaper or magazine, or to be told an entertaining story. Occasionally there was a request to be read to over the telephone instead of visiting. For myself, it was rather unexpected to discover just how many people wanted other people's help to read a book or hear a story. As I saw how, slowly but surely, the number of members increased, I was forced to accept that my wife's judgment had been correct. There were a lot of people who offered to be narrators, perhaps because they had trouble finding a job. The clients' levels and tastes varied from person to person so that the books to be read were widely varied, requiring a considerable intellectual capacity, besides which their voice had to be up to the task. Of course, selecting narrators was particularly complicated. Perhaps because it was important to choose a text that corresponded to the character of the job, the role of the narrator and the disposition of the client, training sessions and meetings often seemed to be required. As time passed, my wife came home increasingly late and it seemed inevitable that she no longer bothered with housework. My wife never actually said as much, but I had the impression that she hoped I would stop looking for a job. From the start she indicated that she took it for granted that I would stay home and look after the housework. That was simply the way things were, I'm not saying I was dissatisfied.

Male, 59. Character: reserved and meditative. Music-lover (almost always wears earphones). Prefers aphoristic essays or works of a religious nature. Khalil Gibran's *The Prophet*, Max Picard's *The World of Silence*, Aurelius's *Meditations*, the Bible's *Proverbs* or *Ecclesiastes*. Sometimes asks to go walking together.

My first client, summed up in a few words, seemed to be someone of rather reclusive tastes. Even considering that a reclusive character was to be expected in this line of work, still the contents were sufficient to make me feel curious, surely? As my wife had requested, I washed, shaved, combed my hair and put on a suit. I read the materials my wife had sent while I was on the subway. Together with the basic information on the client, whose name was Han Sang-cheol, there was a file with the text I was to read. It contained an extract from Tolstoy's *On Life* typed in a twelve-point font. I skimmed through it absent-mindedly, thinking it was not very interesting. The thought that the person who wanted this boring piece of writing might well prove to be not very interesting made me feel depressed. That it was boring emerged clearly from the table of contents to the recommended book. I briefly thought about phoning my wife to ask how long I had to spend with this fellow, but then I felt I was being pathetic and gave up the idea.

The man was living in a rural villa not far outside Seoul, surrounded by poplars and willows so that it was not easy to find the entrance. Unable to find the way in, I passed by it several times. The tall, leafy trees looked like guardsmen. But of course there was no way of knowing what it was the trees were guarding. It simply served to confirm a little more my previous image of a man with reclusive tastes. I was welcomed by a solidly built woman in her mid-fifties, her face pale, her attitude restrained. Yet she did not look like the owner of the house. You find people like that. A face gentle yet expressionless. A warm yet dull voice… someone who has been working in a house so long that she seems to have become part of it. Someone who seems to intimately know every corner of the house. Owners are not like that. An owner does not look like part of the house, nor do they look as though they intimately know every corner of the house. Even when in fact they do. As I pointed at the file and introduced myself as the narrator sent by "Seoul, 21st-century Storytellers," I felt rather tense, although I was not lying. I suppose it was a kind of inferiority complex. "The regular narrator is sick and so I've come instead, I don't know if you've been informed," I mumbled on, scratching the back of my head as if embarrassed. My hand kept rising toward the unaccustomed tie I had put on. The woman, seemingly not interested in any such feelings of mine, led me to a chair in the middle of the garden and told me to wait there.

I stood awkwardly in front of the chair and examined the house. Broad-leaved trees surrounded it almost entirely, giving the impression it was cut off from the outside world. The building seemed to be quite old, I could see cracks here and there and places where the paint had flaked off. The garden was quite spacious but it did not give the impression of being well maintained. Overgrown branches and irregular patches in the lawn spoiled the effect. A rectangular wooden table and five wooden chairs had been set up and I had just sat down when I heard someone approaching. I quickly rose again. The woman who had welcomed me before had come out pushing a wheelchair. My eyes turned naturally to the person sitting in the wheelchair. It held an elderly man whose skinny frame and small stature contrasted with those of the woman. Deep wrinkles and unfocused eyes, a lack of expression suggesting a complete loss of interest in the world that reminded me of a mask, while his thin body with no sign of vitality gave off the feeling of a dry log. If this man was indeed the music lover with a taciturn, meditative personality whom I was supposed to read to, his age ought to be fifty-nine. That was what was written down. But leaving aside the taciturn, meditative personality, the term music-lover did not appear to suit him at all. Even more impossible to believe was the age of fifty-nine. On his ravaged, old face the shadow of death lay more thickly than shades of life. As for his expression, there was one, of course, but there was no guessing what his vacant stare was directed at, and it made my flesh crawl. You might even go so far as to imagine he had emerged from a graveyard. I doubted if this man was a fifty-nine-year-old music lover with a taciturn, meditative personality, but I had no reason to suppose he was not Han Sang-cheol.

The woman brought the man to me, bowed her head in greeting and withdrew, and at that moment I had the impression that she was being re-lieved of an impossible load. Feeling burdened by the unaccustomed role that had been thrust upon me, I again muttered that I had come instead because the usual narrator was unwell. I saw the old man's eyelids slowly open then equally slowly close again. Perhaps on account of the speed, he looked extremely bored. I also saw his fingers twitch slightly as they lay on the armrests of the wheelchair. For some reason I felt that looking at his fingers would be impolite and averted my gaze. He had earphones in his ears (at first I had thought it was a hearing aid) that seemed to be con-nected to the small cassette player he had on his lap. Music after asking someone to come and read? The thought struck me that it would not do, but I felt no desire to ask him to remove the earphones. I was thinking that as far as I was concerned, all I had to do was read Tolstoy's *On Life*, whether he was listening or not. Besides, I found myself expecting him to understand better if he listened with music in the background. In which case there was no reason for me to complain that it wouldn't do. I wished he would say something, but he gave no instructions. After fumbling with my tie and clearing my throat, I sat down on the chair facing him. Then I began to read the prepared text from *On Life*.

Man lives only for his own happiness, for his own good. If he does not feel a desire for his own welfare he no longer feels himself to be alive. Man cannot think of life without a wish for his own welfare.

As I read, from time to time I observed the old man. There was no change in his expression. There was no knowing if he was listening atten-tively or not, and I felt worried. At one point I even began to wonder if he could hear my voice. Not whether he was listening to my voice but wheth-er he might not be so deaf that he could not hear anything. If that was the case, what on earth did I think I was doing? His persistent lack of response made me feel awkward, puzzled, apprehensive, mortified, and finally reduced me to self-pity. It was the pointlessness of having to keep saying something on and on to someone incapable of understanding. Thanks to the myth of Sisyphus, surely everyone knows what a dreadful punishment it is to be obliged to keep repeating a meaningless gesture. Being obliged to keep rolling a rock up a hill that constantly rolls back down again is a dreadful punishment, not because it is physically arduous but because it brings humiliation and boredom.

"Shall I stop reading?" I asked. If he nodded, that indicated consent and I could stop; I had decided that if he showed no response at all, that would prove that he was deaf and could hear nothing, so there was no need to go on reading. But my expectations proved wrong. Not that he expressed himself. He neither nodded nor shook his head. He simply slowly opened his eyelids and silently looked at my face. That's a response, isn't it? I tried to read some message in his face, but failed. I could read nothing, but the fact was he had shown a response; by showing any response at all, the fact was he had shown that he was not deaf and I could not ignore that. That meant I could not put an end to my assigned task. What was I to do? I had to keep on acting as narrator. I tried to control my irritation. Frankly speaking, I had for some time been feeling intensely frustrated and humiliated on account of the way my meaningless action had failed to provoke interest in my audience. My feelings of frustration and humiliation were similar to the discomfort felt on having one's inner feelings observed unilaterally by someone wearing dark glasses. Dark glasses are an excellent means for observing without being observed. While I was reading Tolstoy's *On Life*, the idea kept pursuing me that my audience was deciphering the flimsy, conventional and feeble text entitled "Myself." And through some kind of association, a forgotten memory of something that had happened fifteen months before came into my mind. For a long while after I had left the company in the wake of the restructuring, I kept wondering why I had been the only member of our section to be forced into early retirement. Finding the answer was difficult and painful. I reflected belatedly on how uneasy I had felt the whole time I was working there. Once I realized that sensing the atmosphere in the office or reading the boss's mind had always been the most difficult things for me, I quickly understood why I had felt uneasy. I had found it hard to laugh when the boss laughed without knowing the reason. There had also been several occasions when I had provoked an icy atmosphere in the office by a single phrase spoken in jest. Now I finally realized, as I stood scrutinizing the expression of an immobile old man sitting in front of me while I read Tolstoy, that while people could easily read me, I could hardly read other people, if at all. I felt that it was an important realization. Immediately I grew anxious and found myself unable to continue my meaningless reading. I could not read Tolstoy.

Still, it was less than fifteen minutes since I had entered the house, there could be no question of my simply leaving already. I felt sorry that I had not asked my wife how long I would have to act as a narrator. But what was I to do? I was obliged to decide and act for myself. I was being paid, I thought, so surely I would have to stay there for an hour at least. It was dreadful to imagine spending the remaining forty-five minutes imitating a poor radio actor. At the thought that I was not so much like a poor actor as a broken-down radio, I felt as though I was crawling across mudflats. I grew impatient to see the old man lower his eyes once again; in that case I would be forced to go on being a poor actor and a broken-down radio, something I disliked intensely. I just had to catch another glimpse of his eyes before his eyelids covered them again, even if they looked like black holes. I felt convinced that for that to happen I had to stop reading and talk to him.

"Have you heard?" As I spoke freely my voice naturally grew faster. "It seems there's a tribe somewhere in Asia that worships turtles as gods. When a turtle lays eggs, someone is designated to take care of them care-fully, serving as a nursemaid. Turtles are herbivores, but if they only eat grass they grow weak so from time to time they are fed tonics. I wonder what those tonics might be made of...." I gave up reading like some poor actor and adopted the tone of someone making conversation. It seemed that would be the only way of awakening his interest. I really had no wish to go on pointlessly pushing a rock uphill. Nor did I want to be seen through. Of course, I had no other text ready beside Tolstoy's *On Life*. I was impatient because I had no idea what to talk about. Luckily, you might say, just then I recalled a program about a strange tribe that I had seen on television one morning. My wife had already left for her work and I was feeling relaxed as I drank my coffee and enjoyed the morning, while strange tales emerged from the television, that was on out of habit. I was simply watching, without any particular pleasure, but seeing the way in which that came to mind just when I needed something to talk about, I suppose I must have been feeling some degree of interest. The old man's eyelids had been drooping occasionally but now he looked up. Success. It was not clear what he was focusing on, but once I could look him in the eye I grew more confident. I continued talking. I probably made things up when my memory failed me. "Lizards. The villagers catch lizards and press the juice out of them. That's the tonic they give the turtles, to help them have many children. Those villagers believe that if a turtle is hurt, even by accident, they will fall seriously ill. They claim that there have been several cases where people have injured a turtle and died before the day was out. Stories like that being handed down would explain how turtles came to be vested with divine powers. The people believe they are under the curse of the Turtle God. It does not matter if turtles really have such powers or not. People simply believe it. Who knows, after all, some regime needing to maintain their grip on power by the spread of such myths might fabricate something of the kind. That's the way things generally are. The outside appearance is not the whole story…." The old man was concentrating on me. His gaze was still as vacant as ever, but I could sense it. How hard he was panting, deep inside… at least, I had been able to stop being a broken-down radio. Fortunately.

My wife smiled brightly as she questioned me: "How did you do it? How on earth did you do it? That difficult old man…." Behind her incredulous expression I could read indications that she found it wonderful that I had such talent, but I decided not to let it affect me. What did it matter? As a matter of fact, I was equally incredulous. What had I done, finally? In place of Tolstoy's *On Life* I had talked about adopting turtles as gods, after which I talked about a movie called *The Village* I had seen on a borrowed video tape about a year earlier. Because I had to keep on talking, no matter what I said. It was about an isolated village that invented a myth that said a monster was living in the forest, in order to keep villagers from going outside. Like the tale of the turtle, that too was not part of the program. It would be hard to claim that there was any clear similarity between the two stories. I suppose that some kind of association brought both tales to mind but I am incapable of explaining the process. And what was I going to say next? It did not take very long to tell those two stories, and then I had to start on something new. But I had nothing ready, so perhaps that was why I began to talk about the landlord of the place I was renting. Maybe because the apartment block had been built nearly thirty years ago, every time we turned on a tap a stream of rusty brown water came pouring out. Then from a few days back there had been a tap from which water continued to drip, even though it was turned completely off, enough to half fill the bathtub overnight. Surely that's a serious matter? I called the owner and asked him to have it repaired but, well, he shouted back in a loud voice that it was up to the person living there to mend it. How dare he? Was it my property? I protested. It was not as though it was my fault if it was dripping, it was because the building was so old, so why should the tenant have to mend it? At that he asked sarcastically where I would ever find an apartment that large at so low a rate, which drove me up the wall. He seemed to be saying that if I was dissatisfied I should get out and it really upset me. It was true that the rent for that old apartment was cheap but surely that was no reason for replying as if I was complaining for the mere sake of doing so. Was it? Then, as I went on arguing, the fellow hung up as though he was fed up with listening. It was really weird. All of this I told the old man. "There are so many occasions when common sense fails to get across. Surely, even if an apartment is cheap, what needs repairing has to be repaired. I was so angry… I felt like rushing out and planting a fist in the fellow's goddamn face. That bastard!" As I spoke, I grew increasingly worked up. I sensed that the man's hand resting on the arm of the wheelchair was trembling a little more violently, but I had no idea what emotion that was meant to indicate. The more I denounced my landlord, the more my agitation turned into an odd kind of pleasure, so I went on at some length. That was all. You couldn't say that I had played my role of narrator well. But so what? What had I done, after all?

When I left the house after filling up a whole hour, I was feeling famished, and at the same time I wanted to go somewhere where I could lean back and relax. It was in part a sign that I had done some hard work for the first time in months, but also a result of the fatigue that came over me as the tension wore off. I undid my tie and removed my jacket. My shirt was soaked. I had not realized that talking to someone consumed so much energy. The stories in our heads exist as a mass of images. Unraveling them as stories involves giving them bodies. A chain of trivial details forms a story because they form a body. After the mass of images has been divided carefully into details, each has to be joined to the others in a chain. That is what happens inside us whenever we talk to anybody. The details mainly have to be summoned up by the memory but when that fails to happen, when the memory does not function, they need to be invented. That was when I discovered that not only making things up but even simply recovering memories is really hard work. I was close to exhaustion. As I gazed up at the poplars and willows that surrounded the house like a fence, I murmured to myself that I was really not cut out for this kind of work.

Whether or not people blamed me for still not having found a job, I had no wish to do it a second time.

But, perhaps as a kind of strange provocation, that difficult client kept asking for me to come again. "What do you mean? You're asking me to go back there? To that grim old man?" At first I suspected my wife of wanting to turn me into one of her employees. I thought she might be saying that the client wanted me as a way of appealing to my self-respect. Because I had left the house not at all convinced that I had satisfied him. To the very end, his mask-like lack of expression had not varied. Having to pour out an unending stream of some kind of words toward his unfocused, in-animate eyes had been equally grim. Moreover, I had begun to wonder, although I could not be sure, if the old man was not simply taciturn but actually incapable of speech. There was no telling if he could hear, but perhaps he could not speak... which was why I asked her whether the old man had expressed that wish himself. "The gentleman didn't tell me himself. It's always that woman who contacts me. You must have seen her at the house." My wife was sitting in front of her mirror, removing her makeup. "She doesn't seem to be his wife," I said, "Is she some kind of relative?" "She's been working in his house for a long time now," my wife explained. I remarked that there seemed to be too great a difference in their ages for her to be his wife, which reminded me that on the client description form his age had been given as fifty-nine, and I asked if they hadn't got his age wrong. When I said that he looked too old to be only fifty-nine, she vaguely agreed but then added indifferently, "Maybe he's not well." "Even if he's not been well, I still don't believe it. And that fellow is more than taciturn; he can't talk, can he? He never said a word for a whole hour. Have you ever heard him speak?" My sharp-witted wife immediately understood my meaning. "You think I'm making it up, don't you? Why would I say what wasn't true? So what if he said nothing for an hour? It shows he's taciturn." Then she put on a serious expression and added: "I'm running a business, not a hobby in my spare time." Well, that put me to shame. There are times like that, aren't there, when you kill a conversation by trying to check a viewpoint or a position... I felt wretched and decided to shut up. My wife turned her face toward me, shiny with the cold cream she had applied, and went on: "I think he just refuses to talk, really, that client; he's twice sent away narrators we've sent, he seems rather hard to please. Of course the narrators find him grim, too. But he likes you, doesn't he? It's never been like this before. Why would I say something untrue? You're really remarkable." That was what she said, but I did not think I was remarkable at all. I could agree that he was grim, but not that I was remarkable. Moreover, I had not entirely freed myself of the suspicion that her "remarkable" might be no different from a hand intent on pushing me into that grimness. I kept reminding myself of my decision never to go back to that house.

In the end, I was unable to keep to my decision. Not on account of my wife's stubbornness (though she certainly is more stubborn than I am) but because my resolve was not firm enough to sustain the decision I had made. My wife kept repeating, "The client wants you, you know." No doubt it was my victim mentality, but her words sounded to me like a voice saying: "There's nobody else asking for you, is there?" I'm not sure if my wife was really harboring that intention or not, but I had no other choice, apart from the image of my shrunken figure spending the best part of every day with job ads spread out in front of me.

I suggested that for this client we should choose storytelling or even conversation, rather than reading. It was not that I had any particular reason behind it, only a thought to that effect had struck me. I said that I had no idea why that old man wanted me but it might be on account of the way I had talked about things seen on television and criticized my landlord instead of reading Tolstoy's *On Life*, and my wife agreed that it might be so. "That's the hardest part, deciding on a selection of texts corresponding to a client's tastes. Some of them make up their own lists, but not the majority. Choosing texts that correspond to their taste, level and situation is the most important thing. The way you speak matters too, of course." I asked the reason why Aurelius, Tolstoy and *Ecclesiastes* had been chosen as texts for me to read to the old man. My wife recalled that the woman who looked after him had said that he wanted religious, meditative texts. Hers had been the first call "Seoul, 21st-century Storytellers" had received. That suggested a high probability that the woman had taken the initiative in choosing the texts. I suspected that whether or not it was the woman's decision, they were not to the old man's personal taste. She might have chosen at random, but even if she hadn't, even if they reflected the old man's wishes to some extent, which I conceeded was certainly possible, even so, she clearly did not know what he really liked. I also think I insisted strongly that the manner of speaking was more important than the contents. My wife looked quite moved as she praised me, "You're a born narrator." I wished she would stop making such statements to encourage me. I was on the point of telling her that, while it might be alright for her to talk to the others in that way, she should not treat me just as she did the other narrators, but stopped myself because I reckoned that such a request would naturally imply that I was a narrator.

Despite such feelings, I found myself obliged to act as a narrator twice a week and obviously could not go chattering on aimlessly as before. My wife, who according to her business card was "Head of Planning, Seoul, 21st-century Storytellers," said she would leave the choice of texts to me, as if she was doing me a special favor. I concentrated on finding stories. Of course, I consulted various books. But instead of taking books along and simply reading from them, I chose a method that would be more like storytelling. I had quickly discovered on the first visit that in this way I could avoid sounding like a broken-down radio. If my wife's evaluation of me as wonderful was based on that, I had no reason to deny it.

As a narrator, it was pointless for me to organize the tales I would tell in a systematic order. Suffice to say I had discovered that variety was the very essence of storytelling. For example, I drew on myths and legends, television dramas, fables, comedies, newspaper articles, even Buddhist and Christian sermons. I introduced my personal experiences here and there as well. It would not be difficult to make a list of the different stories later. Instead, I changed my mind, seeing that this was not particularly important. On the first occasion, I had had difficulty filling an hour with this and that story, but now I would be capable of expanding a single story to fill any amount of time. Should I say I was a veteran now? That was what I had meant by saying that the manner of speaking was more important than the contents.

Not that there was any visible change in the way the old man listened. The change was in me. Becoming able to accept the old man's mask-like expression, his inanimate dryness and dark emptiness as time passed, I think that can be termed a change in me. The times I spent at his house grew longer, at first it was a matter of a cup of tea but later they happened to coincide with mealtimes and I started eating with him. "I'll just add another spoon," the distant relative who looked after him spoke in a kind though toneless voice, almost like a whisper, then added: "The gentleman doesn't usually eat with other people." It sounded as though she expected me to express my gratitude for a special welcome, a request I found it hard to respond to. While I waited for the old man, she used to make tea and bring it out to me, at which times we would make light conversation, usually about the day's weather or mood. One day I happened to ask who the old man was. She stared at me for a while as though it was an unexpected question, if not a forbidden one. In order to show that I had not asked out of real curiosity, I shrugged my shoulders and lightly waved a hand. To which she replied: "If you knew what kind of person he is, you might be surprised." Thereupon I grew curious and asked again what kind of person he was. She did not reply at once and I did not press her. I felt it would be wrong. She sat there in silence for a while then, having checked that my teacup was empty, as she stood up holding the tray she spoke in a kind of mutter. "A man who has spent thirty years of his life in hiding, waiting to be called for, that's who he is. Pretending to be deaf, then dumb. I don't know how it's possible. All the time believing in one vague promise... until his body is in its present state. Now he'd be no use even if he were to be called for, yet he lives waiting for that one message. When you think of it, you can't help but feel sorry for him...." I had already guessed that there must be some kind of story so I was not surprised, and hearing that much only made me more curious to know the full story, but I could not interrogate her directly. She went into the house carrying the cup and after that made no further reference to the story.

On a few occasions I took the old man on a stroll, pushing his wheelchair, but we never went beyond the fence of poplars and willows. Far off between the trees a railway line was visible; we used to stop there and silently watch the trains passing. I stood behind the wheelchair holding it steady and told him a short story by some writer about the fuss when a venomous snake being kept in a plastic bottle on the veranda of someone's apartment somehow vanished, or the happenings that ensued after an elephant broke through the wall surrounding a zoo and escaped. After a few things like that, I told him at length about how I had come to be a narrator. I likewise explained the reasons and process by which my wife had come to start her work. Then at one point I told him how I had been fired. Starting at one point, I mean, I mainly talked about myself. The department head deceived me to the very last moment. Although he had already put my name on the list of those qualified for voluntary early retirement, even when we were out drinking together in the evenings he expressed exaggerated trust in me until the very day before I was notified. I had not been capable of reading his inner thoughts. Indeed, I had never so much as thought that I ought to be reading them. How he must have been laughing to himself. Even now my face flushes and I grow angry when I think of it. As I told the story, I became agitated, my voice rose, I may even have sworn a few times. I always feel better after that.

He seemed to hear what I was saying and at the same time not to hear. I did not care if he was listening or not, I just went on talking. I no longer even worried about the old man's earphones, that had previously worried me so much. Nor his vacant eyes like black holes. Turning into a bro-ken-down radio and telling stories to the unresponsive old man had been so burdensome, but now I felt it didn't matter, so it didn't; I wonder how that came about, sometimes I surprise myself. Is it true, as my wife said, that I'm a born narrator? Anyway, from a certain moment I, the narrator, no longer paid any attention to the preferences or opinions of the old man, the client, but simply selected and told this or that story as I wished. As I went on expanding my stories, it finally dawned on me that perhaps I was not telling stories for him to listen to but rather he was listening so that I could tell stories. If the benefit I got from talking was greater than that which he received from listening, who is dependent on whom? Surely humans are closer in nature to being "speaking beings" than "listening be-ings"… and suddenly I wondered if the reason why high-class ladies from the women's quarters or girls from the *gisaeng* houses or playboys who had lost their official positions all called for the old-time storytellers might simply have been so that they could hear stories.

That kind of strange, symbiotic relationship between Han Sang-cheol and myself continued for a while. Without acknowledging it to one anoth-er, we were using each other. Indeed, after a while I even began to look forward to the times when I went to meet him. Meeting him had become part of my dull, boring everyday life, and the dull boredom tightened its grip. It was like a comfortable sofa. I had the feeling that once I was on a comfortable sofa, I could spend forever lounging there. But my time on the sofa was not to last long.

The incident happened when the old man finally opened the mouth he had kept shut for so long. I am truly obliged to call it an incident, for the old man opened the mouth he had never once opened since I first began to visit the house. The wind was blowing hard that day. Occasional raindrops had been falling since early morning. To avoid the wind and rain we had moved into the living room. As always, the old man was sitting in the wheelchair, his earphones were in his ears, his arms were neatly laid on the armrests. I was sitting opposite him telling some kind of story. I don't recall exactly what. Occasionally it was something serious, mostly it was something light. The old man was looking off in some other direction. I used to talk without looking at his eyes. It was more comfortable that way. Worse still, I sometimes talked while thinking about something else. Of course, he probably thought about other things as he listened, too. It had all become so natural that nothing was a problem anymore.

Then all of a sudden, the old man raised a hand, pointed at something, gasped out a cry, and fell forward. I don't know why, but he seemed to try to stand up too quickly, lost his balance and fell, at the same time as a great shock made him lose consciousness. That was my guess. It all happened so quickly that it was hard to grasp the situation. I urgently called for the woman then looked in the direction the old man had pointed, but I could not tell what he had seen there. Wind coming in through the slightly opened window was making the curtains shake, there was a framed picture of the lake at the summit of Baekdu Mountain, a television set and two orchids in pots, I could see nothing unusual. The television was not on. Had he observed some ghostly eyes that I could not see? As I was thinking, the woman who cared for him came rushing in. "What happened?" she asked as she raised the fallen old man. I said I did not know and shook my head. I was rather worried she might think I had given him some kind of shock. I helped her put the old man back in his wheelchair, and he gave a groan as though he had recovered consciousness. The voice sounded hoarse, divided, disagreeable. "You'd better go and rest. Come along, let's go and rest." The woman pushed the wheelchair into the next room. Confused, I could only stand there in my uncertainty. I still did not realize that, although it was only a cry, I had heard the old man make a sound with his vocal cords for the very first time.

"It looks as though you'll have to go back home for today." The woman did not emerge for a long time after taking the old man into the other room and I had been wavering as to whether I should simply go; finally she came out and indicated that indeed I should. I too thought it would be better. Yet there was some kind of uneasy feeling that kept me from leaving at once. It was rather as though I felt I would be leaving the scene of an accident and sneaking away. At least, I reckoned it would be cowardly. Surely it was only natural that I should think that the woman would know the reason for what had happened, while I did not. This was not the moment to quibble over whether it was natural or not. Nourishing the hope that she might be able to satisfy at least a little of my curiosity, I asked: "What happened? For goodness' sake, what happened?" The woman glanced toward the room where the old man was and sighed deeply. She showed signs of hesitating briefly, then gently closed her eyes and spoke.

"It's all over. The long wait to which he sacrificed his whole life is finally at an end." Her words sounded to me like a Zen riddle. I was bewildered. I could not help asking her what was over. "I told you that you would be surprised if you knew who that old man was, didn't I? I don't know if you will remember. Many years ago, a powerful former high-ranking official met a suspicious end. It provoked a great uproar for a long time. The truth about the incident was never made public and the years ticked by. A lot of people have forgotten all about it. But that old man has lived on, never forgetting. He spent half his life hidden and silent. Waiting for the day when he would be called for. If he never spoke, it was not because he had forgotten but because he had not forgotten. Because he could not forget. He was not permitted to forget. The highest-ranking official over him had said that if he hid and kept quiet for a little while, he would call for him. It has been thirty years now. Too long for a little while... yet...."

How was I to understand that the old man had never lost hope in the promise of his former chief to call for him, even though his body was overshadowed by death? Life is not a lonely thing, surely, it's just as vulgar as a magazine cover. But it seemed that wait had ultimately become less urgent, nothing much more than a habit. Why did he not understand that a magazine cover is vulgar because it's like life? Just as a magazine cover can never be lonely, a human life cannot not be vulgar. That day, on the radio that he was always listening to through his earphones, the news came of that chief's death. That was why he had been shocked, cried out, collapsed, she said. Just see how vulgar a human life can be. No matter how lonely it may look, life is bound to be vulgar. It was the woman who told me, but later I was able to verify the facts from the lips of the person most directly involved, Han Sang-cheol. Yes, the old man told his own story. Of course, at the time I thought that day would be the last. But about a month later, the old man called for me again. I felt rather uncertain but I couldn't not go. Indeed, there was no reason for not going. What stories should I tell? I was a bit worried. I thought I knew him a little, but in fact I hardly knew him at all, so that choosing stories was difficult. I went with a few tales ready: the man who passed through walls, the man who sold his shadow, the man who sold real estate in the stars.

The poplars and willows surrounding the house were the same as before. The untended garden, too. But the man had changed. The emptiness gaping like a black hole, the shadow of death as if he had just emerged from a graveyard had vanished completely.

On entering the house, I found the old man in much better health than before, even declaring that he'd soon be up out of his wheelchair. "Today, I'll be the narrator. Today, I want you to listen to me." With that, he launched straight into his own story. He related without pausing to rest. His story was long and dark, amazing and passionate. He told his story with such passion that as I listened I wondered how he had been able to live until now without telling it. Then, once he had finished telling his story, another thought struck me. Maybe what he had been waiting for had not been someone else's voice calling for him, but his own voice. Maybe he had been waiting for a time to come when he would not have to wait any longer. Maybe he had been waiting for an end to waiting. Maybe that was why he had been listening to the radio without ever for a second removing the earphones…. Of course, he did not say as much himself. Those are just my conjectures. Who can know what lies beyond things said? We should never forget that, as someone once said, under the surface of our lives flow long and dark, amazing and passionate stories that there is no way of knowing unless they are told. The old man died not long after telling me his story, so it might be considered a form of sacramental confession. Of course, I could tell the long and dark, amazing and passionate story I heard from him. A long time has passed but I still remember it almost word for word. But that's enough for today. I'm too tired. I've told too many stories already. I need to rest awhile. Be careful as you go out.

AN ANONYMOUS ISLAND

Yi Mun-yol

Translated by Heinz Insu Fenkl

익명의 섬
이문열

A critique of this short story was published in the Koreana magazine in Winter 2009 (Vol. 23 No. 4, pp. 85-87).

© Cha Jae-ok

"Tsk-tsk."

It's the end of a long evening, and my husband clicks his tongue at the TV as if he were watching something despicable. On the screen there's a group of men and women hunched in the corner of a police-station waiting room. The camera catches them from various angles, hiding their faces with their hands or with some article of clothing. I think they might have been arrested for gambling, but it seems they were dragged out in broad daylight from some dimly lit secret basement club where they were dancing. The announcer doesn't say they were dancing—he uses a more suggestive phrase: "They were rubbing their bodies together."

"What the hell is the matter with our generation?" my husband complains. "How did it get so easy to be anonymous?"

I've heard the same thing from him many times, and I can guess where he's headed before he has even finished: *Get off the bus one stop past your neighborhood in the city and you hardly recognize anyone. It's so easy to hide these days—there must be huge numbers of people living anonymously. It's the moral failing of our generation, a major factor in the corruption of women's sexuality.* He pushes on like that and eventually gets around to how much he misses his childhood home, a rural village with only one clan.

"We all knew each other," he'll say nostalgically. "It was like looking down into the water at your own reflection…. Most of the people were blood relations, so it was practically unthinkable for a woman to be unfaithful. Once in a while someone went off to a nearby village for that sort of thing, but sooner or later it was found out."

Whenever my husband goes on like this, it makes a repugnant memory resurface in my mind and I feel sorry for him. Maybe I should feel some shame for myself, too, but it's something that happened ten long years ago.

That spring, I graduated with a degree in education and took my first job at an elementary school in a rural village, which I will leave nameless. It was sixty *li* from the county seat, up past two high, rugged mountains in a valley where it seemed no one would want to live.

I got off the bus and stood on the slope at the bus stop for a while, feeling desolate and alone. The mountains encircled me like the giant walls of a prison that would confine me for the rest of my life, and the village of about a hundred houses that I saw in the distance looked abandoned—like a ghost town. The school I was looking for must have been hidden behind a ridge. I couldn't see it anywhere.

The few people who had got off the bus with me had already disappeared, so I went to the store nearby to ask for directions. I had gone only a few steps when I felt something like a sharp beam of light pierce my skin. I stopped to look for the source and saw a young man sitting on the back porch of the store, silently watching me. His pants were so stained and dirty that I couldn't tell what material they were made of, and the sleeves of his dyed Army jacket hung in tatters.

His face was dark and weathered, with a prominent nose and high cheekbones. I stared at him without realizing it. Just then the light seemed to prick at my skin again. It was hidden behind a veil of madness, but the source was unmistakable—it was coming from the man's eyes.

It's as if I were on a forest path. I see a snake through the thick foliage and the fear stays with me until I leave. No simple fear but a kind of primal thrill that dissolves into a hollow regret when I'm safely through and the danger has passed. That's how it made me feel, the light from his eyes, until the shopkeeper opened the door and came out, breaking the illusion.

"Ggaecheol, you idiot! What are you doing still sitting out there?" Although the man must have been five or six years older than him, the shopkeeper talked down to him, as if he were a child. The man was apparently not some vagrant just passing through—he belonged to the village. He didn't even pretend to hear the shopkeeper, but just kept looking at me with those vague hooded eyes. His expression wasn't lewd or disgusting, but for some reason it frightened me.

"You deaf?" the shopkeeper said. "Get up!" He went over and gave Ggaecheol a loud thump on the back, and as I cautiously approached he called out, "Welcome! Are you looking for something?"

It was only then that I was able to shake Ggaecheol's clinging gaze from my body. I asked coolly, "Where is the elementary school?"

"Ho! So you're the new lady teacher they said was coming." The shopkeeper's face suddenly overflowed with kindness. He turned just as a boy, who looked about six, came out from the back of the store. "Hey, come over here," he called.

"What is it, Mr. Togok?" the boy said.

"Looks like this is the new teacher. Show her to the school before you go." He looked toward me with a hint of pity, and muttered, "The school's the size of a booger, and it's way out in those hills."

Obediently, I stepped forward to follow the boy. Ggaecheol's eyes were on me again, but I had recovered my composure. I shot him a fierce look as I left.

Walking to the school with the boy, I realized how quickly I was being introduced to the peculiar dynamics of the village. The boy nodded in greeting to each man we met, calling him "uncle" or "grandfather." I had grown up in the city, and my only exposure to relatives was when I visited an uncle's house once or twice a year; the closeness of this place felt strange to me.

In the classroom, half the students had the same surname and even those with different surnames seemed to be first cousins. Later, I learned that this was because the village was surrounded on all four sides by layer upon layer of high mountains, with a single road threading through from north to south. The village produced nothing special, so there was virtually no influx of people from other family lines.

After my first encounter with Ggaecheol, I forgot about him for a while. Of course, he was constantly lurking about the village doing nothing, and I would see his shabby form and feel that hooded gaze several times a day, but this was my first job and the first time I had been far away from home by myself. I was busy cultivating my new life and I paid him no attention.

But, as I more or less adjusted to my new life and had some time to think, I gradually became curious about my surroundings, and the first thing that came to mind was Ggaecheol.

What initially struck me was the question of his origins. He wasn't born in the village and he wasn't related to anyone there either by blood or by marriage. He had drifted in by chance, however many years ago, and had been living there since. He was over forty, and yet he was known by the childish nickname Ggaecheol, to adults and children alike.

The next unusual thing was how he earned his living. At first I assumed he did physical labor or odd jobs, but then I saw that he spent his days doing absolutely nothing. Even so, he was able to get three meals a day and had a place to sleep every night.

This is what he did when he wanted to eat: he would burst into any house as the family was gathered around the table, and announce, "Give me some food."

Just as no one ever spoke politely to him, he never used the polite form of address, either. It was strange how the men of the house reacted. Not only were they not annoyed by his intrusions; they actually seemed to welcome him. They would say, "Even an idiot like you has to eat to live. Mix up a bowl for him, dear."

The wife would fill a large ceramic or brass bowl with rice, soup, kimchi, and whatever, stir it all together, and push it to Ggaecheol, who would take the bowl and slurp it all down, sitting on the corner of a straw mat or the edge of the raised wooden floor. As he left, he would announce, "It was good. I'm going now."

"Don't you say thank you?"

"What for?" he'd say. "I ate my food and now I'm going." He'd wander out and there would be neither hide nor hair of him in that house again for a few months. According to my calculations, the number of days he stayed away was approximately equal to the number of households in the village.

It was similar with his sleeping arrangements. Usually, he slept outdoors in a pavilion or in a common room, but when it grew cold—or if it was a day when no wood had been prepared for the heating fire—he was sure to go around the village saying, "Let me sleep in your house."

"You can sleep here if you take a bath first."

"You won't need your blanket," he'd say. "You're just gonna go lie down next to your wife, right?"

That was the usual procedure, and it all seemed a bit too comfortable to me.

When I thought about it, there was clearly something strange about Ggaecheol's relationship with the villagers. The men all treated him like a half-wit or a madman, but it seemed as if they were trying hard to mask their anxiety that perhaps he wasn't really like that. The women, too, seemed to consider Ggaecheol dim-witted or mad, but beneath their strict maternal façade they hid a protective impulse that went beyond mere sympathy. What I couldn't understand, no matter how much I thought about it, was why the villagers supported him in this way, like a member of their own community. He did no work, he had no special skills, and he never earned their good will with his wit or humor.

But then something happened that hinted at an answer to my question. One day, after I had been there for six or seven months, I was walking home from work when I witnessed a disturbance in the vacant lot in front of my boarding house. A young man was literally pounding Ggaecheol into the dirt, but it was odd—neither the attacker nor the victim indicated any reason for the fight. The young man, with a staff in one hand and a piece of firewood in the other, was wordlessly thrashing Ggaecheol wherever he could find an opening. Ggaecheol was curled up like a porcupine, periodically spitting out a groan.

As I watched, not knowing what to do, villagers gathered from here and there, and they ended up explaining the brutal violence.

"What the hell are you doing, Hwacheon? We look out for each other in this village! How can you behave like this?"

"Tell us, Hwacheon, what could this idiot possibly do?"

"That's right, Hwacheon! You're losing face and bringing shame on your family. Our ancestors have been here for three hundred years, and not once did a woman get thrown out for adultery."

All the men were trying to make him stop, but to me it sounded as if they weren't so much trying to convince Hwacheon as reassuring themselves.

"Look, Hwacheon, you've got to think about your wife's dignity. Are there no other men in the world that a woman would rather do it with an idiot like him?"

"That's right! She's got her own perfectly good snake with Hwacheon here, so why would an idiot . . . Don't go killing him now!"

"You've got to behave like a man of your standing. He's over forty and impotent! Can't even dream of getting a wife."

Even the older women helped calm the young man down, and their tone, too, suggested that Ggaecheol's being an idiot was his saving grace—a sort of magical charm. Strangely, not one of the younger women came forward to help, and their angry looks were directed not at Ggaecheol but at the young man wielding the staff.

The disturbance didn't last long, but it was through that unexpected event that I was able to get a sense of why the villagers permitted Ggaecheol to live among them. The fact that everyone in the village was related by blood or marriage also meant that they looked out for one another, especially where issues of morality were concerned. I was now certain that Ggaecheol played some peculiar role in the sex life of this closed village.

My suspicions were confirmed one day when I accidentally overheard some village wives whispering by the bank of a stream. It was a hot and humid summer night, and I had gone there so that I could at least cool my feet. The water must have reflected the sound of their voices, as I was able to hear them from quite a distance.

"Don't you think Yeoung'gok's baby looks like Ggaecheol?"

"Be quiet! Do you want poor Ggaecheol to get killed this time?"

"What did I say? I was just talking."

"Even so. Ggaecheol's just an idiot with no place to go."

"Right, he's an idiot. Ggaecheol's just an idiot."

They seemed to end their conversation by tacit agreement, and I thought I heard an intimate tone of conspiracy in their voices. I was finally able to guess why I sensed that strange protective quality for Ggaecheol among the women even when they spoke of him contemptuously. Ggaecheol never worked, but he got three meals a day and a place to sleep every night—and the women were half the reason. But the other half? I couldn't figure out why the men put up with his presence in the village.

I worked in what was nominally a school, but there were only six grades, and sometimes the classes were only half full. Inspections were rare in such a rural mountain village—they were practically never done. So, distracted from the monotony of my daily life by my curiosity, I had plenty of time to keep a close watch over Ggaecheol and the villagers.

But when the second semester began I no longer had that leisure. During summer break at home that year, I went to the seaside with some friends and met my future husband, who was a college senior. What at first seemed a passing fancy between us slowly heated up. Being in the same city helped, but our interests and temperaments were similar, and we grew close more quickly than I would have thought possible.

When I returned to the village for my second semester, my nights were spent just trying to read and answer his flood of letters. My head was filled with thoughts of him, my imagination swirling around the city where he lived. Unless it related to him, nothing at all in the world could get my attention.

The remainder of that year passed, and the spring of the next year came around. Neither of our families objected, so we became engaged when he graduated. But then he immediately had to enlist for his mandatory military service. By that time, I had become a woman with intimate knowledge of a man; we had gone on a three-day trip over winter break, but after we were engaged, during the end-of-year break before he was due to enlist in the Army, we were practically inseparable.

After he enlisted, the torrent of letters began again, and I responded to them even more fervently than before. There were times, once in a while, when Ggaecheol would suddenly pop up and look me over with that gaze, but though he sometimes startled me he was not of interest.

Five or six months after my husband enlisted, his unit was mobilized for the war in Vietnam. I'd thought that all I had to do was wait quietly for his three-year tour of duty to end, so I was stunned when I heard the news. In those days Vietnam was considered a death sentence, and I was gripped by a terrible despair. And beneath my fear was a longing for my husband that burned not only in my mind but also in my body.

I wrote to him without embarrassment. Just once, if only for a moment, I wanted to be in his arms again. I wanted to feel the warmth of his body and the heat of his breath. Whatever he had to do, he had to be with me first. His answer came quickly. Before shipping out to Vietnam he would have a weeklong leave, and he promised to set aside a few days to come and see me.

At five o'clock on the last day that my husband could have come, when the last bus went by without stopping, I was so disappointed that I wanted to collapse right there. I regretted, until my bones ached, that I hadn't missed work to run to him, but by then it was no longer possible. What I couldn't understand was why my body didn't know to cool off when I was so terribly disappointed. I had spent the last week imagining myself in my husband's arms, and now, when I knew for certain that he wasn't coming, my body burned even hotter.

I staggered away from the bus stop in a delirious fog until a sudden noise brought me back to my senses. I was standing in the middle of the road. Though it was already early fall, what I'd heard was a cloudburst, and the rain poured down like a monsoon. I noticed a storage shed by the side of the road and ran over to it. At first my plan was to stand under the eaves and wait it out, but then the rain fell harder and the wind picked up, forcing me back against the corrugated-metal door.

I waited a long time, but the rain only came harder, so I opened the door and stepped inside. Normally the shed was stacked full of fertilizer, but today it was completely empty and quiet. I remember thinking that someone might be in there, yet it didn't occur to me to look around. I just stared out at the rain through the half-open door. It wasn't that my mind had gone blank; it was that I couldn't rouse myself from the exquisite heat that tingled like tiny insects swarming over my body.

It was a mistake not to look around the storage shed. As soon as I was completely inside, someone rushed from a dark corner, shut the door, and quickly drew the bolt.

"Who's there? Open the door! I'll scream!" Filled with a sudden, instinctual fear, I let out a sharp scream.

"It's no use," a slightly hoarse voice said. "You see anyone out there walking in the rain?"

A hand clamped onto my wrist. It was Ggaecheol—I had suspected it the moment I saw the blur of his shadow, and, strangely, now that I knew who it was the fear that had gripped me was gone.

"Ggaecheol," I said. "Let go of my arm!"

I tried to intimidate him the way the other villagers did, but he just pushed me down onto the straw-covered floor and roughly grabbed a handful of my skirt.

"If you don't want to go back all messy, undress nicely," he said.

I used all my strength, struggling to get away from him. He lay on top of me, and I felt his hot breath in my ear. "This Ggaecheol may not know much, but I know exactly when you women need me," he whispered. "Right now your body's hot and ready."

When I heard those words my body suddenly relaxed and the strange tingling fever, which I had momentarily forgotten, came back.

Again, he whispered expertly in my ear, caressing my body, "I was watching you the whole afternoon. All the time you were waiting so nervous, at the bus stop."

He had already become an abstraction of a man to me, an image with no relation to his shabby clothes and ugly face. I did not resist as I fell into a dreamlike state—I just let go of everything. I'm embarrassed even to remember it, but I didn't feel victimized. I'm not so sure that I didn't enjoy it, as if he and I were having an illicit love affair. If I could offer up a single defense as another man's woman at that time, it would be that at the moment of climax it was my husband's face that I saw.

For a long time afterward, I was worried. I was afraid that Ggaecheol would come bursting into my room, or that the whole village would find out and do irrevocable harm to my life. The fact that I don't recall feeling a sense of moral shame or of having sinned against my husband makes me feel strange now, though not remorseful.

Contrary to my fears, Ggaecheol did not once come near me—it was remarkable. I had experienced a major catastrophe, but not a single rumor had spread through the village, and in the end I remained unsullied. It was only after a few months of restraint and closed lips on Ggaecheol's part that I realized his silence was his own protective shield. If he pushed me into the situation I feared, I would deny that anything had happened, and it was obvious that he would end up the loser.

It was the same for his relationships with all the other women of the village.

After the incident, I understood the village women more completely. To put it bluntly, he was the lover or potential lover of every one of them. But I did not yet understand why the village men accepted his behavior.

One cold afternoon before winter break that year, I was sitting by the stove, in the teachers' lounge, across from one of the male teachers who had grown up in the village. Only the two of us were still there in the empty schoolhouse, so I got him to talk about Ggaecheol—something I should have done earlier.

"He's an imbecile. And he's impotent."

The phrasing was a little different, but his assertion was the same as that of every other man in the village. Seeing him react so defensively annoyed me, and I methodically laid out what I had observed about the village. Of course, I omitted my own story.

He listened quietly until I was done. "You have remarkable observational skills," he said finally, with a helpless look. "I was born and raised in this village, but I only recently guessed at this. I didn't realize you were watching the villagers so carefully, Ms. Han."

I used that opening to ask another question. "But how can the men of the village allow Ggaecheol to behave like that?"

"There are probably lots of reasons, but I think there are two worth mentioning. One is vulnerable pride, and the other is utter pragmatism."

"Pride and pragmatism?"

"Pride means a man doesn't want to see himself as the victim. If a man wants to feel superior to Ggaecheol, he can't consciously know that he lost his wife to someone like that. What's more, he's got to believe that the other man is an idiot even if there's nothing wrong with him. It's a convenient rationalization. Pragmatism? That's what makes the men forgive Ggaecheol, because some other husband has suffered the same thing.

As you know, this village is made up of just one family clan. Everyone's related by blood or by marriage. Instead of suffering the shame of incest or having in-laws be discovered belly to belly, isn't it better to save face by letting Ggaecheol do what he does?"

That kind of logical explanation wasn't what I wanted. I wanted the pleasure of hearing about the villagers' fear of some kind of demonic violation; I wanted the vicarious joy of identifying with Ggaecheol, who was so free, shaking off the yoke of their tradition and their morality. But that seemed too much to ask, so instead I asked, "What about the man who beat Ggaecheol up in the middle of the village?"

"This is just my observation, but I think even Ggaecheol has certain rules. For example, avoiding young girls, or not going after the same woman twice. The young husbands tend to throw punches a bit too hastily, and even the older men wouldn't put up with it if their wives did that sort of thing too often. When Ggaecheol got beaten up that time, it was probably because he didn't stick to the rules."

It must have occurred to him that I wasn't a member of the clan, and that I wasn't married yet, because he suddenly blushed and started to stutter, bringing our conversation to an end. "W-well, it's all guesswork on my part. I just made some haphazard comments after your detailed observations, Ms. Han. W-what we just talked about, please be careful not to repeat it to the villagers. It would create problems."

His words, and even the expression on his face, were like those of the other middle-aged men in the village. When I finally got around to asking about Ggaecheol's past, he had already lost interest in the topic.

I left the village a little over three years after I began teaching there. When I got a letter from my husband saying that he had been discharged from the Army and that he had found a job, which he still has today, I submitted my resignation to the school so that I could prepare for our wedding. But there were only a limited number of teachers there, and if I had left immediately my classes would have been discontinued until my replacement arrived. So I had to stay on for three more days.

My replacement happened to be an alumna of my college, and on the day I left the village she walked me to the bus stop to see me off. Who knows when he showed up, but there was Ggaecheol, crouching on the back porch of the store, watching the new teacher with the same look he had given me on my first day.

Seeing that, I was going to tell her about Ggaecheol, but in the end I decided against it. In a village full of people who were so closely related, all tied to the same lineage, he was the sole drifting island of anonymity. Perhaps if she was like most of the village women—or like me two years ago, feeling unbearably trapped and sexually frustrated—she might have need of that anonymous island.

Instead of warning her about Ggaecheol, whose eyes clung to her almost hatefully, I shot him a cool look. He met my gaze with the same coolness. I might have been mistaken, but at that moment I thought I saw a faint laughter in his eyes. Just a glimmer. Then he turned his head toward the village and the paddy fields stretching out on the slopes below. There was not a piece of land or a fistful of dirt that he could call his own—or a house or a room where he could lay his head without the owner's consent—yet he gazed out over that land like a great man, the possessor of everything, an emperor.

NOODLES

Kim Sum

Translated by **Brother Anthony of Taizé**

A critique of this short story was published in the Koreana magazine in Fall 2015
(Vol. 29 No. 3, pp. 88-89).

© Kim Si-hoon

Right. Now it's kneading time. A time when I have to add water to the lightly mounded flour, one, two, three, four spoonfuls at a time, mixing it in and molding it into a lump of dough. A time when I have to mix and knead until the lump, its skin as rough as a blistered heel, grows smooth like a baby's face coated with milk lotion. I have to give it a vigorous massage….

I had just been rummaging in the kitchen cabinet, trying to find some perilla oil, when I came across a bag of flour. The moment I glimpsed the four-kilogram bag, its top sealed by a twisted yellow rubber band, I found myself seized by an urge to boil up a serving of noodles made with my own hands: kneading the dough, rolling it out, slicing out noodles one by one. I immediately took a large brass bowl and poured the flour into it from the bag. I shook the bag until it was empty; there looked to be enough flour for three or four bowls of noodles. I could not guess how large a lump of dough that amount of flour would yield, or how many strands of noodles it would produce. If the bag of flour had not caught my eye, hunched there behind the packs of seaweed and glass noodles like some neglected old man, I suppose I would now be boiling up some rice gruel. After pouring a handful of soaked rice into a saucepan and stir-frying it in perilla oil, then adding the water saved from washing the rice, I would be stirring it with a rice paddle to keep the grains from sticking to the bottom of the pan, until they began to come bubbling up. Grains of rice rising like futile thoughts… all of them….

I am waiting for the grains of salt to dissolve in the water. The grains of salt, that resemble grains of sand, have settled to the bottom of the drinking glass and show no sign of dissolving. In the glass, which is marked "Chilsung Cider," the water is quite still. The salt may be melting, moment by moment, but far too slowly for my inept, impatient eyes to be able to see. Until the grains of salt have vanished without a trace, am I supposed to wait forever, absentmindedly? Instead, with the time remaining… I finally take a spoon from the box. Using a spoon with a phoenix on the handle, I stir the water in the glass. It must measure about five centimeters across. In the narrow glass a whirlpool forms and the grains of salt rise upward, around and around… As I stare into the vortex I start to feel giddy. I have the sensation I am being sucked into a powerful eddy.

Little by little, parsimoniously, I pour in the water, where the salt grains have finally dissolved, and blend it with the flour. The flour grows damp, clumps roughly, sticks to my fingers. Rubbing the flour between my clenched fingers, I shape it into a lump. Pressing until the joints of my fingers bulge like bulbs... using my fingers to scrape off the wet flour sticking to the basin like chewing gum... Perhaps I had some vague premonition that one day a time like this, kneading time, would come to me; a time, I mean, when I would have to endure while repeatedly clenching then spreading my sluggish fingers. The kitchen window full of afternoon sunlight like a squashed persimmon... sitting like this, my back turned indifferently to the window.

As I keep firmly kneading the dough, I look around the kitchen. The plain yellow linoleum, bulging and scratched in places, the gray sink, the wallpaper with its pattern of purple morning glories, the Goldstar fridge, the rice cooker that could cook the rice then keep it warm, the green plastic pot with aloes growing in it, the pale green trash can, the calendar from Nonghyup, and the bamboo good-luck charm coated with dust, the neatly stacked, darkly stained saucepans, the rice jar decorated with the ten longevity symbols, the round portable dining table with its legs folded, leaning against the fridge... kneading time must be different from vegetable peeling time, or the time spent scraping the scales from half-frozen croakers, or brushing perilla oil on sheets of seaweed spread on a tray. Or the time for rubbing hard at macerated dried seaweed, or the time for crushing a handful of garlic, or the time for dicing radish, or the time for peeling burdock stems, or the time for roasting perilla seeds in a frying pan. Five in the afternoon, when all the world's shadows always fade... normally I would be out shopping or taking down and folding the washing. But I wonder why I feel as if I have mixed and kneaded flour in your kitchen like this before, not just yesterday but the day before and the day before and even the day before that as well?

For some reason the dough refuses to become less lumpy, repeatedly popping and splitting. I am still a long way from kneading the dough into smoothness, yet already there seems to be a smell of noodles being boiled. It is as though there is a cauldron somewhere in the house full of noodles, tangling and disentangling as they boil. The smell of noodles boiling... how can I describe that smell? The smell given off by noodles made of nothing but kneaded flour as they boil, I mean. Somehow serenely, calmly and subtly savory, that smell that slyly awakens a long-forgotten hunger… that smell is quite different from that emitted by boiling noodles produced and dried by machine—how to put it—just as the sounds of an organ and piano are different. I recall a scene where a cauldron of noodles was set down near a meal table. Leaning to one side, with the cover off. The layer of newspaper cradling the smoke-blackened cauldron, a white cotton cloth wrapped around its handles, the pile of nickel bowls like a tower beside it, the noodles scooped into the bowls, the steam rising from the noodles, the finger casually sweeping up the noodles dangling from the bowl….

The dough is still too dry, not soft enough. I'm going to have to add a little more water. Just a drop… no, not enough. Two drops… right, just two drops more… the more water I add, the soggier the noodles will be… and maybe the dough will be easier to handle, right, it will become more malleable, but on the other hand, the noodles I produce after all this effort may become too floppy and not stay firm.

At last the dough seems to be coming together into a lump. Yet still I have the feeling that the dough may be too hard. I recall once again the sight of you huddled like a visitor to one side of the wooden porch kneading dough. Pressing hard on the dough until I worried you would wear away the lines in the palm of your hands… things you dug secretly into the dough, obliged to just press and press… what could they have been? Was it really twenty-nine years ago already? That means that when you came to live with us you were the age I am now. You were forty-three then, now you are seventy-two and I am forty-three… The day you arrived, the family elders were gathered in this room speaking in hushed voices about the barren woman… Was it because I overheard them talking about how you had been divorced because you could not have children? To my childish eyes you looked crestfallen, like someone merely brought in as a domestic servant. Father, who in those days was selling tools in the central market, brought you home before heading back to work. Once the family elders left, you went into the kitchen and came out carrying a basin. In the bowl, which was used to serve sweet potatoes or kimchi, or for washing rice, you had put some flour. While shadows fell over the porch which had been full of sunlight, the dough you pressed and kneaded, the noodles you produced, then boiled… in those noodles there were no slivers of potato, pumpkin, or leek, no sliced egg. Without even adding any seasoning, you served them up and placed a bowl before each of my younger brothers and me. I must have felt upset and angry about something, I am not sure what… Using a spoon I cut up the noodles you had worked so hard to produce. All the noodles in the bowl, chopping away….

My wrists are already going numb. How much longer do I have to knead and rub until the dough is properly firm? How much more… *thud*… Intent on continuing to work at the dough, I start to feel myself growing old. By the time I lightly sprinkle flour on the dough, before flattening it with a rolling pin, I may feel as feeble and old as you. Once your husband, who was like a cold chimney, was dead and your stepchildren had left home, how many kneading hours did you spend while you cared for this house all alone. As I was making the noodles, I began to think of you… *thud*… From time to time you used to phone me and mutter those words. "Noodles, you say?" It seems you never realized that my taste in food was like Father's, not fond of dishes made of flour such as noodles. Moreover, as the eldest daughter, I had inherited a hard-hearted character just like Father's, hadn't I? Still, you felt anxious that you could not treat me to a bowl of noodles you had kneaded and cooked with your own hands.

I wonder why my fingers look so unfamiliar as they knead the dough on and on? I feel as though I have stolen someone else's fingers and am mindlessly using them as my own to go on kneading. Your fingers, I mean, as you lie in there sleeping. I recall the noodles you first cooked and placed in front of us; if there had been some sliced egg perched on those noodles, would I still have been able to cut them up with my spoon, I wonder… or if at least some scraps of dried seaweed had been sprinkled over them…?

"It's my tongue…."
"What about your tongue?"
"My tongue…."
…
"It ached and throbbed so much that I had to stop eating noodles."

…?

"Even just touching the noodles made my tongue hurt as though it was being smoothed with a plane."

…

"They say I need to be examined at a major hospital."

Seized by a sudden urge, I feel like throwing the dough away. If I go to the store, I can find lots of noodles that are softer and stickier than those I could produce with my own hands, so why make such a wretched effort? I feel myself growing irritated.

Not only the dough; I barely manage to control an urge to hurl down the brass bowl… maybe… *thud*… *thud*… it may be that I am enduring this kneading out of a sense of repaying a debt. Indeed. Since some time ago, whenever I think of you, I start to feel as though I am running away charged with a debt that I can never repay, even if I keep on paying for a whole lifetime.

"My tongue…."

…

"Cut out my tongue, please…."

You called at two in the morning and after I hung up, you can't imagine how shaken with anxiety I was. Not out of concern for your tongue that was hurting so intensely that you wanted to have it cut out… not because of concern for your tongue… It was only two months later that I had you come up to Seoul and took you to a hospital. Blood tests, urine tests, ultrasound tests, all kinds of tests. The three hours of tests left us both exhausted. More than the tests themselves, it was going to each examination room, one after another, then waiting your turn, that wearied you. As though everyone in the world were sick, you remarked, every examination room was crowded like the waiting room in a railway station. Once we left the hospital, I took you to a noodle restaurant. The tests had you fasting since the previous evening and there seemed to be no other restaurant suitable for me to take you to except for the noodle restaurant. The noodles were served in stainless steel bowls about ten minutes after we ordered, and were different from those you would make. They were the same noodles, but a quite different kind of food. With one bowl costing seven thousand won, they served the flat, thin noodles garnished with zucchini in a milky bone broth... you only took a couple of spoonfuls of the broth.

The noodles you used to prepare... there were just two occasions when I really longed to eat those noodles. It was back in the days when I had moved up to Seoul and was cooking for myself while working. One evening, coming home from work, I bought flour from the store in front of my home and prepared some dough. Not having a proper bowl, I poured one whole pack of flour into a saucepan, and dribbled in water. Crouching before the television, I kneaded the dough until the moist mixture clung to my fingers. Cooking for myself, I had no rolling pin, so finally I wrapped the lump of dough I had prepared in a plastic bag and put it into the vegetable container of the fridge. As I took it out later, when cleaning the fridge, the lump of dough had turned as hard as stone and was covered with dark blue mold. I reckon that lump of dough I tossed into the trash must be roaming the world like a stone. It must simply be rolling here and there... rolling, rolling until it scatters as gravel... at last turning into grains of sand... I remember reading somewhere that there is sand that goes flying beyond Earth's atmosphere and reaches Mars. Come to think of it, that lump of dough even looked like Mars. Mars, where sometimes sandstorms arise. To tell the truth, that day, I had been fired from my job... Perhaps because it was my very first job and I had only been working there for five months when I heard I had been fired, standing in front of the coffee machine, my only thought was that I wanted to eat some noodles. That I wanted to put a portion of noodles your hands had made into my mouth and chew them like a docile, sluggish ox... Nine months passed before I was employed again but I never let you know my situation.

Perhaps because it is so quiet, with me making dough and you sleeping deeply, we seem to be the only humans on earth. How much longer must I rub and knead and mix before I have produced dough suitable for making noodles, I wonder. What you once poured salty water onto in the basin and kneaded on and on, I think, must have been time, rather than flour. Suddenly such thoughts... *thud*... I never imagined I would one day be kneading flour into dough in your kitchen... *thud.*

Just a bit more, a bit more pressing.

You came to visit my house only once, right? It was in my eighth year of marriage, when I was in bed recovering after losing the baby I had been pregnant with after AI and all sorts of difficulties. My husband contacted you as he was leaving for a few days, away working in Busan; the next day you took the bus at dawn and arrived at my house. I said I wanted noodles to eat… so you kneaded flour into dough in my messy, unfamiliar kitchen and prepared a bowl. Crouching huddled beneath the table, just as on the day you first came to us. Making broth with a chicken, cooking the noodles in it, slicing thin strips of the flesh, seasoning them with sesame oil and perilla seeds, using that as a garnish… chicken noodle broth that seemed sure to act as a tonic if I only consumed one bowlful. You served it up with water kimchi you brought from home in place of a sauce.

"If you wait quietly, one will come. If you just wait, it will come naturally…."

After you left, I flushed the bloated noodles down the toilet. Before the elevator carrying you had even reached the ground floor from the fifteenth, cursing your fate and mine. Flushing and flushing until the toilet had swallowed up every last strand… in that way I was transferring to you the blame for my not having a baby. Blaming you, with whom I had not a drop of blood, not a scrap of flesh, not a sliver of bone in common. Perhaps because I wanted to believe that your fate had taken control of my fate. Just as two strands of noodles, that should stay separate, somehow stick together as they cook and form a lump, your fate and mine seemed to have clumped together….

If I wait, you said?

Perhaps it was because I learned far too early that there are sometimes things that do not come, no matter how long one waits. My mother setting off for the house of her brother, who ran a dry cleaner's… Mother had said she would be back before evening and though I waited she never came back. I waited as the evening grew ever deeper, festered, ready to burst, until day dawned bright just as mold blooms on a festering spot… On the day you came to us, too, I think I spent the whole day waiting for Mother. It simply seemed that if I only waited Mother would come back alive. If I waited earnestly… And I think I spent the whole time you were in charge of us in place of Mother waiting for her. That might be why I never once called you "Mother." While I had striven to repudiate you and keep you at a distance, it seemed that if I ate a bowl of the noodles you had prepared, my body that had so pointlessly expelled the baby would somehow recover. Noodles with clams, noodles with red beans, noodles with potatoes, noodles with dumplings... there are all kinds of noodles, but even one bowl of the exceedingly plain, austere noodles you prepared... that rolling pin you left behind in my kitchen... when we moved house, I left it behind.

The cancer in your tongue had already spread considerably, resection surgery was inevitable, but how should I tell you the doctor's explanation? Would it be better to wait, saying nothing, until you had taken several mouthfuls of noodles and then bring it up...? *Thud....*

Maybe because the consistency of the dough has become so firm and sticky, I begin to feel as though I am kneading not a lump of flour dough but a lump of resentment. It's as though I am engaged in a wrestling match with hard, tough resentment. Exerting reckless stubbornness in an attempt to see if you win or I win... The angrier I become, the more my fingers attack persistently and tenaciously, while this resentment only grows stickier. And yet... somehow, despite the resentment, something seems to be loosening up inside me. Something tight and deep like this cursed resentment... something that no other word comes to me to explain: resentment, softening... I wonder if for you kneading times were not also times to soothe and loosen the resentment inside you?

This lump of dough is the size of an average face. Perhaps because of that, I feel as if I am making dough, not to produce noodles but simply to make a certain form. If I shape this dough into a form, it will turn out to be your face, I guess. A resigned, inscrutable face, with joy and anger, sorrow and pleasure, various contradictory emotions, jumbled together until even a single emotion can barely be detected on it... Even if I leave the dough as it is, I have a feeling it will take on a form exactly resembling your face, without any hand to guide it. Indeed, it seems that the dough is, little by little, of its own accord, taking on the shape of your face.

I try to imagine piercing a hole in the dough, that looks exactly like you, and puffing breath into it.

Puffff.

I wonder how many strands of noodles I shall be able to produce from this lump of dough. The noodles you used to make were neither too thick nor too thin.

"Shall I cook noodles for you?"

With that voice, that sounded like a dried fish being torn, I turn around in surprise. Am I hearing things? Yet it had been clear... Beyond the sliding door, I do not see you in the living room. It must have been an auditory hallucination.

Will one hour be enough? The time for the dough to mature, I mean. During the time it is left unfussed, undisturbed, the dough would grow soft and sticky. Once the dough had been worked enough, you used to wrap it in plastic and set it aside, covered with the bowl. One hour, two hours, sometimes half a day might pass and you would leave it alone, as if you had forgotten it. You knew for sure that while it was being ignored in that way, the dough would grow deeper and come to full maturity. How else might I express that ripening time? A time of withdrawal? A time of alienation? A time of inner silence? A time for introspection? I remember reading somewhere that, scientifically speaking, four or five hours is the optimal time for dough to mature. Also that keeping it in a fridge rather than at room temperature is effective. Four or five hours... only I don't have time to leave the dough that long. This evening I have to catch the express bus back home. At the latest, I have to leave here by eight if I am to reach Seoul before midnight. Then you will be alone in this house again. Feeling impatient, I long to roll out the dough, cut it into thin slices with a kitchen knife and make the noodles straightaway, but... just for one hour... I want to leave it alone for at least an hour so that the dough can have time to mature. I have kneaded it enough, so one way or another it ought to yield reasonably good noodles now, but I should wrap it in plastic... I feel sure that somewhere in the kitchen you keep a pile of wrapping cloths. Cloths folded the size of my hand, neatly piled in a drawer of the cabinet... pale green, golden, orange, purple. The purple one will do. After wrapping the bowl in the purple cloth and putting it in a dark corner of the kitchen, I feel numb and hollow….

While the dough enjoys its ripening time all by itself inside the purple wrapping cloth, what am I supposed to do? I get pins and needles in my right hand. The fierce earthquake-like tremors that visited my right hand that felt like ruined land seem unlikely to subside for quite some time. I quietly clasp my right hand with my left. Is it because I have passed through the kneading time? My right hand seems like your hand, not mine. Just suppose… if the first food you placed before me and my siblings had not been noodles, what would have happened? If it had been, not mere plain noodles, but presentable, creditable food, I mean. *Japchae, bulgogi, gimbap…* or a saucepan full of well-boiled pork and kimchi stew. Or even noodles, only garnished with beef, I mean. Or if you had served up the noodles cooked in a broth made with dried anchovies and kelp, with chopped potatoes and leeks.

While I was kneading, five calls had come in and remained unanswered on my mobile. Three were from my husband, two from the gynecology unit. I did not tell you I had decided to make one more attempt with AI. The appointment at the hospital to have the procedure had been today. At about ten I left home to go to the hospital and took a bus that passed via the bus terminal. After spending an hour in the terminal's waiting room, I took an express bus and came down here. Was something suddenly drawing me toward you? You were due to come up to Seoul in six days' time, after all. You asked nothing, as though you had been expecting me. From your deeply lined face, both cheeks sunken like ravines, I could vaguely guess the pain your tongue was enduring.

Blindly. Will there ever again be a day when I come visiting you blindly like this?

I once saw an old man eating noodles alone in a restaurant. It was not a restaurant specializing in noodles, it mainly sold rice and soup. The old man was eating noodles alone at a table in one corner. Clutching chopsticks in a hand shaking so much I wondered if he suffered from a hand tremor… lifting the noodles… inserting them into a mouth like a small dish. Lifting five or six strands at a time with difficulty, he seemed to be uprooting them from deep underground... The noodles were so precariously pinched between the chopsticks that by the time they reached the old man's lips only a couple were left. How he must have wanted to eat them to have ordered noodles alone like that in a restaurant... The idea that he was not eating noodles simply to serve as a meal seemed to come from something about the old man's appearance, suggesting some kind of desperate effort. Was it that the old man looked needy and pathetic? If it had been at all possible I would have liked to slyly place a bowl of your noodles in front of the old man. I had been intending to eat soft tofu stew, but on an impulse ordered noodles instead. The noodles submerged in a broth tasting of artificial seasoning were a disappointment, not worth the five thousand won they cost. Not that I had expected anything better. The zucchini sliced into half-moons, three or four of them, was almost raw and gave off a metallic taste. The meat of the clams, perhaps deep-frozen, was shriveled and wretched like scraps of spat-out chewing gum. All other things aside, the noodles themselves were dreadful... neither sticky nor soft, but slippery and tough, they were just like slivers of thick paper... When I exited from the restaurant, leaving half of what I had ordered uneaten, the old man was still silently consuming his noodles.

There is no time to stay gazing blankly into the distance; I have to prepare the sauce to go with the noodles. Why, I had nearly forgotten about the sauce. Hoping that there might be some sauce you had made, I explored the fridge but there was nothing besides some leftover stew made from bean curd dregs and a few side dishes. Surely the sauce was the highlight of your homemade noodles? Since you do not add any seasoning while cooking the noodles, without sauce there is nothing to savor but the taste of flour. You wouldn't have forgotten how important seasoning is for food? No matter how fresh or fancy the ingredients used to make a dish are, if the seasoning is wrong it ends up spoiled. The sauce you used to prepare separately to provide the seasoning... It was only after adding a couple of spoonfuls of that sauce and stirring it in that your noodles yielded their true taste. Finely chopped chives and chilis, chili powder, sesame seeds, starch syrup, perilla oil, Joseon-style soy sauce... I prepare a mental list of the ingredients needed for the sauce. I will have to go out to the store to buy the chives and chilis, at least. As I emerge onto the porch holding my phone and purse, I glance into the bedroom where you are lying motionless, turned toward the wall, before walking to the sliding door. I put on your slippers and pass through the entrance gate where my eyes suddenly fall on the doorplate… Father has been gone a long while but it still bears his name… and after all, the owner of the house is my younger brother, not you. In addition, this rundown neighborhood is bound to be redeveloped within the next few years. It was only when I was getting married and went to the local office to obtain the copy of my family register I needed to register my marriage that I realized you had never been added to it, you had always lived as a kind of ghost. There was no sign of your name anywhere in the copy of the family register I received. I forgot to wash my hands. The flour that adhered to my fingers, palms and backs of my hands while I was kneading is now coming off like dead skin. After hesitating whether to go back in again and wash my hands, I go on walking down the alley. Though mixed with starch syrup, sesame seeds and perilla oil, I still always disliked sauce made with Joseon-style soy sauce; its bitter taste is stronger than that of the brewed soy sauce we call Japanese-style, and in addition I find its rich, stale taste and smell unpleasant… so I used to dislike mixing the dark brown sauce into the cloudy broth of the noodles, to say nothing of the way the noodles emerged coated with chili powder, chives and sesame seeds….

One bunch of chives, one bag of chilis, a kilogram of flour, a box of soy milk packs, a box of strawberries. Then going in the butcher's shop beside the store, I purchase a pound of beef for making soup. Unable to just pass in front of the bakery, a castella and some red bean jelly, too. The counter clerk at the bakery, who must have been about my age, flinched as she was about to hand over my change. She must have seen my hands and been startled by the bits of dough from the kneading that still clung to my fingers. "I've been making noodles, you see…" I muttered, embarrassed. "My goodness, you mean there are still people who make their own noodles?" At the clerk's incredulous response, my face flushed and I quickly left. She seemed to be looking at me the way people look at old-fashioned or eccentric people… a pointless inferiority complex I had. All the while I was kneading, there had been one thought that refused to leave my mind, I could not rid myself of the thought that I was making a fuss over nothing… There is something we have never discussed, something I do not want to discuss, but once you are gone, where are you to be buried? The plot beside Father's grave is occupied by Mother's. She had been buried there early, after giving birth to the four of us, and had then been waiting for Father. What would have happened if even one of us had been your child?

Indeed, perhaps I had been wanting to ask you bluntly. And therefore… perhaps that was why I had so abruptly come to visit you. Perhaps I wanted to hear you answer while your tongue was still intact… what it was like to live a whole lifetime as a woman without ever bearing a child. Living in this world with its six billion inhabitants without a single being to whom you gave your flesh and blood… without one being so absolute and intense that the words "my baby" come flowing out automatically… like a string. The idea that children are strings is something I once heard a friend say. Not simply a string linking you with your husband, but one serving as a link with the world, she said. Just as the bakery clerk's words had suggested, unlike the women of today, my friend married early and had four children. Come to think of it, noodles do look like strings. Long and thin like the white laces of sneakers… I wonder if the noodles you produced were not your strings. It might be that you used to knead flour dough and produce noodles in place of the strings we call children. Maybe it was because you hated to see those strings swell up then droop uselessly that you used to stuff them into your mouth as you did? I no longer remember when it was that I noticed you did not bite off the noodles with your teeth. Instead, you somehow used to pull them up with your chopsticks till you reached the end. Hauling them up… rolling them into your mouth. Down to the last drooping, slippery strand. While I chopped up every one of those noodles with my spoon… all… Were you hurt? I once asked you that. As you were stir-frying chopped radish in perilla oil in a deep frying pan for Father's Memorial Day offerings.

"Hurt? Not in the least…."

You murmured, as if speaking to yourself, and poured a ladle of the water used to wash the rice into the pan. As I watched the half-fried chopped radish being swamped in the rice water, I thought that your reply was not honest. "How could one not be hurt?" I asked abruptly, in a spurt of defiance. Were you really not hurt?

"What could there be to feel hurt about…?"

Probably the life bringing up us four children was the best for you. Having already produced three sons as well as a daughter, Father would not have had any desire to have more children with you, while you as a woman must have been content not to have to fear being abandoned again. Nowadays people declare frankly that they are not going to have children, but when you were young, things were not the same. One day, about four years after you came to live with us, your mother paid a visit, I recall. She suddenly dropped in, bringing seaweed and dried anchovies like some peddler, ate a bowl of noodles you prepared for her, then left for her home again. I can clearly recall her appearance, as she adamantly refused your urging to go into the main room and ate the noodles sitting on the wooden porch. Her appearance as she stared at us four children with bean-like eyes while quickly scooping up the noodles with a spoon. One noodle strand after another… one strand… one… I wonder if she was wishing we were children you had borne. The thousand-won notes she gave to me and to each of my younger brothers before she left… those crumpled banknotes were somehow like slices of her flesh… so similar were they to bits of her flesh sliced off and given to us that I immediately went rushing out to the store to exchange mine for cookies. Then only about two months later news came that she had died and you hurried down to a place called Jinan in North Jeolla Province for the funeral. When you came back five days later, you had a pin in your hair with a white ribbon attached. Have I ever told you how much I worried in suspense during those five days? I felt you might never return… like Mother, you too… I wonder why her image has remained fixed so indelibly in my mind, although like you she and I did not have a drop of blood in common. Unlike the way the appearance of my maternal grandmother, whose blood I share, completely faded long ago.

Lifting the purple wrapping cloth, I prod the dough with a finger… then removing the plastic wrapping, I try feeling it. Is the dough still too hard, even though I added more water in the middle of kneading it? While it was maturing, it should have gained elasticity and consistency, and tough-ened up. If the dough is too dry to begin with, I think it is because I was afraid it would turn out too soft after all my efforts, so soft that the only solution would be to make dough flakes instead of noodles. Or the noodles might stick together even before they are put into the boiling water. Dough for noodles is a real challenge, though making dough for flakes is easy enough. In any case, surely there would be no point in trying to add more water then kneading the already matured dough again. Since its viscosity would have increased, the water would not be able to penetrate evenly into the dough. The surface of the dough might become so wet that it would make rolling impossible… in fact adding more water to already matured dough can only be thought of as sheer willfulness. Although I can't say it is against the natural order of things, it would certainly be like changing a process that is right and proper. Nevertheless, it is also impossible to start making dough again… you might wake up while I am making new dough, and besides, I simply can't start all over again.

Just a single strand. Yes, if only your tongue could roll up a single noodle without any pain… that tongue of yours that smarts and stings when even water touches it, let alone a grain of rice.

Whether the dough is too hard or too soft, I must get on with rolling out and slicing the noodles. Noodles as fine as silk threads, if I have my way. For that, I will have to roll the dough until it is as thin as a sheet of paper. Then I will have to uniformly fold the evenly, smoothly rolled out dough like folding diapers… and slice that while pressing skillfully with my thumb, middle finger and index finger.

The way you sprinkled flour over the dough you had rolled as thin and wide as a wrapping cloth, the way you folded it comes to my mind. Sitting with one bent knee raised, close to the chopping board, slicing the dough… with your head tilted to one side….

One bowl of noodles….

My brothers and I only realized that there were many kinds of food you had never even seen, let alone tasted, when we took you to supper at a shabu-shabu restaurant for your seventieth birthday. You said that it was the first time in your life that you ate shabu-shabu, all sorts of vegetables and beef dunked quickly in boiling broth at the table. You said you had never tasted monkfish stew, that so many people eat. Then have you ever eaten assorted seafood and vegetables in mustard sauce? Five-spice pork? Tuna sashimi? Pufferfish soup? Mung bean jelly with beef and vegetables? Steak?

The kitchen is so dark I have to have the light on. The sound of the noodles being sliced rings like a hallucination. I find a clean cotton wrapping cloth and spread that on the kitchen floor, then lay the wooden chopping board on that. Opening the bag of flour I bought at the store, I take a handful and sprinkle it evenly over the board. I lay the dough onto that and press it down... as you used to... you would lay it on the board then, before rolling it out, you would pat it gently as though soothing it, press it down, shape it. As though helping it relax.

I recall the sight of flour-coated noodles scattered over a round, silvery tray. Also the sight of the noodles dancing and swaying as they loosened up in the boiling water. As well as the sight of the whitish noodles growing ever paler as they cooked, and the foam seeming ready to brim over the edge of the cauldron.

Ah, in the meantime, the dough has been hardening. Moving on my knees, I draw closer to the chopping board and sit down. I pick up the rolling pin, that has been accustomed to your hands for more than thirty years, and lower it onto the dough. Gently pressing down, I push the rolling pin forward. Your two hands, that would start resting together at the center of the pin used to slide outward. Just as positive and negative repel each other, your two hands would separate. Then bringing your hands together again at the center of the pin, rolling forward... after sprinkling flour like rain drizzling down, again rolling... all the time turning the dough so that it did not grow uneven but spread out in a circle....

When you were rolling out the dough, it almost looked as though you were performing full prostrations in a Buddhist temple; if I told you that, you would surely shake your head from side to side.

Near the supermarket where I usually do my shopping, there is a man who parks his small truck at the roadside and sells ready-to-cook noodles. Dressed like a cook in a Chinese restaurant, he stands there energetically rolling out dough and making fresh noodles. I wonder what circumstances led him to sell handmade noodles from a small truck. Not cooked noodles in broth, but just plain, uncooked noodles. Four or five helpings? Even when there are no buyers in sight, every time I see that man, he is busily making more noodles. Amidst all that noise and pollution and mess, standing there silently, rolling out dough.

For some reason, despite the effort going into my wrists, the dough refuses to spread properly. It seems as though, instead of a lump of flour dough, I have a lump of lead from somewhere that I am trying to roll flat. Was my aim of producing noodles as thin as silk threads a mere wild ambition? The way the dough is refusing to spread properly, even though I apply all my strength in pressing down on the rolling pin, is surely not simply because the dough has hardened. It's because my body linked to the rolling pin cannot get into the rhythm. Whereas when you rolled out the dough, your body was filled with rhythm. Not just your hands and wrists but from head to toe. With a slow yet heated rhythm you rolled and the dough gradually spread out.

The noodles you produced were neither too thick nor too thin. Not too tough, not so soft as to break easily, or swell up and burst.

Neither flat nor round, the dough seems to be stretched and pulled here and there in every direction at random. No matter how carefully I slice, it will be so irregular that I doubt if noodles of similar thickness and length will result. How was it that I could only roll the dough into something looking like this? With this self-reproach, despondency surges over me. What should I do? Unwilling to put down the rolling pin, I sprinkle the dough with flour and fold it in half. Then sprinkle more flour, fold it again… until it is half as wide as before… then raising my right knee I draw close to the chopping board… *snip… snip, snip…* The stuff I am now cutting with the kitchen knife resembles cardboard or paper rather than dough.

I scatter the noodles on the silvery tray. I am supposed to separate and scatter the strands using slack fingers like someone combing their few remaining strands of hair. Fumbling as I raise them so that the strands hang loose between my fingers… one by one I separate strands that remain folded together because I pressed too hard as I was cutting. As I look down at the noodles floating in a white cloud of flour, the thought that they look like strings strikes me more acutely... like a connection linking you in there and me out here... long or short or thick or thin or crooked, one by one, all of them... all....

A sudden urge comes take to take the noodles I cut as best I could and crumple them together again.

Now I must quickly put a cauldron of water on to boil. To boil the noodles. Before my hands obey my whim and crush the noodles together. The kitchen echoes with the sound of the flame on the gas range flaring up. Now I only have to wait for the water to boil and keep the noodles from tangling together as I put them in; then it will be finished. I pick up the little folding table leaning against the fridge, unfold the legs and wipe it with a cloth. Taking out the bowls for the noodles, I rinse them and set them ready... To the previously chopped chives and chilis I add two spoonfuls of soy sauce, half a spoonful of starch syrup, half a spoonful of chili powder, half a spoonful of sesame seeds, and half a spoonful of perilla oil, and stir them together. It looks as though I will not be able to go back home tonight. It's already past eight.

I hear the sound of the water boiling behind me. You still have given no sign of life and the noodles are hardening helplessly. From beyond the window comes the sound of feet returning home. Water will probably be boiling in some other person's kitchen too, not only yours. The sound of water boiling seems to be bubbling from inside of myself. From some time back, something seems to have been boiling somewhere inside me. Without my realizing it, something has reached boiling point... I stand up, carrying the tray. As I take off the lid, steam rises like a flock of freshly hatched white butterflies. It overlaps with memories of something I once saw on the television, a cloud of butterflies emerging like smoke from a tree whose stump alone remained... and I grow blank. Having been cut down, unable to stretch out branches, bloom with leaves and flowers, and thus incapable of bearing fruit, the trunk of the tree sending out a cloud of butterflies; the scene had been a quite wonderful spectacle. Clouds grew heavy like rocks, the wind raged fiercely like a wild ram all night long, then came the sight of it releasing into the air the thousands of butterflies it had been embracing carefully inside itself. Only suppose… if that tree had been a solid tree, if there had not been an empty space like a cavern inside its leftover stump, how would it have been able to embrace all those butterflies? Likewise, weren't you a leftover tree stump for us? On a chaotic night when bats fluttered, gladly embracing us… no matter how wildly we raged, you put down strong roots. Never shaking… Then once the butterflies had flown up from the tree stump, they scattered into the cobalt-hued dawn without once looking back.

I wait for the steam to disperse, then pick up a handful of noodles. I scatter the dry, stiff strands into the boiling water. I stir them well to make sure they do not clump together, then another handful… the noodles dance lightly, white foam rises, threatens to overflow… Turning down the gas a little, I go on stirring with the ladle….

While I kneaded the dough, cut up the noodles then boiled them, much time seems to have elapsed. Not just three or four hours, much longer than that. It seems people began making and eating noodles around 2000 B.C. Traces have been found in the Yellow River basin, the oldest datable evidence of the existence of noodles, apparently. I remember hearing that those noodles were made with sorghum flour, not wheat.

From 2000 B.C. until now, a period of time too long to calculate, it all seems to be contained in one bowl of noodles.

I suppress a longing to improve things with a sprinkling of egg garnish. From the beginning I wanted to offer you a bowl of noodles no different from those you first served us, noodles no simpler and no more elaborate than your own. Clasping the table, with nothing but the boiled noodles and the sauce on it, I cross the kitchen threshold. As the edge of the table touches the sliding door, the opaque glass shakes.

You must have woken up at some point; you are sitting forlornly to one side of the room. Perhaps you have been awake this whole… The sound of the grains of salt melting in the water, the sound of rubbing and kneading as I poured the salty water into the flour, the sound of the dough being pounded, the sound of the cutting board shaking and banging while I was rolling out the dough, the sound of the dough, folded like a diaper, being sliced with the kitchen knife, the sound of the noodles boiling, the sound of the table's four legs being unfolded, perhaps you have heard all these sounds without saying a word....

"Why, you've cooked noodles."

Smoothing your disheveled hair, you approach the table. Holding the spoon, you scoop up the sauce and transfer it to the bowl of noodles. You stir it around in order to mix it in evenly. Changing to chopsticks, you stir again a few times, then lift up some noodles. Five or six strands dangle from the chopsticks as you raise them.

Before you can open your mouth, the noodles you have labored to pick up slip off. Even the last, barely remaining strand finally falls from your chopsticks. After all, it looks as though your tongue is not up to the task of dealing with the noodles, so I pick up the spoon. I begin to snip and cut the strands. Just as I did long ago to the first noodles you ever served to me. Only my feelings then and my feelings now as I snip at the noodles are clearly different. *Snip, snip... snip.*

SAMPUNG DEPARTMENT STORE

Jeong Yi Hyun

Translated by Brother Anthony of Taizé

삼풍백화점

정이현

A critique of this short story was published in the Koreana magazine in Summer 2008 (Vol. 22 No. 2, pp. 85-87).

© Cha Jae-ok

At five fifty-five in the afternoon on June 29, 1995, Sampung Department Store, located in Seocho-dong in southern Seoul, collapsed without warning. It took less than one second for each floor to collapse onto the one below.

In the spring that year I possessed many things: somewhat right-wing parents, a clean, super single bed, a translucent green Motorola pager, and four handbags. In the evening on weekends I went out with a boyfriend who had recently begun to work for a securities company. Our dates followed the directions found in *Dating Manual for Model Exchanges With the Opposite Sex* to a T, though I have not checked if such a book actually exists. I was quite convinced that I could become anything I wanted if I put my mind to it, only there was nothing that I wanted to be. The fact that we were still barely halfway through the 1990s perplexed me intensely. I was poised to say, "Well that was a beautiful year, wasn't it?" But on second thought I felt irresponsible, as if I had become one of those telemarketers who dial numbers at random and urge people to invest in real estate. At the very least, I resolved to remember to say that 1995 had been special in some way.

I had embarked upon regular education some twenty years prior to 1995. My mother, who nourished optimistic expectations regarding the education our country provided for small children, seized her barely four-year-old daughter's hand and went along to visit the local nursery school. It was the place with the best reputation in the neighborhood. The directress, butterfly-shaped horn-rimmed glasses perched on the tip of her nose, scrutinized my face carefully. "Why, she still looks like a baby." Mother's feelings were hurt. "You think so? But she's much more forward than she looks." I had no wish to disappoint my mother, so I kept my lips shut tight as a clam and focused all my energy into making my eyes shine. I still do the same thing, sometimes, when I want to protect myself from an adult I am meeting for the first time. As the directress agreed to take me, she uttered the following curse: "It's time now to start learning about the order of life in the community." The mighty order of life in the community! Waking from the same dreams, shouldering the same kind of book bag, arriving at school at the same time, learning the same songs and actions, then eating from the same lunch menu.

Four years old. Constantly late. I was completely unable to understand why day after day I had to be forcibly wakened from sweet morning sleep by someone else. I was unable to accept it. Every morning Mother was obliged to pick me up and go running down the alley with me on her back. Our home help Suk-ja, who in those days worshipped the celebrity Nam Jin, ran along with us, supporting my behind with her hand. The class teacher expressed curiosity about the reason for my repeated lateness. "It's not my fault, Miss. I get up as soon as the round sun rises. That's what you taught us, isn't it, Miss? 'The round sun rises.' Getting up, first I brushed my teeth, brushing my upper teeth and my lower teeth, washed my face and combed my hair before I got dressed; then I was ready for the next step, having breakfast. But, oh no, I found that Mother and Suk-ja were still sound asleep. Nobody was making breakfast for me. You know, don't you, Miss? I'm still only four. I'm much too young to prepare breakfast all on my own, aren't I, Miss? So I woke Mother, then waited for breakfast to be ready, ate it up, then set off, but I arrived late. As side dishes I had beans in soy sauce and fried dried anchovies, with seaweed soup, I like all those, Miss." Being legally responsible for a student who repeatedly arrived late for school, Mother was soon summoned. She must have found it unfair, but she could not allow her daughter to be considered a failure, so Mother told me she had promised that in the future, come what may, she would get up before her daughter and have breakfast ready on time. Those were days when I only had to open my mouth for a flood of lies to come pouring out as if I were possessed.

Unfortunately, my parents did not seem to take symptoms of social maladjustment, such as laziness or lying, very seriously. Rather, they very likely felt proud that my command of language was so far superior to that of other children my age. That was especially true of my father, who was already thirty-five when his first child was born, quite late for those days. His boast at his daughter's first birthday celebration, when she managed to haul herself upright by holding on to the table, comparing her to the winner of the Olympic marathon, was an example that remained in the memories of all the family members present at the party. Before I started school, if we had a visitor, Father would summon me to the living room and make me read from the newspaper in a loud voice. "Why, how has she mastered the alphabet so soon?" When the visitor politely pretended to be amazed, he would modestly reply with another question: "Well, surely every child can do the same nowadays, can't they?" I shyly hid my mouth and laughed as befitted one who was "a prodigy, at least." My heart would race at the idea the guest might ask me what time it was. Apart from the occasional Chinese character, I could read the editorials in the morning paper quite clearly, but I was incapable of telling the time. The moment figures appeared, I suddenly used to grow dizzy like someone suffering from amnesia, and the world would start to whirl about me. Likewise, for a long time I was unable to tell my left hand from my right, but that problem found a natural solution when, at the age of eight, I slashed my left wrist against a glass door.

"If it had been just a fingernail's width further up, it would have caught the artery; she's a lucky kid." The doctor in the neighborhood clinic, which provided a vast variety of treatments, from obstetrics and gynecology, through internal medicine, pediatrics and otorhinolaryngology to orthopedics, sewed my gaping skin together in a rough and ready manner. A long, jagged, slanting scar remained on my left wrist. "Whatever will become of a girl with a thing like that on her body?" Mother wept, but I was flying high. Now I no longer had to blush with shame and shoot furtive glances at my neighbor at the words, "Everyone raise their left hand!" Now all I had to do was shoot up the hand with the scar on it. In later times, the scar produced by bad stitching used to enrage my friend's boyfriend, who was a national representative for doctors specializing in orthopedics, but strange to say I never once felt ashamed of it. One day in the 1990s, in a fit of utter boredom, I even calculated the length of the scar using a tape measure; it was no less than eight centimeters long. That was about the same as the height of the platform shoes that were fashionable at the time. When I found myself confronted in the street with a woman wearing such shoes, a slight sense of affinity and an unexpected feeling of melancholy used to strike me.

On June 29, 1995, the weather was stiflingly hot. At three minutes past five I entered Sampung Department Store through the front door. "We apologize to our customers for a failure in the store's air-conditioning system. It will be repaired by tomorrow." The elevator girl spoke with a warm smile.

In the spring of that year, I was the proud owner of the email ID "myself," of twenty-four friends who were either university students, or on leave from university, or had already graduated, of the first three albums by Seotaeji, and of the latest model of the Le Mot 3 word processor. In my desk drawer student cards issued by several well-known language institutes were rattling around. In the early 1990s, I had certainly spent far more time in English conversation institutes located near Gangnam Subway Station than on my university campus up in Seongbuk-gu. That was even more the case if time is not something absolute, but relative. I chose the nickname Sally for myself. My classmates in the conversation class asked if I'd taken it from the movie *When Harry met Sally* but actually it was adapted from the Japanese anime *Mohotsukai Sally*. So long as I did not have to be addressed by my real name, I felt it did not matter in the least if I was called Sally, Candy, Iraija, or even Pipi. It was the time when Jeong Hyeon-cheol, transformed into Seotaeji, was at his peak.

1995 was the year I was ejected from the national education system. Then as now, the fact that Seotaeji and I are the same age made me feel proud and inferior at the same time. In March 1992 it was their first hit, *I Know*. In August 1994, they released *Dreaming of Balhae*, "There's one thing I hope for; when shall I be able to meet friends from this divided land? We lost each other as we hesitated." I suddenly came to my senses and realized that my final autumn in university was almost over. "Now we're going to turn into old women," one of my friends sighed. I proceeded to stare at her glistening lips. I was curious as to the brand of lipstick she was using. Someone in possession of a job and a boyfriend was a gold medalist, someone with neither was a wood medalist, for sure. Another friend cracked a cruel joke. According to her criteria, since at the same time as she was starting her final semester she had started work as an intern with a prestigious investment banking firm, and she had a boyfriend attending a national university, she was a laurel-crowned gold medalist. I could not get to sleep at night. For the past ten years, every time I applied for a part-time job I had written, without lying, that I was a "student." I had never once thought that, after graduating from high school, there might be a direction I could take other than becoming a university student or a student at a cram school before reapplying for a university the following year. It was no different now I was graduating from university. After an extensive online search I visited the photographer who took the best ID photos in Seoul. Hoping to appear docile, reliable and sociable, I smiled at the camera and said "whisky." It was a method I had learned from a friend who had recently passed the exam to become an air hostess for the national carrier. With my teeth half revealed, the corners of my mouth turning upward, it was hard to claim that the me on my curriculum vitae was not really me.

I prepared ten copies of my personal statement on my word processor. "I am a solid individual." That was how I began the personal statement I submitted to a brick company. The statement for a stationery goods company started: "I have a pen made by your company beside me as I write." Then it went on: "For your company, I will be like a pen, sacrificing myself when all the ink has run dry." When it came to a company whose activities I could not in the least fathom, I wrote: "I was born of loving parents and grew up in an ordinary environment. I am eager to see my youthful dreams and passion ablaze in your company; please give me a chance." A call came from the company. It was a movie company. I could not remember what I had written in my self-introduction for them. It was only when I went for an interview that I realized why I had passed the initial screening.

The movie company's offices were at the top of a five-floor building with no elevator. Once past the office space, with old leather-covered sofas like those you find in estate agents' offices, metal filing cabinets, and clustered office desks, an unexpectedly luxurious president's office appeared. The president was a short, scrawny guy in his forties. He stared hard at my face. Have I got a spot under my eye? I'll have to have that removed before I get married. Ah, yes, in case he asked which I would put first, marriage or a career, I resolved to reply that I figured for young women nowadays choosing between marriage and a career is no longer a problem, but the question did not come up. "Are you good at English?" Ah, yes, whenever anyone had to check one of the boxes "good, average, poor" for their English ability, they always choose "good." But after all, I had graduated from the intensive English course at the Pagoda Institute. "Tell me now, are you any good at writing?" The president's tone suddenly became more familiar. I could not immediately grasp what he might mean by asking if I could write. I looked blank. "For goodness' sake! I mean, when you were a kid, didn't you ever take part in any kind of writing contest? English and writing skills, we're looking for someone who possesses both." "Well, when I was in high school I did take a class in creative writing, and I won a prize once for some poems I'd written." I got that far, and began to feel extremely awkward.

The president did not conceal his suspicions as he asked another question: "Okay, then what erotica made the strongest impression on you? Huh? You don't know what erotica means? Men and women together, that kind of thing!" "Ah, well... *Nine and a Half Weeks* and *Red Shoe Diaries*." The president started to smile. "Aha, now we're getting somewhere." As the president explained at length what would be required of me if I joined the company, the implication was clearly that he wanted to hire me. "You've heard of cash-cow movies, haven't you?" Cash-cow movies? I had no idea, but did not dare shake my head. "Ultimately, our company's aim is to import hitherto unknown art films from the Third World and introduce them to Korean audiences. At present we're waiting for the right moment; soon specialized cinemas for arthouse movies will be opening. So what is most urgent first of all? Obviously, guaranteed funding. When it comes to doing business, you can't always just go ahead and do what you want to do. There are times when you have to hold back, in order to see your dreams come true." After he had thus expressed in touching terms the dreams he held for his company engaged in importing porno movies to his only job-seeker, the president informed me that my job would be to review the draft translations of the imported movies, mostly adult-only porn which would be marketed as videos without ever being released in cinemas, smoothing them out and improving them. "It's mostly groaning, so it shouldn't be too difficult. You can start next week, can't you? Huh? Why aren't you saying anything?" "Well, I need time to think." The president's eyes widened. He took my voice full of diffidence for that of a village maid turning down an earl's proposal. "Dear me, either still too young or not hungry enough yet." Taking the white envelope an employee held out, I left the office in some confusion. "Interview fee" was written on it in large letters. It contained two stiff ten thousand won notes. Is this normal? As I walked down the stairs from the fifth floor, I was invaded with a sense of regret that I was spurning the chance to work in such a respectable and conscientious company. I was a typically fickle kind of person then, as I still am now.

The Q-brand outlet was located at the far end of the women's department. I walked past slowly but my friend R was nowhere to be seen. Another employee in a pink uniform was idly tapping on the keys of the cash register. Maybe she had gone for a snack. She liked spicy noodles with half a boiled egg perched on top. She used to complain that they always left off the egg in the store's employee restaurant.

My new friend.
Nobody knew about her; I had first met her that spring.

R and I were graduates from the same high school. While we were at school we had almost never spoken. There was no particular reason. She was so quiet you never noticed if she was there or not. In our first year, we had been in the same class but our student numbers were not close, our height and our grades were not similar, we had no close mutual friends, either, and we took different roads to and from school. Our high school was located to the north of the Han River, but for the thirty percent of the students who lived south of the river the school operated five buses. Less than thirty months after it had been included in the eighth school district, news came it had been assigned to another district for unavoidable reasons; the parents declared they could not accept it, and there was a mass movement to register their children in other schools. In order to calm things down, the school was obliged to put on a show of good faith. "We will undertake steps to ensure a safe journey to and from school." Of course, coming home proved more problematic than going to school. "To avoid unfortunate incidents, the students will be dropped off on their very doorsteps." The moment the evening study time ended, I was obliged to rush out in order not to miss the school bus home. I only learned much later that R's home lay only twenty steps away from the school's back gate. When we finally met again, we recognized each other at once. That was in February 1995.

It was about one week before the graduation ceremony. A phone call came from a friend S. "I'm in trouble! They demand that we come to work in formal dress." She told me that the employees in her finance company wore uniforms—"Great, isn't it? No clothing expenses!" I could not think of any suitable reply. "Well, I don't know. Surely wearing what you like is better than everyone being dressed the same?" "Yes, I suppose you're right. By the way, what are you wearing for graduation?" "What? I don't know. Anyway there'll be the black gown covering everything, so how can anyone see what we're wearing?" "Oh, yeah. Anyway, it doesn't matter. Let's go and buy some clothes. I'll be going to Sampung." The department store where I agreed to meet her was five minutes from my home. As I sauntered between the apartment blocks, I fingered the pager in my coat pocket. I could not feel it vibrating otherwise. I was waiting for a final decision from a magazine specializing in beauty products and a company producing tailor-made kitchen furnishings. No other company had offered an interview fee, so I was feeling an odd nostalgia for that first movie company. One evening a few days back, drunk after a few glasses of beer, I had phoned the movie company instead of the first love I had just broken up with, and listened to the phone ringing for a full five minutes. It must be a really good company, they didn't even work late. I could not believe that after one more week, I would be an independent person.

S wanted to try on all the clothes that the mannequins in the women's department were displaying. One velvet one-piece did not really suit her, she being on the chubby side, but she bought it anyway. "Q-brand slacks are always nice." So we headed for the Q-brand outlet. And there was R, wearing a pink uniform. "Why, hello!" R greeted me first. "Oh, hello," I replied. That was our first conversation. "I work here," R stubbornly insisted on telling me something I already knew. "Well, I never! I didn't realize, I often pass by here." "Hmm, I recently moved here from the Lotte Store in Myeong-dong." I felt strangely awkward. S threw me a look as if to ask "Who is she?" but I pretended not to notice. There would have been no adequate explanation anyway. I could always say: "We attended the same high school, we often bumped into each other," but there was no point in whispering something like that. S selected a pair of khaki slacks and went to the changing room to try them on. There were no other customers. R and I were alone. I laughed awkwardly. R spoke up: "You haven't changed a bit. You're still just as pretty when you laugh." When had R ever seen me laugh before? I had been born in the city. I had learned that if someone offers you a compliment, you should make one in return. So I said: "You're a lot prettier than you used to be." R smiled in an off-putting manner. "I was rather plump when I was at school." In that case, she seemed to have lost a lot of weight. We fell silent again. "It's odd, they seem to have changed the design of their slacks. They make me look short, don't they?" S was examining the clothes, turning this way and that in front of the mirror. "Oh, no, they suit you, miss. It's only because they are on the long side." "I'm not sure." S seemed not to like what she saw of herself reflected in the mirror. "Let me try turning up the hem." R knelt at S's feet in order to turn up the bottom of the slacks. Her hair was tightly curled up and held in place by a black gauze net. A few stray hairs were spread across the nape of her neck.

In the end, S did not buy the slacks. "I'll be going. Nice to see you." "Right. Enjoy the rest of your shopping today and drop by next time you're passing." "Okay, see you later." "Hey, hang on." R called out to me as I was turning away. "Write down your pager number for me. I'll let you know in advance if we're having a sale with special offers." In return I asked for her number. She inscribed her pager number, beginning with 015, and the outlet's phone number that began with a 5, on a piece of note-paper bearing the circular logo of Sampung Department Store. Another week passed, and there was no news from the magazine specializing in beauty products or the company producing tailor-made kitchen furnish-ings. I did not attend my graduation ceremony. The winter vacations were long, but on the first day of what was no longer vacation I had a different feeling. In early childhood I had been briefly mistaken for "a prodigy, at least," but now my parents surely must have complex feelings about their daughter being an unemployed graduate, yet they did not push me. They were sufficiently well-off not to need their daughter's salary to supple-ment their income. Instead of inviting them to the graduation ceremony and having a photo taken with them wearing my mortarboard, I was able to avoid being blamed for unfilial behavior by agreeing silently to meet a possible future husband.

They told me that a man studying dentistry in the United States had come back to Korea in search of a bride. He began by explaining that his field of research was going to restore dentistry's damaged state to its for-mer glory. Stopping in the middle of the street, he pointed at a ten-story building. "If I treat just three patients a day, I can put up a building like that in no time at all." It was the first time I had ever seen someone speak with that kind of self-confidence, outside of a television soap that is. As my contempt for him grew, my mother seemed to become more enthusi-astic about him. "Mom, are you crazy? How can you expect me to go and live in a country where I can't communicate with people?" "But haven't you been attending English institutes all this time? After the fortune we've spent sending you to those classes, why can't you communicate?" "Anyway, it's no good. I absolutely can't go and live in another country." "Why not?" "Because I'm someone with a high command of advanced Korean." It was only then that I became aware that I had studied English not in order to leave Korea but in order to stay here. It was nearly March.

I had no sooner opened my eyes in the morning than it was already past midday. I picked up a leather shoulder bag, left home and went to the National Library of Korea in Scocho-dong. At the entrance I produced my student ID instead of my national ID. The man giving out admission tickets glanced at it without showing any interest in details like expiration dates. In the periodicals room all the magazines published in the country were available. After reading *The Happy Home*, *Working Woman*, and some literary reviews I had never heard of, the inside of my head felt numb. I had only once tried the library restaurant's watery curry rice consisting of nothing but potatoes and carrots. For my late lunch I ate a bowl of instant kimchi noodles with a can of Pocari Sweat. I did not take off my winter coat, for spring had not yet come. This was the fifth such day. In the library's convenience store, as I poured hot water into the bowl of noodles and split apart the wooden chopsticks, I felt a chill run up my spine. The library was frosty. Simply dumping the remaining noodles into the trash bin, I left the library. I took the neighborhood bus and headed for Sampung Department Store.

The spicy cold noodles on the store's fifth floor were amazingly tasty. Squeezing a good helping of mustard onto the scarlet noodles, I stirred. It was so spicy, tears sprang to my eyes. Taking a gulp of broth, I scalded the roof of my mouth. Riding the escalator from the fifth floor, I went down one floor at a time. The fourth floor was sporting goods, the third floor men's clothes, the second women's clothes. I explored each floor carefully. When you're feeling bored, there is nothing better than a department store for passing a pleasant hour or two. In the outlet in the right-hand corner of the second floor, I noticed R serving a customer. Standing in front of a middle-aged woman whose large girth seemed unsuited for Q-brand clothes, which did not go beyond a size sixty-six, she was smiling politely. I went in and tapped her lightly on the shoulder, then turned and walked away. I tested a new brand of eye shadow at a makeup counter on the first floor, fingered a pair of Hepburn-style sunglasses with round lenses, then put them down again. Going down to the luxury goods counter in the basement, I bought a pencil case made of red cloth decorated with images of Winnie the Pooh. Then standing in the adjacent bookstore, I read from cover to cover a collection of works awarded a literary prize, the contents of which I have completely forgotten. Some time later, though I looked all around, there was no way of knowing how much time had passed. Then as now there are no clocks in department stores. Growling sounds were coming from my stomach. I emptied out my bag as I searched for the page R had given me. I entered a phone booth in the store's first-floor lobby, elegantly decorated like a street in Paris, and phoned up to R on the second floor. "Ah, it's you." R got my name right, too. "Just wait two hours more. If I hurry up, I can get out by eight." Once 1995 had faded into the remote past, I sometimes used to wonder why she replied so calmly to my call. Had she been counting on me to make the first move? Or had she too been feeling the need for a new friend, someone who knew nothing at all about her?

As soon as eight came, a flock of young women erupted toward the outside parking lot. The girls looked pale and lively, dressed in their everyday clothes instead of uniforms. R tapped me on the shoulder first. "You been waiting long?" In her jeans with a hooded jacket, she looked exactly as she had in high school. "I'm starving. Let's go." She slid an arm through mine in an utterly natural gesture. We walked down toward the Express Bus Terminal. "Wow, I'm crazy about noodles, and it sounds as if you are too! Still, you ought to avoid eating flour-based food two meals in a row. Otherwise your stomach gets all messed up, like mine is. People with our kind of job eat at irregular hours, we all suffer from indigestion." I nibbled some picked radish and asked: "You been working long in department stores?" "I began when I was twenty, so this'll be the fifth year." After leaving high school, I had never heard even the smallest scrap of news about her, so of course I had not realized she had not gone on to college. "I see. Has it been interesting?" "So-so. Earning a living's all the same, isn't it? They say that being in sales is like a drug. They all run around saying they're going to quit, it's too hard, but they're never quite driven over the edge." Our noodles arrived. We silently devoured the noodles from which thick clouds of steam were rising. R did not ask me what work I was doing. She did not ask me if I had graduated, either. As we were leaving, she was carrying the bill. I quickly pulled four thousand-won bills from my purse. That was the cost of my share of the noodles. Going Dutch, with even the small change being shared exactly, was the usual custom among female students in the 1990s. R stubbornly refused to take them. I was obliged to put back my four thousand-won bills. "Then let me pay for coffee." R took my arm again. "Frankly, I think going somewhere for coffee's a waste of money. Shall we go to my place? There's a direct bus from just down there."

We got off the bus at the stop by our old high school. Following her, I made my way through a maze of gloomy lanes until I saw the familiar wall with the back gate of the school. We had taken a shortcut. I had studied there for three years, but never knew it existed. "Our house is really close to the school, isn't it?" I nodded. "I reckon I got to class the quickest out of all the kids in school. Sometimes I used to be sitting in the empty classroom when the sun rose." She laughed shyly. To reach her home, we had to go in through the gate then climb a long flight of cement steps up one side of the main house. It was dark, and each step was quite high, so it was a bit awkward. R turned on the light switch in the hallway. The space inside was small but there was a wonderful view of the lights of Seoul stretching beyond the window. "Wow, what a great nighttime view!" My exclamation was a bit forced. "And if you look over there, that's Namsan, isn't it?" R added, as if it were something improper. "I knew you'd like it." The low table was covered with a piece of purple cloth. She pulled the table over in front of the window. The sweetish coffee slipped smoothly over my tongue.

Waiting for R to get back, I took the escalator down to the first floor of the basement. When it came to the structure of Sampung Department Store, the open spaces were all so vast you could find your way around with your eyes shut. Going to the counter selling fancy merchandise, I picked out a hardcover diary. After hesitating between a waterdrop pattern and a zebra pattern cover, I opted at the last minute for the zebra pattern. It was so stuffy that breathing was difficult. Four or five salesgirls in uniform were gathered by the cash register, chattering. "Have you heard? Just now the ceiling in the fifth-floor cold noodle shop collapsed. What's going on? You don't think it's all going to fall down today, do you? I mustn't die today! I wore my new pair of jeans to work!" All the girls burst out in a shriek of laughter. It really did sound like a shriek. "That will be 4,900 won, please." Clasping my hundred-won coin change, I walked away.

Early in the spring of that year, I rapidly grew close to my new friend.

Perhaps because all twenty of my other friends were busy, my green Motorola pager never rang. Also, I never made the first move to contact friends apart from R. The March daylight hours were short, as usual. I would complete one job application each day in the reading room of the National Library of Korea. I ran out of copies of the photo where the corners of my mouth were turned upward. I was obliged to take the negative of the photo taken by the best photographer in Seoul to the instant photo corner in Sampung Department Store and have ten more copies printed off. "What do you do all day long at the library?" R asked. "I just read and study, that's all." "Don't you get bored? What are you studying all this time?" Since I had never once studied to the point of getting bored, I felt a stab of conscience. "If you have nowhere to go during the day, shall I give you a key to my place?" I had no other friend who would ever have said such a thing. I just laughed. "Since it's empty in any case, you can make yourself at home, cook some instant noodles, read books. So long as you wash up the dishes you use." It was certainly a very simple condition for the loan of a house. As she pulled out a silver-colored key, I felt an inexpressible sense of obligation. I shook my head stubbornly. "No, it's alright. What would I do all alone in your house if you're not there?" "Still, take it. After all, you never know. Suppose I have a heart attack and die in my sleep, you can use this key to let yourself in and discover me." "Hey, why do you say such gruesome things?" "Or else you can rescue me when I've slipped on the bathroom floor and fallen down." "Right, but before I call the emergency services, I'd better put some clothes on you." "Ha ha, sure, you'd better." The key that was passed from her palm to mine looked small and incomplete.

I have no memory of ever having put that key into the keyhole and entering her home on my own. When the library closed, I used to head for Sampung Department Store. Either I took the neighborhood bus or, once the days grew warmer, I walked. Sometimes I would turn right from the library and go past the junipers at the Seocho Station intersection; on other days, I used to cross the road in front of the library and cut across the grounds of Saint Mary's Hospital. The two or more hours I had to spend waiting for R would pass quickly. Reading books, choosing a CD, examining clothes, eating ice cream, I did every imaginable thing you could do in such a place. That's what a department store is for. If I was at a loss, I used to go to the Q-brand corner and assist R. Since I seemed to be a customer just like them, women who emerged from the changing room wearing clothes they were trying on would trust my comments more readily than those of R, she being a salesperson. "Frankly, you know, rather than an achromatic line, a pastel system suits you far better." "Rather than the gray jacket you're wearing now, the light green coat you tried before was ten times prettier." "Even if it's a trifle expensive, if I were you I'd surely buy that." Once the customer had left with her arms full of blue shopping bags, we would look at each other and grin. "I think you have a special talent for this kind of thing," she used to praise me. "It's because I want you to hire me as your deputy," I would giggle.

As closing time drew near, there were fewer and fewer customers. Once closing time had come, the loudspeakers began to play the song *Sorrowful Parting*. Though I used to hear that tune every day, played in a quick, cheerful tempo, it always sounded strange. "Dear friend, whom I have known for so long, why talk of sorrowful parting? Is it merely a matter of going away? Go where we may, we shall never forget one another. So let us sing, looking forward to the day when our friendship will bring us together again." Humming the words to myself, I would leave the store first and wait for R to come out after changing into her jeans. She and I took turns paying for supper. "You don't have any money." She used to try to stop me but I could never imagine letting someone else treat me regularly. In actual fact, my financial situation was not so bad. It might not have run to pizzas or steaks in family restaurants, but when it was a matter of noodles or rice rolls, I could afford that kind of thing every day. I never told R that I was still receiving pocket money from my parents.

After supper, we would go to R's place and watch a video or drink beer. With the beer we would nibble peanuts or onion rings. R flatly refused to buy squid-flavored crackers. She never ate roasted dry squid, either. She said she could not stand to see the dried squid squirming around like that when it was put on top of a gas flame. I urged her to shut her eyes. "It'll be okay if you don't see, surely? I'll roast them," but she pretended not to have heard me. "It's too cruel, isn't it, not only the way those squid that have been living deep in the sea get pulled up onto dry land and dried for days on end exposed to sunlight, I mean, but then the way they're roasted over a scorching hot flame?" Hearing her, I agreed. My longing to dip roasted squid into mayonnaise and chew on it with my molars vanished. The beer always ran out before the onion rings. Once the beer was finished, I would stand up. R used to accompany me to the bus stop. Compared to a few days before, the evening air had grown warmer. The forsythias along the road around Namsan were starting to open their first buds. Dappled by lamplight, it was impossible to tell how yellow they really were. I was not even sure if they were forsythias or azaleas. Come to think of it, I never once saw R's face in broad daylight.

If I'd asked I suppose she would have told me, but I never did ask R why she was living alone. According to my standards, I thought that was being polite. I felt that possibly it was something that made her feel sad. Gauging the right distance between one heart and another was something difficult for me then, and it still is. I was curious about the poetry books on her bookshelves, too, but my lips remained sealed. The volume of selected poems by Gi Hyeong-do in a series with caramel-colored covers was a book that I also owned. "There was a long time when I was unable to write. The weather here was bad and I could not stand that weather. In those days, too, there were streets with cars driving along them." When I re-read those words on the book's back cover in R's house, I realized that what I could not stand was not the weather here, but myself.

Going into a phone booth on the ground floor, I dialed R's pager number. R had not even recorded a commonplace word of greeting. Hmm. Composing my voice, I left her a message: "It's me. I dropped by but there's no sign of you. Are you having a snack? Are you okay? I'm sorry I haven't been in touch more often. It's what happens when you're working in an office. Get back home, wash up, and you're asleep in a flash. Today I managed to escape in the middle of things. I got out, only there was nowhere to go. Take care, I'll come by again later." I wonder if R ever heard my message. I still don't know.

It was a Saturday. I had got up late and when I came out of the bathroom, the telephone number of the Q-brand outlet was showing on my pager. "Can you come and work here, just for today? Our manager has had to leave town in a hurry; her grandmother died suddenly. The main office say they can only send someone to replace her tomorrow and it's sales time, there'll be lots of customers, so give me a hand for today, please." I replied that was no problem. Then I opened my wardrobe. I reckoned I would do well to wear Q-brand clothes, so I took out one of their previous year's spring models that I had bought, a white, short-sleeved sports shirt, and put it on. Beneath it I wore a black skirt I had bought at a store near Ewha Womans University. R had once mistaken it for a traditional Korean skirt, exclaiming, "Why, that's our Korean style of dress!"

At the Q-brand outlet, R was with a man I had never seen before. He turned out to be the brand's local agent. She introduced me: "She's going to be employed here just for today." He took my ID card and jotted down a few details. "Get into uniform," he said. R seemed more upset than I was. "She's only working here for today, why does she need to wear a uniform?" "It's the rule, isn't it?" "We haven't been following it recently." "Having people work here who weren't wearing uniform was a mistake, that's all." "But she's only a student, and she's my friend, so she's helping me out just for today. Let her be for just this once, please." Since I was no longer a student, I winced. R's attitude hardened. Anyone passing might have thought that the agent was trying to make me wear convict's garb, rather than the uniform of a salesgirl in Sampung Department Store. I interrupted R. "It's fine by me. Let me go and put it on, okay?" R looked at me. Her eyes were gentle like a cow's. "Is it really alright for you?" I laughed weakly. "Of course. Where is it, now?" "And you must pin a label on her chest saying she's a temporary assistant." The uniform was a perfect fit. My generation had been allowed to wear whatever clothes we liked at school, so it was the first time I had been in a uniform since I wore a girl scout outfit way back in my primary school days. It was heavier than I had expected, oddly enough. Or at least that was how it felt to me.

Compared to when I had been standing around dressed casually and saying whatever came to mind, everything was different. Once midday passed, customers began to come crowding in. Being slow-moving and with many things to do, I was clumsy. Having to find the right size in addition to selecting clothes that suited each customer, I was soon perspiring. R did all she could to cover for me, but when she was off fetching stock from the storeroom or dealing with another customer I was at a loss as to what I should do. While I was inserting pins to mark the hemline for a customer who had come in first, another who had come in after would do her best to distract me. "With a thirty percent discount, how much is this blouse?" I was at a loss how to calculate a thirty percent discount when the price was not 150,000 won but 148,500 won. After all, I'm someone whose head starts to spin at the mere sight of Arabic numerals, aren't I? I glanced toward R. She was fully occupied in selecting a coat to go with some white slacks a customer seemed to like. The cashier at the counter also looked extremely busy. "Come on, what's the matter? Hurry up and tell me how much it costs. I'll take these four, so work out how much that is with the thirty percent discount." I carefully tapped at the keys of the calculator. The problem was that the busy cashier did not bother to check my sloppy arithmetic.

The customer handed over a million-won check, took the change, and left. Moments later, she reappeared. "What damned idiot added up this bill?" She swore without so much as blinking. The insult was directed at me, but I did not realize it. R stepped between us. "What's wrong?" "It wasn't you just now, it was that girl there who dealt with it." "Why, she's just a temporary assistant. I'm the one you need to talk to." "What are you employing an idiot like her for? Didn't she finish middle school? She doesn't even know how to add and subtract!" Since I was undoubtedly just an ignorant temporary assistant, I just hung my head. "I am so sorry. Let me quickly recalculate your bill for you." R bowed deeply several times. It involved adding some 40,000 won somewhere, I couldn't follow the process. Having received the money owed to her, the customer threw a withering glance in my direction, then pulled a scarf from the neck of one of the display mannequins. "I'm so furious, I'm not going to leave so easily. Because of that stupid girl there I've had to waste my time here, so I'm taking this as compensation. Deduct it from her wages or whatever." R snatched at the scarf she was holding. "No, that is an original design, I can't allow that. We can give you gift vouchers instead." The customer grabbed the scarf again, and raised her voice. "Who wants your no-good gift vouchers? I've told you I like this, and I'm taking it, so why argue?"

The dispute was only settled by the sudden appearance of the agent I had seen previously. The customer finally went sailing out, tucking the scarf into one corner of her bag. As she listened to his barbed scolding, R kept her lips clenched tightly. As for me, all I wanted was to go running away from there. Once the agent had left, R spoke: "I'm so sorry, it's my fault." In hindsight, those were words I should have spoken, but I could hardly open my mouth. "Are you alright?" R's eyes were shifting quietly. "Of course. It's not a big deal at all." She brushed some dust off one shoulder of my uniform. "You worked hard today. The busiest period is over now, so you can go." I was unable to answer. "I'll work out how much you've earned later. Hurry up and change." "Will you be alright on your own?" "Yes, I'll be fine alone; go and change quickly." She pushed me into one of the customer changing rooms. There I took off the uniform of a Sampung Department Store salesgirl and changed into my own clothes, a white, short-sleeved sports shirt and black skirt. Though they were not the uniform, they too felt heavy. It was as if an iron bar was pressing down on my shoulders. Barely four hours had passed since I entered the Q-brand outlet. I left R standing there and dashed out of the store. The pink Sampung Store building seemed to be bounding after me.

It is not uncommon to grow apart from someone you were once close to, especially once you've grown up. After that incident, it was not long before I got a job with a company importing food for animals. I was amazed to discover that there were so many animals in the world. I was assigned to the marketing team and sold food for animals being used for experimental research. Hamsters have to consume ten to fourteen grams of calories per day and rats need fifteen to twenty grams. Rabbits meanwhile need at least one hundred and twenty grams. R and I did not call each other by pager. The milk coffee produced by the machine in the office corridor was a far cry from the coffee she used to make. I was so busy paying visits to all the hospitals and university research institutes in Seoul and the surrounding areas that used our company's products that I did not notice the way spring was passing at a dizzying rate. I took the subway to the offices in Anguk-dong. On weekdays we had to wear formal dress but on Saturdays we could wear jeans. That was the one thing I liked. Several times I lifted the phone, then put it down again.

A boyfriend appeared, too. He was newly employed in a securities company and whenever we met, we mostly talked about life in each other's offices. He said he liked me because I was cute. "What do you mean, cute?" "What I say. You're not pretty but you look cute, don't you? You've got pale skin and when you smile three creases appear at the corner of your eyes." He probably thought that Gi Hyeong-do was the name of an island somewhere off the South Coast. But he was kind and bright, not bad at all. In the spring that year I possessed many things: somewhat right-wing parents, a clean, super single bed, a translucent green Motorola pager, and four handbags. They were all obsolete. Spring had ended and, feebly, summer was coming.

Sampung Department Store had opened in December 1989; it was an ultramodern building with five floors above ground and four basement levels. June 29, 1995. On that day the air conditioners were not working and it was suffocatingly hot inside. Perspiration flowed like rain. When did summer start? Five forty: I was walking up and down in the lobby, muttering. Five forty-three: I walked out through the front door. Five forty-eight: I arrived home. Five fifty-three: I opened my zebra pattern diary. I had just written "Today, I..." when I heard a great crash. It was five fifty-five. Sampung Department Store had collapsed. It took less than one second for each floor to collapse onto the one below.

Then several things happened. My translucent green Motorola pager filled up with messages asking if I was alright. The woman living in the apartment below ours had gone to the supermarket in Sampung Department Store to buy some tofu for soup prior to making supper and never came back. I heard that she'd left half a leek lying on her chopping board. The rainy season came. A few days later, the morning paper printed a list of the names of those dead or missing. I did not read it. On the page facing that was a special column written by a female celebrity. It suggested that the collapse of Sampung Department Store in the Gangnam area, reputed for its luxurious lifestyle, might be God's will, a warning to a country increasingly tainted with extravagance and pleasure. I called the newspaper to protest. They replied that they could not give me the writer's phone number, so there was no alternative and I screamed at the man in charge of the reader's department. "Did that woman ever once go there? Does she know who was in there?" I was panting hard. I felt sorry but there was no avoiding it. I still feel grateful for the way that newspaper employee kept hold of the phone without hanging up until I had stopped crying.

On television I saw one young man rescued after holding out for two hundred and thirty hours inside the concrete wreckage. There was also a girl who emerged after two hundred and eighty-five hours. I did nothing but watch the television. My boyfriend worried about me. "Once you're born you're bound to die. When I was doing my military service, I saw several deaths. My maternal uncle's a general, he could have helped me avoid serving, but my dad forced me to go." I cannot say that was the only reason, but we eventually split up. He immediately started seeing a university student four years my junior who looked as cute as a Japanese doll.

After June 29 I never once went to work at the office and soon received a dismissal notice in the mail. The reason given was absence without leave. That was an accurate expression. Three hundred and seventy-seven hours after the collapse, they discovered a nineteen-year-old girl. Her first words were, "What day is it?" The total number of victims of the collapse of Sampung Department Store on June 29, 1995, including thirty who remained unaccounted for, was finally given as five hundred and one dead, nine hundred and thirty-eight wounded. If I had been ten minutes later in leaving, that would have been that. People told me how lucky I was.

I put the small, incomplete-looking silver-colored key in the bottom drawer of my desk and let ten years go past. I sometimes happened to open the drawer if I was looking for adhesive tape or a poultice in a hurry. I never heard from R. Her pager number and mine both vanished from the face of the earth. People kept changing toys, from pagers to mobiles, from the "I love school" online community to the "Mini-hompi" site.

As I began to write this, I did a search for R's mini-homepage using Cyworld. There were twelve girls born in 1972 with the same name as R. I clicked on the names one by one. It seemed the twelve Rs were mostly not maintaining their homepages, too busy perhaps. At the age of thirty-three, we seemed to be passing through what might prove to be the most real moment of our lives. On the thumbnail for the eleventh mini-homepage there was a photo of a little girl. She looked to be about three or four years old. I enlarged the photo and gazed at it for a long time. Her eyes were gentle and large. On closer inspection, the rounded line of her jaw looked like R's, too. I longed to see other, clearer photos, but that was the only one there was. I sincerely hoped that the girl might be R's daughter.

Many things have changed and many have not changed. The site of Sampung Department Store remained empty for a long time, but in 2004 a towering complex of apartments and stores arose there. A few years before it was finished, I moved to another neighborhood, far from there. I still pass by occasionally. Sometimes I feel a pain on one side of my chest, and sometimes not. One's birthplace is not necessarily a place you always feel a deep nostalgia for. It was only after I left there that it became possible for me to write.

THAT WOMAN'S AUTOBIOGRAPHY

Kim In-sook

Translated by **Brother Anthony of Taizé**

그 여자의 자서전
김인숙

A critique of this short story was published in the Koreana magazine in Fall 2007 (Vol. 21 No. 3, pp. 85-87).

© Hong Ju-mi

"Do you like cats?" That's what he asked me, the first time we met. I was listening closely to what he was saying, because I reckoned it would surely be no ordinary question, but an attempt on his part to try to understand me first. I had no need to feel uncomfortable. So far as our relationship was concerned, if there was a need to understand and investigate, it lay on his side, and probably for that very reason he would feel a wish to get to know me. The question whether I liked cats was something I associated with the first part of a psychological test. Depending on whether the answer was yes or no, the direction of the arrow indicating the next question would vary.

"My wife likes cats." Unexpectedly, he did not wait long for me to reply. "She has a gray Abyssinian. Have you ever seen one?" This time the answer, "No," emerged quite easily. He nodded. "The same here. Until my wife bought hers in Japan and brought it back, I'd never seen one, either. She brought it back from Japan! She's the kind of woman who buys cats abroad; amazing isn't it? Quite extraordinary! If there's a cat in someone else's house, I've been inclined to stroke its back once, at least. But this cat lives in my house... if I hate my wife, at least I can get a divorce, but this is a cat, what can I do? So when I want to be quiet without the cat, I sometimes use this hotel. So naturally I started to work in this hotel room with the person I was working with before."

The arrow seemed to be pointing in the wrong direction. Certainly, one might associate questions about cats with psychological tests, but my anxiety must have been excessive. He and I were not young things in their twenties meeting for a tryst, nor were we a patient and a psychiatrist meeting for a counseling session. Yi Ho-gap was fifty-two. At that time, the only things I knew about him for sure were his age and his name, nothing more. Of course, before we met, the materials I had been given had taught me more about him than anyone else I knew, but that kind of information could never be of much use. I once again prudently considered this fifty-two-year-old Yi Ho-gap, the way he had said he wanted to work with me in a hotel room, and had started off with a question as to whether I liked cats. It was not that he looked younger than his age, or excessively endowed with stamina, but at least he was not fat and his hair had not fallen out. At least there was nothing repulsive about his outward appearance.

On our way up to the room, he and I were alone in the elevator. A curious sensation tickled the soles of my feet as I stood on the soft carpet.

None of the men I had ever had a "relationship" with would have invested in such an expensive hotel room for the sake of his relationship with me. If my meeting with this man had not been because we were working together, but for a relationship, what would I be feeling as we rode the elevator together up toward a suite in a luxury hotel? But I shook my head to myself. What I was going to be obliged to do from now on was to ghostwrite the autobiography of a wealthy man who hoped to enter the world of politics, without bringing into play a novelist's imagination. At the twenty-third floor the elevator stopped. As the doors slid open, I glimpsed a corridor where the afternoon sunlight lingered on the brown carpet, extending in silence into the distance.

The reason I had agreed to ghostwrite his autobiography, no matter what external reasons I might have put forward, was ultimately on account of the money. When an older friend, who had already completed perhaps half the work for that autobiography, found himself obliged to give up the task midway for personal reasons, he said he would let me have everything he had done on the condition that he didn't have to give me the money he had received as an advance payment. When I received his unexpected call, with its talk of "ghostwriting an autobiography," I found myself assailed by a disagreeable feeling of "Who does he take me for?" but at the end of the conversation I simply replied, "I'll think about it," which was pretty much the same as accepting.

Yet once I'd hung up, I experienced an overpowering feeling of disgust. Ghostwriting an autobiography… For the past ten years what I'd been longing for was to be able to spend a couple of years, or even just one year, writing what I wanted to without having to worry about money. And this was a job that would enable me to write what I wanted… Despite that feeing of disgust, there was no way I could look down my nose at the fact that the fat sum I would be earning by ghostwriting this autobiography was larger than anything I had earned in the past ten years.

That same evening, just like any other day, I was sitting at my laptop. On the television that stood on the other side of the room from my desk, home shopping advertisements were replaying over and again. Someone once wrote how, when they started to write, they could not stand even a speck of dust on their desk, could not endure the sound of the hands turning on the clock; I, however, was inclined not to be able to stand silence. For a time I had worked with a CD of classical music playing; then for a while I would listen to a radio music program; nowadays, I turned on the television when I came in. No other sound was as soothing to me as the sound of home shopping advertisements, echoing behind my back. Then, instead of hammering away at my laptop's keyboard, or reading a book, I would turn around under some kind of compulsion and grab the telephone. Even as I was pressing the buttons, the numbers indicating sales of bedding sets, fitness machines, the latest models in household goods, would be climbing dramatically. Pick me, pick me. Impatiently watching adverts promising bonus offers to a fixed number of customers as if hoping for a jackpot, I would go so far as to shout aloud, "Pick me! Pick me!"

Yet that evening I did not purchase anything. It was almost as though the windfall that had materialized before my eyes had abruptly made that kind of petty urge to buy things vanish from within me. Unable to write a single line, incapable of reading one page from a book, but also not hurling myself at the telephone to become the fiftieth purchaser of packs containing ten sets of lingerie, the night advanced....

A typical self-made man. Those words were especially underlined in the materials my friend had given me. Below that sub-heading were set out details of his family background, upbringing, and achievements(!). He had been born into a wealthy farming family, but with his father having squandered the family fortune, he had spent his childhood in wretched poverty—typical, indeed! He had begun his youth working as a delivery boy for a store selling rice, but thanks to the generosity of the store's owner, who recognized his tenacity and sincerity, he was not only able to earn the equivalent of a high school graduation diploma by the national qualification examination, but was even able to buy a share in the store—surely that too was a story I'd often heard somewhere before? Having accumulated the basis of his wealth by selling rice, his first stroke of luck came with a rise in the price of the land in his home village, which previously no one would have looked at twice even if they were offered it for nothing. From that moment on he began to actively invest in land, and that became a decisive factor in his accumulation of an immense fortune—a part of the text that my predecessor had underlined in a different color. At least, we might say, none of that was worth making widely known. He entered university when he was already quite old, and he had chosen to major in social work, because he wanted to plough back into society the money he had accumulated—at which point what more could be hoped for? After that, he had set up a welfare foundation, a scholarship foundation and so on.

Perhaps because my friend's notes were so very well organized, there was no need for me to spend a long time reading them, pondering every word. As I browsed through the pages of notes, what made me ponder was not so much his career, but rather the words "a typical self-made man" that he had underlined. It looked as though that had been the direction which he had intended to take the autobiography as he wrote it. Nothing could be more "typical" than the case of someone who becomes a millionaire, as a result of an increase in the price of the land he or she owns, while yielding a valuable lesson in life, to focus on real estate investment. Not only had a youth who was nothing but the delivery boy for a rice seller gathered together, one by one, the grains of rice falling from the rice sacks until at last his own sack was full, then gone on to establish welfare and scholarship foundations, but he had even become rich enough to devote a huge sum of money to the ghostwriting of his autobiography, and there could be no doubt that in our society this was truly atypical.

For a while, the work went smoothly. As my friend had said when he handed me the nearly finished work, as though I had suddenly won the lottery, it seemed there would be no difficulties. All of the documents concerning him had already been recorded; things that should be discarded and things that must not be discarded were clearly indicated by separate labels. I hoped that having a female author undertake the autobiography would be satisfactory for the client, but it rather looked as though the choice of a woman had been his. The only misfortune in the life records of fifty-two-year-old Yi Ho-gap—not for himself but as far as the autobiography was concerned—was the record that, formally at least, he had been divorced twice. He did not wish to reveal all the details of that in his autobiography, but it looked as if he reckoned that, in order to avoid any misunderstandings that might provoke women voters, the writing needed to be such that would make them happy. When I showed him my first drafts, a month after starting to write, that was precisely the part that satisfied him the most. In actual fact, I knew almost nothing about the kind of people his wives had been; I did not even know how many of them there had been. If there was one thing I knew, it was the fact that his present wife had bought a gray Abyssinian cat on the way home from a journey abroad, instead of some prestigious brand of perfume or handbag. Considering the most recent trends, I could portray her as an animal lover, and to that extent as a woman abounding in love and devotion.

Yet no matter how smooth a piece of work may be, some part of it is bound to offer difficulties. At the very heart of his autobiography, what he hoped would be most clearly expressed was, as he put it, "his own contribution to democracy." That utterly preposterous coinage seemed to have been the result of laborious efforts on his part. To his great regret(!), he had never been in prison; he had never been implicated in any political incident during the preceding decades. Even more regrettably, he had accumulated the greatest part of his fortune during the period that had been the most repressive politically. Unlike his two divorces, which he wanted to be passed over lightly in a sympathetic manner, he wanted this particular part to be expressed as clearly and accurately as possible, that among the groups receiving support from his foundation, there had been one opposition organization, and funding had been provided secretly to a certain famous person within that group; admittedly, it had not been during the most repressive period, but even at that time it had still been an extremely hazardous thing to do; he had nevertheless decided to provide the funding despite the apprehensions of the foundation's board, and he considered it to have been extremely necessary in order to advance the restoration of democracy in society....

I understood what it was he wanted. Times had changed, and in these changed times, a record of activism during the previous periods had become as much a required element in a person's curriculum vitae as graduation from a reputed university. Understanding him was not difficult, but it took him some time to accept what I was doing. I kept reminding him that what I was writing was not his biography but his autobiography. Therefore what was doing the writing was not me, only my hand. I was under a duty to write whatever he wanted, no matter how far from sincerity or the truth it might be. I stayed up all night writing, on and on, and all I hoped was that the job would soon be over and the money would come into my hands. But when it came to that section, he was not prepared to be easily satisfied with my draft.

"You there, Author." That was how he always addressed me. "Authors are good at inflating words that aren't there; can't you put some flesh into this?"

While I was writing his autobiography, home shopping advertisements poured day and night from the television behind me. While the writing was advancing smoothly, I played the commercials simply as background noise, without paying attention to the contents, but once the work became complicated, I started to listen compulsively again. Things bought by home shopping filled my wardrobe and kitchen sink, to say nothing of the shoe cupboard, and the space under my bed. In an attempt to control my impulsive buying, I shifted the telephone into the living room. As I went running to the living room instead of hammering away at the keyboard of my laptop, I would stop as though I had tripped over the frame of the door, suddenly struck by the thought, "What am I doing?" So far as compulsive shopping was concerned, it proved more effective than I had hoped, but by the time I was back sitting in front of my laptop, the will to go on typing had vanished.

In those days, amid all the various kinds of advertising spots for this and that, unexpectedly there was one for books, for multi-volume sets of works. I listened to the hosts, whose voices were about an octave higher than those of ordinary people, proclaiming in piercing, seductive tones how entertaining, how full of literary quality, and how instructive this or that book was, until I was deafened. For some reason, although I used to feel an urge to buy even male sexual stimulants, I experienced no desire at all to buy in response to that commercial. In the end, I turned off the television; a little later, I also turned off my laptop.

In my childhood, the bookcase standing in the hall of our poor home was full of sets of works—biographies of famous men, of historical novels. Father was extremely devoted to his books. Whenever he had a spare moment, he would dust them, and if any had been put back in the wrong order, he would earnestly correct it so that everything was arranged tidily. But as a matter of fact I never once saw him take out any of the books and, while reading, moisten the pages with his spittle as he separated them, or fold down the corner of a page as a bookmark. Thinking back now, I have a feeling that he was less intent on reading than on collecting. Still, he used to summon his son, when he was still only a child, in front of the bookcase packed tight with those sets of volumes, and address him:

"You've got to read books. Because in them you have the whole world, you have truth, you have the way ahead."

He also used to say: "All the things that I can't teach you are in them, you see."

His voice used to sound rather sad when he said that, unlike when he was talking about the world and truth and the way ahead. But to a young boy's ears, it was all just an immensely boring peroration. As Father's words went on and on, my brother would squirm, shifting from one leg to the other. As a daughter, I was felt not to need to hear such speeches, and I was therefore all the more eager to listen to those lengthy, tedious addresses. I already hoped to become a writer, and I only had to imagine the day when my book would take its place in Father's bookcase for my breast to swell with pride. Late at night, after climbing back up onto the wooden veranda on my way back from going to the toilet across the yard, I could be seen sitting in front of Father's glittering bookcase. I longed for people to draw me from the shelf and smear every page of my life with fragrant spittle and the smell of tobacco-impregnated hands. I believed that my life would be saliva-stained, creased, increasingly tattered, but made glorious by all kinds of splendid incidents. Really, I wondered whether it was not a writer but a book that I longed to become. It seemed that Father had anticipated that, because when I told him I wanted to be a writer, all he said was:

"I said you should get married. Writing? How could you choose such a harsh fate… a job where you'll earn nothing; what will become of you…?"

Now I felt as though my dead father's voice was echoing, tut-tutting in the silence of the house. Unable to endure that illusion, I pressed the power button on the remote control to start the television again; just then the telephone rang. "Home shopping here. Which product do you want to buy?" My hand felt as light as usual as it held the phone.

"Hello?"

There was no immediate sound from the handset. I repeated my "Hello?" "Which product do you want? If you say you want the Mystery of Longevity Tonic, as the hundredth purchaser you will receive one bonus set of stamina panties. If you say that you wish to purchase the stamina panties, as the hundredth purchaser you will receive one bonus set of the Mystery of Longevity Tonic."

"Hello?"

"It's me…."

The moment I realized that the cautious sounding voice belonged to my brother, all the lightness left the wrist holding up the phone. Brother only called cautiously like this when he needed something. This time it seemed he'd done something that meant his business had been abruptly closed down, at least temporarily. The previous night the police had staged an unexpected inspection and it turned out that the youths drinking in the main room of their chicken restaurant were under age. He'd spent the night being questioned at the police station, and had just got out; he said that naturally, his business had been closed down for the time being, and it looked as though there would be a somewhat excessive fine. As he hesitantly explained the situation, he repeated several times that he had not known the youths were under age. Even if he had not kept repeating that, I had no reason not to believe him. He was not the kind of person to lie to me or to anyone else. He had always lived as he had decided he should, and his wife was full of poverty-stricken right answers. "I feel really sorry toward you," was what that simple, honest man kept telling me. And so he should feel sorry. The cost of that simple, honest life placed a wearisome burden on him, of course, but also on the rest of his family, as he could not help but realize. I told him to wait a bit, since I might soon be coming into a large sum of money. Since it couldn't be helped, I strove to speak as affectionately as I could, but inside of me, indignation and rage seethed like a mass of insects. This was the brother who, after Father died, had paid my entire university tuition, and when he sold off our old village home, had put aside my share and provided the key money for a semi-basement apartment for me to live in. This was my brother who had never once, on all those occasions, lost his expression full of goodwill, although there was no knowing whether or not he too felt insects squirming inside him.

Once the writing began to sour, there seemed to be no way of sorting things out. I could see no way of filling out the portion that Yi Ho-gap was dissatisfied with. To make matters even worse, just then I got a call from a woman who said she had been his first wife. I sometimes received calls from Yi Ho-gap's secretary, but there was no reason for me to receive calls from his wife, let alone from his ex-wife. While I was repeating, "Yes, yes," as if I knew nothing about anything, the flood of words poured out by the woman indicated that Yi Ho-gap was the world's worst swindler, a complete bastard, even a homicidal maniac who had killed any number of people. At the start I had repeated, "Yes, yes," but after a while I simply held the receiver without saying anything, and finally she seemed to take my lack of response for an insult:

"Agreeing to write such a person's biography for a few pennies—aren't you ashamed?"

With that unexpected put-down, she hung up. Even after that I remained there, holding the phone in a daze. Some time elapsed before the thought occurred to me that I had simply endured it one-sidedly, and I felt a certain resentment. I kept saying, "Hello," into the phone even though I knew she had hung up. Now look; what I'm writing is his autobiography, you know, it's not a biography. That means he's the one writing it, not me.

But in that case, what am I?

"You there, Author."

When I told him I'd received a strange call from his ex-wife, Yi Ho-gap addressed me using that extremely awkward title, as if it was something trivial, an everyday event.

"No one knows me as well as my author, do they now? For all I know, you may know me better than I know myself. In that case, what my author thinks of me may really be the truth."

Without asking what had been the contents of the strange call, he gazed at me fixedly as if asking if there was anything more that had to be explained. Yi Ho-gap was someone who spoke well. So well that it made me wonder if he hadn't taken courses in conversation at some speech academy in preparation for his entrance into the world of politics. But the moment he mentioned truth, I realized that the problem was not a matter of his oratory skills. I suddenly developed a headache, while a booming sound echoed inside my mind. Regarding my relationship with Yi Ho-gap, what was I? The person who was going to have to provide the answer to that was not his former wife but Yi Ho-gap himself, and I myself. That I was merely a ghostwriter, that the money I was receiving was simply for my work, that at least there was no reason why I might be up to knowing the truth about him, so that I knew nothing about him being the world's worst swindler or a homicidal maniac—the thought struck me that I ought to say something about at least one of those, but that was the best I could do. On top of the headache, I was struggling to control a growing feeling of nausea in my stomach.

When I called my friend later that day, he said he was preparing his lectures. What lectures? To my abrupt question, he told me a vacancy had come up at our alma mater and he was able to teach there several hours a week. I thought he'd hit the jackpot, but it was not a full-time professor's position, only a few hours per week as a part-time lecturer. But it seemed that for him, since he had failed in several applications for full-time jobs, just being able to build up a teaching record at a university in central Seoul was something worth celebrating.

As soon as we met, he said I didn't look well. The same could be said of him. He had written several novels that no one remembered the titles of, and had served on the planning committee of a publishing company no one had ever heard of, and was even a nominal member of the executive committee of some kind of NGO. But among the various business cards he carried, there did not seem to be one that truly satisfied him. I was not even sure that, if ever he obtained a business card as a university professor, it would prove to be his happiest.

"Hasn't his second wife turned up yet?"

That was his response when I told him I'd received an unpleasant call from a woman claiming to be Yi's first wife; he seemed unsurprised. I was about to reply that his jokes were not funny, he was trying to put me in a bad mood, but I sensed that his words were no joke.

"That woman who claimed to be his second wife says her former husband is a criminal without an equal anywhere in the world. It looks as though she wasn't his legal wife at all, but anyway it seems he'd set up house with another woman even before he left her. Besides, she says he used to beat her at the least provocation. She also said she was keeping twelve or thirteen medical certificates that can prove his beatings...."

My face must have turned pale. Leaving his light tone, my friend continued in a more serious voice.

"To my way of thinking, they're all after just one thing. They each hope not to figure in the autobiography of Yi Ho-gap. The problem is not the kind of person he is being portrayed as; what they're worried about is the impact on their own image if they figure in it at all. Only there's no way they can protect themselves. Except by making Yi Ho-gap out to be a really bad guy, that is."

"Do you mean to say you reckon he's not that bad?"

My friend looked taken aback at my words, He even adopted a slightly baffled tone, as if to say that he had never for one moment expected me to ask him such a question.

"A penniless fellow who inherited nothing yet gets to be as rich as he is now, and in addition says he's dreaming of entering politics? Surely the answer's obvious?"

Really? Was the answer so obvious? It struck me that I was not asking him about the truth concerning him as a human being. But to the question I was asking, again no reply was forthcoming. While I simply fidgeted with my coffee cup, he continued to speak.

"What percentage of the things Yi Ho-gap tells you do you reckon are true? The story about him becoming a rice delivery boy because his father had squandered the family's fortune; do you think that's true? And his high school graduation by the national qualification examination? His university graduation? The foundations? Do those foundations really exist?"

"What do you mean?"

"What do you want to know about that person? Yi Ho-gap is merely Yi Ho-gap. He's not the main character in your novel."

I looked at my friend rather dumbly. I knew that Yi Ho-gap was not the main character in my novel. I knew better than anyone that what I was writing was not a novel. But if he was not the main character in a novel and if what I was writing was not a novel, what was reality and what was fiction?

"Why did you stop work on the autobiography?"

I asked the question in an uncertain voice that I could not disguise. After all, even if he had got a job as a part-time lecturer, as he had said, that was not so time-consuming a task that it would oblige him to abandon work on the autobiography. He seemed to hesitate for a moment, then began to speak as though he had no choice.

"I told you that my father nearly died of stress caused by accumulated anger, didn't I?"

I seemed to vaguely recall something of the kind. It had been about a family burial plot. He had told me how, all through his life, his father's only talent had been to cultivate his land. Then one day some people from Seoul had turned up, who treated him to a meal, and to drinks, then having got him in the right mood, they had virtually robbed him of the family's burial ground... only, surely, the person who had been brought to the brink of the grave by fury had not been my friend's father, but he himself? After all, he had been impatiently hoping to sell the burial plot to raise some cash. If he ever thought of that land, that had disappeared for next to nothing because of his "stupid father," he came close to dying of rage; yet in fact it was really a stroke of luck, since if it had not happened, he would surely never have seen a day when the burial plot was turned into cash. That was about the time when my friend moved into a roomy apartment he had bought.

"But you see, that had something to do with Yi Ho-gap's foundations. When he heard that I was writing Yi Ho-gap's autobiography, the old man went into a towering fury…."

"You mean you didn't know?"

Instead of answering, he gave a brief snort of laughter. I did not question him further. Of course he did not know. It was easy if you thought of it. The same was true regarding Yi Ho-gap. In any case, the name of the ghostwriter would not figure in Yi Ho-gap's autobiography.

I went off to visit my brother, carrying a parcel of high-powered kitchen detergent I had purchased through home shopping. My sister-in-law opened the door of the restaurant, her eyes swollen from crying, as if she had had a row with my brother. I carelessly laid the bag of detergent on a table, then a little later hid it under the table. Whenever something happened, there was only me, his little sister, that my brother could call, and I would arrive carrying just detergent or something similar, but we were merely equally pitiable. Without even thinking to ask my sister-in-law about the suspension of their business, I opened the door and went outside again, where I could see my brother sitting on a bench in a corner of the shopping precinct. Seen from one side as he stared at the madly speeding cars, holding a pack of cigarettes in one hand, my brother looked just like our father had been long ago.

"They say genes never lie; he's just like your father…."

That was what Mother used to say, whenever she anxiously considered my guileless brother. Even while Father was still alive, Mother would say that at the least pretense, and Father never responded, no matter what she said. His silence on such occasions appeared to indicate a kind of assent to her insults. It was as though he had raised his son as he wished and his son had grown up according to his desires, but father was still not satisfied with the son he had produced. On every possible occasion, father would summon him, settle him down, and expound on the lesson contained in a book, but his son seemed inclined to ignore it. How did great men become great? To father, what mattered was not the life of great men but the fame, the success, the wealth their family achieved. The fact that a great man can be poor, but that a poor man can never become great; the fact that a great man can deny success but a man who fails to succeed can never become great; and above all, the fact that someone poor and incapable can never figure in the pages of a set of volumes… these were the things he hoped his son would learn from books.

Father died before he reached retirement age; he had spent his whole life working as a clerk in a middle school in a small rural town. His work failed to bring him satisfaction. He dreamed of becoming a teacher and throughout his entire life he prepared to pass the teachers' qualifying exam. But just as he failed to read all the sets of books that filled his bookcase, likewise he never opened a study guide to questions likely to figure in the teachers' qualifying exam. Father was the only person who did not realize it, but his dream was not in fact to become a teacher. What he really dreamed of was waking up one morning to find that the value of our small, dilapidated old house had suddenly skyrocketed, or that the business plan he had written out in minute letters and figures in a notebook had turned into reality and money was pouring in—things of that nature. There was no reason any such dreamlike stroke of luck should ever happen to someone who had simply worked faithfully all his life as a clerk in the middle school of a small rural town. If Father bought those sets of books and prepared for the teachers' qualifying exam all his life, it must have been because he did not want his children to find out how tawdry his life was, at least. He wanted to be a father who would be revered by his children, and to that end he spent his whole life deceiving himself.

Luckily or unluckily for Father, my brother truly revered his father and just as he had spent his whole life as a clerk, he in turn dreamed of becoming a civil servant and living an honest existence. When I told him I was going to become a writer, Father clucked his tongue and said: "That son of mine's not a patch on my daughter." Yet even then, my brother did not realize that in some way he was a disappointment to Father. Brother received a certificate for perfect attendance every year without exception all through his school days; he never once failed to do his homework; just once he "fell under the influence of bad friends" and missed one hour of class, for which he felt such remorse that he wrote a full-length letter to Father. Such was my brother....

"You're here?"

Belatedly becoming aware of me standing there beside him, he put on a show of being extremely surprised. As I sat down beside him on the bench, the breeze felt cool. After I looked out at the cars for a moment, I abruptly asked him:

"You remember the old days, back home, I mean?"

He stared at me as if wondering what on earth I was talking about, suddenly going on about home... What he wanted to hear was whether I had raised some money, or how long he would have to wait, that kind of thing... I stopped talking, looked out at the cars, then made an effort to speak cheerfully:

"About ten days, can you wait that long? I've got a book coming out. They're printing a big first edition. They reckon it'll sell well."

He stopped looking at me and mutely directed his gaze at the ground, then spoke again after a lengthy pause. He always used to hesitate like this when he was going to say something difficult. "You know, I... I was always proud of you."

He wouldn't say something like that because he felt sorry about asking for money. Brother could never tell a lie; when Father handed him a book to read, he was never once able to discover a phrase saying it was alright to tell a lie; my brother spoke as he was.

Do you like cats? In the novel, not the autobiography, the person asking is not Yi Ho-gap but I myself. The "I" who is the main character of the novel speaks first, before Yi Ho-gap replies. The I in the novel does not want to give Yi Ho-gap a chance to speak. I've owned a cat, too. It may not have been a gray Abyssinian breed, but it was a pretty little kitten.

Really. It was a pretty cat. Besides, that cat had been a present from a boy I was having a relationship with at the time. One evening, as he was coming to my house very drunk, he'd seen a hawker selling kittens and puppies late at night by the roadside. Making the taxi stop, he'd bought the cutest looking puppy. Rolling drunk, he rang my doorbell and the moment I opened the door, shouting "Surprise!" in a childish voice, presented his gift, only it was not a puppy after all, but a kitten. He'd been so drunk he couldn't even distinguish a cat from a dog; so drunk that he'd even forgotten that the reason he absolutely had to meet me that late was to break up with me. That night, for the last time, he listened to an outline of my novel, lying with his head pillowed on my leg. "Come on, tell me, what kind of things do you write?" The first time he asked me that, I'd felt insulted. What, doesn't this boy know the difference between what you can say and what you can't?

Still, any relationship is bound up to end up taming you. It did not take long before I began to stammer out the plot of my novel, and later I even began to invent new tales just so I could let him hear them. While I was talking, with him lying with my leg as a pillow, he would fall asleep and sometimes even start to snore. But just as I was coming to the end of my tale, he would suddenly open his eyes and say: "It'll be a great novel, but it won't sell well."

In those days I wasn't interested in things like sales. Yet it's true that I longed to write a novel that I would hear my boyfriend speak well of. As a result, I even longed to expound to him, not the outline but the way into my novel—my life, my happiness and my pain, everything… When I start to think like that, I always seem to turn into the fiction I am writing, and that fiction has always been more wonderful or more terrible than real life.

Once the boy who'd brought the cat left, what made life impossible for me for a while was an inky-dark confusion where what I was and what I was not were blurred and mixed together. My home was a semi-basement unit in a terrace and in that unreal space there was a cat. I had no idea at all what to do with that cat. We'd kept a dog in the yard when I was a child, but I'd never once had a cat in the house. Unlike a dog, I reckoned, a cat doesn't beg to be petted, it doesn't deposit its excrement brazenly in the middle of the yard or the room, it doesn't ask to be washed, and it doesn't ask to be taken for walks. I felt that all that was required was for me to show that I existed whenever and wherever that independent animal decided on its own that it needed me. Then once affection was established, it would lick the back of my hand with its rough tongue, or if its owner was sick in bed it would bring the fish bones left over from its meal and deposit them beside my pillow.

In any relationship, the first taming is important. But my little kitten seemed to have no thought of letting itself be tamed. The moment he put it down, the cat sped like lightning to hide on top of the bookcase, and showed no thought of coming down so long as I was in sight. When I got up in the morning, clumps of dust from the top of the bookcase were littered over the floor. I dragged a chair over and tried to pull it down, but the only result was nasty scratch on the back of my hand. I tired tempting it with smelly fish placed at the foot of the bookcase, but it was no use. That cat would never even touch food unless I had gone out somewhere. On damp days the whole place seemed to smell of the cat's piss.

I was helpless. If I didn't mean to starve the cat to death, I was obliged to leave the house whenever feeding time came along; only after breaking up with that boy I had nowhere particular to go. Each night I had to go to sleep in the bed on the other side of the room from the bookcase. If I woke late at night, startled by a bumping sound, I would see the kitten, clambering down hungry amid a cascade of books, then quickly scrambling back to the top of the bookshelf. And the steady gaze of its yellow eyes....

At that point I could not feel any liking for that little kitten. It was not that I disliked it. All that I felt regarding that cat was a realization, that I had no need to share with anyone, that I was helpless, that therefore I could neither like it nor loathe it; there was no such thing as truth here; no matter how many dozen times, how many hundreds of times I reflected, I was helpless.

So how did the cat disappear from the house? By brother's face comes to mind. Unable to overcome his wife's complaints that a rank-and-file civil servant's salary would not be enough to send their children to university, he'd started a so-called business; after which he often visited me. He'd just been passing... that was what he always said, whenever he visited my house, sitting down amid the books that were piled up in a disorderly fashion all over my small room, he would drink coffee and eat the apple I'd peeled for him. On days when the room was so chaotic there was no real place for him to sit, he would lower his behind onto a pile of books. He used to look comfortable, as if he was in the only place where he could go for a rest. When he came visiting often, there were times when I would crossly wonder if that was why he'd bought me the place, really. Just like Mother said, he left me feeling anxious, too. After he had left, I used to open the window, disturb the books that he had arranged neatly in order when I wasn't looking, volume one, volume two, and evacuate the smell of musty tomes that filled the damp space of my semi-basement.

On that occasion when my brother visited me, I could not so much as offer him a cup of coffee as I usually did. Cohabiting with the cat had left me completely exhausted. Seeing that I was looking off-color, he asked what was wrong. I replied angrily that I couldn't write on account of the cat. Only the anger I felt was not directed at the cat but rather at my brother. He might be my brother, but I wished he didn't live so narrowly; and that he'd bought me a proper apartment instead of this semi-basement in a terrace; but, far more than that, if only he wouldn't come visiting me looking so miserable….

Seeing my brother ignore chair or cushion, and instead settle his behind on the pile of books the kitten had brought tumbling down, I let myself down onto the bed briefly, where I must have fallen asleep. When I awoke it was already dawn, and in the darkened room there was no sign of my brother, nor of the cat. All I could see was the pile of books where he had been sitting, and the cat piss splattered on every page. It was no time to be phoning, yet that day at dawn I called my brother. He answered before it rang for long. I said, "I just called," like he always used to say when he visited me. And he simply replied, "Sleep well."

In the end, I found I could not ask my brother about the cat. Did you take my cat away? Then did you get rid of it in a dark park or in a corner of a marketplace? The thing that I had only dreamed of every night, until I became fretful with the unbearably wretched wish and the sorrow? At the moment when you were ridding yourself of a living creature, were you happy that a chance had come for you to do something for me…? Instead, I quietly put down the phone.

The very next day, I got rid of the baby that had been lodged in my belly for nearly the past five months. I knew it could be dangerous beyond four months, but as in the past, the operation was simple and trouble-free. I bought a bowl of ox bone soup in the restaurant on the hospital's ground floor. Determined to consume the broth to the very last drop, I scraped the bottom of the bowl with my spoon, consumed in thought. Got to go on living, just like scraping defiantly at the bottom of a bowl of oxtail broth. I had to think about something or other, if I was not to fall into sentimentality, but thoughts like "Got to keep on living" were worse than not thinking at all. Yet nothing else came to mind.

"Just a minute." After excusing himself, Yi Ho-gap had gone to the toilet. Then, instead of returning to the table where I was sitting, he went into the bedroom without saying a word. Touching up the final draft once again, I waited about thirty minutes but still he failed to emerge from the bedroom. Had he fallen asleep without saying anything to me? Or having found my draft as unsatisfactory as ever, was he catching his breath after a sudden fit of anger? The thought struck me that, if he was angry, the day I got my money would be delayed a little longer, but now there was nothing more that I was afraid of. If he wanted, I felt that I could even try giving him a lifetime as an independence fighter. Anything difficult at first, once started, would not prove so difficult. If Yi Ho-gap wanted, or rather, in order to get my hands on some money, I reckoned I would even be capable of making out he was God.

After waiting a further thirty minutes, and not being prepared to wait any more, I was about to knock on the bedroom door when it slid open silently as if moved by a breeze, not having been completely closed. He was standing at a window that looked out onto the river. The side of his face was red. Incredibly, he looked as if he had been crying.

"I've really had a hard life."

In a voice from which he was unable to banish his emotions, without turning he addressed me as I stood outside the door.

"Whatever insults people hurl at me… it doesn't matter. I tell you I've really had a hard life. But who is there who understands that?"

I nodded, though he was not looking at me. It was true; how could anyone understand that? The miserable poverty of his childhood, the adolescence he had been forced to start as a mere rice delivery boy, then the wife he had been obliged to exchange for another several times, then being slanderously labeled as human trash, a homicidal maniac, and then... then that gray Abyssinian cat so impossible to like, who could understand that? Who could understand the notorious criminal, the killer, the immoral lump of greed that he was?

Gazing at his bowed shoulders, I quietly closed the door. Having seen him burst into tears instead of exploding in anger, there could be nothing more to improve in the draft. I returned to the table but, having nothing to do, I sat there quietly for a while. Then, turning around the chair that had its back to the window, I began to look at the view outside that Yi Ho-gap had been contemplating. Soon the sun set. I could see the riverside highway along which the streetlights were beginning to glow faintly. I had a feeling I had once gone speeding with a poverty-stricken lover along that road as the lights were coming on. That had been a time when I had not yet got rid of anything, before I even knew what getting rid of something meant. Getting rid of means being got rid of, not by another but by oneself... such thoughts are always accompanied by a feeling of sadness. Perhaps, if this were not a hotel suite, I might cry a little, as I always have done at such times. But at present I feel as if this hotel room is mine.

Once the streetlights came on, before long a nightscape began to emerge beyond the window. The sky grew dark in the twilight, the streetlights cast a brilliant glare, the helplessly gaudy high-rise buildings shone out with a glow of breathtaking temptation. Beyond the window of the suite, Seoul by night looked beautiful. Or rather, it was beyond beauty. It looked like the symbol of a breathless moment of life, one that only those capable of possessing it could comprehend.

What Father had dreamed of, what Father had dreamed for his son was surely just such a moment. I recall those sets of books that filled Father's bookcase in our childhood. When you reach the point where fiction becomes truth, truth becomes fiction—there must have been such a phrase in one of the books that filled his bookcase. Might it have been in the preface to *Dream of the Red Chamber*? Yes, words like those were concealed within the covers of that Chinese classic, deemed unsuitable for children to read, glossy and shining without a speck of dust, let alone any trace of spittle or a folded page.

"You see, the things that I can't teach you are to be found in them too."

As Father's melancholy voice comes into my memory, I try to imagine Yi Ho-gap's autobiography inserted in his bookcase. Father disliked books that were not part of a set, Yi Ho-gap's autobiography would have to form a set of several volumes. I see my little brother and myself standing by the bookcase. My brother, well-behaved and docile from infancy, unable to resist his sister's importunateness, pulls the thickest book out of the bookcase. I am determined to dry a leaf between its pages. Father only collected books, he never read them, so that my brother feels no anxiety that he might discover such a sacrilegious act. Once a day my brother and I pull the book from the shelf to see how much the leaf has dried. As the pale green leaf's color fades and the living creases it had when alive slowly vanish, it grows more beautiful than reality, more everlasting than reality. Brother and I pull petals and leaves from all the flowers and trees in the garden and insert them between every page. Yellow and red and green juices seep softly into the paper. By night a flowery scent wafts from the bookcase standing in the hall and fills the whole house with its fragrance. Every night, my brother and I dream sweet dreams. On such nights, even the yowling of marauding cats is heartwarming. On our little faces, virtuous, warm smiles are spread.